THIS SAVAGE SEA

TIDES OF FATE: BOOK ONE

A.P. WALSTON

First published in the United States by Alexandria Walston.

THIS SAVAGE SEA.
Copyright © 2022 by A.P. Walston.
All rights reserved.

Printed in the United States of America.

ISBN 978-1-7373891-2-5 (hardcover)

ISBN 978-1-7373891-1-8 (softcover)

ISBN 978-1-7373891-0-1 (ebook)

First U.S. Edition: January 2022

Alexandria Walston

For my brother and sister—the real inspirations for the love and devotion Markus and Anna share.

And for Andrew Giddings,
for being the first one who said I could.

EARLIER

Anna stepped in close, burying a small blade between the pirate's ribs and twisting. She swallowed back bile as he hit the deck, his blood mixing with that of so many others. It was such a waste of life for such an itty map. Markus slid next to her, rapier in one hand and pistol in the other. He met her gaze before stepping forward and countering another pirate's swing.

"Last I heard from Father," he called as Anna ducked. She strained to hear him, the echoing booms of cannon fire and the screams of dying men were so much louder than her brother. "You had been kidnapped by pirates!"

She slammed against the taffrail, chest aching from where the pirate's foot had connected. Anna twisted to the side, watching as the pirate's cutlass bit deep into the polished wood. "*Kidnapped*—"

"Were you, or weren't you?" her brother snapped from several feet away, metallic clangs punctuating his every word.

"Well, Father wasn't jesting."

Her brother cursed, quickly followed by a dense thump. "*Anna*—"

She lunged forward. "I had a lead, Markus—"

"*Anna*—"

"It was time sensitive!" she screamed before breaking the pirate's hand and disarming him of his blade with the next flick of her wrist.

"ANNA!"

1

This time the voice didn't belong to her brother. It was grittier with a slight trill. The familiarity caused her to turn right into the swing of some blade. She looked down and saw a river of red running from her chest between fissures of skin and bits of bone. Bugger, she felt like she had been torn nearly in two. Anna coughed and dropped to her knees, a shock of red hair in her periphery. A pistol went off as the world tilted on its axis.

Markus dropped to the deck next to her, hands hovering above her ruined chest. "You'll be fine, old girl. I promise this will all be fine," he whispered, wiping his eyes.

Her brow furrowed; the pain in her chest certainly didn't feel fine, but hearing her brother's voice reminded Anna she had something to give him. She disregarded her brother's worried speech as she reached into the front pocket of her blood-soaked shirt and slapped the map into his hands.

"Anna, is this a *scalp*?" Markus questioned as the world faded to black. When he spoke next, his voice was a soft hiss. "This had better not be what I think it is!"

CHAPTER 1

Anna had been nine years old when she realized the company of the dead was preferable to that of the living.

Sixteen years among stuffy academics and Bellcaster high society had done little to change her opinion on the matter. The dead didn't argue and they didn't doubt her. They didn't try to place her in a gilded box built with the preconceived notions of who she should be or what she should want.

The deceased were a little smelly, of course, but so were the living.

Unfortunately, ceremonial flowers did little to hide the stench of decay, especially when one sat so incredibly close.

Anna adjusted her arm beneath her head and stared into the empty eye sockets of a bleached skull. Based on their hips, the skull likely belonged to a woman.

"Do you know where the khan is?" she asked the thousand-year-old woman.

The woman kept her silence, her jaw askew.

"You realize if you tell me where he is, that open seat on the Board of Antiquity will be mine? Those crotchety old men will have to let me sit in it."

Still, nothing.

Anna sighed quietly. "As a woman gifted to the khan's harem, I would think you'd want to help me. Designated to breeding and child-rearing. A life not your own, no choice in the matter because you were not born a man." She shook her head and dropped her voice to a whisper. "I'm fighting that, you know; the standard that we marry young and have little babies and do not go on adventures. Finding the khan will do just that. This goes beyond notoriety."

Moisture somewhere in the cavern dripped into a puddle. It was the only sound beyond her breathing and the scratching of her clothes against stone. Delicate dried petals adorned the sparkly grey slab, part of a mortuary ritual Anna hadn't quite cracked yet. She had removed most of them, but the few she'd missed had been crushed to dust beneath her weight.

She tucked her legs underneath herself and sucked on her teeth. "Why keep secrets for a man who murdered you? The marks are easy enough to see on your vertebra—clean, deep cuts, at least. It was fast, wasn't it?"

Anna thought maybe the woman's eye sockets had darkened, but that wasn't possible, not really. Stare into nothing long enough and the mind was bound to play tricks. The shadows and the dark were mischievous entities, tricksters and bargainers, granting what one wishes without telling the price.

Staring into the empty eye sockets of the dead was no different.

Shadows, tricks, and desires with an unknowable cost.

Despite Anna's staring, the thousand-year-old woman did not utter a secret. Not with words and not with her bones. The dead did not speak a language many understood and this woman was determined to keep her secrets even from Anna. Rolling to her back atop the stone altar, she stared at the cavern ceiling hundreds of feet above. Clues often hid in the landscape of a tomb as much as they decorated the inside of one.

Paint crafted to glow adorned the dark stone in pale blues and greens in absolutely stunning whorls. She cocked her head. The specks mimicked the night sky. They weren't necessarily placed correctly, but Anna knew the khan hadn't cared about accuracy, favoring only constellations related to the sea. She hadn't figured out why yet, but she would one day.

The *Kraken* peeked around a stalactite, glowing a soft green. Just above Anna sat the *Fishmonger* with his *Great Net*. And there, twined together like serpents, were the *Tides of Fate*, always pointing to the North Star, guiding men and women ever forward whether they knew it or not.

Granbaatar Khan had pulled nautical symbols and water into his spaces whenever possible. Even here, old stone buckets filled with water surrounded the altar, each one large enough for her to stand in comfortably. A brief glance in them had revealed little boats filled with dried water lilies. One of the bottles of incense she'd opened had smelled of the sea, of seaweed and sand.

Anna sat up, looking at the candles lining the path of crushed shells to the altar and then back to the ceiling. It was a tiny room, carved straight up. Originally, she had thought this would be a treasure chamber, full of iron coins and jewels fit for a queen.

Instead she'd stumbled upon a chamber containing a favored consort and a sweet little apology letter scrawled into the ground. It was an old dialect, one she hadn't studied at university, but Anna had understood the gist. Something about not realizing the woman could die from what had been done, that she drank from a sacred cup, gifted by Granbaatar Khan himself, and it should not have been possible. That bit was repeated quite often, the impossibility of what had happened.

An absurd notion, really.

Remove anything's head and surely it would die.

She sat back on her hands and hopped to the floor, careful of the shells beneath her feet. Another turn in place revealed about as much as the woman had. Not enough.

Anna huffed, placed her hands on her hips and tipped her head back. It was an apt description of the predicament she found herself in as well.

Twenty-five and unwed and not enough to show for it— not for a senator's daughter.

But there was an entire step pyramid to continue exploring. Anna had only happened upon this chamber by chance while jogging. She'd spent weeks in the ruins above already, brushing at scripture carved into the wall and avoiding booby traps.

The khan had a strange sense of humor.

He built a massive step pyramid, inviting all who could see it inside, and then armed it to kill.

She dusted off her hands and carefully walked back into a tunnel and up into the sweltering jungle. The sun hung high in the sky at barely past seven. Plenty of time to go spelunking through the step pyramid, aptly named GB-SP21 by the Board of Antiquity.

Anna squinted up at the stone structure, one hand up to blot out the sun.

She hadn't been to the top yet; maybe it was time she looked around.

CHAPTER 2

Was there an actual reason why jungles were so unbearably hot?

Anna couldn't think of one—not right then, anyway. A bead of sweat rolled down her temple and dripped from her jaw. She looked up, glaring at the cutout in the ceiling. Perhaps if a certain builder had not added that splendid feature, she would not be sweating quite so terribly right now.

Not yet noon and already her clothing stiffened with sweat. Anna rolled her sleeves past her elbows and unbuttoned her shirt to her sternum, abandoning her leather underbust altogether. There wasn't much more she would be willing to part with, not even in this heat.

Good God, this must be what it felt like to live in an oven.

Narrowing her gaze at the ground, Anna cocked her head. Her focus slid from the safety of the jaguar next to her boot to the line of pictographs just on the other side. They ebbed and flowed like a well-fed stream between the animals that marked some of the tiles. She followed the trail of phrases and prose to the far wall.

The writing itself was indiscernible, just a scrawling of pictures posing as letters, but Anna knew what had been carved into the stone. The khan's accomplishments and adventures, even the ones which ended in agony. They painted him a hero, a destroyer, a lover beyond compare. There were thousands of tales—too many for any man to have lived in a hundred lifetimes—and each one smiled upon the khan.

Anna had come across much of the same in his other temples and pyramids, in all the other places that once belonged to Granbaatar Khan. But one infuriating fact remained: *None* of those places had contained the famed builder.

Just booby traps.

Lots and lots of booby traps.

Anna would find the old chap eventually, there were only so many places he could hide. She took another slow step forward, watching which tiles her boots landed on. Nudging a vine with her toe, she squinted down at the picture beneath. Eagle. Bugger, she couldn't walk there.

"Did you find him?" Batu called from behind.

"No," she exhaled, gaze focused on the task at hand. "The khan remains as elusive as ever. I did find a very pretty kitty, though."

Another step, another heavy pause where even the step pyramid seemed to sigh.

"Careful," he whispered.

"I *am* being careful," she replied, fingers stretching. Not close enough. Anna slid another foot forward, her focus on the dusty floor. Was that another jaguar or a monkey? "I'll have you know that careful is my middle name."

Batu snorted. "Temple of Dogs?"

Anna blew a stray blonde curl from her face. "That was one time, two years ago. When the warning said, '*Prepare for drowning*,' I did not think the floor would drop away into an underground river. Though, considering we were in the middle of the desert during a summer drought, it was a splendid surprise. Cool water, strong current, an excellent life guard."

"You and I remember things very differently."

"Say what you will, Batu, I had a lovely time." Anna shifted, crossed her steps. The stone jaguar sat within reaching distance. Licking her lips, she glanced down and reached forward, its gold eyes staring down its nose at her.

What a pretentious little thing.

It could be haughty all it wanted, she was still taking it—and before the looters caught whiff of its gold eyes, too. Normally the nasty little buggers followed her like carrion birds and it was a bit surprising she hadn't found evidence of their ilk yet. They were little tells, things like supplies askew or new tracks in a chamber she hadn't explored yet. The devil was in the details and she always noticed.

Once the jaguar was firmly in her grasp, she paused and surveyed the room.

Nothing.

The ground remained intact. The walls stood. Not even the heavy vines draping the walls changed, their itty white flowers blowing in that infernal breeze. Swallowing, she lifted the stone jaguar from its resting place and paused, squinting about the room.

Surely if something had to go terribly wrong, it would be now. But nothing came, not for her and not for Batu. Anna half expected the tiles to drop away into a bottomless pit or, God forbid, another underground river. But here she waited, looking silly standing as still as the stone statue in her grasp.

Frowning, Anna reached for the buckles of the satchel at her side and tucked the statue under her arm as she turned. Something about this was entirely too easy, but she wasn't one to complain about a rare stroke of her brother's good luck.

"See, just like I told you, Bat—"

Anna froze, mouth open.

Four men stood in the dark depths of the corridor behind Batu, one with what looked like a pistol in his hand. That was a bit of a relief; at least these looters hadn't gotten their hands on any revolvers yet.

Batu's hands shook in the air next to his head and sweat poured down his face. It soaked the front of his shirt and stained a sizable area around his armpits.

"Looters?" she asked, squinting at the men in their mismatched brown clothing and floppy hats.

The men behind Batu shared his medium brown skin, a stark contrast to the warm honey of Anna's. Her tan had absolutely nothing to do with heritage and everything to do with the time she spent in the sun. These men were locals, most likely from the village that had sprouted up on the outskirts of the jungle. Descendants of the men and women who had built this step pyramid all those years ago.

The man directly behind Batu hissed a sentence in Haidenian. It was tonal and rough but Anna understood the words easily enough. Understanding was one thing, speaking was entirely another.

"He—" Batu's throat bobbed, the whites of his almond-shaped eyes visible. "He said—"

"I know what he said," Anna replied calmly, putting the jaguar on the ground and sliding it in their direction with her foot.

She wiped her sweating hands off on her breeches, focusing on the approaching man. He brushed vines from his path, picking his way to the jaguar. She stared at his feet. One misstep and he could solve this problem for her. Then again, one misstep and he might bring all three steps of this pyramid down. A bead of moisture meandered down her spine, her heart nearly beating its way through her chest.

But the looter stepped exactly where she had, using the places where her boots disturbed the blanket of dust along the tiles as a road map. So, they weren't complete idjits. Splendid. While extremely relieved the looter wasn't about to incur the wrath of a dead khan, Anna was also slightly disappointed. She glared at the man and his grubby little fingers as they roved over the stone jaguar.

"Take care of that," she said quietly. "I'll be taking it back shortly."

The looter sent her a blackened smile and tipped his hat, exchanging a quick conversation with his partners. In her experience, looters were never friends. Friends did not shoot each other in the back for the chance at a larger cut of the deal.

Anna paid them and their pointless conversation little attention; instead, she busied herself watching their hands, following the jaguar as it passed from one to the next. She marked the looter it ended up with. One of his boots was taller than the other, his was coat short at his wrists, and as he turned she noticed the back of his jacket was split down the middle. It flapped at her, looking like it waved goodbye.

She didn't see what happened next, but she heard it.

Batu cried out and Anna spun to him. He clutched at a bleeding wound on the back of his skull. His eyes pinched shut from the pain and he stumbled forward. Good God. Anna's eyes widened and she threw her hands in the air, yelling for Batu to stop, to look where he stepped, to—

His foot landed on a tile, one which had remained tucked tightly beneath a blanket of dust.

A plume of stale air wafted up like smoke and the tile hissed as it slid an inch into the floor. He lifted his foot, staring at Anna with wide eyes. Breathing deeply, her gaze skipped from one side of the chamber to the next.

The step pyramid buckled.

Anna careened left and then right as dust and debris rained down and clogged the air. She wiped the grit from her eyes and spat it from her mouth. She couldn't breathe and she couldn't see, but she knew what direction she had to run. Anna sprinted across the path she had carved earlier. Batu remained on the ground, hands over his head.

"Come on, Batu! Now is not the time to be sleeping on the job!" she said, fingers tight around his bicep.

Batu stumbled to his feet and shook her off, hardly able to run in a straight line. Blood dripped from beneath his thick, straight hairline and between his eyes. He glared at her fiercely, his gaze nothing but dark pinpricks. "You are an omen! This is the last time I work with you, Miss Savage."

Anna laughed, unable to contain the giddy buzz from the adrenaline flooding her veins. "That's what you said the *last time*, Batu. And look at us now!" She grinned, sliding around the first corner in the corridor. "Out-running certain death yet again."

Batu continued to grumble beneath his breath between deep, wheezing gasps.

He was not in the best of shape.

She focused on the coat flapping just around the corner in front of them. The looters might have the lead, but Anna had lived in this ruin for weeks. She had breathed its stale air and walked its deserted halls. No one knew its twists and turns better than she did.

Not the looters.

Not even the rats.

Anna slid as she rounded the next corner. The hall opened into a straight away and there, halfway down, the looters faltered and shuffled as the ground shook beneath their feet. She bent low and scooped up a sizable rock—a bit of the ceiling, Anna realized at second glance.

She tossed it, testing its weight, and glared at the men before her. Searched for the mismatched boots, one taller than the other. The short sleeves. That despicable coat. Rock connected with flesh. The looter screamed at the impact, from surprise or in pain, Anna wasn't sure—nor did she care.

All was fair in love and looting.

Her mother had made sure she learned that much.

The man tumbled and rolled, unable to catch his balance between the bucking floor and the stone she had thrown. The jaguar cracked against the stone tiles and spun ahead of them, one of its feet flying off into the distance. A section of flooring popped up, throwing Anna to the ground as the ceiling above cracked and split, then collapsed.

A gust of dirt and wind washed over her with enough strength to tear some of her pale blonde hair from its bun. Anna blinked rapidly, trying to clear the stars from her eyes.

White noise buzzed and a bit of blood dribbled from her nose.

She coughed, clearing her throat, looking for that damn—

The jaguar laid directly in front of her face, its golden eyes gleaming in the pyramid's newly-minted skylight. The underside of the jaguar faced her, a single pictograph inscribed on its belly.

Anna squinted, lifting to her elbows and licking her lips. Its meaning didn't immediately register. She crawled closer. It wasn't from this region, but it was very old, probably cousins to what she had seen in the woman's little chamber earlier. In the best of cases, this particular dialect would have been spoken and written by Granbaatar Khan's priests, and in the worst of cases, by none but the khan himself.

Tracing its flowing lines, its edges and curves, she searched for meaning in the deep depths of her memory. Nothing came. Not immediately and not otherwise. Anna should know what this symbol meant, which word it translated into, no matter how obscure or archaic. It should have waved like an old friend in passing, and yet it hadn't.

Bugger.

Bugger it all to—

Anna cocked her head.

Was that an E?

She sucked on her teeth and nodded slowly. It had to be—

The pyramid belched out another gust of putrid smelling detritus, reminding Anna of her priorities—lying prone on the floor of a dying temple certainly wasn't one of them. She pulled to her feet, sliding the stone jaguar into her satchel. The floor steadied to a slow, rolling rumble but Anna still held to the wall for balance. "Batu, it's time to—"

13

Her voice cut off and she dug her nails into the stone, something dark and tight welling behind her ribs. Batu laid beneath a section of ceiling along with two of the looters. The other two were just starting to rise. Wiping her stinging eyes, Anna spun and set off down the remaining section of hall. Compared to some of the other chambers, it was a relatively straightforward dash from the top of the pyramid to the exit down below.

The distance wasn't at all the problem.

The problem was the pyramid's integrity.

Walls blew out in whole sections as the pyramid crumbled in earnest. She ran with her hands up to shield her head and eyes. Obscenities followed her down the hall, screamed from the men that chased her. She ignored the cobwebs and spiders, skipped over fallen stonework and torch holds. A mosaic spread out beneath her feet, relieved of dirt and grime, showing yesterday's interest.

A shadow stretched before her, two or three times the depth of her own. One of the khan's pits. Anna's lips thinned at the sight of its dark expanse, about the length of a man lying down. She knew what waited at its bottom: sharpened sticks or rocks and the skeleton of every victim it had ever claimed. Inhaling deeply, she leapt the abyss.

For a second, the chill below clung to her skin, grazing and scratching like a lover's fingers.

Her feet hit the ground on the other side; she tucked and rolled back to her feet. A body in motion remained in motion and she didn't have the time to stop. A scream followed her and then a grunt. Anna turned, squinting into the dusty haze that trailed her. Only one of the looters had made it over.

She scanned the ground as she ran, boots falling lightly against the blank ceramic tiles. This hall turned several times, zigging and zagging back and forth at a downward slope. The wall on her right erupted and a chunk of stone slammed into her ribs. Anna cried out, sliding from the momentum. Her foot came down hard on a ceramic tile.

It cracked—

Broke.

A cascade of grating clicks tore through the air, the clacking of stone work and metal permeating just above the growling of the pyramid's death throe. Anna hit the ground, eyes prickling with tears, hands over her head. Arrow ports opened in the walls and stone-tipped arrows with red fletching flew above her head like spurts of blood.

She ignored the whistling of arrows and the scream of the last looter. She crawled forward on her forearms and stomach until the narrow corridor opened into a vast hall. The stone staircase had never looked so beautiful.

Anna winced on the next inhale, holding her ribs, and plunged down, taking the stairs two or three at a time. Pillars carved in the shape of men with jaguar headdresses lined either side. Halfway down, the stone men no longer supported the step pyramid, instead they held intricately carved beams overflowing with flowers.

From the corner of her eyes, Anna caught glimpses of the jungle. Her thighs ached and her knees wobbled but she buried the discomfort deep and focused on her heart. The furious, excited thumps. She felt them with every step, heard them with every breath.

She lived.

She lived.

She lived.

Several grinding cracks resounded loud enough to drown out the growling from the temple. Anna looked over her shoulder and stumbled. Bugger. The pillars had cracked in half, trembling from the additional weight of the collapsed temple. Swallowing, she stepped backward, gaze fixated on the stone men. One exploded and then another. Anna whipped around with a groan. Stone pillar after stone pillar erupted behind her, tumbling to the ground like dominos.

Anna ran straight through their camp, little white shells crunching beneath her feet. She jumped over the fire pit and wove between two tents. One blink revealed their climbing supplies and in the next, Anna saw their pots and pans, even the little stone bowls Batu insisted they used.

The ground beneath her feet rumbled. Looking down, Anna tightened her jaw. The thousand-year-old woman with the apology note had been hundreds of feet beneath the step pyramid. If there had been more chambers and the khan had rigged them to collapse...

"Oh, you absolutely brilliant ass," she coughed.

Anna was halfway to the jungle line when a sound like mountains colliding roared from behind her. The next percussive blast threw her forward through the air and straight onto her hands and knees.

She didn't dare turn around, instead pushing herself to her feet. The ground splintered before her eyes, fissures opening and forcing sections of earth up. She looked back, only able to see a cloud of dust.

If this step pyramid didn't kill her, the Board of Antiquity very well might.

The jungle proper started in small bushes and colorful plants with large paddle-like leaves. It quickly grew into towering trees and snaking vines the size of her thigh. Sliding to a stop, Anna sucked a breath in and immediately regretted the decision as coughs wracked her. Swallowing past the grit in her throat, she turned around and froze.

It was gone.

The sheer amount of devastation—she had never seen anything quite like it. The maw that swallowed the step pyramid was deep enough that she couldn't see if anything remained of it. Thick clouds of dust billowed upwards on strong drafts, looking like plumes of smoke.

Anna wiped at her mouth with the back of her hand. Despite her brother's penchant for unbelievable tales, Markus wasn't going to believe any of this; but if anyone could appreciate a story about treasure, it would be him. Perhaps not all the harrowing, life-threatening portions, but he'd enjoy the rest of it.

Anna slumped to the ground and kicked her legs out in front of her. Her knees were skinned, breeches torn, and every breath was a minor agony, but she lived.

Which was more than she could say for others.

After several minutes of listening to birds settle and the terrified brays of donkeys in the distance, Anna looked to the sky. She had plenty of time to make the trek back to the village. But it would take twice as long without the donkeys. Hearing them was one thing, finding them would be another.

"I hope you were worth it," she said, glancing down at her satchel.

The pictograph she'd seen on the jaguar's belly fluttered before her eyes, there between blinks. She pressed her lips into a thin line, rustling around in her bag until she held the stone kitty in her hands, its belly facing her.

Anna blew at the symbol, rubbing away some of the grime and dust with her thumb.

Well, well, well, what was this?

Not just one pictograph, but one carved crudely on top of another.

She squinted, sifting from one language into another, and then finally into a language that, frankly, didn't make any damn sense.

"That can't be right," she muttered.

But there wasn't anything else it could be.

Eero.

It was a name, one that wasn't from this region. A frown tugged at her lips. An Aepith name, a seafarer's name. But what was it doing here in the middle of a jungle that wasn't really a jungle? Try as it might, this bit of foliage wasn't a jungle at all, but the largest oasis on record, tucked away in the center of a desert, surrounded on three sides by mountains.

Anna set the jaguar back in her satchel and pursed her lips at the greedy abyss before her. What was she going to tell the curmudgeons on the Board of Antiquity? That she had collected a stone relic belonging to the khan with an Aepith name on it, but had decimated the step pyramid in the process?

Months of work, of research, of writing proposals and requesting grants—all a waste. She blew at a stray hair, that dark sadness tightening behind her ribcage once more. The effort she had put into this expedition hadn't been the only waste. It had been the least of them, actually. Batu hadn't...

She shook her head and closed her eyes.

Everything could change and it could do so between blinks.

But that was life, wasn't it?

CHAPTER 3

"G'night, miss," the steward called after her.

Anna waved a hand over her head, sagging in relief as she stepped from the late-night train. There was hardly a soul left in the station and she knew from experience it would be the same on the streets. Even this late at night, she wasn't worried about trouble. The Bellcaster Watch was far too vigilant for that.

The bags that pooled about her feet were lumps of floral-printed fabric in the dark. The train staff hadn't realized who rode in coach and Anna preferred it that way—sneaking into the capital of Briland before sneaking right back out, unbeknownst to her father.

Rolling her neck, Anna rubbed at the aching muscles between her head and shoulders, stomach rumbling and demanding sustenance. She had forgone dinner in exchange for additional sleep. The donkeys had never revealed themselves and she'd been forced to walk the entire way back to the village. Exhaustion was not a strong enough word for what she felt upon stumbling past their gates and then onto the train.

She looked down. At least her feet no longer felt like some obscure extension of her ankles.

The train pulled from the station, too late for a whistle. Wind stirred her hair, cold and crisp with the changing of the season. Gas lights blazed at equal intervals down the cobbled street, barely cutting through the layer of fog that descended upon Bellcaster at the beginning of every autumn. It was a stubborn fog, one that would refuse to lift until spring—and even then, it could be caught slinking about in the early hours of summer.

Anna shouldered her bags with a grunt, her breath fanning out in front of her face, and began the walk to her flat. She carried one bag at her back and another under each arm. Her satchel draped over her right shoulder, the golden-eyed stone jaguar still confined within. She'd drop the overgrown paperweight off at the Board in the morning. Though after decimating that step pyramid, she doubted there would be anything she could do to impress goodwill upon them. It would take years and some considerable donations to work herself back into their neutral graces.

Treasure hunter, some would glare.

Adventurer, others would sneer.

And the worst of them would say, *Just like her blasted mother.*

She looked from one building to the next as she trudged along. The windows of some were flooded with light and laughter but most would hold their dark vigil until morning. Not many establishments remained open at this hour, but those that did were far from reputable. Gentlemen's clubs, taverns, and gambling dens, every one of them a favorite haunt of her brother's. Here near the train station, outside the central hub of Bellcaster, they were a common enough sight.

She hummed along to the varying tunes sneaking beneath doors and through carelessly cracked windows. Some were slow piano numbers coupled with smoky feminine voices. Others were loud and raucous, sung and screamed by drunken men and women as they danced or stumbled into the street.

"Oi! Did you hear about what happened in Tremble's Bay?"

Anna paused, tipping her ear toward the open tavern window. News was a rare thing to hear at this hour, especially above the laughter and good-natured fun. Tremble's Bay was a small, warm thing with crystal blue waters, located just north of the Charleston Naval Base.

"The way I hear it, Senator Savage's knickers are in a knot. Apparently, a whole pleasure barge was snatched up by the Pirate King. A bloody riot even broke out, people wanting to know what the Senate will do now that the blasted scoundrels are in our waters."

"Think they'll increase patrols?"

"Do they have the men for that?" a third voice questioned.

A pause.

Anna shifted the straps of her bags and leaned toward the window.

"Does it matter? Fathers are worried about their daughters and wives. Shit, they've got to worry about their sons now too. They're not just plaguing foreign soils. The Senate will have to do something."

Anna exhaled hard. Her father would do nothing, as he had done nothing when she had been taken by pirates. Nothing but sweep her disappearance under the rug, lest she embarrass him. It wasn't entirely fair to think of her father as a heartless man who cared only about his power and reputation. Nine out of ten times it would have been true, but her jaunt in the slave trade was the one time it wasn't.

As she lugged her bags through the empty streets, the missing pleasure barge and the Pirate King's tie to it was all anyone talked about. That, and the Pirate King's latest scuffle with Carsyn Kidd, one of the five Coalition chiefs.

Anna wanted to tell them not to hold their breath for anything beyond a public briefing on the barge matter. Security on the water was difficult to come by, there was simply too much of it. That had been the entire reason for crafting a treaty with the Coalition of Pirates to begin with.

But they were pirates for a reason and honesty was not in their repertoire. And as honorable as the five pirate chiefs of the Coalition supposedly were, the Pirate King was the worst of them. No one knew that better than Anna.

She turned down a narrow alley lined with trellises. In the spring and summer, climbing roses bloomed along them. Now there were only thorns and green leaves so dark they appeared black. She passed under an archway. The iron rod gate closed behind her with an eerie creek, the latch clanging shut.

Anna followed the path to the right. A staircase wound around the cobbled courtyard, circling ever higher. Her flat loomed at the top and each step was a twin to the ones she'd descended in her haste to escape the collapsing step pyramid. Every breath ached and one of her bags pressed painfully against her side. The village doctor had claimed Anna had broken a rib and at the time it seemed unlikely. Now it seemed plausible.

Higher and higher, she climbed, passing framed window boxes and large oak doors. Some had elaborate knockers, others adorned with decorations to celebrate the coming of autumn. Wreaths of orange and yellow leaves and braided straw. Pumpkins sat just to the left or right of most doors. The flames of little black candles arranged next to pumpkins flickered in the breeze, throwing a spiced scent into the night.

Anna blew hair from her face and slumped against the wall, trying to adjust her bags without dropping them. She looked up from under the brim of her hat and wilted. The last set of ten stairs might kill her, she was certain of the possibility. But she'd made it this far and while the bed in her flat wasn't comfortable, it was better than the ground out here—and it had blankets. An entire mountain of them.

Her door did not have decorations, no pumpkin sat at its side. Nothing differentiated it from the other doors except for maybe the amount of dirt that had collected in front of it.

Looking up, Anna sighed and dropped her bags to her feet. A cloud of dust wafted from them at the sudden impact, the sound echoing up and down the spiral staircase. Anna winced at the jarring sound but if the residents living around her weren't used to her late-night comings and goings by now, they never would be. She rolled her neck and reached into her pocket, digging around for the brass filigreed key. Her brows drew together and she dug deeper.

Nothing.

Anna turned out every pocket on her person and patted down every surface available to her. She leaned back against the railing, one hand sliding to her hip as the other pinched the bridge of her nose.

She'd lost her key.

Again.

No matter, she was more than capable of handling a locked door. She plopped down in front of her door and picked through the pins in her hair until several lock picks and a hammer sat in her fingers. Anna couldn't help the soft laugh that bubbled up. Here she was, breaking into her flat in the middle of the night— and not for the first time in her life.

At least it was a bit of excitement, a small spark of something interesting. The mountains of paperwork the Board piled on her desk for filing certainly wasn't doing Anna any favors. Nor were the low-profile digs in places considered perfectly proper. Going out into that step pyramid had been the culmination of months of begging and bribing.

The lock clicked and then with a swift twist of the brass knob, her door opened. She threw her bags into the entry hall and pulled herself to her feet, a hand braced on each knee.

Anna stretched, closing the door with her foot. She picked up the mail from the floor and tucked it under her elbow, turning a knob by leaning against it with her arm. Brass fixtures flickered to life, a bit of flame held within glass cases.

Her satchel bumped against her hip, the considerable weight of the jaguar reminding her it rested within. She glanced to her old leather bag, unbuckling the sides and reaching in. The jaguar's golden eyes glowed in the low light of the gas lamps. Tossing her satchel with her other bags, she stared into its gaze.

What a curious little trinket.

Weighty, as expected from something made of stone with solid gold eyes. But it was more than that. She squinted at it. The jaguar had…presence and it was cool to the touch even here. Anna flipped it over to reveal the nonsense carved on its stomach.

Eero.

Could it really be an Aepith artifact?

Curious, so very curious.

She set the jaguar down on a thin entry table to her right. Next to it sat a small crystal bowl with soft peppermint candies. A diamond-shaped mirror with a gilt frame hung behind it, revealing just how haggard Anna really looked. She leaned forward, inspecting the bags under her eyes. No one ever said archaeology would be a glamorous career, but Anna would have liked it if someone warned her about the sleepless nights.

Leaning back, she stepped away from the mirror and stared down the hall. It was so silent, this flat. Her shadow loomed long and anemic in the low light. She crossed her arms and looked from the golden wallpaper to the elaborate runner along the floor and the dark wood beneath it.

Something exhausted Anna about returning to a perpetually empty space. She didn't consider this home, just the place she occupied between her various travels. Somewhere to put her things until she found something that felt right. Her own personal limbo.

Her stomach growled, interrupting the silence and making itself known. There was never any rest for the wicked, not truly. Anna toed off her boots and pulled the mail from its resting place snug beneath her arm. She snatched a mint from the entry table, popping the fresh delicacy into her mouth as she sorted her mail. The unimportant letters she flicked over her shoulder.

Her father's reelection campaign. Her father's birthday gala at the end of the month. Anna cocked an annoyed brow—was it that time of the year already? She could have sworn they'd just celebrated the damn thing. She stared at the envelope for a long minute, the way her father had written her name in perfect script.

With a sigh, she tore into it, looking for the date and time. She found them, but could only focus on the scrawled note on the inside.

> *Daughter,*
>
> *I highly doubt you will grace us with your presence, but I cannot recommend attending enough. It would do your standing some much needed good.*
>
> *J.S.*

The chuckle tore itself from the space deep inside she reserved for annoyance with her father. Do her standing some good? God, he had to be kidding. Bellcaster nobility thought little of Anna, believing her hardly noteworthy beyond an excellent source of gossip. She preferred it that way and even if she didn't, one outing would hardly change her standing among those pompous asses.

She tore the letter up, throwing its bits and pieces over her shoulder like confetti, and returned to the rest of her mail. Three baby announcements and five engagements in just the last month. Anna leaned against the door and sucked on her mint. Maybe babies were what kept one well entertained in their mid-twenties?

Is that why Anna felt this stirring in her soul, a restlessness that demanded attention? Was she supposed to be filling it with little ones? Or was she just bored? She traced the rose gold script of the last baby announcement, moving the mint to her cheek with a sigh.

Anna would put her eye out before ever admitting her father had been right all these years. Become a spinster just to spite him. A spinster who wore an eyepatch and chased the locals with sticks, claiming to be a witch. A small grin flashed; he'd hate that. Especially after all his attempts to marry her off.

Her nose twitched.

Was that chamomile?

Anna tossed the announcement over her shoulder and crept toward her kitchen, brows pinched. She had left tea out before, but chamomile wasn't her tea of choice. Leaning around the corner, she spied two tea cups at her round, white-washed table, steam billowing up from their tops. Anna was quite sure they had not been there when she'd left last month, and even if they had been, they wouldn't be steaming now.

Anna squinted. Those were her good china cups, the ones with hand-painted lavender curling up their sides. She only got those buggers down for special occasions. Normally she took her tea in an over-large red cup that may or may not have been a bowl in its past life. Her hand slipped to her back pocket, procuring a small knife as she eased into a crouch.

"There will be no need for that, Anna."

Her muscles relaxed at the familiar cadence, chipper and bright as if they had no worry in the world. Anna slid the knife back into her back pocket and straightened, putting her hands on her hips. "Those are very brave words for a man who dresses as fine as you and doesn't carry a knife while traipsing around in the middle of the night."

"And how would you know I don't arm myself?" he asked, clearly amused.

"Because I know you," Anna grinned. "And you, Mihkel Tamm, have never carried a weapon in your life."

"I suppose there's never been a reason on account that I don't start a ruckus everywhere I go. Unlike someone I know."

"How very dull."

Mihk carried a tray of delicate tea sandwiches toward her on a large silver platter. Anna recognized them immediately even though she only had a quick glance. Her stomach rumbled again, reminding her of her hunger. Tomato-cheddar on white bread. Ham, brie, and apple on French. Open-faced smoked salmon sandwiches with dill and crème fraiche.

There was even a salad of fruit in a small bowl. Freshly cut strawberries, blueberries, raspberries, and sliced oranges. Mihkel Tamm was not one to forget the littlest of details.

"You've really outdone yourself, Mihk."

Anna turned, catching sight of the little desserts on the platter. Rectangles of lemon loaf with lemon frosting. Slices of carrot cake smeared with cream cheese and chopped pecans. Chocolate eclairs and scones with raspberry jam. Her mouth watered, stomach making a ridiculous noise that might have embarrassed her had it been anyone other than Mihk standing in her kitchen.

"Someone has to make sure you're well fed. We both know it's the first thing you put off."

"You've seen my thighs, yes?"

"Yes." Mihk sighed. "And you're absolutely stunning, darling."

"I know that, I just wanted to make sure you've seen them." She motioned down to the soft muscle of her legs, the ample curve of her hips and rear. Anna struck a pose against the doorframe. "I really am a vision."

"And so modest, too."

She grinned briefly, exhaustion making it difficult to sustain. Mihk set the platter atop the table and turned, allowing Anna her first good look at him. He'd always been a wisp of a man, about her height with an even daintier frame. Tonight, he wore a thick burgundy robe with a black shirt and long pants beneath. Slippers kept his steps silent. Had he been staying here in her flat?

He sat, motioning for Anna to join him as he brushed golden hair from his face. The fair coloring of the flaxen strands only called attention to his large olive-green eyes and the sharp elf-like qualities he possessed. A pointed chin and narrow face, straight nose, and slightly angled eyes. Mihk was a handsome gentleman, though he'd denied any compliment he'd ever received.

"To what do I owe this pleasure?" she asked after sipping, brow raised in question.

He swallowed, dropping his gaze to his tea. "I hate to be the bearer of dreadful news, Anna. But…" He paused, running his finger along the rim of his cup.

"What could be so terrible it warrants tea and sandwiches?" she joked, picking one up and stuffing it completely into her mouth.

He flinched. "It's your brother."

Anna rolled her eyes. "It can't be that bad," she said around her mouthful.

Mihk only appeared more interested in his tea.

Bugger, what had Markus done now?

"He's been arrested," Mihk said quietly, feet dancing nervously beneath the table. "Anna…he was detained by marshals. I don't know what for yet, only that it happened."

Her breath caught in her lungs and she nodded slowly, entirely interested in her tea as well. "Is there anything our father can do?"

Occasionally—not very often, but occasionally—it paid to be the child of a senator.

Mihk shook his head. "No…I don't think it's public knowledge, nor do I believe it will be."

Detainment by the Senate's dogs was not common practice and it bothered her a great deal that her father's considerable influence would be null in this instance.

Anna exhaled, slow and focused. "How did you find out, then?"

He laughed nervously, turning his gaze to the ceiling. A blush fanned across his face. "I've been seeing a captain. His father is privy to such things."

"And when did this captain find out?"

"Yesterday. The same time I did, considering we were in the closet of his father's office." Mihk coughed, rubbing his neck. "We overheard the conversation."

The grin fell from her face and she squinted at the blond. "It's not Bastian Hayhurst, is it? Because if it is, I owe Markus a fair amount of money."

Mihk looked away, throat bobbing and cheeks flushing in embarrassment. "It might have been. But never mind that. I remembered you would be home this week for a short time before shipping back off to the step pyramid and decided to wait you out. I took the liberty of cleaning your bathroom. It was absolutely atrocious."

"I have been gone for a month."

"Before that."

"Well, before that I spent a month in Xing, and before that I was in the Emerald Isles for four months excavating a long-lost king beneath the ever-watchful gaze of your father."

"He's still bitter about that."

"I would be too," she agreed. "Three of his ships went down. I told them not to send me to the Emerald Isles, but alas," Anna teased. "I'm more interested in my closet. Did you find anything interesting in there, Mihk?"

"*Anna.*" He laughed, raising those olive-green eyes to meet her bright blue ones.

She laughed too. But her gaze slowly dropped to her hands around the little tea cup and any humor she'd found speaking with Mihk dried up. There and then gone, a creeping chill replaced their light mood. Anna tore at a piece of lemon loaf.

They remained quiet for several minutes as Anna contemplated her options, not that there were many. She would rescue her brother. But to even contemplate spiriting him from the marshal's clutches would be mad. A sure way to find a hangman's noose. Daunting and rife with danger.

She shook her head—he'd be fine. Their father would prevail. And if not, Markus had gotten himself into plenty of trouble, perhaps it was time he learned how to get himself out. Of course, escaping and then evading marshals would be a feat unto itself.

"No. Oh, no." Mihk put his cup down, some of the tea spilling over the edge. "That is treason you're contemplating, Anna. You would lose your fortune and your credibility as an archaeologist. If you're lucky, you'll be detained as well. If not, it'll be death, Anna. *Death.* Even if Markus is innocent—"

Anna snorted.

Oh, no, Markus had done something, all right.

"Even *if* he is innocent," Mihk repeated, glaring at the interruption, "of whatever they have charged him with, it will take time to clear your name too. A very long time, I'd wager. All of that very long time you would be in jail, probably Chesterhale—which is worse than death, in case you've forgotten."

"I did not come here to send you to the noose. I came to tell you because you deserve to know. Because he is your brother and I care deeply about you both. Now, I have a plan, Anna. I think we have a chance if we post bail and petition the Senate to—"

"Splendid speech." Anna pushed her tea cup away and popped another bit of lemon loaf in her mouth. "But you see, all of that is only relevant if I'm caught. I'll be in and out with none the wiser. If they take him to Chesterhale, I might never see him again—no, no it would be better to grab him while I still can."

Mihk dragged his hands down his face, groaning. "This is a quarter-life crisis. Too many so-called '*tedious*' assignments from the Board. You'll see once it all blows over—please, Anna, please do not do anything rash. We can post bail and meet with the Senate. I'll bring my father in, you'll see. We do not have to go on some grand adventure to be successful."

Something sparked in her soul. Something related to adventure, something quite possibly cousins with thrill. Whatever it was, she had missed it the way a suffocating man missed air. If nothing else, this outing promised to be entertaining. It promised to likely take several years off her life too, considering the trouble Markus had gotten himself into.

But it would be leaps and bounds better than sitting behind a desk and sifting through field reports—or explaining herself to the Board.

"Anna…" Mihk begged.

She held up a finger, gaze narrowing in thought. "I'm going to need my best dress and a few favors from you, my wonderful, naughty, partner in crime."

He sighed, head falling to his hands. "Please don't call me that."

"Does Captain Hayhurst call you that? It does have a nice ring to it." She grinned, sitting back in her chair. "Now, here is what we're going to do. Do you still have those wigs?"

It would be dangerous.

But some of the very best things in life were.

CHAPTER 4

Markus coughed, a bit of bile rising in his throat. He vomited again, stomach muscles spasming wildly. Bollocks, these marshals hit hard, and with his arms hoisted high above his head, his sides were left vulnerable, each rib ripe for the picking.

He spat a wad of blood to the ground and wiped his mouth along his bicep. He'd been right when he had suspected a bit of light torture. With the general noise of the train, it wouldn't matter how loud he screamed; no one would hear him. Not that anyone in the Borderlands would care.

"What's next, gentlemen?" He coughed, letting his head dip forward, sweat dripping from the tip of his nose.

The chains holding him creaked and scraped against each other, the manacles at his wrists chafing his skin bloody and raw. There were several marshals in the train car with him. Honestly, Markus felt rather flattered by the number the Senate thought they'd need to keep him under control. It was a splendid little compliment in its own twisted way.

His slow clockwise spin halted.

Markus lifted his gaze, staring into eyes nearly as blue as his. He eyed the marshal's uniform, tracing the gold stitching. This was the prick who had been put in charge, sporting bruised knuckles and a split lip. Markus grinned; he'd gotten a good shot in when first loaded into the empty train car. Well, empty save the chains that kept him suspended and the various crates.

Oh, and the spiders.

He hadn't seen one of the nasty little buggers yet, but the webs in the corners and along the roof spoke to quite an infestation—one he reminded the marshals of quite frequently. Arachnophobia was a more common fear than one would think, and if Markus couldn't sleep because he was forced upright, then the blasted marshals wouldn't be able to either.

The blue-eyed marshal squinted at him, tilting his head. The hair along his head was a rough stubble. All marshals sported a similar cut, it was one of the many reasons Markus had declined the position when it had been offered. He crossed his arms against his chest. There was nothing nice about the gesture; even the slim grin that peeled his lips apart seemed closer in kin to the glint of broken glass than it did a smile. He could have been handsome, if not for the dead look in his eyes and the severity of his face.

"You could tell us where it is," he offered in what Markus suspected was the marshal's best attempt at sounding sincere. It was not sincere. "Sources say you were the last bloke seen with it."

"Do they now?" Markus stated merrily despite his growing unease.

If the marshals knew without a doubt that Markus had that blasted map, chances were they knew that Anna had given it to him.

The blue-eyed marshal smirked. "Aye, we know your sister gave it to you. You see, we're hoping you'll be more forthcoming and cooperative...otherwise we'll be paying a visit to that sweet sister of yours next."

Markus cocked his head, brow raised.

He couldn't help it—he laughed.

He laughed hard and loud, the sound ripping itself from his lungs before descending into a choked snort. They thought they'd get information out of *Anna*? She was the most stubborn person he knew. Besides, last he'd checked, his sweet sister was gallivanting about in an undisclosed location in a god-forsaken jungle, off in search of something or other.

It would take a small army just to find her.

"I wish you luck." Markus finally grinned, tipping his head back and rolling it along his neck. "You're going to need it. Anna...she is not what I would describe as cooperative and she has a rather excellent knack for being unreachable when you're looking for her. I'd know. I grew up with her."

The marshal's gaze narrowed further.

He made a great show of considering Markus in all of his filthy glory, then he nodded and turned, pacing off as another marshal replaced him.

Ah, let the beating commence.

Markus was at the end of his ropes, he knew that. It would only be for a few more days, anyway. Then they'd reach Bellcaster and his trial with Admiral Kray would begin. A trial he would lose, despite his parentage. Markus would hold out, though; he wasn't about to give the Senate's dogs anything. If he told them anything before speaking with his father, there was no guarantee he'd be able to help.

No, best to hold out and see what strings his conniving sire could pull.

The brown-eyed marshal stepped forward, knuckles popping in warning. Markus did his best to brace for the next shot to his ribs. It came. It thumped and cracked. Markus wheezed, spinning from the momentum. He caught the next punch against his face, splitting the inside of his lip and tasting blood in his mouth.

Bruised but not broken, his ribs ached with each breath and everything stung, especially his wrists—he could probably thank the desert sand permeating the air for that. At least he looked damn good in only his undershorts, a grimy button down, and a pair of barely-laced boots.

Anna would laugh herself hoarse if she could see him.

But she was far away from here and it would be weeks before they could even come close to finding her. Markus held onto that thought as the brown-eyed marshal stepped closer, his grin turning rather wicked.

Anna was far away from here.

So splendidly far away.

CHAPTER 5

She'd gone from the devil's frying pan and straight into his oven.

At least this had nothing to do with pirates or travel on the open waters. That would complicate things she would rather not be complicated. This excursion would be difficult enough without bringing her pesky smudge into the equation. Not that she believed in ridiculous pirate lore—but inexplicable things had happened before. She looked to her left and right, noting how certain men and women lingered on her jewelry or the cut of her dress.

Ah, nothing quite like traveling through the Borderlands.

This stretch of land operated under the illusion of the law, which was to say that the laws were only abided when the lawmen were present. And lawmen were rarely present on account that the Borderlands straddled two governing bodies that assumed the other was doing the governing.

Once one got past the theft and murder, it really was a rather charming fresh hell with its tumbleweeds and sand.

"Ticket!"

Her head snapped up, counting the people between the train's ticket master and herself. Four, maybe five, individuals stood between Anna and fresh air. Looking down, she couldn't see the worn floorboards through the heavy skirts and pant legs around her. The sheer quantity of people looking to board certainly didn't help. This must be what sardines felt like once they were stuffed into tin cans. Bugger, there had to be two hundred people clustered around her, every single one of the bodies hot and inhaling something they had lit on fire.

Anna snapped open a fan from a hidden pocket, waving it delicately in front of her face. The boning of her corset sat uncomfortably against her broken rib, but God help her, she loved this dress.

It was sleeveless with a high neckline that did nothing to relieve Anna from the heat and everything to hide her scar. A diamond-shaped cutout sat atop her cleavage, allowing her breasts some air in their attempted jailbreak. It was a splendid thought, though they were too small to actually go anywhere.

Her dress was a dazzling shade of navy with multiple layers of tiered silk and shimmering organza, some a lighter shade than others. The bustle collected at the small of Anna's back, giving her an incredible figure. Lacework crawled from her bust and dripped down her waist in convoluted webbing. Small sparkling opals adorned it at random, making the entire gown look as if it had been plucked from the night sky.

It was an absolutely gorgeous dress and it did its job remarkably well.

Anna stifled another cough as a waft of smoke curled beneath her nose and approached the front of the line. Her little fan wasn't making this experience more bearable, but at least she would be boarding the train now.

She offered up her ticket as sacrifice, feeling the action more than seeing it, and lifted her monstrous skirts just enough to not tangle her feet. She climbed yet more steps into the cooler air of the train. Honestly, after this adventure, Anna would sell her flat and buy something without steps. There had been far too many the past month for her comfort.

She sighed in relief, the cool air kissing her skin. Anna paused only for a moment, gaze on the floor as she breathed, a hand resting on the headrest of one of the many coach chairs. A man turned sideways, murmuring his apologies as he squeezed past, accidentally knocking his elbow into her broken rib. Anna looked to the ceiling, praying to those petty gods to give her patience with Markus once she found him alive and whole.

Wainscot the color of molasses separated the velvet green carpet from the woodland-themed wallpaper as she left the leather coach chairs behind. Animals of every sort hid in the pattern of bare branches along the wallpaper, its base a fine sand color. She paused only for a second, spotting a hummingbird with bone-like brushstrokes. The artistry was breathtaking.

Anna followed the lovely pine-colored carpets to the private chambers on the train. The brass finishing along the walls and corners had been shined until one could see their reflection as they passed. Anna saw hers and paused. She had sported thick, ash-blonde curls since birth; it was a strange thing to see herself with dark hair.

She nearly grinned. No one would suspect Anna was on the train. Not with her dark wig and not with Mihkel Tamm strutting about Bellcaster. From a distance with a wig and a bit of padding on his rump, he could pass as her any day.

Stopping in front of her private compartment, she curled her fingers around the polished brass handle. From here she could rest and gather her thoughts—and potentially pace a track into the floor until it was time to rescue her idjit of a brother. There would be no going back, no returning to a previous state, after this. Anna swallowed hard and laughed at the ridiculousness of waiting to enter the train car.

She rarely looked twice at any one of her decisions, this should be no different.

The door slid to the side with a crisp snap.

Anna entered, head down and focused on keeping her gown from snagging on the door. Once inside, she dropped her skirts, moving them to a more comfortable position. Anna raised her gaze from the pine carpet to the matching wallpaper to the handsome man—

Her thoughts blanked and muscles tensed, eyes widening in surprise.

Handsome *what?*

Her breathing completely and utterly stopped. A man sat in her private compartment, lounging as one does when alone. Anna dragged her gaze from the tips of his polished boots to the wine-red hair collected atop his head. Two green leather benches sat opposite of each other, a wooden monstrosity of a table cutting between them. And this man took up the *entire* right-hand bench.

He stared right back, face void of anything she could identify.

She sucked on her teeth, feeling rather annoyed by this development.

"Excuse me." She cleared her throat. "But what are you doing here?"

The man's gaze wandered around the compartment before leveling her with a look that bordered on withering. "Sitting," he finally said, turning to look out the window.

She squinted at him, bristling at his poor manners and the bit of brogue that roughened his tone. Anna gritted her teeth; pretending to be a woman of Bellcaster high society meant she could not beat a man to death in a train car for poor manners.

This was splendid.

Just absolutely splendid.

"Ah." Anna paused. "I believe you, sir, are mistaken."

He shrugged one massive shoulder, forehead now pressed against the cool glass and dark eyes closed. She turned her gaze on the hustle and bustle outside. Children ran by the train and a bird crowed as men and women ambled by at a leisurely pace.

Anna pressed her lips into a thin line as the man continued to ignore her. It would appear the monstrous oaf wanted to do things the hard way. Fine. She clenched her jaw and smoothed her skirts, peeking her head back out into the corridor. A minute passed before she flagged down one of the train staff, a woman with a clipboard tucked beneath one arm.

The woman was tall of frame and long of limb, dressed in the drab grey uniform of the train staff, a red kerchief tied around her throat. Her dark hair was knotted at the base of her neck. "Yes, miss?" she asked quietly, a smile gracing her lips.

It made the woman appear at least four times prettier. Anna leaned her weight to her other leg and cleared her throat. After another unsure glance at the infuriating man behind her, she looked to the woman's brass name tag. In looping, elegant script, it read: *Ruth.*

"Ruth," she started, motioning vaguely behind her, "I paid for a private cabin, but…"

"But?" Ruth asked slowly, looking over Anna's shoulder.

She turned with Ruth, finding the man immediately. He leaned back against the window now. His elbow rested on the table between the overly large bench seats, his chin sitting atop a leather-clad fist. Anna watched as he propped one of his overgrown legs on the bench, an invitation in and of itself.

She shook her head curtly.

The man was daft.

Ruth's throat bobbed. "Oh."

"*Oh,* indeed."

They both continued to stare at him. Anna wrung her skirts in her hands and tipped her chin in challenge. She wasn't scared of the brute. Oh, no, she was annoyed by him. She had planned everything to the tiniest detail and now she had this mountain of a man dropped right on top of it all.

He lifted his head slightly as well. Anna sucked on her teeth as he shifted his hips, slouching deeper into the bench, drawing her attention like a moth to flame. He filled his clothes nicely, dressed in a uniform of sorts. Both his trousers and jacket were made of black swatches of cloth, cut and stitched together with silver thread. The fabric was most likely some blend of cotton and canvas. Matte buttons traveled from his midline to the center of his throat, all of which appeared about ten seconds from bursting at the seams.

Thick, red hair tickled his collar along the back of his neck, though the sides had been shorn shorter. And he'd shaved recently, he was clean-shaven and a scab sat beneath the line of his jaw.

He cocked a brow, a slow smile curling at his lips. It looked predatory, not an ounce of kindness in it. Her nostrils flared at being caught staring and she moved her focus past his head. Just out the window, smoke curled upward toward the rafters and a little boy pushed his way through the crowd in a bowler cap.

"Can I help you, miss?" he asked, voice deep and dark.

"No." Ruth blushed, averting her eyes toward her clipboard. "It'll be just a moment."

Ruth's fingers flickered through the papers rapidly. She licked one to speed along the process. Just as Anna's patience waned, Ruth's gaze narrowed, flipping a page back and forth. Her deep grey eyes widened, lips pressing together tightly. Ruth turned to Anna, looking incredibly uncomfortable.

"It would…appear this cabin was accidentally double-booked, miss," she said carefully, glancing from Anna to the man behind her.

"Double-booked," Anna repeated on an exhale.

"I'm afraid so, miss." Ruth cleared her throat. "An error in booking. I am terribly sorry for the inconvenience. If you would like, there is a private room available at the next change over. Would you like me to pencil you in? We will provide a full refund for the inconvenience."

Bugger it all to hell.

Anna blinked several times, turning to face the mountain of flesh. She clasped her hands tightly, thumb tapping against her wrist. She didn't need a private compartment later, she needed *this* one *now*. Making more of a scene would only draw attention Anna didn't want. She supposed she could make this work; she'd find a way to deal with the bugger.

Cocking her head, she considered him a moment longer.

41

"I have to ride with *him*?"

At least he wouldn't be difficult to look at.

"Afraid so, miss, but only if it's okay with the gentleman. His purchase was technically before yours," Ruth said quietly, wincing.

They both turned to the redheaded man in question.

"Couldn't fucking care less." He shrugged in response.

"Splendid," Anna said, less than enthusiastic despite the favorable outcome.

Ruth left without another word, head bowed as she closed the door. Remaining where she was, Anna wound her fingers in her skirt, her back straight. The man dragged his gaze from the hemline of her skirts to the curls piled high on her head. And then he *snorted*, tucked his legs back under the table, and turned to the window, as if he deemed whatever scrabbled across the damn platform more interesting than her.

Her teeth ground together and she glared at the back of his head. If he wanted to act an ass, that was just fine with her. She didn't have to like him or interact with him. The man turned to face her, looking like he felt her attempt to glare a hole in the back of his stupid, brooding skull and was not amused by it.

Good.

Neither was she.

She met his gaze, running her tongue over her teeth. Bugger, his eyes were dark. There wasn't a difference between his irises and pupils, from this distance they were both a rich charcoal. Would they be blue or brown upon closer inspection? Or an incredibly dreadful shade of green?

Not that she intended to get much closer.

Anna sat across from him, tucking her skirts beneath her knees. Frowning, she looked down and pulled at the fabric until it sat comfortably. As Anna raised her eyes to meet his once more, something winked from around his neck.

Her gaze dropped curiously.

Then her stomach did.

So did her chances of rescuing her brother.

There at his neck, nestled in the stiff fabric, sat a matte black pin in the shape of a lion's profile, its paws outstretched and mouth gaping open. It was on his right side, which is why she hadn't seen it earlier. The man was a marshal. One of the Senate's dogs. This is the exact situation she'd been hoping to avoid by paying for a private compartment. She and Markus were twins, it was only a matter of time before the man recognized the similarities for what they were.

He continued to stare.

Unsure of what else to do, she opened her mouth and promptly closed it. What could she say? She didn't know what words to bring forth, or if she even should. Anna cleared her throat, smoothing her hands along her skirts. He leaned his temple against the window and crossed his arms against his chest. How in the world hadn't his uniform torn at the seams yet?

Anna looked away; the last thing she needed was the marshal catching her staring. Again. She pretended to pick at bits of this or that off her skirts and then dug through her pockets until she procured a little book, keeping her eyes down.

The train pulled forward and Anna flicked the cover of her book open, hoping to appear occupied while she puzzled through this conundrum. The marshal shifted at the momentum. Anna looked through her eyelashes at him. He didn't look like any marshal she'd ever seen. From his hair and the downward pull of his lips to the utter lack of weapons and tight leather gloves.

A curious thing, really. She had seen marshals with daggers, pistols, rifles, and sabers; she had even glimpsed one particularly nasty man sporting a mace, of all things. The Senate even commissioned revolvers for them, a new brand of gun that did not require powder like pistols did. They truly were a breed unto their own and the only thing worse than a marshal was a pirate.

She tapped her foot to a lullaby her mother used to sing, turning from his broad frame and back to the pages of her book. Something needed to be done about the marshal, she simply wasn't sure what. Anna considered his lack of steel rather worrisome; perhaps he possessed enough skill that he needn't carry a weapon. Her stomach twisted and Anna swallowed hard past a knot in her throat.

Bugger, she suspected she would have to kill him.

What other option was there?

It was this marshal or her brother and Anna would pick Markus every time, in every situation. There was no room for thought, no room for premeditated grief. If taking this man's life meant saving her brother's, she would cut him down without a second thought.

But the chances of doing just that were rather slim. Even if she took him by surprise, Anna doubted she would be victorious in such a fight. The man was at least the size of her brother, with more muscles than the brute probably knew what to do with. The close quarters of the compartment and her dress certainly made things even more difficult. No, a straightforward fight wasn't something Anna could win. It was a splendid thing that she had come prepared for just the situation.

Anna continued her tapping and the marshal adjusted how he sat, the bench groaning beneath his weight. He dropped a hand to the tabletop and drummed his fingers once. Anna glanced up, just catching his head twitching in her direction. His eyebrows pulled together in thought even as he continued to stare out the window.

Curious.

She looked at her book, imagining her feet beneath the table, and then back to the marshal. She cleared her throat, humming the first few notes of her mother's lullaby. He shifted again, this time cocking his head. The drumming of his fingers started back up, gaining in speed and weight. His lips twitched, barely moving in time with her hum, whispering the words of the lullaby to himself.

The marshal scrubbed at his jaw. Anna tracked the motion, taking advantage of his distracted state and studying his face more closely. Long, dark lashes framed his eyes and eleven or so freckles cascaded over the bridge of his nose. A few had even lost their way and made their home high up on his cheekbones. She frowned. She couldn't recall ever seeing a marshal quite as handsome as this one.

It was unfair, really.

Then all at once he stopped and turned toward Anna, the action deliberately slow.

His eyes widened a fraction.

She flicked her gaze from the marshal to the window and back. She cleared her throat and lifted her chin. He drank her in, that damning crease between his brows the only evidence that he remained undecided about one matter or another.

Had he noticed the similarities between Anna and Markus?

Is that why he stared so hard?

Bugger.

CHAPTER 6

No.

Bloody fucking hell.

It couldn't be.

But it was.

Trevor's mind whirred from one thought to the next, no' a single one of the fucks helpful. Just when he'd given up all hope of ever finding the lass, here she was sitting across from him, bedecked in finery few possessed. Jewels on each finger wi' a dress that cost more than a wee ship. She'd been a redhead last he saw, but now the lovely female had hair as black as his soul.

Shite.

Here she was and she was alive. If no' for singing that lullaby and the blue of her eyes, Trevor never would have guessed it was her. Every one of his thoughts dropped away until just the bloody one remained.

Had she heard about Markus Savage and come to rescue him—in *that*?

Fuck, that didn't sit well wi' him.

Trevor swallowed hard and slid his sweating hands down his legs. Didn't help any wi' the gloves on, but bloody hell, he honestly didn't know what to say to her and needed something to do. It had been three years. Three years and she clearly didn't recognize Trevor and he wasn't even wearing a disguise. No' unless ye counted the marshal's uniform, which he didn't.

He hadn't aged a single day in years.

Same wine-red hair and black eyes.

She stared at him expectantly, hands clasped below the table. Her hair was pinned atop her head, wee strands framing her face and curling around her neck. And, shite, that dress...her breasts pressed together, staring him in the face. Normally, Trevor thanked the man crafting windows in gowns, but no' this day.

Trevor swallowed and shifted in his seat.

The lass leaned forward, raising a brow at him. All he could hear was his breathing and the sound of his heart hammering against his ribs. Bloody hell, was he really breathing so loud? Could she hear it too?

For fuck's sake, he was already making an idiot of himself and he hadn't even said two words.

If Tate were here...

If his rake of a brother was here, he'd flirt and converse as if the act alone was his air, the damn breath that filled his lungs. And no' just because she was beautiful, but because he was a good man and loved conversing and meeting new people. Also loved the sound of his bloody voice, but that was neither here nor there.

Could he do that, at least for a wee while?

Trevor gritted his teeth. Felt dishonest, no' disclosing who he was and pretending to be something he wasn't. But it was better than nothing until he thought of something else. And he wouldn't be lying, no' exactly. The lass hadn't asked who he was. She hadn't asked for a name or a title; she hadn't even said hello yet. Maybe she'd even reveal why she was on the bloody train.

There was something calculating in her beautiful blue eyes, like a blade made of glass.

Trevor quirked a brow, focusing on the sparkle of steel in her gaze. "Lovely...?"

She blinked once, then again. Her cheeks flushed lightly, a pale pink like petals on a rose. Trevor's heart kicked into a ragged rhythm and his hands started sweating again.

He breathed out hard, speaking slowly to curb the way his words came. "...maybe I could provide a wee bit of company?"

Trevor clenched his jaw, holding the grimace back. He sounded like a bloody child, voice quiet and unsure. Pathetic. Absolutely pathetic. It was a damn good thing Tate wasn't here, cause the shite would be on the ground laughing.

She looked up and then back at her book.

Fuck.

Trevor cleared his throat, trying to ready his voice and make himself sound like the bloody man that he was. But then she smiled nervous and wee. Just a tip of her lips, but it stilled any words that might have come out.

Why was she smiling at him?

Pretty females like her did no' smile at idiots like him.

Anna leaned forward wi' a wee sigh. "I suspect that will help pass the time. We still have a stretch ahead of us."

Scrubbing at his jaw, Trevor nodded.

That wee grin of hers took a mischievous glint and he wasn't at all sure what to do wi' himself. His hands felt too big and his breaths too deep.

"Well, mister marshal?" One of her lovely eyebrows rose, voice dropping into a soft whisper. "Or are you concerned I'll bite?"

He fucking hoped so.

Trevor's stomach fluttered and he stared at the wee pearly whites in her mouth. He had a rogue sensation of her teeth scraping against his bloody neck. He knew what it felt like, she'd done it before. A shiver worked its way up and down his spine, trousers getting a wee uncomfortable and no' at all because the damn things were too tight.

He swallowed past the knot in his throat, mouth dry, and then pasted his most Tate-like smirk onto his face.

Fucking *be Tate*.

How hard could that be?

CHAPTER 7

What a serendipitous turn of events.

A switch visibly flipped in the marshal. His cool appraisal of her turned intrigued and a little delighted. Whatever he had decided apparently involved acting like a gentleman instead of continuing his brutish behavior.

Just when she'd decided to kill him.

Splendid.

A lazy smile stretched across his face, very male and very mischievous. "So, lovely…what do you suggest we do to pass the time?"

Her brows drew together.

Was he trying to smother his accent?

It was nearly imperceptible but with all her travel, Anna had an ear for them. His voice clipped here and there with r's that trilled in a delightful way. Each word rolled lazily from his tongue like a cat stretching in the sun. Anna hadn't thought one could ever describe brogue as soft, but his was.

The marshal stretched out and dropped his elbows onto the table, clearly waiting for something from Anna—words, perhaps; though from the glimmer in his eyes, Anna suspected he preferred actions. She matched his movements, leaning forward and arching her back. Her breasts strained against the cutout of her dress, but to the marshal's credit, his gaze dipped no lower than her lips.

He knocked his knuckles against the tabletop. "I could make some suggestions, if you like."

Anna watched his knuckles drum against the tabletop. The cuffs of his sleeves were tight and a bit short, but the gloves concealed the skin of his wrist. She looked back up just in time to see the marshal lick his lips. Something tickled at the back of her mind, like a cool wind blowing through tall grass.

"I hope you don't mind me asking..." Anna paused, rearranging her skirts. "But what has taken you this far west?"

"A wee bonnie lass." He shrugged, accent growing a bit thicker.

"She must be quite the woman," she mused.

"Aye." He glanced away.

She squinted at him while he stared out the window, feeling a bit apprehensive. Such a rakish sparkle to a man who should otherwise be less entertaining than a well-trained rock.

It was more than a little suspicious.

As were his gloves.

"You're not from around here," Anna observed.

He chuckled. "No. Before the sea, I called an island further out home."

"Emerald Isles?"

His head tilted, brows raising. "Aye, lass. Aidanburgh. You ever been?"

"Not to Aidanburgh, no," Anna admitted truthfully. "I've only been to Lochland. I was there several months ago for an excavation. A supposedly famous king. He led a revolt across the isles and started a council to help him rule. We found his wife entombed with him. Their coffins had been carved out of ash wood in their likenesses. Some of the best woodwork I have ever seen has come out of the Emerald Isles."

"Aye. We tend to have a way wi' wood." He grinned.

Anna looked to the pin at his throat. "And you uphold the law?"

"I...I do. At least, I do the best I can."

She sucked on her teeth, turning to the window.

Nothing but buttery dunes, some painted in burnished orange and others in canary yellow. The sun lived high above, brightening the clear blue sky. She stared at his reflection, tracing his profile with her eyes. The marshal was talkative and confident. Perhaps she could get some more useful information from him. He'd said he lived out at sea.

Did he know her brother personally or just know *of* him?

Anna and Markus were two sides of the same coin; she was fair and feminine, he was sharp and masculine. No one could mistake their resemblance, even from a distance. It would be a horrible turn of events if the marshal recognized Anna based on her likeness to her brother.

"Were you in the navy long before becoming a marshal?" she asked, turning back to him.

The marshal's jaw tightened, gaze dropping to look at her critically in a stiff sort of appraisal. One that claimed the curiosity Anna possessed had killed all those cats and it might catch up to him as well, whether he liked it or not.

"I've always been on the sea for one reason or another."

"Always is a very long time. It must have been terrible."

He shook his head, looking down in thought. "Sea's got moods, like anyone else, and it isn't an easy living, but it suits me."

Anna blinked.

The man was daft if he enjoyed life at sea. She didn't have much experience with it, but her brother certainly didn't enjoy it. The rations weren't favorable, the sun and work were hard on the body, and the time spent between docks, and potential pleasure, was nearly unbearable. Markus had complained on more than one occasion about the plights of being stranded at sea with nothing but his hand.

And that was without the inevitable threat of pirates looming above a sailor's head.

"Haven't been on land long but already I miss my stars." The marshal sighed. "No lights out at sea. When we're in warmer waters, on nights when the moon is full and the stars look like spilled sugar, I go swimming. There's not a—"

Anna snorted, the sound quickly disintegrating into an uncomfortable chuckle. She cleared her throat. The marshal leaned forward, brows raised and lips parted. He cocked his head, waiting. Bugger, she'd offended him.

"I'm—I'm not laughing at you. That sounds absolutely splendid, but I'm usually sick for the first few days and I can hardly swim." She paused, rubbing the inside of her left palm with her right thumb. "I'm actually more accomplished at sinking."

The marshal laughed but Anna remained quiet, face neutral. She hadn't been jesting and he would realize that soon enough. His laughter descended into a dull chuckle and then his brows furrowed and his smile drooped into a confused frown.

His dark gaze ran over her once more, hurried and sporadic. "You can't be bloody serious."

Unfortunately, Anna was.

"I'd drown before I was much use to anyone."

And that wasn't even the worst of it.

He seemed to turn the new information over in his head, considering Anna and what she had said. His lips pressed into a thin smile, trying to strangle the new bout of laughter as it caught in his chest. She cocked a brow at all the words he left unspoken. "Yes?"

"Nothing, lass." A childlike sense of wonder smoothed the harsh planes of his face as he turned toward the window once more. Square jaw, high cheek bones. Feminine eyelashes she'd consider murder for.

And his *freckles*.

Anna followed his gaze to the desert wastes beyond.

There wasn't much to see if one didn't know what they were looking for. Just sand, rocks, and more sand. But for those who did, for the men and women who spent countless hours in the desert like Anna? It held its own sort of captivating magic. A still-ness that lent itself to ideas, a twilight that crafted more hours than one knew what to do with. As an archaeologist, she appreciated such advantages.

His leather-clad knuckles started their rapping some time later. There was a tune there, one Anna couldn't quite place. Good God, it was frustrating. The words rode the tip of her tongue, unformed but carrying the weight of the world nonetheless.

The swell of a crew gathered in her ears, the snapping of sails off in the distance beneath the gurgle of the ocean. And just like that, Anna smelled the sweat and piss of the hull she and many others had been kept in, remembered the way her nose had stung and muscles had ached. She slid a finger beneath her collar and snagged the notch in her clavicle.

Anna's stomach flipped, her skin sticky with remembrance. Cannon fire and screams. The cruel bite of steel and the metallic taste of blood as it bubbled up her throat. The wet slap of leather hitting her brother's hand before everything went dark.

The marshal said something, but the words sank beneath the churn of her memory. They were a curious thing, memories; a construction of the mind that roared to the surface when one wanted them least, for nearly inexplicable reasons.

He cleared his throat.

Anna turned, meeting his gaze, eyeing him carefully.

His grin flickered once and Anna breathed deep in response, feeling the beginning of a blush. The marshal outstretched his hand, waiting for Anna to grasp it. She stared at the thing and then looked back at his face. Did he honestly want her to shake that? That couldn't be it. The marshal, a supposedly heartless dog of the Senate, wanted to *shake* her hand?

The grin on his face said that was exactly what he wanted.

But Anna wasn't entirely sure. Supposing there was a first time for everything, she slid her hand into his. His glove warmed her skin, its smooth surface warmer than she would have thought possible. He rotated his hand, sliding his fingers beneath hers.

"'Tis a pleasure to meet ye, miss...?" He paused in bringing her fingers to his lips.

She blinked.

He wanted to kiss them?

"Annaleigh," she stated, jaw clenched.

"Miss Annaleigh," he repeated, lips soft as they brushed against her knuckles. "Anna for short, aye?"

She nodded, pulling her fingers from his grasp. Anna dropped them into her lap where he wouldn't see her wiping her palms against her skirts. They were sweaty, traitorous things, her body equally hot. At his continued consideration, Anna angled her head away, only providing him with her profile.

She turned her wrist over, looking at the watch hidden amongst her bracelets. There wasn't a terrible amount of time left and something still had to be done about the marshal. It was him or Markus. It was an easier decision than Anna would have liked to admit. But a life without her brother was no life at all, and so her decision had been made for her.

"All right, Miss Anna, what are your reasons for traveling?" The marshal paused, tilting his head in a rather predatory fashion as he leaned back against the bench. "Most men don't let their ladyloves out and about without them."

He couldn't be serious.

"They don't...?"

The marshal shrugged. "Shite, no. I wouldn't. No' if my wife looked like you."

Unbearable heat flooded her cheeks and flowed down her chest.

Anna swished her skirts, needing something to do with her hands. She met his gaze, slightly hunched over in her attempt to right the fabric around her legs. She pressed her tongue to the roof of her mouth and bit back the grin.

"The poor hypothetical woman. You can't just lock your wife away, mister marshal. That is quite primitive. Honestly, I'm a little disappointed in you." Her grin broke through, giving light to her words.

"Poor fem?" He huffed, eyes alight with amusement. "Poor *me*. I'd have to beat the other men within an inch of their damn lives to keep them at bay. End up locked up on assault and possible murder charges, most like."

She eyed him suspiciously. "You sound suspiciously like my brother."

"Bloody smart man, that one."

"I suppose he is on occasion." Anna paused. "Luckily, I am unwed—despite my father's scheming. I'm free to do as I please and travel as I wish. No need for a man to think he can sort my affairs better than I can."

They stared at each other a moment longer, her bright blue gaze meeting the veiled shadows of his. His voice softened. "Aye. Good thing, that. Can't marry you otherwise, can I?"

His attention drifted to her ring finger and settled upon her mother's wedding ring, a silent question. Anna refused to answer, folding her hands. She owed this man nothing, least of all an explanation for wearing her mother's wedding ring.

The reason her mother had married her father had never been lost on Anna or her brother. She had decided at a young age that she would never marry for anything short of bone-crippling love, no matter all the pretty privileges a husband might come with. Anna would rather be unwed and happy than married and miserable, and wearing her mother's ring sometimes helped her remember that.

Other times, simply standing in a room with men who wore too much cologne did the job.

Anna grinned despite herself. "I doubt you'd know where to start with me."

"Aye. It would be a steep learning curve, marrying a female such as yourself, but well worth it." The marshal pressed his knuckles to his lips and cocked his head to the side, the perfect image of a philosopher of old. He blew out a hard sigh and ran his hands through his hair. "Lovely…I'm stuck on the fact that you don't have a man."

"I assure you, I am perfectly capable of handling things myself."

The marshal's eyebrows shot toward his hairline. A sly grin grew across his face even as a light blush heated his cheeks. What had she said? Anna ran her words back through her head, pinching her lips together.

Bugger.

She tucked a strand of hair behind her ears and the marshal bit his lip to keep his laughter in check. He leaned forward, clearly very amused. Oh, yes, the mold had been broken with this man. Anna could grudgingly admit that he had a charming personality, but it didn't explain his behavior. It wouldn't seem so strange if it wasn't coming from one of the Briland Senate's personal enforcers.

Her gaze narrowed on him.

Was he a marshal?

She cleared her throat, chest tightening. "Not—not like that."

"You fancy men? I mean, nothing wrong with liking a fem, if they're to your taste. I can certainly relate."

She was embarrassed and uncertain and not entirely sure what else to do, so Anna laughed, the sound just as much of a surprise to her as it seemed to be for the marshal. Unfortunately, her amusement only encouraged him. His smile grew, showing off straight white teeth.

"I—" Anna stopped and shook her head. "Yes. I mean no. I like men, yes. But I'm not interested in any. Currently."

She felt the last part was rather important.

Why was she telling him *any* of this? If Markus could see her floundering and flushing in front of a man, she'd never hear the end of it.

Anna swiped her palms against her skirts and swallowed hard. He grinned at her, eyes glimmering like spilled ink. It distracted her nearly as much as the growing warmth in her cheeks.

He angled his head and drummed his thumbs on the tabletop. "No' even right now?"

"I wasn't aware I was in the company of a man. If you see one, point him out."

"You wound me, lovely."

Anna forced her lips into a thin line, cheeks twitching in their attempt to smile at the oh-so-very sad and fake look on his face. The marshal drew closer as Anna picked at imaginary things in her skirt, leaning his elbows and forearms onto the tabletop.

"What?" she asked, feeling the tension between them down to her very bones.

"Must be bloody lonely is all," he said quietly.

She sucked on her teeth, looking away from him. "Like you when you were a sailor, mister marshal, I have my own crew. Friends. Colleagues. Even my brother. I don't have time to be lonely."

"'Tis different, luv. I don't go looking for a bit of crumpet from my mates. I have an image to keep."

Anna grinned at the surprise and horror on his face. That the very idea of intimacy with one of his crew members put it there. That was the loneliness he was describing without using his words, wasn't it? Mental and emotional closeness, where you could break open your soul and share more than just your bed.

Anna had never possessed such a thing.

And, apparently, neither had he.

"A bit of crumpet?" She quirked a brow.

"Haven't heard the term?" He smiled idly. "Ye know, 'the ol' in-out, in-out?"

Anna blinked, hearing more of his accent creeping into his words.

Ye know, the ol' in-oot, in-oot.

Her brain stuttered to a halt, the laughter cracking from her chest. Anna held her arms around her middle as the sound cascaded around the cabin. She hadn't been expecting that. Bugger, she hadn't been expecting any of this. But here it was, and she'd be lying if she said it didn't feel good to laugh with someone so freely. She wiped beneath her eye, small guffaws breaking the silence between them.

The marshal stared, eyes wide and lips slightly parted. Stunned—that's what that was. Not necessarily surprised, but stunned all the same. Then his grin grew into a brilliant smile.

Oh, no.

"Cleaning the cobwebs wi' the womb broom?" he teased, a wicked glint in his gaze. "Parting the pink sea?"

Her mouth dropped open in a subtle gasp. "I never—"

"Releasing the kraken?"

"You, sir, are shameless." Anna smothered her laughter, motioning between them vaguely. "I'll have you know it is unbecoming for an unwed woman to be discussing *this* with a strange man who she only just met."

"You've made it bloody well clear what ye think of being unwed." He winked, sitting back with a victorious smile on his face.

She nodded. This was clearly a punishment from some spiteful god or goddess. It had to be. What were the chances it could be anything else? A supposed marshal with an adorable brogue and those eleven or so freckles? Anna doubted it could be anything other than divine intervention. Unfortunately, she didn't prescribe to such mythology and she didn't believe in coincidences.

So what was he doing here?

Despite the air, her breath tightened in her chest. It was such a shame. He was a fine enough man, a breath of fresh air compared to the men in her circle. If circumstances had been different, she might have taken the time to get to know him, if for no other reason than to figure out why he wore a marshal's uniform.

The more she thought about it, the more Anna doubted the man fell in line for the Senate, which meant he shouldn't have ties to them. But why would he be masquerading as such a horrible mess of a human being? Could he be encouraged to help her save Markus? The man looked strong enough, at the very least he would make an excellent shield.

He returned his attention to the window and the sand that lay beyond. Anna studied him and the light hum of his sea shanty. He wouldn't be humming or knocking his knuckles to the tune of a pirate without cause, would he? He had admitted to a life at sea once, but…She bit her lip. Something familiar hid in the shape of his eyes and the curve of his jaw.

He turned, hands stilling.

Anna opened her mouth to say something witty, but the sliding door opened with a quick snap, startling them both. Anna slid across the bench, her focus on the door, fist in a pocket of her skirt. The dark-eyed man didn't move a muscle. He was entirely relaxed except for the hand resting on his revolver.

In the frame of the door stood a very nervous elderly gentleman, his attention trained on the revolver at the pretend-marshal's hip. Upon noticing the elderly man's gaze, the redhead slid his hand away from the weapon. Clearly part of the waitstaff, the old man sported a uniform the same drab grey as Ruth's. A brass name tag sat at his breast as well. It read: *Sylvester*.

He stepped into the cabin, dabbing at his forehead with a red silk cloth. He was bald, but a full mustache graced his face. Every white strand of hair Sylvester had ever lost atop his head must have regrown above his lip. Anna squinted, not entirely sure where the lip in question even was.

Sylvester cleared his throat. "Is there anything I can fetch?"

"Tea, please," Anna said automatically. "A jade from Xing, if you have it."

Sylvester tipped his head, turning to go. But the redhead spoke up, voice deep and rich, his accent completely smothered. "Maybe something sweet for the lady?"

"Does the lady have a preference?"

The redhead turned to her, brow raised.

"Madeleines, if you have them."

"Of course. Miss," Sylvester said politely, gaze straying to the pin at the man's throat. "Marshal."

He left, the door slid closed with a hush and a click. Anna stared at the man across from her, gut tightening. He wasn't a marshal and, while initially relieved at that, she didn't feel any better not knowing what he was—let alone *who* he was. The man hadn't offered a name and she hadn't asked.

It would be better this way.

All the little details she learned, the ones that made this man who he was, would be with her for the rest of her life. As an archaeologist, she knew well that language shaped the known world, how one perceived it and made meaning from it. People assigned names to things they wished to keep, things they desired to have meaning, and Anna severely doubted the dark-eyed man would become a fixed point in her life.

How could he be?

She planned to poison him.

Their sliding door opened once more.

Sylvester entered as quietly as a wraith in the night, pouring two cups of tea and setting other items to the side. The man across from her frowned at the cups. Anna spied a carafe of cream and a bowl full of intricately stacked sugar cubes. He left the tea-pot on the table, steam billowing from its spout. Then, with a bow, Sylvester left.

Anna and the redhead reached for the cream and sugar at the same time, fingers brushing. He coughed and Anna's gaze dropped to where their fingers touched. The leather had been soft, but why wear the gloves at all? Did he have something to hide beyond the fact that he wasn't a marshal?

"Allow me," she said past the knot in her throat. "Cream or sugar?"

"Sugar, please, Anna."

Bugger, hearing her name upon his lips struck her chest like a physical blow.

She had killed before—always in self-defense or defense of her findings—and always it haunted her. It was them or Anna with only a split second to decide as fate held its breath and awaited the victor, so she bore it. But there was something sinister and intimate about planning it first. To look upon the man and know she would take his life.

And she would, if he refused her offer.

"How many sugars, mister marshal?"

"Three."

His focus dipped to her hands, where they had touched. She watched his gaze flicker from one ring to the next, nine in total. She whispered, "They were my mother's."

The marshal ran his lip through his teeth, the unease in his tone making their cabin feel all the smaller. "Don't mums give their baubles to their boys?"

Anna choked on her laugh.

Oh, her brother wasn't dead yet.

But he might wish he was when she caught up to him.

"Oh, no," she said with a nonchalant wave, muscles relaxing a hair as she fell back into conversation. "He's still alive. Though, once I'm done verbally flogging him, he might wish otherwise. Our mother couldn't trust him to hold on to anything for when he settled down, you see."

"Why's that?"

She couldn't meet his eyes, not while spinning the ring on her right index finger. Anna looked at his ear instead. Impeccably shaped with a freckle hiding on his lobe. "My brother is prone to gambling, drinking, and other various forms of increasingly dubious debauchery."

"Sounds like my kind o' fun."

Anna rolled her eyes. "Yes, well, because of all those *fun* little habits, the tradition of holding onto our mother's priceless heirlooms fell to me."

"Must be a terrible shame, having to wear all those fine baubles." He smiled, though it quickly slipped from his face. His gaze took on a considering quality, one she didn't particularly enjoy. "But 'tis a dangerous business for someone like ye to be traveling alone wi' none to help. Speaking of which. What are ye doing out here? We're far from civilization, practically on the edge of the world."

It certainly felt like they were and Anna preferred it that way. There wasn't anything quite like exploring thousands-year-old ruins and temples, many of which slumbered in this very desert. The khan had spent most of his time toiling under the blazing sun among these very dunes, which, in turn, meant a great deal of Anna's toiling happened in the sun amidst the dunes as well.

Occasionally she got lucky, as she had with the jungle temple.

Not often, but occasionally.

His gaze skipped from her dress to her jewelry. She saw the words, the musings, in his eyes and agreed. It did look like she taunted fate, pleading for robbery or something far more nefarious. He wouldn't have been far off. She had employed the exact same tactic to encourage abduction by pirates a few years back. It had worked a little too well and all Anna had to remember the experience by was the splendid little scar and the dark smudge on her palm.

"I'm here," she started, "on familial obligations. My brother's poor choices occasionally determine the destination of my travels."

It wasn't a lie and Anna was rather proud of that.

"You're a good sister."

Anna didn't wholly agree with that statement despite the urge to soak in the compliment. Good and bad were subjective, after all. She planned to poison this man to aid in her brother's rescue, which at least made her a committed sister, if not a good one.

His eyes didn't stray from Anna's, not even when she plopped the sugar cubes into his cup and stirred it with a small spoon. He didn't notice when the center cut gem of her right index finger opened he didn't notice when a fine powder sprinkled from her ring into his tea. Anna swallowed stiffly, looking at their cups.

He raised his cup to his lips and studied her face. Again, with that intense stare. He took another greedy gulp of his tea. Anna wasn't sure if he slammed it back because he enjoyed it or because he wanted to do away with it as quickly as possible, like ripping off a bandage.

She turned her sight downward to a small leather strap intermixed with bracelets of copper, silver, and gold. She flipped her wrist and stared at the small watch. She had exactly twenty-one minutes. She couldn't wait any longer, not even if she wanted to.

There were no more seconds to steal.

Anna settled her attention on him like a weight. There it was, that critical glint to his obsidian eyes as he studied her. The crinkle of his brow, the purse of his lips, the tilt of his chin. He shifted, noticing the change, feeling her mood as it hardened into something colder.

"Luv?"

This would be awkward.

Anna adjusted her skirts and then clapped her hands in front of her. How did one tell someone they had been irrevocably poisoned? That if they wished to live, they would have to cooperate? Did she just say it outright, or did she try and break the news with a little more courtesy?

Clearing her throat, she catalogued where his hands sat, just in case he reacted rather poorly. Anna frowned. Of course, the man would react poorly. She thought anger was a rather appropriate response, all things considered. She would have certainly been angry if their roles were reversed—furious, even.

She drummed her fingers on the cool wood.

Straightforward it was.

"There is something I must confess," she said delicately.

He stiffened, distrust bleeding across his face as if she had nicked an artery of caution. He leaned hard into the seat, pressing his lips into a thin line. The plain suspicion on his face didn't physically hurt her, but it did remind Anna that she didn't wish to kill him—not really.

It was Anna or the man in front of her.

The man or Markus.

"I poisoned you—"

"Bloody hell, fem, *what*—" he choked.

"—and if you don't help me rescue Markus, I will kill you now, where you sit. If I suspect foul play at all from you, or if he comes to harm, I will not give you the antidote. Not even under the penalty of death or torture. And I assure you, I am far more stubborn than you and I will not cave."

"'Tis no' possible." He shook his head.

"How many sugars, mister marshal?"

He looked down at his empty cup of tea and then back at her. His nostrils flared in irritation, a hot red flush creeping up his neck. His gaze narrowed to black pinpricks. Anna blinked several times. His eyes looked like a shark's right now. He opened his mouth to speak but Anna cut him off.

"And…" Anna held up a finger, gesturing for him to wait.

"There's *more?*" He gawked, dropping his head into his hands.

"…the antidote is not on my person. So, the choice is yours. Die in agony or help me spring Markus."

The man glared skyward, running his hands through that wine-red hair with a low growl.

"Fuck."

CHAPTER 8

Be Tate.

Oh, aye, mimicking his babe of a brother went and got him poisoned.

No fucking surprise there.

Trevor tried swallowing past the disbelief anchored in his throat, mouth tasting like that gods-awful tea. Who the hell thought boiling leaves would be a good idea? He shook his head, looking Anna up and down, trying to figure her out.

Bloody hell.

The wee fem couldn't be telling the truth. He waited five seconds, then ten, for her to laugh and proclaim 'tis all a gods-damned joke. To see that infernal smile light up her face. She didn't laugh. Didn't even fucking smile. Not even a twitch of those rose-red lips.

She remained stoic, her gorgeous wee frame corded tightly, expecting him to hit her and needing to prepare for the blow. His first instinct was to tell her he wasn't in the habit of hitting women. His auntie and mum had raised him better than that.

But bloody hell, Tate was right. He hated it when the wee shite was right.

Anna was trying to kill him.

Again.

Trevor didn't have much cause or love for words but even he knew to use them instead of poisoning someone. Hell, she could have just asked him for his help. Didn't sit well wi' him, of course, that the wee fem was doing all this to save fucking Markus Savage of all gods-damned people.

He frowned. She must care for him, *really* care for him, to go to such lengths. There probably wasn't a line the lass wouldn't cross to help him. Did she love him? The idea made him sick.

Anna raised a single dark brow.

Trevor managed a calming breath, but his voice cracked as he spoke, "Ye—what?"

"*Poisoned*," she said slowly, pulling his attention to her lips. "I have *poisoned* you. And unless you help me, it will result in a very slow and very painful death. Body tremors. Fevers. Asphyxiation. Expulsions of fluids from every orifice. It really is a dreadful way to go. But alas, the choice is yours."

He didn't know what an orifice was, but that did no' sound like a fucking picnic.

Trevor remained seated, arms crossed as he eyed her.

Did she truly want to play this bloody game wi' him? The lass would to be rather disappointed when she discovered he wasn't so easily killed. Trevor could wait her out; he had all the time in the world. But the lass clearly possessed a plan to get to Markus Savage and he did no'.

In a whirl of skirts, she stood, tilting her chin in challenge.

His lip twitched at the corner, still amused with the vicious female even as bile rose in his throat and his gut twisted itself into knots. Never in his life would Trevor have predicted he'd help rescue a prick like Markus Savage. He'd every intention of stealing the man away and beating him wi'in an inch of his life for information on the map's location. But there was something to be said about offering a bit of bread instead of beating a man wi' a chain.

The fem tucked an inky strand of hair behind her ear. "We don't have all day. Now, if you wish to live, follow me."

And just like that, she strode to the door.

Didn't even look back to see if he followed. Completely unconcerned wi' the fact that Trevor just might choose to die. He laughed, a wee frustrated and angry. He hadn't been able to tear the lass out of his head for three gods-damned years, thoughts always circling back to her like a wheel going around and around. And here she was treating him like a pawn on the chessboard when he was the bloody king.

For a breath Trevor thought he might just sit there on his ass and surprise her. Arms crossed out of spite and fucking jealously. He knew what this feeling was and didn't like it one damn bit. But then she turned, *finally*, and flashed her very best grin, one wee hand pressed against the sliding door. It stopped his heart a bit, a brief spasm of surprise tightening his chest, and just like that he made his decision.

Bloody hell, what was he getting himself into?

CHAPTER 9

Anna pressed her hand against the door, pausing.

Would the man follow her or would he stay and die? She supposed it really depended on whether he believed her, and right now he stared at her hard, a deeply contemplative look on his face. His dark eyes narrowed, distrust and something nastier swelling behind his irises. Anna had been surprised his fists had not followed her declarations. Perhaps he was a good man caught up in some sort of business with the Senate?

Why else would he be parading as one of their dogs?

No good reason Anna could think of.

"Now, why the hell would I go and do that, lovely?"

"Because you do not wish to die. What other reason could you possibly need?"

She looked out into the corridor. Nothing but green velvet carpets and closed cabins, woodland creatures staring back at her. Splendid. Anna looked over her shoulder, making eye contact with a grin on her face. Her smile fell at the hollow look in his eyes. Something cool and sad and endlessly lonely filled the spaces between his irises.

Anna shifted her weight, growing guiltier by the second. Instead of wallowing, she turned and walked out the door, skirts lifted and clenched tightly in her hands. Anna didn't see him stand or follow her, but she heard the creak of the bench and the surprisingly soft sound of his boots on the carpet.

"We're in agreement, then?" she asked without turning. "Your aid for my antidote?"

He grunted in response.

She was willing to admit she deserved that.

Anna swept down the corridor with utmost haste. There were six train cars to get through before they'd find Markus in the rear. His was the second of five cars, holding only provisions. Or at least, that's what Mihkel Tamm had told her. It had taken the poor man nearly a full twenty-four hours to track down that information and had cost Anna a fair amount of her savings.

They maintained a strained silence through each of the train cars, making their way without incident. Before Anna could throw the door open and cross the second-to-last threshold between her and her brother, the man's arm shot out. His fingers closed around her forearm, hot against her skin even with the leather gloves. Anna tilted her head just enough to catch his gaze. His brows were pinched, lips set into a thin, grim line.

She cleared her throat, her own fingers tightening on the latch of the door. "So, you court death, then."

Had he decided to protest her actions now? Or had he been waiting to corner Anna somewhere other travelers wouldn't hear her? She swallowed. There wasn't a single soul who would hear her scream this far back. An icy tingle tip-toed its way up her spine. If the redhead thought she'd go quietly or willingly, he was about to learn the error of his assumptions.

His grip loosened and Anna exhaled as his hand pulled away. Perhaps he stayed her hand to tell her something instead of readying to club her. Turning, she looked up to meet his gaze. He didn't look like a man about to strangle her. Then again, men who made a habit of killing women in secluded places rarely did.

It was a rather splendid thing the redhead didn't want to fight, he was monstrous. Anna wasn't lacking in height by any means, but his frame dwarfed her completely, his shadow enveloping her like a blanket might. He grinned, a bit stiff, several more seconds passed before his voice rumbled cool and deep from within his chest.

"Death 'tis no' a fem I'm interested in. She's as cold as a crypt and a vicious bitch at that." He paused, brows raising. "I prefer ladies."

Anna scoffed, leaning back against the steel door. "I hardly imagine you'd know what to do with a lady."

"I know exactly what to do wi' one, Anna," he said quietly, a tinge of pink flaring across his cheeks.

"I think I'll be the judge of that."

He cleared his throat, stepped back, and then nodded to the door. "Is there any kind of bloody plan, or were ye hoping I'd just take care of them?" he said, flicking his fingers as if they were revolvers.

"My plan is to save Markus by any means necessary. Our only requirement is that we have to be on the roof in"—she looked to her watch—"eight minutes. Splendid. I don't know about you, sir, but I find I do my best work under pressure. Shall we?"

"The roof? Bloody hell, fem, I—"

Anna threw the door open.

They were immediately blinded by the sun and blistering winds tore at her exposed skin. She stopped mid stride, squinting against the sun's glare. Good God, that was bright. She grimaced, holding a hand up against the light. Two marshals stood across from them. Their attention skipped over her completely, assuming she could not possibly be the threat, before anchoring to the man at her side.

Anna tried her best to stuff the feelings of resentment back down into her chest. She was perfectly threatening, the man just happened to exude it a little better than she did.

The redhead stepped forward, gaze narrowed on the Senate's dogs across the way, issuing a silent challenge. The marshal on the right's hand darted to his revolver. In the time it took the marshal on the left to follow suit, only a hair behind the other's draw, two shots rang out. The desert swallowed the sound. Right looked down in disbelief even as Left stumbled to the side, eyes wide. Then they both slumped over the edge of the railing and were lost to the sands.

Anna whistled, impressed. "That was rather anticlimactic…well done, sir."

He grunted, his revolver tucked away by the time she turned. A strained breath left his lips, puffing his cheeks, his attention entirely focused on the door across the way. He squinted, then his eyes widened. Anna whipped around and saw what he had.

A hole had punched through the train car where one of the bullets from his revolver had surely gone through.

Gunshots rang out from inside Markus's train car. Anna and the man she had dragged into this god-awful mess hurdled the gap, ducking to either side of the steel door to avoid the curtain of bullets. She inhaled hot, dusty air and pressed the back of her head against the train car. So much for sneaking up on the marshals unaware.

Bugger, this was not how she had planned to do this.

A bullet punched its way through the steel above her head. Anna flinched, ducking down lower and looking around. Steel frame. Hot sands. No ladder to climb. A man who was apparently an excellent shot. She glanced at her watch. They didn't have time to wait.

Anna hefted her skirts and leaned across the door, throwing the lever and shoving it open. She jumped back as another stream of bullets cut through the air.

The redhead threw his hands over his head, his revolver still clenched in his right hand.

"Fucking hell, lass!"

"You didn't expect that?" she shot back, annoyed.

"Oh, aye, and *ye* did? A warning'd be bloody fantastic!"

Anna rolled her eyes and shouted into the doorway, "*Markus!*"

It was silent for too long.

She inhaled.

Exhaled.

Her hands grew sticky and warm, her head starting to swim. Markus couldn't be dead. He just couldn't be. Anna would have felt it—that was a real twin thing, right? Panic flooded her, hands shaking at her sides. She cleared her throat to speak.

"Anna?" Markus called back, voice cracking on her name like a branch breaking over a knee.

Relief. Relief like she'd never known before roared through her veins.

"*What* are you doing here!"

"Oh, I don't know! It probably has something to do with you being an idjit!" she called back, noticing how the man studiously checked his revolver. He looked anywhere but her, eyes roving over their surroundings. His jaw tightened, knuckles turning white.

Curious.

She looked to her skirts, frowning. The dazzling gown had served its purpose, but it was time for it to go. Her hands flew to the knife hidden in a pocket and pulled it forth. The man on the other side of the doorway stared at her warily, but once she started sawing at her skirts, his brows rose in surprise.

"Luv, what are ye doin—"

"Patience, my good sir. All will be revealed in time," she said, slowly working her way through the gown's ten thousand layers.

"Anna, I do hope this—" Markus abruptly stopped on a ragged cough. The marshals inside the train yelled back and forth, but she only had ears for her brother. "Oh, bugger off, *mutt.* I hope this plan of yours doesn't involve disrobing!"

Anna breathed deep, pausing in doing just that. "Not *one* word, Markus!"

"Why do all your plans involve taking off your blasted clothes?"

"And yours don't?" she yelled through the door.

"Well…about *that*…"

Anna made quick work of the skirts, chest tightening only briefly at the horrible end of her favorite dress. Deft fingers gave way to smooth, precise cuts by her thin blade. It wasn't long before she tore them away from her body and stood. She stepped out of them, and not a moment too soon. The wind caught the scraps of silk and ripped them over her head and around the side of the train car.

Another shot rang out. She flinched away from it and turned to make sure her companion hadn't been shot. A tear had been rent in the metal of the train car wall near his thigh and he was leaning around the frame, returning fire.

She couldn't clearly hear anything in the train car with the scream of the wind and the roar of the train's engines. Her eyes stung with engine smoke, but she was nothing if not focused. The man turned quickly, throwing his back against the wall of the train car and fishing into his pockets for more bullets.

Ah, the benefits of masquerading as a marshal and stealing their uniform. Only the Senate's dogs were allowed these new revolvers; everyone else still had to use copious amounts of gunpowder and pistols. Well, everyone except for Anna. How she had acquired the matching pair of revolvers hanging from the belt at her hips would remain a mystery to anyone who asked.

Anna turned away from him, wearing dark breeches and high, supple leather boots, a knife sitting in each of them. On top, she still wore her orchid blue corset. It was cinched tight to give her the right shape in her dress. She loosened it enough to breathe easier. If not for the broken rib, she wouldn't have bothered with the small comfort.

She pulled a white, long-sleeve button up from around her waist and over her arms, fastening the buttons with ease. She stopped at the center of her sternum, having no reason to continue; she didn't have enough cleavage to warrant covering it.

"Are you ready?" she asked, fingers dropping from the last pearlescent button before starting on rolling her sleeves up to her elbows.

The man glanced in her direction and proceeded to miss the chamber several times. His throat bobbed. Anna couldn't help the grin that pulled at her lips and dimpled her cheeks. His jaw ticked, tightening and then slackening as her grin widened. Her heart thundered in her chest, a joyful glee flooding her veins.

This promised to be entertaining at the very least.

She couldn't wait to tell Mihkel Tamm about their success.

And they would succeed. Anna would accept no other alternative.

CHAPTER 10

His sister was here.

His sister was here and she was about to see him in nothing but a ratty button down, a pair of unlaced boots, and his undershorts. If they survived this, Anna would never let him live this one down and rightfully so. God knew he'd do the same if their roles were reversed.

Markus shook his head as crippling confusion and panic threatened to overtake him. He could think of only one reason Anna would be here now. She had found out. But how? It couldn't have been that long since the Senate's dogs had ripped him from his bed and forced him to board this blasted train.

Then again, time had a funny way of distorting when one hadn't slept in a week.

The marshals shouted in the background and even though his chin bobbed against his chest, his gaze was trained on the cut out of sunlight across the way. Only minutes ago, this dark and dingy train car had been ensconced in shadow with only the lamps to throw light about the space.

A searing wind ripped at his blond curls and stung his eyes, the door blown open to reveal the steel of the car in front. To think his blasted sister was just feet away when she was supposed to be leagues away, trekking through some god-awful jungle and swatting at an infernal number of mosquitos.

But she was *here*.

Deep down, Markus wasn't surprised by her arrival. It was such an Anna thing to appear when she was least wanted, when all Markus wished was to be as far away from her as possible. She wasn't going to be happy about the reason for his arrest. But since she was here, he couldn't wait to tell her it wasn't his fault this time.

The blue-eyed prick from earlier leaned over—unfortunately, it was at just the right angle where he wouldn't catch a stray bullet. Such a shame; he would have looked lovely painted in red. "You should have said you were getting us a present."

Markus snorted. "The only gift you'll be receiving is a bit of steel in the throat."

"'Tis best when they put up a fight." The marshal's brows pinched even as a grin pulled at his lips. "No one likes a cold slab of meat."

Bile rose in his throat even as anger seared his veins. Anna would be fine, he believed that. They had gotten themselves out of similar scrapes in the past and she had always pulled through. But it was only his sister against an obscene number of marshals, each one in possession of an itch that the blue-eyed dog thought best scratched by her.

They could have him, but a version of reality where Markus would let them have Anna did not exist.

Markus looked away from the marshal and toward the rectangle of light. Every marshal in the train car had their revolver trained on the exact same slice of light.

Someone leaned over the door's threshold, casting a monstrous shadow upon the ground and blotting out the light. They disappeared in a second, the sound of gunshots echoing in their wake. The marshals yelped and Markus turned just in time to see the blasted marshal with brown eyes slump to the ground, his entire right eye and part of his nose missing.

He blinked, staring at the gory cavity.

Anna hadn't done that; she had never been that good of a shot.

His whole head whipped back toward the open door, searching for a sign of who was out there. The shadow was much too large to be his sister. At least whoever they were, they were a damn good shot. Then her head appeared, eyes scanning the room before a boot shoved her back.

Anna wore another of Tamm's wigs, this one coarse and black. He knew his sister just by looking at her eyes. They were framed in thick, dark lashes, eyeliner, and a beautiful smoky eye—more of Tamm's handiwork. But beneath all that was a matching set of crystal blue eyes, as if his and hers had been chipped from the same stone.

Markus shifted, lifting his head.

Anna burst through the frame with a wild look on her face. Arms raised, a revolver like the marshal's in each hand. That wasn't what held his gaze, though.

His sister hadn't come alone and Markus did not like who accompanied her.

A man roughly his size followed her, right hand raised and gaze trained on any number of marshals. Thick waist, broad shoulders, and thighs that looked more like trunks of some felled ancient tree. Markus frowned. The man had hair as red as wine and wore gloves.

Markus's nostrils flared and his voice cracked as he screamed, "Who the hell is *that*, Anna?"

CHAPTER 11

Anna leaned over the threshold and scanned the interior, looking for where her brother hung and how many of the Senate's dogs they'd have to kill. Her search only lasted the length of two blinks before the man shoved her to safety with his boot. She stumbled backward, slamming her palm against the hot steel of the train car to keep herself upright.

Anna glared at him. That was unnecessary.

Absolutely unnecessary.

He shrugged, unapologetic.

Bugger, it could have been worse but it also could have been better. Fifteen marshals and Markus strung up like a slaughtered cow in the corner, missing his *pants*, of all things. But the roof hatch wasn't locked, so that was splendid. Anna rolled her shoulders and pulled the two revolvers from their holsters. She held them up, cocking the hammers back with her thumbs.

Show time.

With a revolver in each hand, she stepped across the threshold, gaze skipping from one side of the train car to the next like a rock across the pond. One of the marshals stepped in front of her, his face flushed and peeling from the sun. It was there and then gone, blown clear off his head.

Anna's arm kicked back, already searching for her next target. Three times she pulled the trigger, three times she heard the dull echo of a body hitting the ground.

"Markus!" she roared, making eye contact with him in between one shot and the next. "*Where* are your pants?"

"You know I don't sleep clothed!" His arms were pinned high above his head, the balls of his feet just touching the ground.

Anna spun, rolling to the side and coming up behind a set of solid crates. She scrambled backward on her hands to make room for the redhead. He slid in next to her, breathing hard with eyes just as wild and alive as she felt. His lips settled into a grim, annoyed line as he met her gaze.

"Next time, I go first." He swallowed.

"Who says there will be a next time?"

"Trying to get rid of me, lass?"

She laughed. "Get rid of you? Short of my antidote, I can't imagine why you'd wish to stay."

"'Course ye wouldn't." He shook his head, turning his attention back to the task in his hands.

He reloaded his revolver while the marshals scrambled behind them, fussing about like ants who'd had their nest kicked in. Anna couldn't take her eyes off him, the relaxed angle of his shoulders, the deft movement of his fingers. He nipped at his lip, completely oblivious to the look on Anna's face.

Oh, she knew his calm for what it was. The steady breeze before a storm, the quiet focus of a man who had spent too much time steeped in adrenaline. Did he even notice the gunfire as it rained around them? She didn't think so. And she didn't care, not right now.

"You're enjoying this," she mused.

"Aye," he said, gaze down as he shifted the revolver in his hands. "I'll worry about them, ye worry about your man."

"My what?" She gawked but he was already standing, taking quick strides around the crates.

Anna shoved to her feet, tossing her revolvers to the redhead. He caught them without looking and tucked one into his belt, his focus somewhere down the train car. What a serendipitous turn of events, indeed. Perhaps the spiteful gods and goddesses of old hadn't been trying to hinder her with the handsome man. Maybe, if they existed, they were trying to help her.

79

She sprinted toward Markus, eyes darting left and right, up and down as he catalogued the marshals in the train car. She shook her head with a snort. Oh, yes, the man would deal with all those marshals while she dealt with *her man*. What a curious choice of—

Anna blanched.

As soon as they rescued Markus, she would explain that they were not lovers.

Good God, just the thought disgusted her.

Anna's leg buckled on the next step, she stumbled and it took a few steps to right herself. Her eyes widened and she inhaled deep. Bugger. A sweat broke out across her lower back and on her upper lip. Every step pushed the pain farther and farther away.

Markus floundered, screaming just in front of her. His dirty hair stuck up in every direction. Anna focused on the locking mechanism above him, the one keeping him suspended. Her brother stuck his leg out for her to climb, throwing his head as far to one side as he could. It would be a tight fit, but Anna didn't have much choice in the matter.

She propelled herself off his knee, threading her leg through his arms. His ear pressed firmly against her stomach, his shoulder digging into her rump. Wavering briefly, she ducked at the deafening sounds of bullets leaving revolvers. Anna flinched at the first scream rent from one of the marshal's throats. The pain and fear in it sent a trembling shiver down her spine, but Anna didn't have the time, nor the sympathy, to investigate.

Anna leaned precariously, searching for a better view of the lock. Reaching into her hair, she procured a few sharpened pins from the wig's curls. She never left home without a good set of lock picks; one never knew when they might be useful or required.

"My God," Markus groaned from below her. "Anna, how much weight have you gained?"

"Don't you dare bring my ass—" Anna stopped abruptly, squinting at the lock for a second. Well, hello there… A low impressed whistle left her lips. "Bristolian, circa 15th century. Manufactured by Gideon Thatcher. Second edition, by the looks of the symbol."

"Absolutely fascinating, old girl," Markus said dryly.

"It really is, Markus. Locks aren't made like this anymore," she muttered over the redhead's grunts and the marshal's continued screaming. "It has a high iron content, I can see the flecks."

"Less appreciating and more springing!"

"You have absolutely no appreciation for hist—" Anna flinched, ducking a bullet that ricocheted off her brother's chains. Close—that had been too close. She gulped, wiping a sweaty hand off on her leg, and leaned back into the lock.

Something cracked, big and abrasive enough to cause even Markus to jump. A funnel of heated air tore through the train car, ripping at her wig and stinging her eyes. She shook her head and wiped her face against her forearm to try and clear her vision.

Another scream, high pitched and whining.

"Come on, Anna, come on!" Markus started muttering, something trembling in his voice.

The tumblers slid and *clicked*.

Anna had nary but a second to grin triumphantly before Markus plummeted to the ground, taking her with him. She tumbled from her perch on his shoulder and rolled to the side the moment his knees cracked against the floor boards. Her leg gave out, sending her crashing to the floor with a yelp. Anna propped herself up on her forearms. It took her less than a second to find her brother, face down and unmoving. Her heart thundered in her chest.

Anna scrambled forward, leaning down to check him for injuries once she spied his chest rising and falling. Markus cradled his arms in front of him, slowly pulling his knees beneath him, folding one and then the other. His brows pinched tight, his jaw ticking and veins standing out in his neck.

"Are you—are you okay?" Her hand hovered above his back. He nodded. "I'll be fine."

Anna couldn't imagine the pain of letting his muscles stretch and relax. Her brother braved it rather valiantly. She had expected at least three complaints, but he issued none. Markus rotated his shoulders and tried bending his elbows, an ugly grimace on his face.

A sickening squelch twisted her stomach and then all was quiet except for the air whirling around them. Anna turned only to see the man standing in a field of corpses, the lanterns around him dark. He looked like some vengeful god. His shoulders rose and fell with each gasping breath, his face turned down.

Anna swallowed hard, dragging her gaze from hair that dripped sweat to the blood pooling at his boots. A saber sat limply in his right hand, a revolver in his left—though he was holding it as if he had been using it to bludgeon with, not shoot. At seeing the body at his feet, she winced. The man's face had caved in, completely unrecognizable and looking more like bloody pulp. Only the gold thread in his uniform told Anna who the man had been.

The redhead tipped his head back, revealing a split lip, blood meandering down his chin.

"What about you?" she asked, settling her hand on her brother's shoulder. The man's gaze tracked the motion. Anna cleared her throat. "Are you all right?"

The smile he flicked her way flashed like a blade, all business with no hint of play. Anna turned from the weight of his gaze, choosing to focus on her brother instead. It wasn't difficult to see Markus needed a breather and a moment to get the feeling back in his arms. He massaged them, avoiding the raw patches at his wrists. Blood gurgled from open sores, the skin pale on either side of the bloody mess. She wished she could give him the time to rest and heal, but there wasn't any time left to steal.

"It's time to go, Markus," she said gently.

"Thought you'd never say that." His smile was thin and pale, exhaustion riding his shoulders.

Anna looked at the redhead. "Afraid I'll need some help."

He stepped forward and into better lighting. Blood had splattered across his face, and she was certain he was soaked in it. He dropped the saber first and then the revolver, looking down at his hands. His eyes widened and nostrils flared. Had he just realized he was coated in gore?

The man's throat bobbed and he wiped his face off against his arms and shoulder. "What did ye say?" he grumbled.

"I can't reach and we're exiting through there."

He sighed, looking at the hatch. "Aye, lass."

Markus growled low in his chest when the man took a step in her direction. Anna held her hand up, unsure whether she was motioning for him to stop walking or for her brother to stop growling but it worked on both. Well, this was an excellent start, wasn't it?

"Anna—"

"Not one word," she snapped, limping to the unopened hatch.

The man crouched and Anna threw her legs over his shoulders. He stood in one strong movement. She wiped her sweaty hands on her legs before pressing all her strength against the little door. It creaked and sighed a bit of hot dust at her face but did not open. Bugger. Anna took another deep breath, eyes pinched shut as she strained against the old steel. But it was so heavy and she was starting to come down from the manic energy that had permeated her blood during the fight.

The man raised up onto his toes on her next shove, giving it that extra bit of force needed to open it. The hatch swung back and thumped. A vortex of desert air pulled at her hair and before she could grab the rim, the man lowered her back to the ground. She slid from his shoulders, squinting at him critically. He swung his arms and jumped up, catching the lip of the opening.

"Remember, if you leave us here, you die," she reminded him as he pulled himself up and through the hatch. Markus shot her an incredulous look. "Don't start, Markus. This doesn't concern you."

The man poked his head down, one hand braced on the edge, the other reaching for her hands. "Wouldn't dream of it, luv. Me first, remember?"

Anna considered his hand before slipping hers into it. He could throw her straight off the train if he wished and there would be little she could do about it. She stared into his eyes, feet no longer touching the ground. The redhead raised to his feet, one hand braced on the rim of the hatch as he lifted her with what appeared to be no effort at all.

He set her down as a bead of sweat dripped off his chin, the steel beneath her scalding to the touch. Anna shifted away, but she had yet to break eye contact with him. Something curious swam in those dark depths.

Something wicked, too.

Vicious gusts ripped and pulled at her hair like fingers grasping at straws. Even the short strands of the man's hair danced, drawing her eye. A bruise colored his cheek and he sucked at his still-bleeding lip. He'd cleaned most of the blood off his face, just a pink smear remained at the line of his collar, hardly visible against his skin.

Yet again Anna wondered why he wore a marshal's uniform when he so clearly wasn't one. That was one mystery that would have to wait. Anna swallowed, looking down into the hatch where Markus took deep breaths, a finger in the air.

He wanted more time?

She nearly laughed.

"That man of yours seems to have taken a real beating," the man said from next to her, nearly having to yell to be heard over the wind and engines. "Can't help but wondering what he did to deserve it…"

"He's not my—we're not attached," she said quickly. "Not like that, anyway; I claim him, yes, but he's my brother."

"What?"

"Markus. He's my *brother*."

He stared at her as if seeing her for the first time, brows drawing up, but then for some inexplicable reason, he relaxed.

"*Oh*," he said on an exhale.

"As for your question, normally I'd say he probably slept with the wrong man's something-or-other, but..." Her voice grew quieter, stiffer. She breathed and pressed her palms against her knees. "All I was able to dig up before leaving was the Briland Senate plans on handing him over to the Coalition of Pirates as an act of good faith. I don't know why."

His gaze snapped down to her, eyebrows high with shock. "What the fuck did ye say?"

"The *Coalition*," she annunciated slowly. "They want my brother as an act of good faith. It has something to do with the Pirate King. I don't know what, but I have every intention of finding out once we're safe. If you're alive, and in a position to listen, I'll tell you too."

He shook his head. "The Coalition doesn't operate like that. And—and the Pirate King doesn't make trades or whatever the fuck this is."

"He takes women as tithes and you expect me to think he won't take my brother in a trade?"

The man chewed at his lip and nodded.

"So, *you're* an expert on pirates?"

Anna knew what he *wasn't* and the urge to figure out exactly what he *was* grew by the second.

"I consider myself one, aye."

"Anna, I'm ready!" Markus called, interrupting them. "Now, Anna! *Now!*"

They leaned down, offering their hands. He grabbed them with a gusto that surprised Anna. Her gaze wandered to the back of the train car as they lifted him and—well, bugger. Marshals flooded into the space, revealing her brother's sudden need to climb the hatch.

"Okay, if there ever was a time to share your brilliant escape plan, Anna, now is it," Markus gasped as they dragged him through the hatch.

A bullet zinged past their heads.

Were they coming from the back or the front? Raising her hand to blot out the sun, Anna searched for the gunfire's source. Stupid marshals with their stupid fancy revolvers. Dark figures climbed atop the roofs of the train cars behind them.

She bit her lip; things were not going according to her plans and it was honestly getting on her last nerve. No need to lose her temper, though. She could work with this; she could still get her brother out of this alive.

Anna turned, stopping only to grab her brother's bicep. "Come along, Markus!"

It shouldn't have been difficult for him to keep up with her, but he struggled to keep pace with Anna's smaller strides, which were further shortened by the pain in her thigh. The rhythmic thumping of the man's boots sounded from just behind her and his shadow threw a distorted version of him to their right. They were the only indications that the redhead followed them.

Anna's lips twisted and she closed her eyes for a second. Good God, her thigh might be worse than she had originally thought. At least the marshals had quit shooting, though Anna suspected that had more to do with orders surrounding Markus's health than anything. Her brother couldn't provide them with what the Senate wanted if he turned into Swiss cheese.

They hurdled the gap between train cars. Anna clenched her teeth as pain fluttered up and down her thigh. Markus nearly tumbled from the train, both legs buckling on the landing. She hauled him along with her, the redhead pulling him to his feet without breaking stride.

"We are going to run out of cars!" Markus called.

"Not if we switch trains!"

Her brother laughed, a boisterous cackle that worried her slightly. Heavens above, he must have been worse off than she thought. The redhead, on the other hand, threw her an incredulous look.

"Change bloody trains?" he gawked.

Anna looked at her watch; it was nearly time.

They lunged over another gap and Anna's leg buckled beneath her. Her knee slammed hard, wrenching a steep gasp from her lips. The man grabbed the back of her shirt, dragging her up and along as she struggled to stand. Once upright, he released her, only to hold under her arm when she stumbled again. She sucked in a tight breath on her next step and on the one after that.

It didn't matter. It couldn't matter. Not now. The blasted thing could have been falling off for all Anna cared. She'd get Markus out of this one way or another and her leg would just have to figure it out. Out of all her harrowing adventures and nail-biting escapades, this would not be the one to do her in.

"So," Markus started on a wheeze and looked around, "this train—"

As if in answer to Markus's question, the booming whistle of another train cut across the desert. It drowned out all other sounds around them, including the gunfire. Anna grinned, breathing out hard in relief. About damn time. As the train passed, another gust of air buffed her hard enough that she slid to the left, nearly careening into the redhead.

"Are you sure about this?" Markus called, eyeing the other train warily.

Anna threaded her fingers through her brother's and gave a stiff yank, forcing him to run faster. The man released a string of curses, his accent thick and voice low. As they continued to run, his curses grew more colorful and creative. Markus would have applauded the man's efforts if he had been listening, but as it was he probably couldn't hear over his panting and huffing. He obviously wasn't keeping up on his cardio. Anna supposed that was bound to happen when one moved up in the food chain. More ordering and less working.

"One…more…car," she told them, barely squeezing the words between breaths. If they leapt too soon, the marshals would just follow them over and that rather defeated the whole purpose of the escape and Anna knew Markus would be useless in the fight.

She swallowed hard, looking up at the man. "If they follow us over, will you be able to…?"

"Aye, lovely. I'm always ready for a fight," he said.

She nodded, steeling her nerves and preparing to jump.

But then he continued, "Might cost ye, though."

Anna choked, fully aware of what that price would be. Markus, too busy growling something unintelligible beneath his breath, did not notice her distress. A *kiss*. She shook her head. It was a small enough price to pay for their safety, for her brother's life. She would have given the man far more than that to keep Markus safe, if she didn't already hold his life in her hands.

"I don't know if you're in a position to bargain," she told him, angling toward the edge of the train.

That mischievous sparkle returned. "I can earn it, luv."

She had to bite down on her tongue to keep from grinning. In between one step and the next, Anna jumped to the other train. She wished it was as easy as it sounded. It wasn't.

The roof of this train car was hotter than the one they'd come from. Anna landed on her hands and knees before rolling, scrabbling to gain a hold as she slid down the slope of the roof. One of her nails cracked, catching a rivet, but she slowed. Anna gasped for breath, staring at the sand beyond the train car. She gulped, hoping the worst was over, her body aching and beginning to tremble.

Several thumps followed them over.

Bugger.

Anna rolled to her feet, ducking beneath the first marshal's fist. She swung low into his kidney and threw all her weight behind the next shot to his jaw. He crumpled as she lunged forward, relieving him of his revolver. Her finger tightened around the trigger, the deafening shot a mere echo in her ears. She shook off the sickening feeling in time to make eye contact with Markus and tossed revolver to him. He was a far better shot than she.

The train heading to Bellcaster blew its whistle, and then the last train car passed by. Three marshals jumped only to land among the sand. The man grunted as Markus took aim, arm outstretched and grimy button-down billowing around him, bruised and bloody in a pair of unlaced boots. Gunshots cracked around her, each sound echoing in her head, bouncing and ricocheting from one side of her skull to the next. Her ears rang and the rest of the sounds around her warbled. Markus shouted something and she turned.

Three marshals were trying to bring the redhead down, but in one step he relieved one of his knife, threw another off the train, and then ripped the stolen blade through the third's gut. If he kept this up, he might very well earn a kiss. He shoved the gutted marshal from the train, chest heaving from the effort. He turned, a vicious glare pinching his eyebrows and curling his lips.

Her brother shouted something again. The ringing had quieted enough that Anna heard her name. Markus stood a few feet from her, revolver smoking.

The redhead was breathing hard with an arm wrapped around his trunk. His focus darted from her feet to her eyes, his shoulders rolling back and fingers splaying. A grin twitched at the corner of his lips. Bugger. Heat flooded her cheeks and chest and Anna told herself over and over that she wasn't blushing at the prospect of kissing him.

It was just heatstroke, that's all.

"Where'd ye learn to fight?" he called.

"My brother," Anna answered. "He needed someone to practice on and, luckily for me, I'm a quick study."

"I always let you win." Markus rolled his shoulders and stretched his arms as he followed Anna down to the next hatch. "Now tell me, Anna darling, but who helped you plan this? You're supposed to be in that infernal jungle."

"It's an *oasis*, Markus. And Mihk did. I'd just gotten back and he told me what was happening and offered a bit of help."

"You have him parading as you in Bellcaster, don't you?"

Anna deigned not to give him a response.

He ran a hand through his hair before dragging it down his face comically. "Anna, how many times do I have to tell you to leave that poor man be? Your ministrations are going to get him killed."

The redhead cocked a brow, jaw tightening again. He was easier to read than a book, and so to quell his frayed nerves, Anna coughed and looked up at him. "Mihk only fancies men."

Her brother's hackles raised as he dared an obvious gawk between the two. "Why would he care to know—" Markus's eyes narrowed like a dart hitting home. "You stay the hell away from my sister."

The man chuckled beneath his breath and shook his head, choosing to put his hands in his pockets. Anna glared at her brother, daring him to say *one* more word. She didn't care if he'd been through a rather traumatic event, she'd still knock his silly head off his shoulders. Markus rolled his eyes, looking to stick his revolver in a belt or holster only to find none. He glared up at the sky and tossed the revolver over his shoulder.

They came upon the hatch and the redhead growled in effort to lift it. Once the hatch lay open, she allowed Markus and the redhead to lower her down into the dark, cool train car and then waited for them. As the man was the last to enter, he closed the hatch and looked around.

It was empty, save stacks of dirty hay, but Anna figured she could not possibly smell worse and slumped into the nearest stack.

"We have thirty minutes before we reach a small cargo station. From there, we'll steal horses and ride for Heylik Toyer, the marshals are probably already organizing themselves and this cargo station is where they'll check first. Though I'm sure they'll send a contingent to Heylik Toyer. It'll be rough riding, but I think we can make it in time."

Her brother winced. "I'd really rather not stop in Heylik Toyer, Anna."

"And why not?"

"Someone always tries to kidnap you when we're there, old girl."

"I'm not a child," she said stubbornly. "It's abduction, and we're going."

Markus watched her carefully for a minute before lying down, letting his eyes close. It wasn't long before his chest rose and fell in soft, even breaths. The man waited until soft snores left her brother's nose and then sat down next to her. Brilliant man, really. Markus couldn't be snarly if he was sleeping.

He laid back in the straw with one hand behind his head and the other across his trunk, staring up at the ceiling. Good God, this man. She sucked on her teeth, following the lines of his body. How could one go from gutting a man to this? Relaxed and boyish and not at all dangerous-looking—aside from the sheer size of him.

"So, he's your brother, aye?"

"I do believe that is what I said, yes."

"Makes ye a Savage."

Anna stilled, arms tightening around her legs. She was quiet for a long time before she swallowed and looked down at him. He immediately met and held her gaze; he didn't flinch or shy away from Anna or the connection between them. She had never said their surname and hadn't heard the marshals call it, so how had he known?

"Yes," she finally whispered, "John Savage is my father."

"Pity, that."

If he only knew the half of it.

Anna cleared her throat and looked down to her blood-spattered boots, nausea churning in her gut. "How did you know?"

She heard the deep breath that must have filled his lungs. "Well, I know, lass, because *that—*" he motioned toward her brother with a twitch of his foot—"is Markus Savage. Rather hard to mistake the prick. He's got a reputation out at sea."

And what did this man do out at sea that he would be privy to such information?

"I knew it would be Markus that gave me away."

"Ye don't look like one."

Ah, yes. Anna possessed her father's straight nose and icy blue eyes, clear as a summer pool. Her mother had gifted her with high, prominent cheekbones and full lips—and, though she complained about it often, her mother had also given Anna her pear-shaped frame and lackluster bust.

Of course, she didn't quite look like her father or her brother; being a woman, she was predisposed to growing into feminine features while her brother inherited an obscene resemblance to their father. She was small and sturdy, where Markus was large and hulking.

They both had skin smooth as porcelain that glowed after spending time in the sun and matching curly, white-blonde hair, though hers fell past her breasts and Markus kept his in the same fashion the man did, longer on top and short on the sides. Her brother's jaw was square and sharp. Anna's was soft and round. His face chiseled from diamond and hers molded from clay.

He squinted at her with another warm grin. "Aye...a wee too lovely to be a Savage."

She laughed, looking to his chest, unable to maintain eye contact.

"Savage…" he whispered again before shaking his head in disbelief. "Nice to finally know what to moan." The marshal leaned back and smirked. "Now, why don't ye settle back and relax? I'll keep an eye on things."

Slowly, warily, she leaned back into the straw and tucked her arms beneath her head, rolling to her side so she faced him. She closed her eyes after using a dial on the side to set her watch for twenty minutes and took a deep breath. She was halfway to an exhaustion-induced state of limbo, not quite awake or asleep, when she could have sworn she heard the man whisper—

Tate's no' going to believe this shite.

CHAPTER 12

To think this was the infamous Annaleigh Rae Savage.

Trevor shook his head in disbelief, nearly snorting. He'd always heard conflicting things about the lass. That she was nobility through and through. That she fought in pubs. That she kept to Bellcaster. That she could be found anywhere but there. He didn't know how to make heads or bloody tails of her, but out of every single damn female in the wide, wide world, what were the fucking chances it had been John Savage's daughter that poisoned him?

Tate was going to shite himself.

Bloody hell, just like that, Trevor had more thoughts swimming around his head than he had ships in his armada and he didn't know what to do with a single one of them. Had the first time been intentional? Had her da sent the lass on a quest to kill the Pirate King? Had she come for more than just that wee cursed map?

Did he honestly care?

He wasn't really sure.

On the one hand, he had a complete name now, and it was the loveliest name he'd ever bloody heard. On the other, her da was John Savage and that was...well, super fucking shitty.

If there had ever been a king of the seas that wasn't a pirate, it was him. He'd grown a merchant empire, sailing goods across the five seas after combining his and his late wife's fortune. Most of his ships were peppered with mercenaries to ensure the safety of his cargo. The sailors aboard them were some of the most despicable men Trevor had ever seen.

Fucking hell, that meant her mum was Sara Sommers; the only female to go toe to toe wi' the Viper on more than one occasion and live to tell about it. He narrowed his gaze at Anna curiously. That might explain a thing or two about her.

Since she'd closed her eyes, Trevor had rolled over onto his side and curled his arm under his head. It was almost like they were lying in bed together and the damn thought sent his stomach spiraling.

Anna's face was dirty and speckled wi' blood, black hair falling from the knot atop her head. Did she get the dark locks from her mum? Maybe a grandparent? Trevor didn't care what color her hair was, couldn't care less if he tried. She could have been fucking bald and he still would have been interested if only to get to know the lass who poisoned him on a whim no' once but twice.

Bloody hell, it had to be more than attraction. He couldn't get past that. It was like—like the day he met her, he'd stepped into one of Fate's tides and couldn't pull his damn boot out. No' that Trevor wanted that. The gentle light in her eyes stilled every spiraling emotion in his chest and her smile killed every anxious thought he had.

Tate would call him crazy, thinking one female could make him feel such a way.

Taylee would have mused 'tis about time.

Trevor suspected some kind of bloody witchcraft but couldn't bring himself to care.

His fingers tingled, itching to reach out and touch her, to see if any of this was real or if he was dreaming again. But the fuckers remained firmly at his side. Maybe he'd be brave enough to try later. He hadn't needed to pretend to be his brother by the end of it. She was easy to talk to, words flowing from his soul like water bubbling up from a stream.

Her brother grunted off in the distance, groaning low and in pain as he shifted, the straw about him hushing him back to sleep.

Any thought Trevor held of Anna disintegrated. His jaw ticked. Couldn't fucking believe such a nice lass was related to such a prick. Sure, she was a daft, wee thing. She'd have to be to willingly claim the prick as her brother.

He'd been worried at first, sure as shite she would recognize him—but she hadn't. Then he'd been nervous the bloody prick would and what a twist in the Tides of Fate that would have been. Savage had seen him far more often than the wee lass, albeit from a greater distance. It would have made sense, of course, but Trevor wouldn't have been blood happy about it.

Markus fucking Savage did no' recognize Trevor either, otherwise he imagined the damn man would have been doing a whole lot more than growling pointless threats. So far, who he was remained a well-kept secret and there was something relieving about neither of the twins recognizing him or cowering in fear or worse. Anna didn't have a problem with killing Trevor before she knew who he was and would have even less of a bloody problem after.

Felt a lot like lying, despite all that.

Didn't really matter though.

He still had to find that gods-damned map and as soon as she figured out who he was, Anna would spit in his face and tear out his throat. He grinned. Hopefully she'd try to do so wi' her teeth. Trevor was a wee terrified of the price he'd be willing to pay to have her lips on his neck. Shite, if there ever was a way to go, that might be it. Might be fucking worth it.

Trevor's hand settled between them, fingers curling around bits of straw, watching the rise and fall of her chest.

"Move one more finger toward my sister and I'm cutting the damn thing off," Markus rumbled from a few feet away.

So much for the prick being asleep.

"Piss off, Savage," Trevor growled, closing his eyes. "If I touch your sister, it'll be because she bloody well asked me to and it won't be wi' ye in the damn room."

CHAPTER 13

They'd made it.

Anna squinted up from beneath the cream cloak she'd nicked from the stable. The sun was bright and she had to hold up a hand to examine the mud brick wall surrounding Heylik Toyer. It was thirty feet tall and another fifteen feet deep; sentries were stationed every twenty feet or so, clothed in maroon robes and black headscarves meant to protect them from the sun, curved sabers at their sides and rifles at their backs. Not a single sign of the marshals—not yet at least.

"Relax," Markus hissed from her right.

"I *am* relaxed," the man growled back.

"Are not. Your shoulders are nearly touching your ears and your elbows are at an exact ninety degrees. No one who has ever been on a horse before rides like *that*."

"What's this about my bloody elbows?"

"They look like *this*,"—Markus demonstrated—"and they should look like *this*. Drop your blasted hands, let them rest on her withers."

"I'm no' touching it."

"It is a *she* and *her* name is Daffodil, you prick."

"Fuck ye, mate."

His mare had been the only named horse in the entire stable. The name plate sat above her stall, shined to a near gleam. Anna had initially felt a little guilty about stealing away such a nice girl from whoever had loved her, but there were only three horses in the stables and they required three for the trek to Heylik Toyer.

98

Markus scoffed. "Surely you can come up with something better than that."

Anna sighed.

They'd been arguing or at each other's throats from the moment they stepped off the train. Hissed whispers and scathing remarks had followed her as they'd quietly made their way into the stables, tip-toeing and crouching. It wasn't until she had cracked her brother on top of the head with her fist and glared at the man that they'd gone as quiet as corpses. She preferred the tense silence, full of promised threats. That at least didn't draw attention.

They were dressed like Anna in long cream cloaks that fell to their ankles with hoods pulled high over their heads. Thank God for that because Anna hadn't found her brother a pair of trousers and his pale legs would have given them away immediately.

Markus looked like he'd been born to ride a horse and the man…well, he was certainly born to do something but riding a horse wasn't it. He sat stiff and unsure in the saddle, even after the forty-minute ride to Heylik Toyer. His arms were tight at his sides, gripping the reins until his knuckles turned white.

With the growing hustle and bustle and increase in people before the main gates, the two had grown bold once more. The sun beating at their backs and cooking them within their cloaks probably wasn't helping. She suspected it made them more irritable than they would have been otherwise. It was having a similar effect on her mood.

Anna scanned the surrounding area. People ambled forward like cattle. Some on foot, others in wagons, and fewer still were on horseback. Sentries paced the outsides of the road and stood guard at the gate, ushering people in one by one. They looked under tarps and beneath wagons, had women pull the coverings from their faces and men remove their hoods. Anna stooped a little lower and let the hood slip farther to better cover her face.

Cursing beneath her breath, she leaned toward her brother and their companion. "I think we're going to have to force our way in."

Markus nodded his head in agreement, gaze trained on the gates. "They're looking for us. Did you have a plan beyond getting here? Did you contact…" He trailed off at the nervous grin on Anna's face. Realization flashed on his face right before his nostrils flared. "No, absolutely not, Anna. We were lost for a week last time."

"We were *fourteen*, Markus. One cannot expect a fourteen-year-old to navigate an ancient labyrinth built by *the* khan without incident—"

"You are only proving my point."

"—but a twenty-five-year-old? Like stealing candy from a baby. Plus, I memorized the passages last we were there. It shouldn't be too difficult and no one would dare follow us in."

Markus turned a pointed look on her. "It was a week without food and we stumbled around in the dark avoiding traps. Poisoned darts. Falling rocks. *Scorpions.* There is a reason no one would follow us, sister dear, and it's because they value their life more than you do."

Anna huffed.

Such a baby.

"It'll be *fun*, Markus. Quit being such a worry wart."

"I worry about you sometimes, you know this, yes?"

"Excuse me, lass, but *where* are ye taking us?" the man asked, brow furrowed and shoulders tense. "As it is, I—shite, never thought I'd say this, but, I may be inclined to agree wi' your prick of a brother."

"Look at that, Anna, the man has a brain!"

"Oh, don't let him scare you. I'm taking us into the belly of Heylik Toyer. It's a labyrinth built by Granbaatar Khan late in his life. My brother and I had the opportunity to scout it out as children. We'll be fine, he's being dramatic."

"I've got a scar on my *ass* from the experience. I swore I'd never go back."

"You shouldn't make promises you can't keep, Markus."

They'd sidled up close to the gate, going quiet at the nearness of the sentries. Anna shifted in her saddle, choking up on the reins as she narrowed her gaze at the men. She rode in front, the redhead between her and Markus. They had no saddle bags that needed to be checked, no obvious glint or bulge of steel. She had even shoved her remaining knife far down in her boot to keep it from being seen.

The guards spoke back and forth in rapid fire Kurder, the harsh tones and growl of their voices made it difficult for her to immediately interpret. The language tasted like rust on her tongue and rumbled like an old train just picking up steam. Anna's responses were a few seconds behind their commands as her brain worked to interpret what was being asked.

Step forward, single file.

Halt.

And then—*remove your hoods.*

She breathed deep, attention sliding to the guard's fingers. They twitched toward curved sabers and pistols that were holstered at their hips. The pistols were tucked away in supple leather and the bits of steel sheathed in gilded scabbards.

The guard stepped closer, black boots matching his headscarf, a curious and cautious glint in his bright golden eyes. He repeated his instruction—*remove your hoods…now*—his voice was a rasp from hours of directing, it wasn't unkind.

"Anna," Markus whispered.

She knew—she *knew*—they had to move now, before the ones atop the wall took interest, before the gate thundered down and blocked their entry.

Anna looked between the guards at the top of the wall and the ones standing between them and Heylik Toyer. It wasn't a distance they couldn't overcome but the man clearly was not accustomed to horseback. Bugger, this would be close. She wished for something to wash down the coat of dust that made itself at home in her mouth, sweat dripping down her back and chest.

Anna's heels slammed into her horse's flanks, hands forward, allowing the beast its head. The gelding surged, knocking the first guard to the side.

She heard the screaming, orders shouted over the alarm of the surrounding travelers. One pair of hooves thundered behind her. She didn't have time to turn and look, already the *ticktick-tick* of the portcullis lowering drew all her focus. The thick iron bars were descending and then she was under them, flinching at the sound of gunfire, trying to keep her horse in a straight line as it shied to the right in fear. Once underneath, Anna stood in her stirrups and turned, exhaling in relief.

Her brother ducked beneath the portcullis, one hand forward, allowing his mount to gallop; the other was behind him, his grasp tight on Daffodil's reins. She grinned. With both men in tow it was time to set to work losing the guards.

Their proximity to the crowds and the inconvenience of reloading powder pistols kept the guard from firing, instead they shouted warnings and directions. Those traveling by foot jumped and scurried out of the path of their horses, screaming curses. From the corner of her eye, high above on the wall, Anna swore she saw a shadow of a man on the heels of one of the guards. She bit back a swear and dismounted while her horse was still at a gallop, fake hair whipping about and catching in her mouth.

As soon as her feet hit the ground, her knee gave. She fell forward, scrabbling forward on her hands before standing back up and sprinting into one of the smaller bazaars. Anna turned only once to ensure her brother and the man were following.

She stifled a chuckle, a grin coming to her lips. They were and they were quite the pair. Markus dragged the man by the bicep while the redhead ran a bit bow-legged. Her brother was flagging, though. The small bit of rest and sleep they'd gotten in the straw-filled train car wasn't enough. Anna didn't think a year's worth of sleep would be enough for her brother.

Beneath its sprawling markets and tall mud-brick buildings, Heylik Toyer housed the most complicated feat of construction Anna had seen yet. For as much as the underground structure was a labyrinth in name and purpose, Heylik Toyer was a labyrinth in spirit. Hair pin turns and roads that ended abruptly, close-packed market stalls with pastel-colored roofs to provide the merchants or farmers with shade. The streets wound back on themselves, sometimes peeling and splitting apart, other times coming together.

The buildings were like honeycombs in a great buzzing hive, buildings stacked on top of one another and pressed together. Newer construction sat straight and tall like a newly minted soldier, the older buildings slumped together as if they'd had too much drink. Ladders led up and down to varying levels and clothes lines draped between.

It was a place made for getting lost.

A place where time didn't always seem to tick forward. Sometimes it stood still, holding its breath, and other times it felt as if time were pulled backward by some unseen hand.

They vaulted over carts and wove between people. Anna threw herself underneath a narrow arch and into what was more of a crack between buildings than a proper path. Markus and the man stumbled in behind her, breathing just as hard and just as wild. She pushed forward, the path plenty wide for Anna to walk without touching either building, but the men scraped against the rough walls and groaned at the tight space.

"Fucking hate wee spaces," the man grunted, breaths turning a little uneven.

"Oh," Markus chortled, "you're going to love the labyrinth then, old chap."

The path opened just enough for a ten-by-ten squarish patch of dirt. On their left was a small well and a rusted bucket. On the right, a very rickety ladder climbed all the way to the top of one of the buildings. Three doors lined the brick behind the well and clothing flapped in the breeze above their heads, casting the entire space in shadows. She looked up, unable to even see the sky past the laundry. Anna nodded her head and ran for the ladder. A few more streets, they just had to make it a few more streets.

Anna climbed hand over hand as fast as her fingers could fly until she was pulling herself up and over a ledge and rolling across scalding hot bricks. It was a bit nostalgic, the present superimposing itself over memories of doing this very thing growing up. Only it wasn't marshals hunting them down when they were younger, it was usually the patriarch of a family Markus had offended.

And there was more to it this time, wasn't there?

Another piece of the puzzle.

Anna glanced over her shoulder, watching the redhead keep up as best he could. He hauled himself up and over the edge last and then they were running to the edge of the building and leaping the six feet between this one and the next only to slide down the ladder on the other side, dodging the few bullets that followed them over. The marshals were closing in.

Not for the first time, Anna looked at him and saw something familiar. But what had he been doing dressed as one of the Senate's dogs? It wouldn't have been easy to come by one of their uniforms. He would have likely had to kill one of them. Anna sucked on her teeth. Thinking about the man was like pulling on the thread of a sweater; it didn't solve anything and only served to make a greater mess.

"Anna, what is our heading? It would be quicker to cut across the markets," Markus heaved once they slowed to a stop, pressing their bodies against the shadows of the wall on the second story. Across from them clothes hung, waving lightly in a soft breeze.

She held her breath, raising a finger to tell Markus to *wait*.

Several guards ran by below.

How no one ever managed to look up was beyond Anna.

"Because," she whispered, "I'd like to lose them in the main market and double back. Normal men and women might not follow us into the labyrinth, but I imagine the Senate's dogs might."

"I have been blessed with a brilliant sister." He sighed, closing his eyes and leaning his head against the cool stone.

"No, just one who has had plenty of practice resisting arrest because of her knuckle-headed brother. Now come on, it's clear."

The main market, as its namesake suggested, was the largest and busiest of the bazaars in Heylik Toyer. It was also their best chance of losing the pursuing marshals in the hustle and bustle of innumerable bodies. Anna had zero doubt that the well-trained dogs would try to follow them into the labyrinth. They wouldn't get very far, but she'd rather not feel like she was being chased while trying to navigate the labyrinth's deadly twists and turns.

Anna hadn't lied earlier when she told Markus she'd memorized the paths. But she certainly wasn't as confident as she had sounded. Time had laid a veil of cobwebs over the memory, making her question herself. Could she find her way without trouble, or would Anna lead them to their deaths?

It was hard to say and she wouldn't know for sure until she was staring at the corridors.

The redhead launched up and over a wall before dropping both his hands down. Anna had to jump to reach him. His hand grasped around her elbow as she wrapped both of hers around his forearm. He pulled her up easily enough. Markus was an entirely different story. The man had to brace himself against the wall and then drop down to grab her brother under the armpits while Anna pulled him up by his knee.

They kneeled, breathing heavy, darting glances around as they came to a stand. This particular roof was out in the open, two posts with laundry hanging between them. Across the way, a tall wall shaded a small herb garden. A well-loved ball laid against it. She scanned the surrounding area, the sun bright above them.

It didn't take long for the Heylik Toyer guard to spot them.

It took even less time for the marshals in the surrounding area to fire; they didn't have to worry about reloading powder like the guards did. Anna ducked down, feet already double-timing against the heat of the mud roofs. Their strides ate the space between one ledge of the roof and the next. At the far end there was another ladder. Anna was the first to reach it and in a single motion had thrown her legs over and slid down, the arches of her boots riding the sides.

Down, down, *down*.

Her leg buckled on impact and it took longer than she was willing to admit to stand, taking the precious head start she had on the men to hobble upright. Next was Markus, and finally the mystery man who was choosing to help them against all odds. She looked the redhead up and down briefly—with just the one look, she knew he was a puzzle with a great many pieces, all moving and meant to misdirect. It was quite unfortunate she was a sucker for a good puzzle.

"Are ye all right?" he whispered from next to her.

Anna swallowed past the dry knot in her throat. "I'll be fine."

He took her bicep in his hand and looked down at her. His head tilted to the side, temples glistening with sweat, lip split and bleeding again. The man's chin dipped, brows drawing together. Any closer and they'd be touching. In turn, Anna had to look nearly all the way up. She wasn't short by any means; the man was simply a monster.

They stared.

His bottomless depths, like the backdrop of the night sky, seemed to cling to hers. Such a juxtaposition, his being the color of crisp, cool night, and Anna's the blue of a bright fall morning.

She inhaled, chest expanding and stuttering at the intensity and then time did that funny thing it sometimes did here in Heylik Toyer. It slowed, drawing seconds out into minutes, and then seemed to stop entirely. At least until it pulled in reverse, Anna's feet shuffling backward in the same motion that had brought her close to the man, pulling her arm from his bicep.

Who are you? she wondered. *Why are you here?*

His lips softened from their thin concerned line into the very beginnings of a playful smile. He cocked his head the other way and surveyed her. The bit of brightness sparkling in his eyes seemed to say, *Wouldn't ye like to know?*

And she did.

But Anna had always preferred figuring things out on her own than being spoon-fed the answer.

Markus coughed, gaze narrowed into that of a predator. A rather angry, puffed up one, but one waiting for an excuse to pounce nonetheless. Anna sighed and stepped closer to the man just to make her point clear to her brother. There would be no shenanigans. They had left all of that behind them right along with her patience.

Anna turned away from them both and motioned to the right with a very vague wave of her hand. The main market was just around the corner; they'd be entering from a chronically packed, discreet section on the east side. There would be mostly food vendors on their right when they exited, which was so very unfortunate because the clothes and the entrance into the labyrinth would cause them to turn left. She could smell the desert delicacies, mouthwatering and stomach grumbling loud enough to give them away if a marshal or a Heylik Toyer guard strayed too close.

"What smells so bloody good, luv?"

She grinned, inhaling deeply. The sweets were peppered between savory stalls. There must have been a tent full of confections and pastries just on the other side of the alley. She could smell every bit of sugar and syrup, could picture the flaky phyllo dough and bits of pistachio or almond.

"Where to start?" Anna murmured, mostly to herself. "There's harissa and sticky fingers, baklava too. I like the ones made with pistachio. Growing up, there was a tent on the other side of the street that our mother used to take us to. They served delicious pastries called bird nests, they're filled with syrup and almonds. Difficult to eat in one sitting because of how sweet they are but that was always the best part, taking them back to the dig site and finish them later."

As if in agreement, Markus's stomach growled nostalgically from her right.

"Bit of a sweet tooth?"

"I'll only be living once, sir. There isn't enough time as it is, I'll not be wasting what time I have left eating greens."

"Ye might be surprised by how much time some of us have, lass. Reckon ye'll have longer than ye think too," he said, giving her a knowing look.

They bumped and pressed past men and women dressed in fine silks and cool cottons, adorned from head to toe. Some had face coverings that only revealed beautifully painted eyes in sharp greens and deep golds. Some had fairer skin and others were a warm brown, but all were beautiful.

The men's faces had varying degrees of beards, heads wrapped in scarves, some intricately patterned in checkers or bright colors. A few even boasted a jewel at their center. They wore cloaks to protect their skin from the heat of the sun. Some men went without the protection of a cloak, instead choosing to show off the beauty of their colorful garments.

"They're calling for the arrest of a dark-haired woman and two men in tan cloaks. One blond, one red-headed," Markus whispered, leaning down toward her ear.

"So they are," Anna stated. "I suppose we'll have to change that then, won't we?"

Markus winked at her, one hand darting out and relieving a stand of a small silk scarf. Anna ripped at the remaining pins in the wig, tossing the plain ones over her shoulder and pocketing her lock picks and hammer. Her brother dunked the silk scarf in a passing bin as she carefully dropped the wig on the ground. Poor thing was a bit abused, but it had served her well.

"You're blonde, lass?" the man asked, a wry smile hidden in his tone.

"Savage, remember? Of course, I'm blonde," she told him, unclasping her cloak and letting it slide from her shoulders.

Anna took the cloth from her brother and scrubbed at her face and forehead with a vigor she hadn't realized she still possessed. Within seconds, her eyebrows were no longer dark and the grime of the day was gone. She tossed the rag back to Markus and he started in on his own face.

The redhead followed her lead, letting the rough tan material fall from his shoulders and onto the ground. Markus kept his cloak, an understandable choice with his missing trousers and disgusting button up. Her brother nudged the redhead, a second later the rag passed between them. The man frowned at it before setting in on cleaning his face as well.

In the main market, men hawked their goods to all who would listen. It was a beautiful symphony of voices, all calling back and forth. She heard greetings and goodbyes, questions and answers. Faux alleys had sprung up haphazardly between the large avenues like pockets of clovers in a field. They provided a minimal amount of shade and even less chance of a breeze.

Anna's gaze hopped from one stand to the next, searching the wares. They needed three new cloaks, a stack of candles, and matches. If they could pinch some fruit and skeins of water on the way, she certainly wouldn't complain.

But most importantly, her brother needed pants.

They spun through the stalls, Anna slipping between a narrow gap as her brother forcibly led the man onward. The redhead's neck craned around at a painful angle to keep her within his sight. She twisted, fingers clasping around one dark brown cloak without notice. Another twirl had two navy cloaks draped from her other arm. Anna stumbled forward, hands sliding through silks used to wrap a man's head.

She walked the path of another line of stalls, ducking between shoppers, and bumped into a merchant. Anna whispered an apology in rough Kurder as her finger nicked the skein of water at his belt, flashing him a large smile as she went. The merchant was young and handsome, so she laid on the charm and cleared her throat, speaking a rather forward compliment. He nodded down at her, lips twitching into a grin, and then tossed her an orange, saying something along the lines of hoping it would be sweet like her.

Her brother was nowhere to be seen, but that was how these things typically went. He was large and memorable and as the merchants and farmers selling their wares were largely men, it wasn't exactly easy for him to flirt his way out of trouble. Not here in Heylik Toyer, that is. If they'd been in Xing, it would have been an entirely different story. Anna stumbled, slipping a bit of dried beef off one cart and ducking between two stalls.

Markus waited in the next alley over, leaning impatiently against the wall, as Anna had known he would be. The ground and lower half of the crumbling thing was green with grime and the ground beneath her feet was questionably soft. Anna refused to look down and confirm why, instead focusing on her brother.

"No trousers yet, but I think different cloaks will help immensely," she said, tossing the chocolate-colored cloak and one of the head scarves to her brother. It was a beautiful thing, a solid evergreen that would blend well beneath his cloak. "Still need candles and matches."

Anna held out one of the blue cloaks and the remaining scarf to the redhead. He took the cloak, quickly pinning it around his neck, but he held the scarf awkwardly in his hands. She cocked her head at him with a small smile as she pulled her own cloak over her shoulders and fastened it. He gave her a sheepish look and shrugged, pulling the hood over his head.

"Come here," she said, stepping forward.

He handed her the scarf. It was patterned beautifully in black and white checkers, the ends stitched with tassels, giving it an extra flare. She set to work wrapping his head, careful to avoid a bump along his temple. She wasn't sure when he'd gotten it, but it had to hurt. By the time Anna had finished covering his red hair, Markus was done as well. His fingers were well-practiced at the motion from the three or four summers they'd spent in Heylik Toyer.

Anna went to flick her hood over her head, but her brother held out his hand, revealing a black headdress. He lifted a shoulder. "Hood might come off and those curls are a bit obvious, especially in these parts."

"Excellent thinking, Markus." Anna grinned, slipping it on over her head.

With the three of them a bit more disguised, breathing came a bit easier. She would hate to trip at the finish line. Anna breathed deep, nose crinkling at the smell. Her brother and the man fidgeted on either side of her, Markus playing with the wrap near his ear and the man shifting from side to side. None of them were keen on staying put. Looking from one to the other, she started walking forward, descending deeper into the shadows of this smelly alley.

They were silent as they walked, nothing but the sound of refuse, and God only knew what else, squelching beneath their feet, causing a slick layer to the ground. Anna couldn't hear anyone behind them, no fourth or fifth set of feet and she knew no one was following them from above. The buildings on either side of her had slumped together around the third level, leaning on each other as if they were old friends; it made following by rooftop rather difficult.

The path between the buildings curved slightly to the left. Light broke through the shadows in dim, soft twists. She picked at the cuticles of her right thumb. There would only be one more street to cross. If they were lucky, they would walk across and straight into the labyrinth; if they were not lucky, they would have to run down the avenue, past a crumbling set of apartments, and toward the infamous Wishing Well.

She hoped it wouldn't come to that.

The Wishing Well was a water feature Granbaatar Khan had commissioned when the rest of the labyrinth had been constructed. A gaping whirlpool, fifteen feet in either direction with a low wall of chiseled grey stone surrounding it. It wasn't local rock and Anna had never learned where it had been quarried.

The whirlpool sucked everything deep down and into a chamber in the labyrinth. It was named the Wishing Well not because it resembled a well, which it didn't, but because the citizens of Helik Toyer used to pray to the khan by tossing anything they could into it. Coins, jewels, prime cuts of meat, and even their virgin daughters.

She swallowed hard. She and Markus had found several sets of skeletons near the exit of the chamber, showing where they'd crawled and collapsed, evidence that one could live through that meat grinder. Before then, Anna hadn't thought someone could survive such an ordeal.

But the years had taught her that humans were only as strong as they thought they were; that they would only survive what they thought they could.

And if she believed herself to be invincible now, it was only so she would be.

By the end of the alley, Markus was leaning against the wall, using it to help himself along and to keep upright. The redhead turned toward her with a small question in his eyes, but it was there and then gone before she could think much of it. Another minute and they were staring at the threshold of the smelly alley and the potential freedom across the busy street.

Markus peeled himself from the wall, ear tipping towards various conversations. Bugger, he'd walked off before she could catch his hand. Anna looked up at the man nervously. He watched the crowd with narrowed eyes—looking for a threat, she assumed. Anna wiped her sweaty hands off on her trousers and then threaded her fingers through his.

He stilled, muscles going taut. "What are ye doing?" he asked, voice quiet and hoarse as if she'd taken him by surprise. Anna supposed she had; she certainly would have been surprised.

"Just trust me," she told him.

"Always, luv."

Anna led them out into the bustling crowd. The sun was warm on her side as they slipped between people, but it was a candle compared to the heat that blazed through the man's leather glove. His hand engulfed hers, his strong fingers were wrapped tightly; clearly, he was apprehensive about losing her. Anna couldn't blame him, she'd be worried about losing her chance at living too.

There was something else to his posture, though, something had relaxed. It was almost as if he had slipped into some semblance of control. Maybe this was familiar territory for him, strolling through markets, hand in hand with his lady love. Her cheeks flushed. Anna was sure they were a bright pink based on the heat and silently thanked her brother for the head dress.

She continued tugging him forward at a leisure pace. Markus, ten or so feet in front of them, was making sure to cross the way slowly. The entrance to the labyrinth was considered a haunted place in Heylik Toyer and none walked toward it willingly. She watched Markus bump into a man and then stumble in front of a stall that had candles.

…escaped…

…dogs hunting…train…

…good riddance…deserved…why else…

113

Anna listened to the conversations as best she could but by the time she understood a few words, another three sentences had left their mouths. It was beyond frustrating. It was also a sign that she had been spending far too much of her time in the jungles of the south and not enough time in the desert. Men and women gossiped as they walked, all very concerned about the marshals running rampant and firing their guns in the streets.

The man tugged her closer, their arms brushing against each other. His arm was hard and muscled, much like her brother's, while Anna's was small but toned. He nearly stopped, causing Anna to jerk next to him. She looked up at him to see his brows raised, gaze suspicious as he stared down the entrance to the labyrinth.

Anna cleared her throat and tugged him along, looking over her shoulder before slipping under an intricate stone arch. Jaguars were carved into every side of it and human skulls had been used to decorate its base. The man stared down at those uneasily as they walked past.

What was left of the day seemed to leach away, the shadows here always felt darker to Anna. Despite the dry desert heat, the air was cool and moist. She had the feeling they were being watched, the hairs on the back of her neck prickling with sensation. The man turned around, obviously feeling the same. Anna knew no one would be there, it was just a trick of the space. A stagnant breeze blew from the entrance of the labyrinth periodically like a great giant sighing at the other end.

Markus stood in front of a naturally formed rock wall. It climbed hundreds of feet into the air and was just one part of the plateau that sat behind Heylik Toyer. Anna pulled her hand free of the man's as they approached her brother. She stopped next to Markus and followed his line of sight, heart thumping hard in her chest. The man stood just behind her, his body throwing off more heat than a well-worked furnace.

It would be easy to walk past. The door to the labyrinth was nothing but a slim crack in the face of the plateau, a tall, narrow thing. They stared at it for several moments, the man glared at it rather suspiciously, a bit of color draining from his face.

"That's…?" he trailed off in a whisper. They nodded their heads, choosing not to speak. He cleared his throat, sounding nervous. "This will require a kiss."

Markus laughed outright. "My sister would never—"

Anna rolled her eyes, turning toward the man. Fueled by spite, she raised onto her toes, intending to kiss the redhead on the cheek. He had started turning his head, and so instead of meeting his cheek proper, Anna's lips touched the corner of his mouth. His stubble was rough beneath her lips and his skin was warm. It was a small kiss, one that was short and sweet. Started and then finished in less time than it took to blink.

Markus hissed something foul beneath his breath.

"Never, Markus?" Anna shrugged and stepped forward, tugging on the man's index finger to encourage him. She looked over her shoulder to reassure him all would be fine but had to look away quickly, embarrassment heating her cheeks. The man had a large goofy grin on his face, it was lopsided and full of straight white teeth.

"Absolutely abhorrent," Markus gagged from next to them.

"Oh, please," she grinned, refusing to acknowledge the drop of her stomach as they crept closer to the labyrinth's entrance. Good God, it reminded her of a crack in the earth that would surely lead to hell. "You're just jealous."

CHAPTER 14

Who the hell was this man?

Markus hadn't taken his eyes off the two.

Anna's track record said she could not be trusted with strange, dangerous men, and the redhead was most definitely strange and dangerous. Worst of all, he was handsome. Exactly the kind of man Anna had been known to trail with her eyes. Big and broad with a gorgeous smile and square jaw. The bastard looked familiar too, but Markus hadn't placed why yet or where they might have met.

Anna and the redhead walked ahead, Anna trailing her fingers against the dusty, decrepit wall, while the other held a candle. Squinting, Markus tilted his head, watching the way the blasted man held himself. Shoulders relaxed, steps easy, hands slouched in the depths of his trousers. He was too calm. Much too calm. The prick clearly trusted Anna to lead them through this, and while Markus did as well, he also knew these tunnels to be hateful things.

No one was this easy-going, not after being thrust from one dangerous situation and into a worse one. Not even Markus was completely calm, the bile in his stomach turning and twisting with each step. If he hadn't already been sweating from the heat, he would have been doing so because of nerves, from the bundle of energy deep in his gut.

Anna said something to the man, but Markus ignored it, choosing to drag his gaze from his dirty boots to the back of his stupid head. They stopped when Anna did, taking in their surroundings with a critical eye. Bollocks. Markus knew exactly where they were—and judging by his sister's stiff shoulders, she did as well.

"I am far too young to die!"

"Fourteen is as good an age as any."

"I have so much to live for! In the case of my passing, Anna, I have left my will beneath my bed in a little box."

"You're being dramatic. That snake wasn't even poisonous."

"You can't possibly know that. What are you now, a blasted zoologist?"

"Red touches black, you're okay, Jack," she sang, patting him on the shoulder.

Markus swallowed, allowing the memory to settle over his senses, ignoring the way his and Anna's voices from years ago seemed to echo and twist in the corridor. Nothing quite like watching both present-day Anna and the fourteen-year-old version lean forward to inspect the same symbol on the wall.

He blinked several times, forcing the memory away, back into the vault of his mind. It would do him no good here. None of his memories would. They only served to remind him that his sister had acquired a taste for danger sometime between then and now. A taste he had unintentionally encouraged.

If Markus could go back and hit himself, he would.

Anna raised her little index finger and scratched away whatever detritus had accumulated in the eleven or so years since they'd been here. He knew what she would find—a skull etched into the wall, warning those who knew its meaning of danger.

She straightened and continued forward. "Watch your step."

The memory of rumbling stone sounded in his ears. Markus looked up at the ceiling above. "I learned my lesson the last time."

Eleven years ago, they'd accidentally sent a boulder tumbling from a chamber above. They'd barely outrun it then as energetic, mostly uninjured fourteen-year-olds. He severely doubted he could outrun anything in the state he was in. Markus refused to use the wall to help carry his weight, but only because of the strong possibility a pressure plate was lying in wait to set off a booby trap.

He chuckled, shaking his head. *Booby.*

Forty minutes of walking and he felt no closer to the end of the labyrinth. His gaze wandered yet again to the back of the redhead's skull. What deal had Anna made for this man to help them? He wasn't a marshal, that much was clear to anyone who had eyes.

But what was he doing dressed like one?

The questions circled him like sharks. Markus did not like things he did not know and he liked things he could not figure out even less. Especially when those things were in the shape of a man his sister found attractive.

Where Anna became curious at such prospects, Markus became angry.

The man lifted a hand and scratched at the back of his neck where sweat rolled. Markus squinted at the black beneath his collar where matching tan skin should have been and frowned, nostrils flaring. Only one breed of man or woman that chose to defile their skin.

Damnit.

It was three years ago all over again.

CHAPTER 15

Stepping into the labyrinth was a bit like coming home, familiar with arms open in welcome. Or, well, it was as welcoming as a pit in one of the deeper circles of hell would be, which was reminiscent of coming home for Anna. The labyrinth was staggeringly hot, worse than any heat she had encountered before. Even the air was heavy, scalding her throat as she tried to breathe deep and find that bit of calm within herself.

Had it always been this bad?

It wouldn't surprise her.

The sprawling city outside the plateau had been named after the landmass, after all. Heylik Toyer. *Burning Tower.* The meaning wasn't lost on her now and it hadn't been lost on her then, but she couldn't remember sweating quite like this when she was fourteen. Time had a way of claiming most memories, causing them to grow fuzzy and distant. Perhaps it had been this hot and she couldn't remember.

Anna shook her head; it mattered naught. What mattered was the fact that she was boiling in her skin *now* and with the adrenaline slowly ebbing out of her blood stream, exhaustion and worse was settling in. Her muscles were stiff and her head throbbed from lack of water.

But her *thigh...*

The damn thing could hardly support her weight and the farther she gimped along, the more her vision seemed to tilt on its axis. Anna shook her head, fingers gently trailing along the wall, feeling for the pictographs that would lead them to safety.

As long as they followed the carved jaguars, they'd find the chamber she was looking for. Even without that little hint, Anna had mostly remembered the way. Past fear had cemented every turn and twist; she probably would never forget how to find her way here. Even Markus occasionally pointed one way or another with a tilt of his chin or a flicker of his fingers at his sides and he'd always been hopeless at finding his way.

"Bloody hell," the man grumbled with a rattling breath. His arm was draped around his trunk once more, his shoulders relaxed, if not a little hunched. "Why is it so damn hot?"

She sympathized with his sentiments. All three of them had completely sweat through their clothes within the first twenty minutes of descending the winding paths of the labyrinth. They'd all stripped off their cloaks and head coverings, tying them around their belts for later use—though she loathed thinking about putting the things back on. Anna had contemplated taking her shirt off, but settled for unbuttoning a few more buttons and horrifying her brother.

"Well," she began, tasting the dust and grit along her tongue, "I'm no geologist, but from my understanding there is a caldera far below the labyrinth that has heated the natural cave system for thousands of years. The tribes of people who lived in the area before the khan moved in believed the plateau to be one of the gates to hell. I believe it's the reason Granbaatar Khan chose to build here. He had a bit of flair for the dramatic."

"Oh?" The man raised a brow.

She nodded. "Researching him was a bit of a pet project of our mother's when she wasn't involved with other projects. Markus and I are quite familiar with the temples and ruins he left behind. They're all a bit flashy and ominous so it's not really surprising he chose to build somewhere like this." Anna motioned around her vaguely. "That, and nature had done half the work for him with the naturally occurring caves. He only had to smooth over the edges and lay his little traps."

"I don't know if I would call them *little*," Markus grumbled from behind.

She stopped at a split in the roughly hewn corridor. Both passages were identical in cut and look. Not an ounce of light bled from beyond either of their twists or turns. They'd passed several such offshoots, some leading into six more splits, others continuing to dead ends. This corridor...she didn't quite remember this corridor.

Bugger, why didn't she remember?

"If I remember correctly," Markus began, looking around the small shafts with a curious brow, "this is where you hit your head."

That would certainly explain it.

"And whose fault was that, brother dearest?"

"Not *one* word, Anna. We were running for our lives."

"You *pushed* me out of your way," she said dryly, stepping forward to feel along the walls. Anna looked for that jaguar but they had been immaculately smoothed here.

"I can't believe you're holding a grudge about something that happened years ago."

She ignored her brother, casting a small smile toward the man to let him know she was only toying with Markus. Anna doubted he'd be able to see the smile, but she wasn't willing to light any more of their precious candles. The one cast a soft glow, it wasn't nearly enough light to see by but Markus had only been able to grab three. From their size, she guessed they'd burn for about four hours and she knew she'd need them later.

"Do ye...hit your head often?" the man asked quietly, leaning against the wall she'd just smoothed her hand over.

"No," Anna answered at the same time Markus snorted, "*Yes.*"

She walked from the left branch and to the right. Where were those pesky little jaguars? Certainly, there had to be some to direct their way. She couldn't fail her brother now, not after all they had endured to get here. She closed her eyes and stepped to the middle of the paths and breathed deep, searching her memory for which way they had gone.

"Oh, yes, that poor cranium of hers has taken a beating," Markus continued, surprisingly talkative. Perhaps he would try to convince the man she'd lost her wits and remained unsuitable for marriage because of it. Anna shook her head and tried to concentrate on anything but their conversation. "Just a few years ago, she had a particularly nasty concussion. I imagine she learned her lesson, traipsing about with pirates."

"Pirates? What the hell was she doing wi' them?"

Markus's voice took on an odd tone, slow and intentional. "What, indeed."

Anna's hair stirred. She opened her eyes and inhaled deep, facing the passage on the left. "This way," she told them abruptly and continued without looking to see if they were following.

The passage widened and narrowed, some of the rock growing angled and rough, other parts of the passage were worn completely smooth except for the little gifts the workmen had left behind to find their way. It was a study in futility; Granbaatar had executed all his workers upon completion, but they wouldn't have known that until the very end.

Her brother returned to his sullen silence, following on the man's heels as they stayed on this path. She'd stopped counting at thirty-six connecting paths and ignored the way some of them appeared unnaturally dark or the skittering of critters that echoed back to them. The few times she turned around, Anna caught the man studying the walls and the turns with a critical eye. He tapped a hand against his thigh, the action drawing her attention for more than a few seconds.

Was he trying to map their turns and count their paces?

She wished him luck, it was a nearly impossible task. One that had taken her the better part of a week to accomplish and that was with the aid of their mother's temper hanging above their heads. While a slow death would have been encouragement enough, it didn't match the fear of what consequences their mother could think up.

"Three weeks of latrine duty," Markus mused as if he could hear the direction of her thoughts. "What do you think it would be this time?"

"For entering forbidden ruins or being arrested by the marshals?"

"Mother would have applauded my arrest. She loved anything that infuriated Father."

"Why were you arrested, anyway?" Markus was quiet for a long time, so Anna forged ahead gently, "I know it has something to do with the Coalition and the king. Might as well just tell me and get it over with."

"Can we...can we wait until we've rested five minutes before discussing this?"

"Fine," Anna sighed. Ten more minutes in the dark certainly wouldn't change their circumstances; it would not make them better and it would not make them worse.

Slowly, the path inclined and the trio ascended through Heylik Toyer and out of the depths of the labyrinth. Each step was a grueling challenge, each breath a hot hiss from her lungs. By the time they crested the last bit of incline, her trousers were tight around her left leg and she was growing dizzier by the minute. Nausea bubbled in her stomach and she started feeling clammy, the smell wafting off of them causing her stomach to roll worse.

Then the crude hall turned at ninety degrees and opened into a cavern. The temperature dropped twenty degrees, it was warm but not overbearing. Anna had always believed the heat rose to the cavern ceiling and that was why it was so cool here along the ground. She looked up to those lofty heights now, admiring the glimmer of minerals in the low light brought in through holes the size of her hand. They had been drilled at the upper most reaches of the walls long ago, bringing natural light in.

Anna blew out her candle, stumbling a step forward. Her gaze centered on the natural pool of ice-cold water across the way. It was large enough that it spanned most of this side of the cavern, a rough oval. She had never learned how it had formed, if it was natural or manmade. When they'd been younger, it had been deep enough to stand in and then some, the water like ice and smooth as silk.

She stared at it for a long while, throat parched and eyes burning.

Water had never looked so beautiful or so forbidden.

"Is that...?" the man rasped.

Anna nodded.

"'Tis safe?"

Again, she nodded.

"Can we...?"

She smiled and motioned him forward with her chin.

Markus was already halfway to the pool, stripping what clothes he had as he went. She followed the man closely, gaze never leaving the water's placid surface. He walked in a near daze and stared hard at its depths before tentatively climbing in, clothes and all. He waded forward until his hips were beneath the water and then dropped until she could only see his head.

Anna watched his eyes flutter closed and then his head tipped back with a throaty groan. She swallowed hard at the sound, feeling it deep in her chest and in the flush hot on her cheeks.

"Is something the matter?" Markus watched her closely, already in the water as well.

"Mind your own business." she hissed with a glare.

Her brother lifted his brow.

Anna shrugged her shoulder, lips thin.

He splayed his hands up with frown and a knowing look in his eyes.

She looked away, taking the time to pull her boots off before entering the water. Looking down, she saw her brother had done the same and placed her smaller ones next to his. Next, she dropped her belt with its empty revolver holsters to the ground, placing the remaining knife that had lived in her right boot on top of it. She crawled to the edge of the pool and slid into the water. The cold was a shock, biting into her skin and chilling her bones. She gasped through her nose and closed her eyes.

"All right, luv?" the man asked quietly.

"Mmm," Anna sighed and allowed her bone-deep exhaustion to pull her under.

Down, down, *down* she sunk, until she rested along the bottom.

Her hair had mostly come out of its tight knot and danced around her face, her shirt waved with the slow current that drifted through the pond. Anna would have loved to know how this pool was possible so high up in the Heylik Toyer Plateau, how any of this was possible, but there was something magical in the not knowing.

Her thigh throbbed a great deal in the cool depths, taking its sweet time to numb like her fingers and toes. Finally, her lungs began to burn. When Anna could hold her breath no longer, she grasped a handful of dirt and floated back to the surface. Inhaling slow and deep, she savored how warm the air felt on her face, how it contrasted with the ice of the water around her. Anna took the dirt and scrubbed at her hair, it wasn't soap but it was the best she could do for now.

Markus laughed in relief and then the wet slap of what could only be clothing smacked atop the dusty ground. "God, to be as naked as a babe again."

Anna pinched the bridge of her nose. "Markus, *please* tell me those were not your undershorts—"

"Oh, no. Not one word, Anna, darling. You would not believe the places I've chafed. I earned this."

The man scoffed quietly.

Anna opened her mouth to comment before promptly snapping it shut. Instead of complaining, she settled for the knowledge that Markus was alive and whole, so what if he happened to be naked? He'd be putting those undershorts right back on as soon as he left the pool and the waters were dark enough to hide anything they didn't want to see.

"In that case…"

"Anna…" Markus warned.

"Markus…" she echoed in his stiff, overbearing-brother tone.

Her fingers were stiff and thick as she unbuttoned her shirt. It landed ten or so feet from Markus's and then she was reaching back to unlace her corset and shimmied out of it. It flew and landed with an unceremonious slap. Her breeches were the hardest to remove, all that excessive sweat having nearly glued them to her legs. The swelling certainly hadn't helped matters, either. Anna wasn't entirely sure how she would get them back on once they were dry.

Next went her socks and then Anna was treading water in nothing but jewelry and her underthings. A plain cotton thong and a simple chest binding to cover her far-from-ample bosom. Normally Anna didn't bother with such a useless thing, but she was grateful Mihk had the foresight for one this time. Yet another reason to thank him upon their return.

She dove back down and grabbed two more handfuls of silt from the bottom of the pool and set to work scrubbing as much of the grime from her body as she could. It took a great long while and several more trips before she felt even halfway clean. Anna avoided the most tender part of her left thigh, choosing to investigate it with careful prodding. Submerged in water, and with how swollen it had become, it was difficult to tell the extent of her injury. Hopefully sleeping with it up and dipping into the water every hour would help enough to get Anna back on her feet tomorrow.

By the time she was done, the redhead had his back to her, leaning his forearms on dry land. She took the opportunity to study him a bit more. Why had he looked familiar on the train? She wasn't sure yet but had every intention of finding out.

His hair was slicked back, some of the shorter pieces sticking up straight, and he was fully clothed. She eyed him. Was he shy or hiding something? His arms curled beneath his resting head. His cheeks pink from his time in the sun but additional freckles had yet to make an appearance. The man's eyes were closed, his long, wine-colored lashes rested against his cheeks. His throat bobbed and lips parted ever-so-slightly as he leaned harder onto his arms. His brow twitched. Then his eyes fluttered behind his lids and he stiffened.

Anna stilled, holding onto the edge to keep herself aloft. The man opened his eyes as if he felt the intensity of her attention. Their gazes met and held. Anna had never been one to flinch away from the honesty in someone's eyes and she wasn't about to start now. His lips lifted briefly before settling back into a frown, gaze wandering behind her. It wasn't difficult to guess what had pulled his attention away from her.

"Yes, Markus?" She rolled her eyes.

The man's frown deepened and then the sound of Markus pulling himself from the water echoed around the cavern. Water sluiced off his skin, sprinkling back into the pool. Anna had the good sense to stay facing the man, listening as her brother paraded around naked behind her. He was behaving like a juvenile. She had half the mind to tell him as such when he stopped and wrung out what she assumed were his undershorts.

"Now, Anna," he said, voice low, suspicious. "What is *he* doing here?"

"Mate, do ye have to stand right behind the lass?"

"Yes."

He looked annoyed, pulling himself up and out of the water until he was seated at its edge, glaring at her brother. Anna coughed, looking away. The uniform had been tight before, but now it appeared as if it had been sculpted for his every muscle. Through its fabric, Anna glimpsed every hard, defined line of him. From his biceps to his pecs, straight down to his torso. She hadn't let her gaze drift any farther south in respect for the man. Or at least, that's what she told herself.

Good God, he was handsome.

Why was he so handsome?

"Are you going to answer me?" her brother snapped peevishly.

That's right, Markus had been speaking to her.

What was it he had asked—something about the man?

The man in question cocked a brow at her, glancing between Anna and her brother. Then he looked down at himself and his brows rose genuinely. He looked up at her through thick lashes with a devilish smile. Was he flexing now?

Show off.

"*Anna.*"

The man glanced to Markus before returning his gaze to her. She glared at him. *Don't you dare.*

"She *poisoned* me so I'd help save your sorry ass," he spoke bluntly, leaning back on his hands with a wince. Amusement twinkled in his gaze where there should have been something else—distress, perhaps? Yes, the man should definitely have been more distraught about all of this.

Anna groaned when she saw the expression on Markus's face. He did in fact have his undershorts on, but that was it. Every bruise and cut was highlighted against the pale complexion of his skin, especially around his torso, which was mostly composed of mottled blues and purples. His wrists were red and raw, bits of watered-down blood dripping from them.

But that wasn't what had caused the groan.

"Anna,"—he pinched the bridge of his nose—"you really have to stop doing that."

"If you let me explain—"

"This is a felony. You could go to prison for this—not jail, Anna, *prison*. And trust me when I say, being in the company of marshals," he spat the title, "is less than ideal. Need I remind you who the warden of Chesterhale is?"

Ann waved him off, unconcerned. "They'd have to catch me first."

Markus crossed his arms. "I was afraid you'd say something like that."

"Such an irrational fear."

"Is not."

"Is so," she shot back. "Even if they caught me, there isn't a cell that could hold me. Give it a few days, week tops, and I'd be out with none the wiser."

"That doesn't make me feel the slightest bit better. I worry about you sometimes, you know this, yes?" He then shifted his gaze to the man, frown tugging at his lips. "And how long shall the *marshal* be bunking with us? For the night, or am I expected to clean up your mess and slit his throat as soon as he falls asleep?"

The malice that sprung in her brother's normally calm, cool tone wasn't lost on her. But she was tired and chose to ignore it, and because he was acting like a fool, Anna wasn't going to tell him the man wasn't a marshal. Not yet, at least. Maybe after he'd eaten something and gotten some rest and decided to join them in being a proper human being.

Anna's attention flickered towards the man in question for a moment. She still hadn't figured out what he was, nothing beyond the fact that he wasn't a marshal and he had spent a decent amount of time out at sea. Her lips thinned at his dark gaze as it rested lightly on her. He quirked an eyebrow in question. How long was Anna planning on stringing him along? Just long enough to cure him? Longer if she offered and he chose to stay?

She chewed on the thought, thinking of how easy his presence had been, of how much aid he had offered in rescuing her brother. Whatever his motives for masquerading as a marshal, the reason Markus had been arrested in the first place hadn't been solved yet and it might be good to have an ally like him in her corner.

If she could convince him to stay, that is.

And Markus would absolutely hate it.

"Actually, I think I've decided to keep him." Based on the look on her brother's face, she hit the nerve she'd been aiming for.

"Bloody hell, lass, I'm no' a stray dog."

Markus looked the man over suspiciously. His cheek twitched and then his lips pulled into something that might have fooled anyone else, but Anna was his twin and knew his fake smile when she saw it. It didn't reach his eyes, it was a small, even thing that looked more like a baring of teeth on her brother. "Fine, Anna. We shall keep your dog."

Too easy.

Anna glanced between the two, noticed how stiffly the redhead sat, gaze boring into her brother's. This had better not be a pissing contest. Anna shifted her attention between the two several times before Markus turned back toward her, arms still crossed against his chest. "He's going to need a name, though. We have to call him *something*." He angled back to the man. "Well, boy? What's your name?"

"Matters naught to me what ye call me."

Markus rolled his whole head in exasperation. So dramatic. "You don't understand, if we leave it up to Anna she will bungle the whole thing."

"Will not," she pouted. "I'm sure he came with a name, anyway, I can't just rename him."

"Of course, you can."

The man loosened, looking both intrigued and slightly concerned. Anna grinned at him, wide and broad, in encouragement. Perhaps she could get his true name out of this yet. If he gave it, it was him offering it, not Anna asking for it. One more piece of the puzzle sat right in front of her, just waiting for her to pick it up.

"How could the lass muck something like that up?" he asked honestly.

"If we left it up to Anna, she would probably name you *man*. Anna loves simple solutions to simple problems. When we were children, our father got us a pair of hunting dogs. I named my Jameson. She named hers *Birru*, which means *dog* in one of her many dead languages."

"Venbali," she mused, thinking of that little wiry-coated pup. She turned toward the man in explanation. "It's a pre-written language. All we have left of it is from the oral tradition of a few tribes of nomads in the north—"

"We don't care what it is, Anna, it's dead for a reason."

"Just because it's dead doesn't mean it's useless."

"Well, it certainly isn't use*ful*, is it?"

Anna waved her brother off with a very specific finger. "And I would not call him *man*, that's absolutely preposterous. I would call him…" she stopped short, a shiver creeping up her spine. What would she call him? She certainly couldn't let Markus know she had been calling him that in her head this entire time. "I'd call him Red or something like that."

"Bravo, Anna," Markus drawled with a yawn. "You've done it again. Your creativity strikes fear into our enemies."

Anna braced her hands on the edge of the pool before hauling herself out and sitting down. It was just dark enough that she doubted Markus would notice the wound on her leg. The warm air breathed life back into her muscles even though the water dripping from her hair left a trail of goosebumps in its wake. She wrung her hair out and ran her fingers through it, piling it on top of her head in a loose bun. Anna stretched from one side to the next, standing straight with her hands high above her head.

"Lovely, are we just ignoring the pressing issue of ye poisoning me or—" the man stopped with a cough.

"I suggest you look away, wretch," Markus growled.

She turned around to see the man's eyes wide, hand paused in rubbing the back of his neck. She met his gaze and saw his cheeks flush a little darker before giving her a wink and looking away. He grinned shyly as he put his hand down and focused on watching the water settle in front of him.

Looking down at herself, Anna remembered she wore nothing but jewelry and underthings. It might have been dark enough to keep her injury hidden from her brother, but it was light enough to see her every curve. Let the man stare. She had nothing to hide and held no embarrassment about her body. And if a bit of heat found its way to her cheeks at the thought of him staring, she refused to acknowledge it.

"Oh, hush, Markus. It's nothing worse than a swimsuit and I dare say he saw you naked. You have no room to speak." She paused, kneeling next to her clothes, and looked up at her brother. "Or are you jealous that he was staring at my rump and not yours?"

"Back to the poison, Anna," he said through clenched teeth, forcing her to talk about something else.

She waved him off. "It was just a teensy bit of poison."

"A teensy bit, lass?"

"Don't be a child," she said, pulling her clothes to the pool to scrub them before turning in for the night.

"Don't…be a…" he trailed off, looking up at the ceiling. A small huff of disbelief left his lips in the form of a laugh.

"Aye," Anna mocked in his accent, dunking her shirt into the water.

"Now look who's being a bloody child."

"I'm not—" Anna stopped short at seeing an angry, black scorpion crawl toward his hand. "Don't move."

He stilled, following her gaze toward the nasty little beast. The stinger was bright red, the poison held within its confines straining against its boundaries. They all held their breath, watching as some welled at the tip in anticipation. Markus took a step back; he already had a scar on his bum to mark his encounter with a scorpion and apparently had no intention of asking for a rematch.

She fought the urge to scream as it crawled forward, its muscular legs making nearly inaudible clicking noises against the stone floors of the cavern. They had made it this far and she wasn't about to let a little scorpion be the reason the man died. Oh, no, if Anna wasn't going to be the one to kill him, a damn arachnid certainly wasn't going to get the honor.

The man's throat bobbed. "Let me guess, wee fucker is poisonous."

"Highly," Markus muttered from even farther away. "Today really isn't your day, ol' chap."

And then the scorpion struck.

Its stinger planted in the soft tissue between the man's thumb and index finger as he pulled his hand away. Then his boot came down hard in one swift motion and crushed it. He held his hand to his chest, breathing deep. He took another gulp of breath and it was then that Anna noticed his fingers clasped tightly about his wrist to slow the poison.

Smart man.

The redhead turned toward her, promptly canted his head back, and glared at the ceiling. Anna rolled her eyes; he was either cursing the gods or asking for their patience while he attempted to deal with her. He turned his dark gaze back on Anna and inclined his head dramatically. She crawled toward him and grasped his hand, looking at the puncture marks in the leather.

"We're going to have to suck the poison out," she told him seriously, raising her gaze to meet his.

His eyes had widened again and then his gaze went from her eyes to her lips. "Wh-*what*?"

"*Suck the poison out*," she annunciated slowly, trying to keep the grin off her face.

"Absolutely not! Anna!" Markus called from behind her. "Put his filthy hand down! Put it down now! You don't know where that has been!"

CHAPTER 16

Bloody fucking hell.

He did no' have words.

Trevor sat as far from Anna as he could get. He would have chosen the distance even wi'out her prick of a brother standing guard over her. He still hadn't recovered enough to look at her, except out of the corner of his eye. The image—it was just...*there*.

When he'd looked up earlier, he had seen nothing but cheeks and forgotten what the hell he was saying like a damn lad. Glorious cheeks and lovely thighs at eye level no' five feet in front of him. It was haunting him, like looking at the sun or a bright flash and closing his eyes.

It had taken everything in him no' to muck it up worse. This bloody uniform had already been slicked to him like a second skin and Trevor could only imagine how her brother would take the sight of his cock pointed in his sister's direction.

'Tis no' a wee thing, they sure as hell would have noticed.

Trevor had actually thanked his awful luck the scorpion had appeared.

Right up until the lass said she'd need to suck the venom out. Who the fuck did that? Suck venom out of someone's hand? Shite. Then all he could see was her lips on his skin and feel the ghost of teeth brushing his throat. It had taken him five minutes to convince her she needn't fucking do that. Five minutes of arguing that the stinger hadn't gotten past the bloody leather of his

135

gloves. Trevor wasn't sure Anna believed him even now. She was a smart lass, she could smell a lie a gods-damned league away.

He glared up at the cavern ceiling. It was full dark now and they'd decided to turn in for the night, no' that they'd been given much of a choice. The cavern was decently sized, that lovely pool of water taking most of the other side and leaving them wi' plenty of space to stretch out and sleep.

Anna had already curled into a ball, her brother's cloak draped over her while she used hers as a pillow. Their clothes were spread out, air-drying. Trevor'd never taken his off, that would have given him away real fucking quick wi' the tattoos and all that and he still had a bloody job to do.

He sighed.

Of course, that involved getting the damn man alone. He hadn't figured out how to pull that one off just yet and the wee fem said she was taking him to the market first thing. He and Anna would be heading back out of this cursed place and onto the next task of getting the fucking antidote before Trevor had to explain a few things to her.

Her poison was already at work. His head had been growing heavy and the muscle aches had already started in his chest and arms. It was only a matter of time. He needed the antidote, just no' for the reason the wee beastie believed.

Trevor angled his body, able to see the lass out of the corner of his eye. She was on her side, one arm under her head and the other around her torso. Her lips were cracked from the heat, parted enough to allow soft snores to escape. Bloody adorable. Something warm stirred in his chest, the heat flowing out to his limbs and clouding his head. But that was about when he noticed Markus Savage glaring at him from where he sat against the wall like a lost child.

The prick was the reason he was here but, fuck, it felt like he was a bloody chaperone. Tate was going to lose his shite when Trevor told him about this wee misadventure in getting the blasted bit of cursed leather. Was it enough that it was John Savage's daughter that had poisoned and stole from him? Oh, nay. Of course, John Savage's boy had to play chaperon.

Fucking hell.

Trevor had to focus. The map, the map, the bloody map. Enough flirting wi' the bonnie lass; it was time to start sleuthing. He turned, looking back to where the lass was sleeping, to where her things were placed wi' absolute abandon, to the way her wee chest rose and fell as she slept. A reassuring thing, that.

"I don't know why you're here, or why you bothered to help my sister at all," Markus Savage said from his position next to her, one elbow on his knee. "But I will."

"Ye did hear when I said she poisoned me earlier, aye?"

"That's not the only reason. I know it's not."

"'Tis no'?" Trevor teased.

"I'm going to figure it out, and when I do, you better hope your intentions for my sister have always been honorable."

Trevor thought of her ass just then and grinned down at his hands. "I hate to break it to ye, mate, but I'd be lying right now if I said they were." He cleared his throat and met Markus's gaze. It surprised him again just how similar their eyes were; chips of ice among desert blonde curls. "But I can swear I've never meant her any harm and I never will."

It seemed to pacify Markus enough that he nodded curtly and closed his eyes. A few minutes later and the prick was snoring as well, leaving Trevor to contemplate what he'd said. He didn't trust Trevor, that much was fucking clear. But having Anna around might pay off if Markus thought he was only trying to chase some tail.

He might be able to take Markus by surprise when he asked about the map. Maybe they'd tell him where the map was and save him the trouble. A thing like that shouldn't be floating about, wandering unchecked. It needed to be locked away and he'd been a bloody fool to think it was safe in his cabin on the *Pale Queen*.

Trevor looked at Anna again and grinned.

'Course she would have done something no one saw coming, something no one else would have ever fucking dreamed of doing.

Lass was something else.

Taylee would have liked her.

CHAPTER 17

When Anna woke, she just laid there for a long time with her arm draped over her eyes and listened to her brother breathe. When they had shared rooms or a tent growing up, his snoring had kept her awake often. Their mother had always jested that he could wake the dead. Now was no different; it was loud and borderline offensive, but it was a sign that he was alive and well, that Anna had succeeded.

She'd done it.

She had rescued Markus.

She had rescued him and he wasn't *too* worse for wear.

Anna bent her leg, figuring it was time to rise; surely the man was feeling the effects of the poison she'd used yesterday by now. She shook her head at the thought that she had been boarding the train this time yesterday; just another reminder that time belonged to no man, that it fell at a speed of its own choosing.

She frowned as she tried to bend her legs. Her right leg protested but her left outright refused. Keeping her eyes closed, she rolled her ankles and then tried moving her left leg again. The skin above her knee was tight and the knee itself was stiff and swollen.

Bugger.

Even with waking up and elevating it and going for multiple late-night dips, it was wrecked. She clenched her eyes and added items to her mental list—clothes, food, water skins, medical supplies, and antiseptics. Oh, and then there was the business of collecting the antidote for the man.

139

Anna stilled, listening as another body shuffled along the dusty stone floors. It wasn't her brother. His snores were still reverberating from her right side. If the popping of joins was any indication to go by, the redhead was awake and moving about. Good God, he sounded like an old man. Anna peeked out from beneath her elbow, catching him stretching.

He kept moving, seemingly oblivious to her staring, so she kept peeking. Once done with stretching, he moved on to sets of pushups and sit-ups, breezing through them all. She supposed any man would be compelled to keep up his physique while being held hostage by a woman half his mass in a dusty cave.

This was absurd.

Why was she staring?

"I know you're no' sleeping, luv."

Anna flushed and turned away. There was no point in arguing it or pretending he was wrong, so she sat up and came face to face with him. She stiffened, not entirely sure when he had gotten so close. He was kneeling, elbows on his knees and with that grin on his face, his cheeks flushed—a combination of exertion and fever, she assumed.

Anna leaned back to keep from sharing the same air as him and tracked a bead of sweat as it raced down his face. She was close enough to count his freckles and to realize the freckles she thought she'd seen on his ear lobes were holes—bugger, the man's ears were pierced. It wasn't a practice found among men in Bellcaster or the Emerald Isles and was typically associated with unsavory sorts...

But this close to him, it was easy to picture him with diamonds or something gold. Splendid, absolutely splendid. Just when she thought the man couldn't possibly get any more attractive.

His gaze dipped and then he stood and turned away from her. She glanced down and breathed deep, the cloak she'd been using as a blanket had slid down, exposing her bandeau chest wrap and a bit of tummy. Slouched over as she was, some of her stomach had rolled over the rest, but that wasn't why she clenched her jaw and turned away from him. Her scar was on full display, making her stomach flutter and mouth dry right up. Embarrassment was not something she felt often but it had a habit of rearing its nasty head when it came to her lovely scar.

Who would have thought a single swing of a sword could rent such damage?

"Have you never seen an unclothed woman before?" she teased, reaching for her shirt. "Or do I make you nervous?"

He chuckled, quickly followed by coughing. "No, luv, starting to feel a wee sick and don't want to throw up all over ye."

"How thoughtful."

He shrugged, taking a deep breath through his nose. "Going for a dip, let me know when we're leaving."

She waited until he slid into the water before removing the cloak from her legs, getting her first glimpse at her leg in the daylight. Bugger. Anna ground her teeth together and tilted her left leg back and forth. It was one giant bruise, deep purplish-black with a yellow outline. If only that had been the worst of it. But no, there was a stretch of skin the length of her thumb missing just above her knee.

Anna glared down at it; she knew a bullet wound when she saw one and she was lucky the lead ball hadn't gone through her leg and only skimmed it. Didn't make the pain any less nor change the fact that it would only get worse before it got better. They didn't have time to waste while Anna sat on her rump waiting for it to heal. Clearly the medical supplies would not only be for her brother.

She pulled her shirt on and buttoned it to her sternum before forcing herself to stand with the aid of the wall. What scabs had formed overnight quickly cracked open. Anna fought the groan. She might have to stitch it to keep the bugger closed.

Pulling her breeches on was excruciating, her teeth dug into her tongue and the sides of her cheeks while she pulled the thigh's material over her left leg. Truly, it was a test of will. But she did it, breath growing shallower as she dressed. Next were socks and boots, knife slid into her right one for safe keeping. Anna removed the leather revolver holsters from her belt before threading it through her breeches and tucked her shirt in.

"Ready?"

"Nearly," Anna said, fingers running through her hair.

She stooped over her brother, fingers weaving her curls into a tight braid. Markus was sleeping face down, arms out in front of him, in nothing but his undershorts. No surprise there, her brother hadn't slept in proper clothing since they were babies. She nudged the least bruised bit of his ribs with her boot.

He did not even twitch in response.

"Markus." She nudged him again out of necessity.

He snored wildly.

"*Markus!*" She nudged again, nearly tipping him onto his side.

He did not wake, growl, or grumble. Anna shook her head; clearly, he needed the sleep and who was she to rob him of it? He would not be happy when he woke and found them missing, but that wasn't Anna's problem. She'd tried to wake him up and any conclusions he came to about her and the redhead were his own.

Still, she did not want her brother to worry.

Anna stomped several feet away and dragged her boot through a thick patch of sand, writing her brother a note of sorts. Once done, she placed the orange she'd been gifted yesterday next to her writing. The grin on her face was nothing short of devious as she looked down at her brother one last time. Anna steeled her spine and readied herself to walk as normally as possible. If the redhead noticed she was walking funny, she'd play it off as being stiff and sore from yesterday's events.

She had just finished her braid by the time she walked around the cool pool of water, tying it off with a leather cord that had been around her wrist. The redhead was waiting for her, both their cloaks and head coverings in his hands. His cheeks were darker with the beginnings of a beard. Water trickled from his hair, down his neck, and into his collar.

Which, of course, was still buttoned to the middle of his neck.

What was he hiding under there?

The heat alone should have driven him to unbutton it as she had. Anna doubted the man handled the heat better than she did. He rubbed the back of his neck as she approached, well aware of her careful observations. Did her attention make him nervous? That certainly would have been interesting, but why would she cause such a reaction?

Did it have to do with who he was?

He angled his chin in challenge, his brogue a soft whisper in her mind, *Ask me, luv.*

But she wouldn't—it wasn't often that Anna stumbled upon a truly challenging puzzle and this one was simply begging her to solve it. Her curiosity knew no bounds and Anna knew better than to let it guide her. But the *pull*, the *need* to know, was the very same one that drove her interest in Granbaatar Khan. Insatiable and needy and always there. It was a little disappointing, really, that the man had coaxed such an interest out of her.

"Is your brother coming?" he asked tentatively, looking beyond her to where Markus was still doing his best impersonation of a lump.

"Oh, no." She lifted her gaze to meet his. "I don't think he'll wake before dinner. If we're lucky, we'll be back by then and avoid his ire altogether."

"He have a temper?" the man asked, brows drawing together. Something had changed in his voice, it was harder, flintier.

"Markus? No. Never." Anna paused in thought, holding out her hand for her cloak. "At least never in my direction. I think you have him confused with our father. Markus just doesn't like me gallivanting with strange men he doesn't know."

"Does *that* happen often?"

She cringed, ignoring the question. "I left him a note." A note scrawled in one of those dead languages Markus believed to be useless. "Now, shall we?"

She almost wished she was staying, if only to see the look on his face when he realized what she'd done.

"Aye," he said, spinning on a heel and waltzing out into the passage before Anna could.

"Manners, sir," she chided, trying to step in front of him.

But he barred her path with his arm and continued ahead of her as if it were the most logical and natural thing to do. "Aye, ladies first and holdin' doors may be bloody good manners." He paused to brush a rogue cobweb before it engulfed his face. "But, shite, I'd rather be the one walking into danger first, luv."

"And why would I let you charge into danger without me? Sounds tedious."

"Safe, more like."

Anna snorted; thus far, their adventure had been anything but safe.

"Ye have something against living?" he questioned gently.

"Living?" Anna tilted her head to the side, following him. It would only be a matter of time before they became lost and he asked for her to lead. She just had to wait him out. "No, I have no quarrels with living. I simply prefer actually doing so over the illusion of it."

He didn't reply.

They wound their way down the corridors, sinking into the heat of the labyrinth. Sweat already dripped from every inch of her, stinging the cuts and scrapes she had gotten along the way. The silence between them on the dusty paths was companionable, soft in a way that pulled at the words buried in her chest. Anna didn't think he understood what she had said. And how could he? He hadn't spent a fair amount of his childhood cloistered in the Savage estate being seen and not heard.

144

But for some strange, inexplicable reason, she wanted him to. Maybe it was the quiet that required her to fill the space with words, or the rasping of his boots against grit that was building a pressure in her lungs. He was easy to talk to, she'd figured that out on the train. They had a long walk ahead of them, they might as well pass the time.

"I grew up in the capital, as I'm sure you realized," she blurted, voice cracking and unsure. "The way they go about their life in Bellcaster…it isn't living. It is existing. It is going through the motions for the sake of a comfortable, predictable routine, not out of necessity or any pressing sense of urgency. Not out of the need to survive and thrive. Risks are not taken because there is no perceived reward. Bellcaster is stagnant, unaccepting of change even if it is the right thing to do or the right path to take."

"And you're different from them?"

"I would have thought that much was obvious."

He chuckled, though Anna wasn't entirely sure what part of her statement he found so amusing. After another few beats of silence, he glanced up from his palms and over his shoulder. His gaze settled on her, curiosity sparking in its depths. "And what made ye different?"

"Our mother," Anna answered immediately, swelling with pride. "She was an explorer, you see, the first female archaeologist recognized by the Board of Antiquity. She was a pioneer in her field and no task was too great. Because of her, Markus and I had a rather unconventional upbringing. One full of unconditional love and adventure. Full of life."

"She sounds wonderful."

Anna nodded with a small smile. "She was." Her voice broke over her words, forcing her to clear her throat. She wracked her brain for something, *anything*, that would take away the raw quality that always came with talking about her mother. "Did you get much sleep?"

He did turn fully this time, coming to a stop as he pinned her down with an incredulous look. "After a wee beastie poisoned me? Absolutely no'. I paced the whole bloody time."

That explained the dark circles.

"You said the stinger didn't get you."

"I'm no' talking about the damn scorpion. I'm talking about *ye*." He turned around and made a left down an offshoot.

Despite the situation, he looked comfortable. Well, aside from the blood-boiling heat. How he was so at ease was a bit beyond her—she had poisoned him, after all. The last thing the man should be feeling in her presence was comfortable. A bit of guilt came bubbling back to the surface now that she didn't have adrenaline to drown in, now that she had figured out he wasn't one of the Senate's dogs. Now that it wasn't him *or* them, but rather him *and* them.

She needed to focus.

He wasn't her friend.

He wasn't her ally.

She didn't even *like* the redhead, not even a little.

Well, maybe a *little*.

The tunnels twisted and turned, sometimes the floors sloped and other times they inclined but always the general direction was down. They arrived at the crack they had entered through in record time. Anna praised him for his memory, completely surprised and impressed that he had been able to retain every twist and turn. They couldn't escape into the cool morning air of the deserted alley fast enough. Before entering Heylik Toyer proper, she rewrapped his head and pulled her own head covering down. She double checked the fastening of her cloak and then stared out into the winding streets.

It was going to be a hot day.

Already there wasn't much relief from the sun, but there was something about its buttery kisses that made everything feel better—even her thigh seemed to ache less. She took a deep breath, looking up at the sky; it was clear and bright, not a hint of a cloud in sight. Absolutely beautiful. If nothing else, Anna was her mother's daughter—a child of the sun. If given the chance, she'd bathe in the sun for days at a time, taking in the rich vitamins and enjoying heat-induced naps.

The man cleared his throat, looking down at her curiously.

Anna shrugged off the look and laced her fingers through his as a precaution. He stiffened, angling his body away from hers and staring at their linked fingers, his completely dwarfing hers. The black leather of his glove made her hand appear all the lighter.

He opened his mouth and then cleared his throat, looking down toward the ground while he addressed her. "I—what's this, lovely?"

There was something wary in his posture, the line of his shoulders, the angle of his face. It would appear he wasn't as comfortable around her as she'd originally thought and she couldn't blame him for the sentiment. She wouldn't have trusted herself if she were in his shoes. Despite knowing that, rage sizzled in her stomach that she had to explain *this* to him at all. She fought the frustration, the embarrassment, that came with admitting it.

"It's not safe," she said quietly. His brows drew together, something dark and dangerous peeked out at her from beneath the abyss of his gaze. She took a deep breath. "They—the Pirate King's slavers—they…frequent the area and untethered women become unfindable women."

Once was enough.

"Bloody hell, ye jest?"

"I do nothing of the sort, not about this. *Never* about this." Anna turned back towards their hands, lips curling in disgust. "Trust me when I say, I hate the idea just as much as you. The last thing you probably want to do is hold the hand of the woman who poisoned you."

His fingers tightened around hers. "I don't hate the idea of holding your hand, luv." And then he pulled her closer, placing her hand on his forearm to guide her down the streets.

She smiled, a soft huff of a laugh escaped her lips. "You're not very smart, are you?"

"I've been accused of worse."

The winding paths and open streets weren't quite busy yet, stalls in the market just organizing with the fresh morning light. Without words, the two strolled through the market, the redhead looking like he oversaw their path while following the soft tugs and pulls of her direction. His arm held her tight to his body, unwilling to let the current of individuals separate them.

As they came closer to the main market, it became slow-going, people swaying to and fro with the current of the crowd. They were bombarded with the orchestra of voices, the shouts for wares, the music that was the main market. She loved it, the excited hustle and bustle, the cries of deals. She pulled him to the edge and stopped, needing to rest her leg for a moment. He didn't question the lull in their search, simply pressed himself closer and kept an eye on those around them.

As Anna tried to discreetly bend and stretch out her knee and thigh, she noticed what kind of stands she had pressed them between. One was selling chickens; feathers peppered the air and the birds were pressed into individual cages. Noisy, noisy birds, they only distracted her for a minute before she turned to the stand that was at her back.

It had an emerald green cloth draped over the top to block the owner from the sun. The wood was dark and scuffed, parts of the poles splintering. Small ceramic jars sat at the forefront, filled with God only knew what. It wasn't their beautiful bright colors that caught her attention, but the fliers tacked to the wall the stand sagged against.

Wanted posters. Not just any wanted posters, but ones for the Pirate King's crew. At the top was the quartermaster and next to him was a stern-looking woman with harsh braids, the master gunner. Scattered down the wall were other gunners, the surgeon, and the sailing master. Even a cook; if rumors were true, he'd served as the head chef in the Senate's kitchens before the Pirate King had nicked him.

There were others, mostly for petty crimes, but the wanted poster with the Pirate King's face was missing. Only a weathered paper with his name on it held his place on the wall.

No one had seen him up close in years. She couldn't remember what he looked like and the closest she would ever come to seeing his face again was looking at his quarter master's wanted poster—they were brothers.

In this one, the quartermaster appeared in his thirties, with a well-groomed beard and long hair. He was missing the three paper-thin scars on his right cheek—Anna remembered that much about him. When had this poster been drawn for those to be missing?

She cocked her head at the poster, something eerily familiar about it—beyond the obvious, that is. Something tugged at the back of her mind, though Anna couldn't have said what. The man's breath caught in his lungs. She glanced up at his face only to see it had gone a little pale, his gaze centered on the wanted posters. Then he was tugging her back out into the crowd, ducking his head away from her.

"I know," she said, attempting to make a joke. "It should be a crime for the quartermaster to be that pretty."

He coughed and still did not meet her eyes.

They walked through a section selling food and Anna's stomach growled in time with the man's. Food was certainly an item near the top of her list, but she had no intention of stealing from the masses today. Money wasn't easy to acquire in a place like Heylik Toyer, especially for women. But Anna had been frequenting this stretch of sand for years and knew nearly all the hidden places. With how often Markus ended up in a holding cell, she had learned early on who was willing to work with women.

As they came to a Y in the market, she pulled him to the left. "This way."

"And what's in this direction, luv?"

"A booth," Anna said, leaning another portion of her weight onto his arm to relieve her left leg. If he was uncomfortable or curious as to why, he didn't show it. "I intend to procure funds for our transactions."

"Oh?" he mused, glancing from one end of the crowd to the next, clearly marking certain individuals. "And how do ye intend to do that? Nothing that'll get me in trouble wi' your brother, aye?"

"Watch me work, perhaps you'll learn something."

"Best no' mean what it bloody well sounds like," he grumbled.

CHAPTER 18

Damnit, Anna.

Furious was not a strong enough word.

Markus stared down at the note she had scrawled in the sand. The crude symbols looked vaguely familiar, as if the last time Marks had interacted with the blasted things, he'd been drunk. Which, more likely than not, was true. Closing his eyes, he tried to place where he'd seen them to get a grasp of what the damn sentence structure would be.

Languages, especially *dead*, written ones, had never been within his wheelhouse and Anna knew that. He supposed this was payback for poking fun at the languages she knew inside and out. Markus shook his head, leaning down to squint at the damn things. Only reason Anna preferred dead languages to those of the living was because there wasn't anyone left alive to argue with her. But good God, after this, he was tempted to learn some so he could do just that.

After half an hour of staring at the sand until he was sure a blood vessel would break, Markus swiped his hand through the message. Pinching at the bridge of his nose, he settled against a wall and glared at the, now unreadable, scrawl.

Had he died?

Was this all some blasted, cosmic joke?

If it wasn't, he might kill her.

Markus was supposed to be protecting her; that's what he'd promised their mother on her deathbed. He hadn't done such a splendid job of it thus far but Anna also hadn't exactly made it

151

easy for him. Their father certainly blamed Markus for many of his sister's dalliances. Always skipping about the countryside and deteriorating ruins and temples. Picking the most dangerous men to bat those long lashes at just to get a rise out of their father—which was a precarious game in and of itself.

Their father was the most dangerous man, Markus knew that better than most, and after him the list of unsavory individuals continued in this order: Marshal MacGrath, Carsyn Kidd, Lir, Chardae Badawi, and Jean Black.

Some would argue that the Pirate King and his quartermaster should be at the top of the list, coming before the five Coalition chiefs. But Markus would have told them to bugger off, the crew of the *Pale Queen* hadn't caused much trouble the last ten or so years. They'd been blamed for plenty and there wasn't a doubt in his mind that they were dangerous but—he shook his head.

Speaking of dangerous men.

Is that why the wretch seemed familiar?

The blood drained from his face and his heart clenched in his chest. Anna was with a very dangerous man and she was with him in a place where women were known to disappear. Markus hung his head in his hands and tried to breathe through the new panic that threatened to crack his chest in half. Anna's reckless behavior knew no bounds.

He didn't dare leave. The twists and turns of the labyrinth were familiar enough after last night but he wasn't completely confident in his abilities to navigate the natural cave system the khan had built upon. Even if he left and found success reaching the outside world, there wasn't a guarantee he could stumble upon her in Heylik Toyer. It was a large, bustling beehive of an establishment. One that was quite good at losing its inhabitants.

He stretched out, wincing at every inch of him that was in pain. The best thing he could do for his sister was catch up on his sleep and renew his strength. He had to trust her too, trust her to find her way back. She always had before. But if she wasn't back by morning, Markus would go out and search for her. He'd been battling the slave trade long enough to know most of their haunts.

Sleep didn't come, though.

CHAPTER 19

Anna breathed deep, feeling nostalgic.

"...'tis no' what I expected."

"What? Did you think we were going to a brothel? Or that I was just going to drop my breeches first dark corner we rounded?"

The man rubbed at the back of his neck with his free hand. "Something like that."

"Apologies for any disappointment you may be feeling." Anna stepped forward. "I used to come here when Markus was in trouble and I needed to grease a few palms to clean up after him. Wonderful little family establishment. The father operated it then, looks like the son does now."

"How did ye run about by yourself growing up?" he asked.

"The streets were not as dangerous, the slavers not as ambitious. Word on the street is the Viper pissed the Pirate King off right and true and that's why most of the abductions come from Abu Shazar." She paused, thinking of how much easier it had been when she was little. "And I honestly looked more like a boy. I kept my hair shorter and pinned it back. Chest was about the same size then as it is now; at least my rump and thighs have grown."

The man choked, smothering the smile on his lips.

They stopped at a stall with a ruby covering and a sign in the front that advertised homemade ceramic jewelry. On the tabletop were examples of their work—burnished orange charms and deep blue earrings. Necklaces made with twine and spirals of gold interspersed with shiny eggplant-colored beads. A small smile flickered at her lips. The stand hadn't changed at all. Hopefully, she'd still be able to pawn off a ring or two without being questioned. One paid for this kind of secrecy—and handsomely, at that.

The man behind the counter was younger than he appeared, a thick russet beard covered his face, matching the springy, insolent curls escaping his headscarf. The covering itself was a solid maroon with gold tassels; a gorgeous citrine in the shape of a star sat at its center. His robes were canary yellow with maroon threading. The scar on his cheek bisected his beard. His lips pressed into a thin line and he crossed his arms as she approached. Anna saw the moment recognition flashed across his face.

She wasn't entirely sure if it was a good or bad thing that he remembered her from their youth.

"Trouble again?" the man behind the counter asked slowly, gaze stopping briefly on her hands before trailing back up to her eyes.

Anna shrugged. "Trouble always."

He motioned her forward with a crook of his finger. She slid a sapphire ring from her right hand. It was banded in diamonds and silver leafing, one of her father's favorites. The redhead raised a brow at the man across from them as he inspected the piece of jewelry. His arm had slipped behind her waist, resting on the curve of her hip while she haggled, stumbling through her Kurder pronunciations.

She let out a sigh, pretending to deflate at the vendor's final offer. She accepted it, throwing her best begrudging tone into her voice. The man counted out several small, round disks and put them into a velvet bag. He handed said bag to the man. Forcing a frown onto her face, she otherwise ignored the subtle slight.

"Keep brother out of trouble, savage little girl."

They'd already turned back the way they came when the man leaned toward her. His breath touched the shell of her ear, dragging forth a shiver from her spine. She licked her lips, angling her head closer to better hear him.

"Surely ye know that damn ring of yours was worth far more than that? Sneaky bastard cheated ye."

"I paid for his discretion…" Anna paused, blinking a few times before turning her head to face him. She was a breath away, close enough to count the cracks in his lips. The bottom was a bit plumper than the top. "Wait, *you* speak Kurder?"

He nodded his head, pulling away from her. "Enough to get by. I understand it better than I can speak it."

"How?"

"My ships intercept the slavers here and there. As ye said, many females go missing from this fucking desert and over the years I've picked up a few words and phrases." His voice dropped next, throat bobbing tightly. "Helps when they can understand ye."

Anna's chest tightened, throat closing as well. "That is a very noble cause."

"Nah, fem. Just the right one."

"Aren't they one in the same?"

"No' always, luv. No' always."

Despite searching his face for some hint, some clue to the puzzle that was this man, he refused to meet Anna's gaze. She cleared her throat and turned away, thinking of what he'd said. Clearly, he was a sailor of some sort. It wasn't the first time he had mentioned combating the slave trade and being out at sea. The biggest tell, in her opinion, was that he knew who Markus was on sight. It didn't explain why he was dressed as a marshal nor his reasons for being on that train though.

What other secrets could he be hiding? She tapped her thumb briefly against his arm in thought. From the corner of her eye, she watched him reach up and tug at his collar. What was under there? No one in their right mind would have their collar buttoned up like that in this heat if they weren't hiding something. Suddenly, it was all she could focus on.

The slide of his fingers beneath the fabric, how stiff with sweat it was against his skin.

What was under there?

Her gaze darted away before he could catch her staring. For the first time in a very long time, she was truly interested in what was beneath a man's shirt. She blamed the sun for the heat on her cheeks, grateful for the face covering. It would at least keep him from noticing—

Anna stumbled, her cloak jerking behind her. Her hand slipped from the man's forearm. He whipped around, eyes dark with anger, gripping her wrist and glaring out into the crowd. He dwarfed most of those around them in sheer mass. Men and women parted around them, nothing out of the ordinary except for the overly large oaf snarling at the masses in the middle of the street. She breathed deep, trying to settle her nerves as he pulled her back to him, her hip pressing into him.

"What the fuck was that?" he growled, glancing down at her before putting a hand around her waist and holding firm, fingers wrapped around her hip.

"I—I think someone stumbled on my cloak, that's all. I'm fine," she told him quietly, heart still fluttering from the swift jerk.

But then his fingers started thrumming along her side. Bugger, it was that blasted sea shanty he'd been tapping on the train. Anna bit her lip, heart as quick as a hummingbird's wings for an entirely different reason. His hand was warm, feeling just like the sun beating down on her back.

She directed him toward where the clothes would be. It was on the way to the antidote and they were in need of both. She didn't fancy staying in the market for longer than they had to and she imagined Markus was probably sweating with rage right about now.

They'd walked another mile before the merchants started hollering about clothes instead of food or jewelry. Cashmere sweaters and silks from Bellcaster. Trousers made of supple leather and soft cotton. Some were in the most immaculate patterns Anna had ever seen and, better yet, there was clothing that would make them indistinguishable.

Anna slowed to a stop and surveyed their surroundings. Most in Heylik Toyer were roughly her height and she could see over shoulders and through the spaces between market-goers and to the wares. She and her brother would need several changes of clothing. Markus especially needed pants.

There was something calming about shopping. Somewhere in the methodical routine of it, her shoulders dropped and she stopped clenching her jaw, even going as far as to not bother looking over her shoulder, or his, while they searched for something to wear. The man would need fresh clothes too if he chose to stay. And if he didn't, whatever Anna had bought him would fit her brother.

"I never thought I'd meet a man as large as my brother," she said quietly, holding up a shirt that dwarfed her.

It could have served as a proper tent any day of the week.

"No' many are. Even my babe of a brother isn't this..." He paused, looking for the words. A moment later he motioned to himself vaguely.

"A brother?" Anna asked, angling the shirt up so the collar was flush with the man's neck—too small. She folded it and put it back down, reaching for a blue long-sleeved one made of rough-spun cotton. This one was too short in the waist.

He was quiet, looking down at her with a considering gaze. Anna couldn't meet it and instead continued to keep herself busy, all the while the market continued its hustle and bustle. Another shirt unfolded and she eyed the low v of the front.

Best keep Markus away from it; he tended to flaunt.

"His name's Tate," he said in a near whisper. If she hadn't been looking in the direction of his face and seen his lips move, she would have missed it entirely.

"Handsome name." A slow grin crept across her face, another piece of the puzzle. She looked him in the eyes then; they were such an awfully dark shade. She still wasn't sure if they were green or brown or blue, but they were beautiful.

Tate.

Anna waited several beats, throwing a golden-brown shirt that passed inspection over her shoulder, adding it to a russet long-sleeved and a cream short-sleeved. She looked at an emerald one for a long second before taking it too; it would look lovely with the man's red hair.

Something tingled at the back of her mind, like a memory was trying to force itself to float to the surface. Was it his brother's name that caused the feeling? Or was it something else? Her stomach turned, and a tingling began along the back of her neck. She shifted to look over her shoulder. Nothing. It must be the name, but it was a common enough one, especially in the Emerald Isles.

They paid for the four shirts and he turned her back to the market, his fingers once more glued around her hip. He didn't speak again after sharing that little nugget of information but he wove her from stall to stall, hand always present at her back and gaze always roaming in anticipation of a threat. What a strange man. She'd originally planned on killing him and yet here he was, doing his best to protect her. Was it because she hadn't given him the antidote yet and he was protecting his life more than he was hers?

They stopped for lunch, eating the food with their fingers as they stood in the shade of a stall that carried water skins. Anna pointed to several and the man paid for them before the pair walked down a cluster of stalls that sold fresh fruit and dried meat. They made sure to buy plenty; Anna wasn't entirely sure what would come next but she didn't want to starve.

A stall with fabric the color of flamingos caught her eye first, but her attention held when she noticed the beautiful and bright fabrics, and then firmly fixated on the stall when she caught sight of the stack of bland clothing near the bottom. He seemed to notice her interest and led her that way, his hand only absent when he was facing her while she held up clothing.

Perhaps chivalry has risen, she mused, sucking on her teeth.

"How are you feeling?" Anna asked.

She didn't bother to look up from the stack of cotton pants she was rifling through. She'd added three shirts to his and Markus's growing stack and another three for herself. Now she focused on finding good pants; they'd need to last a rough journey and were more prone to tearing or ripping at the seams. Or at least, that was typically her experience with them, but that could be because of her thighs.

"Sluggish. Bones are achy and muscles are tender," he answered casually and Anna was a little surprised with his honesty. She didn't know many men who would admit to weaknesses of any sort, let alone to a woman. "I assume this is your doin', beastie?"

Anna refused to meet his gaze, though she felt it on her skin and in her soul as if she were sitting in the sun. She snapped a pair of pants in front of her and then held them up to his waist, cocking her head to the side as she looked at the fit. Her eyes drew upward of their own accord, noting the beads of sweat dripping from beneath his checkered scarf and down the stubble of his chin.

Bugger.

She sighed; the pants were a good fit. She started plucking her way through the piles and pulled out five other pairs, all dark in color. They would fit either of the men and Anna could look for trousers for herself on the way back from the antidote.

"Suppose we should find you that antidote before you keel over," she said, holding a pair of leather pants up to him for a quick second.

"I'll last; no sense fretting about me, luv."

"I'm not fretting," Anna lied through her teeth. "Though, I *am* amused you're still standing."

His gaze narrowed, the dark depths becoming nothing but fine, suspicious slits. It was either amusement he was trying to hide or genuine annoyance at her suggestion, she just wasn't entirely sure which. Perhaps it was a little bit of both.

Anna grinned anyway, knowing he couldn't see it. "What? I did say you had two days to sort your affairs, did I not?"

"No, lass," he ground out. "Ye failed to mention that wee detail."

Well that was rather embarrassing; she normally remembered to disclose that sort of information first. Anna shrugged and gave the man her very best apologetic look, throwing the leathers over her shoulder and swatting at his chest playfully. "Apologies."

"Accepted." He slouched, tucking his hands into his pockets. "But I think I'd rather fucking die than watch that prick ye call brother parade around some more in his damn skin. I'll be fine, luv."

"Men and their pride." She dumped the trousers onto the counter. "Which is why we're buying these. Quickly. I'd hate for you to keel over *now* of all times."

He pulled the little velvet coin purse from his pocket and counted out what was needed to pay, flashing her a raised brow as he spoke. "Oh, and why's that?"

Was he fishing for compliments, hoping she might like him to stick around?

Anna shook her head; that was a silly thought. She leaned her hip against the counter and crossed her arms. "Who else is going to carry my bags?" She motioned to the growing stack as the merchant folded the trousers in thin paper before tucking them away in sturdy bags. "Keep it up and this arrangement might have to be permanent. Shopping in Bellcaster is practically a sport."

"I'm a bloody pack mule, 'tis that it? Shite, if only Tate could see me now." The man rolled his eyes, a smile on his face despite the feverish tone of his skin. He hoisted all their bags in one hand and tugged her to him before his fingers claimed their spot around her waist.

"I'm assuming he'd be amused?"

"Oh, aye, the wee shite would be amused, all right."

The man was like a dandelion, letting the wind take him every which way, stopping at any stall he must have found interesting. In that, Anna was absolutely delighted. Each stop to look at something, to pick it up and touch it, to taste it, gave her a little more information on him. It was like getting a rare glimpse inside his head, free of his carefully picked words.

Twenty feet down and across the street, he spoke to a vendor in slow, broken Kurder. To the best of her knowledge, the man asked which ships were docked in the port to the south. The words he used weren't typically ones she spoke with, so her translation might have been wrong, but then the vendor paled and started gesturing wildly with his hands while he spoke. His speech was too fast for Anna to keep up with, though she did catch two words. Two little words that held the weight of the world.

Pirate King.

Seeming satisfied, he thanked the merchant and they bled back into the crowd.

Was he inquiring about the slave trade?

He had mentioned that his ships, wherever they were, had done work thwarting the slave traders. She knew he wouldn't answer any of her internal questions, not unless she asked them directly, but she didn't want to scare him away with her inquiries. It might lead them in a direction she wasn't ready for yet or maybe he'd clam up and decide to keep to himself. She didn't want that, she rather liked drifting through the market with him. It was surprisingly enjoyable, slowly building over the very unpleasant memory of her last time in the market on the arm of a man.

You're…what?

This—us—it isn't working.

I don't understand.

It's not you, I swear it's not. You're lovely and—

Anna's breath dried up in her lungs and tightened her chest. She leaned more and more on him, even going so far as to wrap her arm around his waist. It was thick, his back well-muscled and hot beneath her touch. At first, she wasn't sure what to do with her hand and debated sliding it into his back pocket because it was closer than his far hip. A quick glance at said back pocket had her flushing and looking forward; he'd probably think she was trying to grab his rump.

Based on his grin, he thought he'd caught her staring at it, so Anna settled for looping her thumb in his belt to help steady her arm. He seemed pleased by the action and pulled her closer, gaze still scanning the crowd like a man might search the horizon out at sea.

Around a corner and about a mile later, they stopped at a booth within the shade of one of the mud-brick apartments. This one had a baby blue cloth draped over it and an old withered man sitting on a barrel behind the counter. All around him were blades of every sort. Cutlasses and sabers, daggers and throwing knives. Anna was surprised to see a few marlin spikes clattering in the breeze above her head. It was safe to assume the redhead had an interest in steel.

Did he have a collection or did he have a need for it, like fighting the Pirate King's crews?

She leaned toward the latter; their time on the train had clearly shown he knew how to handle a blade. He was an absolute monster in a tussle. Big beast like himself probably scared plenty of men away by just waving his fists and beating his chest like an ape.

The image was silly enough that Anna had to stifle her laughter and then couldn't contain it when he looked down at her with a raised brow. She cleared her throat, trying to beat back the image of his fists thumping away.

The next stall had children's toys carved from wood. There were elephants, doves, and small foxes, even little ships and trains. The man peeled his hand from her waist, gaze focused and intent. His fingers stuttered above a small carved bear but then the tension in his shoulders slackened and his hand went back to his side, a beat later it snuck back around her waist. His fingers started their drumming again and Anna's brow furrowed; they were turning away from the stand almost in a hurry.

"Do you have children?" she tried to ask casually, motioning back to the stall with a wave of her hand.

"Tate's a bit of a fucking child."

Anna gave him a look.

The man stopped in the middle of the crowd, unconcerned with the market-goers parting around them. "Ye want to know if I've wee ones?" he asked, sounding more like he was talking to himself. He looked down at her, pulling her toward a dimly lit alley. They were still heading in the right direction, hopefully he would last. "Ye know damn well I'm no' married."

"You said so, but that doesn't make it true."

"Well it is. If nothing else, luv, I'm always honest."

"Even so, marriage is not a prerequisite for procreation."

"No," he agreed merrily. "But I'll no' have any until I am."

Her brows pinched. "Why?"

"There's something to be said about waiting."

"Waiting for *what*?"

Waiting to die, perhaps?

Because she certainly felt like that was what the man was doing right now with all this wandering.

"Bloody hell, for plenty of things, fem. Ye've got to wait for all the good things in life—marriage most of all. The right time. The right place." His gaze shifted toward her and he shook his head with a shy smile and averted his attention to the far side of the alley. "The right *female*."

Anna stumbled, completely relying on him to keep her upright.

Surely, she had heard him wrong.

"'Tis a dangerous time, now, and—well, I'm dangerous." He cleared his throat, his tone changing to something Anna thought to be a little sad, resigned to a fate where he would have none of these things despite his hope for it. "The mother of my wee ones is going to help me raise them, no' do it by herself, and bloody hell, she won't be doing it away from me where I can no' protect them. I figure I'd at least have to like her, aye? Means I have to wait for someone I like more than a passing tumble."

Anna stared at him.

This was shock—she was certain this was shock.

He shrugged, glancing down at her wide-eyed stare. "I don't mind waiting. I'm no' in any rush. Time, ye see, it doesn't eat at me like it does most."

Anna shook her head, still a little dazed from what he'd said and unsure of the sentiment of *helping*. That wasn't exactly how it worked in Bellcaster, especially with her primary example of marriage—her mother and father. They had been a political match and while arranged marriages were a thing of the past, neither had refuted the coupling outright. Both came from families with large estates and treasuries.

With the money, her father had started his merchant empire and her mother had been free to travel and explore. So, she dug and discovered and uprooted so many glorious pieces of the past. Nine months after their union, she and Markus came along, as was the primary duty of a wife.

Then their father had claimed his seat in the Senate when they were eight and their mother died some years later. Anna would have liked to say it changed then, that it was that moment in time—that singular event—that had caused the callous, cold efficiency in their father, but John Savage had always been true to himself. That may have been the one thing she had inherited from him beyond looks, for better or worse.

It sounded lovely, though, to be partners, to be a team.

To be loved enough that someone *wanted* to have children with you instead of it being an expectation of marital coupling. She'd always believed children should be a gift given and not a liberty taken.

They exited the alley, Anna still breathless from both her injury and what the man had said, what he had potentially implied. She knew that couldn't be the case, no one wanted her like that. They saw what she came with, what was attached to her, all the gains they could make if they wedded and bedded her. Even Bryce had been like that, wearing blinders and only seeing her value as John Savage's daughter instead of who she was.

And she'd *poisoned* this man.

No matter how it sounded, he could not have meant it like that.

"Do ye find my answer to your liking, lovely?"

She heard the real question, the one hidden between the spaces of his words, behind the grin in his tone.

Do ye find that I'm to your liking, lovely?

Anna blushed furiously beneath her head covering and reminded herself that he was not interested in her. He could not be, it was not possible. She was a thing to men, no matter what this man said. She hated how the idea made her feel but she refused to look away from him as she answered, "Whether it is to my liking is neither here nor there."

"Sounds like an *aye* to me, lovely," he said, grin still on his face as they picked up the pace.

Her thigh protested at the movement but they weren't far from the merchant with the antidote now and Anna had plans to pick out their medical supplies while they were there, too. The warmth trickling down her leg and pooling in her boot was evidence enough that her thigh needed stitching.

She squinted, seeing the shined bronze covering atop one of the stalls several minutes down this makeshift avenue. It was like

a lighthouse calling her home. That wasn't the stall she was looking for, but the antidote was at a stall kitty-corner to it.

Not long now.

She looked up at the man and, despite the circumstances, he
had a pleased, lazy grin on his face. "If I'm lucky enough to have
a daughter," he confided quietly, a new bounce to his step. "I'm
naming her Taylee."

It was a beautiful name, one she hadn't heard.

Anna remained quiet, questions coating her tongue. Just because she had already established the man could have no genuine
interest in who she was as a human being did not make her any
less curious. She had decided the man was an optimistic fool
when it came to topics like marriage, the fact that he believed in
the same notion of love and union as Anna only further proved
her point.

But she wanted to know more.

When she and Markus had been nine, her brother had told
Anna her curiosity would get her killed one day and, bugger, she
was starting to believe him.

"Why Taylee?" she breathed out, glaring when she realized
the question had slipped out with her breath. She nearly groaned
at realizing her mistake.

"Everyone in my family has a name that starts wi' a t. My
brother Tate, my mother Teagan, Auntie Tella…and, and my
sister, Taylee. Well, Taylor. Tate couldn't say her name when he
was babe, but he could say Taylee." His features turned hard and
for a minute Anna didn't think he would say anything else the
rest of the day.

"It's a beautiful name."

He nodded his head, looking pained, and while she wanted
to know what had happened, she decided to leave the festering
wound alone. He had given her another piece, after all—the letter his name likely started with. It wasn't much, but it certainly
was something. Markus would be proud of her.

Not because of her sleuthing, but because of the restraint she was practicing.

The redhead wavered with a rattling breath.

Here reality was, coming back to remind them why they were out to begin with. It wasn't about eating sticky sweets for lunch and watching him lick his fingers until they were clean. It wasn't to shop hand-in-hand. It wasn't to talk about marriage and children. It certainly hadn't been about becoming friends, and they hadn't, but it wasn't hard for Anna to feel like they were getting close.

No, it was about getting this mysterious man an antidote so he didn't leak fluids from every orifice and die before she figured him out.

Anna hastened them along, having to pull him across several alleys. The man's skin started taking on a pale-yellow color, looking almost waxy in appearance. As they continued to walk, his throat bobbed often and his grip around her waist waned. Finally, the small caravan with medical supplies was within her sight. She pushed her way through the crowd, a bit aggressive in her attempt to force their way to it.

Even from this distance she spied shelves piled high with herbs and medicines, all of which she could name. Years in the greenhouse growing up had assured that.

His breath became labored.

Anna glanced up at him, waving the caravan's owner down.

It was yet another man, even though Anna knew his grandmother was the one making all their wares. He stepped forward, wearing a robe the rich color of eggplant and a blackened headscarf, both inlaid with gold trim. He cocked an eyebrow at her and scowled. Anna assumed he recognized her as well. One might say she had a bit of a reputation in these parts. She waved his attitude off with an angry glare of her own.

"How does every bloody merchant seem to know ye, luv?" the redhead asked, voice thick.

She pointed to her eyes. "Don't get many of *these* around here."

He stared at her, blinking slowly. This time when he spoke it was in a whisper and Anna wasn't entirely sure he'd meant to do so. "Aye, they're memorable, all right."

The sincerity in his voice made her chest tighten and that was worse than if she had blushed.

Quickly, Anna pointed to several bottles—antiseptics, antibacterials, and anti-inflammatories. She slid three bottles of pain medication to the pile. While she waited for the caravan owner to pack the bottles, Anna paced in front of the counter, opening and sniffing various ointments.

They were in small circular tins, most were smooth and waxy, but in a few of them she could see the ground herbs they'd been made with. One was light green in color and had a strong medicinal scent. Crinkling her nose, she skimmed the top and rubbed the contents beneath her fingers. The skin of her fingers started tingling and warming.

Anna wiped the ointment off on her pants and placed two tins of the green ointment next to the bottles. After a moment of thought, she slid an ointment with a lavender base to the pile. It was supposed to help with sleep and she would take whatever help she could get in that endeavor. There was another with honey as an ingredient, it would help keep infection away. She handed bandages and stacks of gauze, strips of tape, and even several needles and stitching thread to the pile. If Anna had to she could use her hair, but she'd rather not.

The redhead cleared his throat to hide his cough from her. She met his gaze, noticing his loose grip around her hip not for the first time. He cocked a brow, sweat running down his neck and into the collar of his shirt. She tried not to think about how he was wasting away before her. She tried to ignore the signs of it. But the man was standing a breath away and grinning down at her antics with the medicine and she couldn't help herself.

She tracked another bead of sweat down the column of his throat and then shifted her attention to the swollen veins at his neck. The man's pulse was entirely too slow, but it didn't seem to bother him nearly as much as it did Anna. He was already digging into his trouser pockets and procuring their little velvet coin purse that seemed to be shrinking by the second. With both his hands on the task, he shifted a leg so it rested behind her calf.

"'Tis all?" he asked, counting coins.

"Aye," she tried to tease with a grim smile and then knocked on the counter eight times to a very distinct beat.

The redhead shifted his gaze toward her, sliding another coin across the tabletop, lips moving as he continued to count in his head. Anna pulled another ring from her right hand and flicked it to the merchant. If the redhead hadn't been watching, he probably wouldn't have seen the transaction.

The merchant eyed them both and then picked it up in one swift move, hiding it beneath his robes. It had been a simple metal ring, shined until she could see her face, with a small drop of amethyst at its center. The band was thick and inelegant, something she'd never pick for herself, but it was the exact price of a vial of the antidote the man needed.

With the supplies packaged in thick paper bags, Anna took them in one hand and set out down the street, tugging the man behind her.

"I feel like we're forgetting something," he muttered, fingers laced with hers.

"I feel like if you're a tad more patient, you'll get what you want."

"Wasn't I just telling ye about the merits of waiting, luv?" His attempt at a chuckle dissolved into a fit of coughing. "Reckon no one likes playing cards wi' ye."

"And why's that?" Anna asked, eye on a stall across the way. They'd have to pass it before disappearing into the alley behind it. Just a minute away from heading back to Markus, nothing had gone wrong yet, but there was still light left in the day.

"Your sleight of hand, for one. Almost as good as mine." He shook his head in disbelief. Anna shot him a stern look which was ruined several seconds later when she grinned. Mumbling, he turned away from her. "At least your poker face is shite."

"Yours isn't any better," she shot back, completely focused on the boy across the way.

He was just starting on his first beard, four scraggly hairs sticking out from his chin, full of awkward, teenage energy. He looked at Anna in horror, his eyes shifting from her to the distance between them. The man seemed to pick up that something was amiss and turned toward her.

"What'd ye do to him?"

"Nothing."

"'Tis no' *nothing*, lovely. Look at the lad, he's trembling."

Anna sighed. "He might have heard some stories."

"Some stories? Care to explain?"

"I'm not entirely sure you're old enough to hear them, sir."

The man laughed, loud and boisterous, eyes shining with amusement when he looked down at her. "Trust me, if anyone is old enough, 'tis me."

The boy ducked beneath the counter, shoulder twitching up and down once he was visible. His head was bare but for a little cap, surprisingly light brunette hair sticking out in a mess of straight shafts. Medium brown skin and dark green eyes stared at her as she approached. Anna didn't give the boy a second look, striding past, tugging the man along as he'd assumed they were stopping.

A small vial rolled across the counter.

Without breaking pace, Anna swiped it, inclining her head to the boy for a job well done. She was careful about slipping the vial into the hand at her hip, pulling him toward the alley. "Drink this, you'll feel right as rain soon enough."

Anna did not have to tell him twice.

171

He let go of her hand as they entered the alley and turned down a darkening intersection. She noticed a small hole in the building, cobwebs brightening in the fading light. She stepped away, half her attention on their surroundings, the other half watching the man tip his head like he was knocking back a shot.

That was all it took, that single second of careless motion.

Such an inconsequential frame of time. A second between life and death. A second between love and hate. All it took was that single second to reveal a secret one could never take back. If Anna had blinked, she would have missed what he was hiding under his collar.

In that single second, in that insignificant exposure of his throat, he'd revealed tattoos.

He's a pirate, she thought, surprisingly calm.

That was all the time Anna had to contemplate such things, because in that same span of time when seconds ticked slower, a hand covered her mouth and pulled her into the hole in the wall and into an even deeper hole in the ground.

CHAPTER 20

One second the wee beastie was there and the next she was no'.

Trevor spun in a circle. He hadn't even had the time to swallow the bloody antidote before the lass was stolen right out from under him. There wasn't—shite, there wasn't anywhere for her to go in this alley. Only about six feet from one brick wall to the other, except for the hole in the...

Bloody hell.

He lunged toward the damn thing, hands clenched around the dusty, broken bricks framing it. Hole wasn't even the right word. It resembled more of a crack, if he was being honest. He looked up and down; there was barely enough room for him to squeeze through. He'd have to think some really skinny thoughts.

Trevor inhaled once and then forced himself through, shoulders scraping the brick. A cloud of dust wafted down onto his head and shoulders, stinging his eyes and coating his tongue. On the other side, the ceiling was low, forcing him to duck. He was nearly certain there were four walls, though he couldn't see past the shadows on the other side.

Shite, this was just his luck. Got the antidote so he wouldn't have to explain no' dying to the bonnie lass, but he still hadn't figured out where the damn map was. He'd seen all there was to see of Markus Savage and could confirm it wasn't on the bastard.

But now the lass was gone, disappeared right into a damn hole in the wall and then right into a hole in the ground. He sniffed, lips curling back. The jungle on Tiburon smelt like this too. Old blood and broken bones. It was the same smell that clung to all the dark, cursed places of the bloody world.

"Ahh, shite," he growled between clenched teeth, squinting into the darkness to get a better look at the hole in the flooring.

Inhaling deeply, he caught the barest hint of citrus and silk. Anna had gone this way, which meant he was going too whether he liked it or no'. And he did no'. Fucking hated small spaces. Trevor tossed their bags into a corner, hoping they'd be there once he and Anna came back this way. Trevor exhaled and ran the ten feet though the decrepit building, catching cobwebs and a chill.

Then down into the bloody hole.

He held his breath, grunting as he hit the ground. It was a further drop than he would have thought and black as sin. Couldn't see a damn thing. Trevor went as fast as he dared, the tunnel alternating between straight lines and hairpin turns.

With every step came more confidence and soon Trevor was flying down the twists and turns, listening hard and dragging his fingers along the wall. They'd grown wet and freezing to the touch before warming and crumbling away wi' every brush of his fingers.

He breathed deep, barely able to detect a hint of citrus in the air. Close, he was damn close. The floor inclined and Trevor's toe caught a step; his head cracked into something at the top. A ceiling? A trap door? Shite, he didn't care.

Trevor blinked the dizziness away. He couldn't believe he'd smacked his damn head against whatever this was. He closed his eyes, feeling for seams, and quickly found the bolt, throwing the door open and hurrying into the blinding light. Dazed and squinting, he shook his head.

His vision was shaky at best but, hell, his ears worked damned fine.

Anna was struggling and Trevor heard every growl and swear that left her pretty mouth. His gaze darted around, taking in the rough mudbrick walls and the even rougher window. It was circle-ish, but that wasn't what he focused on.

Nay, out in the distance were several bastards, all about the same height and build with their cloaks and scarves, dragging the wee beastie between them.

Anna's legs were a blur of motion, catching one man as she pulled another over her shoulder and to the ground. She turned, set on running down an ally opposite of Trevor. One of the fucks grabbed her wrist, pulling her to a stop. Anna whirled, swiping her nails against his face and leaving marks deep enough for Trevor to see even at this distance.

Oh, aye, his beastie had claws.

Trevor could do nothing but watch as she was thrown to the ground, rolling wi' an expertise that made him a wee furious. Why the fuck did she look like she'd had practice? The roll was bloody graceful. He couldn't bloody well roll like that.

She popped up and straight into a fist. Her head whipped around, body spinning as it followed the motion, and then Anna was lying face down in the dirt. One of the men pulled her head covering off only to reveal those beautiful, pale curls. They were talking but—but—

He blinked.

Anna wasn't moving.

Nothing made it past the haze in his head.

He was there in his bloody body and then he wasn't, like a wall had been built between who he was and what he was about to do. They dropped Anna just on the other side of a fountain in their haste to outnumber him. One by one the slavers dropped like flies, their tactics damn useless against him.

Trevor didn't feel the pain of his knuckles peeling open beneath his gloves, didn't feel the hits to his body or face. Hell, he did no' hear their screams or his own labored breathing. Didn't fucking care, if he was being bloody honest, because the only thought running through Trevor's head was *no' again, no' again, no' again.*

Trevor straddled the last, fists wailing into his face when he heard it. The soft groan and the scrape of breeches against stone and sand. Turning, his gaze immediately landed on Anna. Something in his chest loosened, his breaths came easier, and the red retreated from his vision.

She was breathing.

He exhaled, muscles relaxing.

Better yet, the lass pulled herself to her wee elbows, squinting at him. Anna winced, working her jaw back and forth. There was a bruise blooming on her lovely cheek and a bit of red stained her right ear, dripping down her neck.

She scrunched her nose, bloody adorable despite it all, and closed her eyes a moment. She coughed, squinting at him again. "Is that *you?*" She sounded surprised.

He opened his mouth to answer but instead of words, a grunt escaped it and pain flared in his side. Ah, shite. That's right. The bastard beneath him still lived and—well, now the poor lass was throwing up and he couldn't hold her hair till he finished up here. Then again, he'd just watched her take bits of that man's skin off with her nails. The lass didn't want to be touched, most like.

Trevor glared down at the male and wrapped his hands around his throat. "Ye fucked up, mate."

Minutes passed and he closed his eyes wi' an exhale, loosening his fingers. The bastard finally quit moving. Now that the lass was alive and mostly well, all the pain and aches were coming in wi' a fucking vengeance. Bloody hell, he'd done a number on his body. Standing, he stretched and dragged himself toward the fountain to wash some of the blood off.

It coated his hands and had sprayed his face. He was a monster, aye, but he didn't want to look the part in front of Anna. She'd seen enough. He slumped onto the rim and splashed his face once, then twice. Swished a bit of water around his mouth before looking over his shoulder.

"Ye alive, lovely?" he called with a grin, feeling the blood dripping from his nose.

If the female cared about that, he'd point out she'd bloody well thrown up and it bothered him naught. 'Tis no' an accident that the wind was blowing the other damn direction.

"No thanks to you," she groaned, rubbing at her forehead wi' the back of her hand.

Trevor motioned to the scene around them just to make sure they were having the same bloody conversation. She blinked, gaze skipping from one dead bastard to the next, completely unimpressed by the work he'd put in.

Bloody hell, this female was something else.

She opened her mouth to say something, paused, beautiful blue eyes wide. Trevor winced, closing his eyes as she turned and threw up again. He sighed, looking away from Anna to glance at the sky. The breeze picked up, blowing a little stronger. Her cheeks flushed and the bit of blood draining from her ear was fucking worrisome. Broke, if he had to guess. Trevor wasn't entirely sure the wee beastie was okay.

She sat back on her heels, spitting the last of the bile from her mouth. "I would have figured it out. I always figure it out. And I told you there were slavers here."

"Aye." He swallowed hard, trying to force the rest of the words from his mouth but they refused to leave the damn nest they'd made in his throat.

"They would have rued the day they forced me on their ship." Sighing, Anna looked up. Her fingers shook and her throat bobbed. She looked just to Trevor's left and he nearly glanced too but—shite, was the lass seeing double? "We should get back before their friends show up."

Trevor nodded, brows drawing together. The lass had put a wall up, something was sitting between them right now and he didn't know what the fuck it was. Could be the slavers but he didn't think that was all of it.

Anna found her feet but she wavered and wobbled worse than a wee filly that'd just found her damn legs. He rubbed the back of his neck and crossed the space between them, wrapping his arm around her waist as he had in the markets, choosing the opposite side in case she couldn't hear out of that ear. She stiffened beneath his hand.

Fucking hell.

Of course, she didn't want to be touched, let alone by him. He'd just used these same hands to kill all those bastards. Had just washed their blood off. Surely, she knew there was no letting them live, that it was her or them and Trevor made the decision wi'out bloody thinking.

"I—"

"Yes?" she said quietly, looking from the corner of her eye.

"I...told ye...I'm dangerous," he whispered.

Her shoulders straightened, the space between them widening. Damn it all to hell, he'd said the wrong fucking thing. Trevor's lips pressed into a thin line and he looked away from her, stomach twisting and skin heating.

"I knew that already. You do recall I was with you on the train?" She sounded exhausted, the words coming out breathy. He looked down. Shite, she could hardly put any weight on that leg of hers. "Where did you leave our things?"

"Safe...I hope." This felt stiff, fucking wrong. Anna was a breeze to talk to, words dropping from his mouth like a bloody geyser. But this shite? Like an anchor, weighing him down. "I— uh, dropped them—to follow ye."

"Oh."

"...aye."

Fuck.

He needed to say something. Well, no' anything. Clearly, he was saying the wrong gods-damned words and he needed to find the right ones. What would Tate say? His wee brother would have something ready to shatter the tension. Something clever— and suggestive to boot. Anna'd benefit from a wee laugh just as much as he would.

Anna stumbled and Trevor absorbed her weight wi' ease. Her gaze remained on the ground. Trevor followed her bright, icy eyes and stopped. He simply stared at the broken body at their feet. Bloody hell. Her foot had caught on the arm of a dead man and that's why she'd stumbled.

Trevor squinted down at the male and his lighter skin—paler than even Anna's. So, he wasn't from around here. He cocked his head, lips pressed into a thin line, focused on the snake bites at his throat. Curious, that; he'd only seen it a few times before.

"Wasn't from here," he commented, leading Anna away.

"They never are. The Kurdish value their women, respect them. But..." She sighed. "But like most boys who are afraid of their toys being stolen away, they've got their fists clenched tight. They've lost too many mothers and sisters and daughters to not become as protective as they have."

"Loss, grief...'tis all just another sea in life," he said, noticing the same bite marks on another man's neck. He frowned; it'd be too easy to blame the Viper, but clearly someone was trying to. "But they can turn even the best men into a damn monster. Reckon 'tis for the best that ye don't have a man wi' all the trouble you get into, luv."

Anna turned to him, smiling viciously.

Fuck, this was the first he'd seen the wee beastie truly angry. Some old hurt haunted her eyes. He saw the mettle, though, and knew it for what it was. Her nose scrunched and she tipped her chin up to him. "What the hell is that supposed to mean?"

Shite.

Abort—fucking abort.

"I—I just mean that I can't imagine any man doing this full time wi'out losing their damn mind every now and then, fem," he stammered, gesturing wildly around them.

Bloody hell, he'd really put his damned foot in his mouth. He should just stop talking. Just shut his mouth and refuse to open it. Trevor could learn fucking sign language and never speak again after this. He could do it. Couldn't fucking read, but he could learn sign language. It was all about priorities.

She laughed and that was when he knew he was truly in deep, unending shite. He opened his mouth before he knew what the fuck he was doing, a wince on his face as she led them back toward the building they'd both crawled out of.

"You're taking this the wrong way, luv, I just—it's just..." He blew out a bit of hot air.

"Just *what?*" she snapped.

Trevor groaned, looking up at the sky. "Any man in love...bloody hell, lass. I'm no' even in love wi' ye and the last thing I want is to see ye hurt, and if becoming a monster keeps ye whole, then... My soul isn't getting much blacker than it already is, so to hell with it."

Idiot, he was a bloody idiot.

Good thing Tate wasn't here, he'd be laughing himself hoarse.

Anna didn't respond.

Did no' even look at him.

He held his breath, stepping beneath the arch and back into the wee mud house, descending the steps and wading straight into the dark. Trevor reckoned retracing their steps would be the quickest way back. Once the lass was off these bloody streets and under the supervision of her brother, he'd be able to relax. To quit looking over his shoulder. The right words might even come then.

Probably wouldn't, but he could hope.

She sighed and Trevor looked to where he knew she was by his side even though he couldn't see her. "I live a messy life. It's hardly my fault no one wants to get their hands dirty and—and I have never settled for anything in my life. Why would I start with the man I marry?"

He almost laughed—the lass was waiting, too.

Anna might have asked a question, aye, but he didn't think she wanted his opinion. He nodded his head. There was something safe about the dark that allowed someone to share their deepest and darkest. Hell, Trevor knew that better than most. He'd whispered to the night sky enough times in his life to know the only true secret keepers in the world were the shadows that lived between the stars.

Between one moment and the next, the hole opened above their head and he lifted her above, setting her on the edge. His hand came away bloody after touching her leg, his stomach twisting at the sight. But if Anna wasn't going to say anything, he damn well wasn't going to either. Nay, he'd wait to pick that fight until they were in front of her prick of a brother—strength in numbers and all that shite.

She leaned against the wall while Trevor climbed from the hole, probably looking like a demon scrambling its way from hell. Felt a bit like one wi' the blood drying beneath his nails. He caught her eyes as he kneeled, wary and bright blue wi' so many unspoken words hanging between them.

Still on his hands and knees before her, Trevor blurted. "Sounds to me like ye need a rogue, luv."

"Or perhaps a pirate?" She didn't even fucking blink.

Trevor nodded quickly.

'Tis a perfect pairing if ye asked him.

The grin on his face felt good despite the split in his lip. "Aye, I imagine a pirate would suit ye perfectly."

"Is that so?"

He settled back on his heels with a shrug. "Hands are already covered in calluses and stained in blood, a little dirt would hurt no' a thing. Bastard probably wouldn't even think twice. I know I wouldn't." He winked, coming to his feet.

"Is that a proposal?" she asked as Trevor lifted their bags into one hand. He wouldn't be letting her out of his fucking sight anytime soon. She stepped closer, brow raised. "Is this the part where we kiss and I turn you into a prince?"

"I told ye, luv, I'm the bloody king."

CHAPTER 21

She should have let the slavers take her.

It would have at least saved her from *this*.

Or at least that's what Anna thought while Markus paced nearby, pinching the bridge of his nose. Her brother was quickly wearing a track in the floor with his alpha-male grumping. He'd been more than a little upset with them for leaving him to roast in Heylik Toyer while they enjoyed the freedoms of the market, right up until he saw the bruise on her face and the dried blood on her ear and neck. Then he'd been downright furious with Anna and absolutely hostile with the redhead—the *pirate*.

Anna laid on her back, legs dangling in the pool and breeches tossed into a corner. They were ruined with her blood and that of the slavers the pirate had killed. It had been brutal and efficient and she had been unconscious for most of it. A stiff hit to the jaw and she'd seen stars, the world tilting on its axis and then going dark.

When she'd come around the first time, the pirate was beating one of the slavers into mush. She'd lost consciousness once more after throwing up her guts. The second time Anna had awoken, he had been washing his face in the small bazar's fountain, blood dripping from his nose and mouth.

Ye alive, lovely?

Why would he go through such lengths to protect her from the slave trade, the very one the Pirate King had created? One only crossed him if they had a morbid interest in death. She had done it once and had vowed never to sail again, having gotten away mostly unscathed. With her hands resting on her stomach, she rubbed at the smudge on her left palm with her thumb.

"*Anna?*"

She sighed through her nose. "*Markus?*"

"Have you been listening at all?"

Anna waved him off, wincing as the pirate stitched the wound on her thigh. He stood in the pool between her legs, head bent over his task. On a normal day, she might have blushed or decided to flirt at having him there, but she was too exhausted. The only thing keeping her from slipping off to sleep was her brother's ravings and the stinging prick of the pirate's ministrations.

Pirate.

She still wasn't entirely sure what to do about that. Or if she should do anything at all. Anna hadn't had a spare moment to ask Markus's opinion, let alone put much thought into it. She laid her forearm over her eyes, hoping to blot out the remaining light as well as her brother's mother-hen-ing.

"You would have been an excellent wet nurse," she told him, fed up with all of it.

"What was that?"

"I'm not helpless, Markus. I knew what I was doing and I knew what the risks were."

"A concussion is a traumatic brain injury," he repeated in a stern tone that Anna suspected he would use on his children one day—if he ever found a woman who could tolerate him for more than five minutes. "I'd hate for you to damage your best asset, Anna, darling."

"I know what a concussion is. And that is hardly my best asset," Anna mused with a wicked grin, peeking at her brother from under her arm. "Have you seen my—"

"Please, have mercy." He closed his eyes, throat bobbing stiffly.

The pirate smirked from between her legs, intentionally dragging his gaze from the top of her head to her thighs and back up to her eyes. Markus cleared his throat and the pirate cast him a goading look, just asking her brother to act like an idiot in his direction.

Little did the pirate know, Markus had never needed an excuse to do so.

"This is your fault. I suggest you wipe that smug look from your blasted face," Markus snapped.

"Oh?" The pirate's grin widened, just as tired of her brother's volatile mood as Anna. "Correct me if I'm wrong, mate, but it was ye strung up like a roast pig on that train, aye?"

It went quiet.

Not the quiet of snow falling from the sky in Bellcaster during winter—peaceful and blissfully soft.

No, this was the quiet before a storm. The quiet in one's head as they watch the shark's fin break the surface and speed toward them. It was a quiet she was rather familiar with. Anna moved her arm and glared at her brother, daring him to open his stupid, fat mouth. He stood several feet away, arms crossed against his muscled chest, still in nothing but those dirty boots and his undershorts.

Bruises and scabs riddled his body, mostly concentrated on his ribs. But the worst of it were the sores on his wrists from where the manacles had bitten deep. He'd immediately bathed his wrists in everything they brought, worried about possible infection. They had been red and weeping but not so much that Anna shared his concern. Since then, Markus had wrapped them in a bit of gauze to keep them clean.

"I own my mistakes, but her head and ear? Those are on you," Markus growled.

"My injuries are on no one," Anna muttered. "No one but myself."

"Suppose ye should put bloody pants on, then? She went to great lengths to get ye those."

Markus grinned darkly. "Does it make you uncomfortable?"

"No' much to look at, mate, just figuring ye might be cold."

"Not one word," she snapped when Markus had opened his mouth.

He glared down at her and then went about his pacing. She breathed out in relief, pleasantly surprised he had backed down immediately. Markus was a powder keg waiting to explode and it was only a matter of time before he erupted. His mood was always the first to foul when presented with no sleep and injuries. Today was no different and tomorrow wouldn't be either.

Anna knew it would take time for him to soften back into the brother she knew and loved. His experience with those marshals had hardened him and he'd raised walls that kept even her out. When he was ready and rested, she would be the first to welcome him back into decent humanness with arms wide open.

But until then, she would encourage him to pick his words carefully.

The pirate knotted the last of the thread and waded back, careful not to touch her. Ever since he'd found her bruised and bleeding, he'd been cautious with his actions, only putting his hands on her when necessary. Anna had come close to telling him she was fine several times, that she wasn't scared of his touch or of him. But then, every time, she would remember he was a pirate.

He was a pirate and he was here and she did not know why.

Normally such a challenge excited her, driving her curiosity, but with Markus's life in the balance she was furious with the not knowing, sick with it.

"Markus?" she asked, staring at the ceiling now. The sky was black through the cutouts, nothing but a candle lighting the space.

"Anna," he echoed.

She pulled upright, leaning back on her palms. "I do believe it's time for you to share what exactly you were doing in the custody of the Senate and why you have a pending trial with an admiral."

"Why do I have to share first?" he whined dramatically. "Shouldn't we ask your *pirate* what he's doing here before I bare my soul in front of the scoundrel?"

"Mar—" Anna's mouth snapped shut, brows furrowing at her brother. "You knew?"

"Near immediately. I'm a high-ranking naval captain, give me some credit." Markus sniffed with a shrug and then gave the pirate a dirty look. "I can smell a pirate a mile away."

"I don't—" the pirate said before rubbing the back of his neck. "I don't *usually* smell. I think we can all agree that I've had a bit of a fucking day."

Markus huffed. "Isn't that the typical day in the gran' ol' life of a pirate? Treachery, deceit, complete lack of honor."

The pirate grinned something terrible, promises swirling in his dark eyes. "I could show ye a lack of honor, mate," he said lowly, hands braced against the side of the pool as he pulled himself from the water. The pirate threw Anna a look before grinning at her brother and tugging his boots off, throwing them in a corner, quickly followed by his socks.

Markus frowned, gaze turning predatory. "What the hell are you doing?"

"Getting comfortable. Cat's out of the bag, no sense in hiding all this." He motioned to himself and then stripped his gloves off, pulling one from his hand with his teeth.

Anna watched in rapt attention, unable to remove her gaze as his strong, tattooed fingers started at the buttons at his throat and quickly made their way down. She gulped, watching his shirt part to reveal sculpted muscle and dark, swirling tattoos—sea serpents, mermaids, pieces of ships and gold. Anna saw the beginnings of tentacles and other sea beasts tucked beneath the fabric.

The pirate tossed a shy smile her way and then smirked at her brother. Markus's gaze shot between them a few times before settling on the pirate with enough intensity to boil blood, nostrils flaring. Anna gave them little attention, instead letting her gaze wander the pirate's exposed skin, trying to memorize every swirl of ink. She had always thought tattoos to be pretty but only pirates had them, which made admiring them rather difficult.

But here the pirate was, letting her drink her fill.

His were stunning and Anna was disappointed when he stopped unbuttoning his shirt between his pecs and started rolling up his sleeves. There wasn't much skin to be seen, aside from the breaks in the ink. They started at his fingers, looking like fingerless gloves from a distance. Even his palms were covered, though they were mostly skin breaks with thin black lines. In a way, the glimpses of his palms reminded her of a map. The tattoos trailed up, disappearing beneath the cloth at his elbows. She assumed they ran all the way up his shoulders before spilling over his chest.

He reached back up, folding his collars down and breathing deep. A red line tapered against his throat from where his collar had been buttoned. It had to have been uncomfortable but he'd obviously been committed to keeping his secret from them. Tentacles reached up his throat and on his forearms—

She squinted and tilted her head.

The pirate cleared his throat. "Bloody hell, 'tis good to breathe again. Now, luv," he said, shifting his attention to her, "I get how the prick knew I was a pirate, but that doesn't explain how ye did."

"Have you seen you?" She grinned, forcing her gaze to remain on his face and not dip down to his exposed skin to trace every inch of his tattoos. "I have four bachelors and two doctorates—"

"Shite," the pirate interrupted. "In what? Sleuthing?"

She grinned as she continued, "—and I dare say I've spent more time among pirates than my brother."

"How'd ye bloody well manage that?"

They were quiet, Anna unwilling to share why and Markus unwilling to even think of it.

Anna returned her attention to her brother, who was more akin to an obstinate toddler at this very moment than a fully-fledged adult. He remained unflinching beneath her scathing gaze. His lips pulled into a thin line and he sighed through his nose while Anna massaged one of the many ointments onto her thigh, dabbed some of the honey-based ointment over the sutures, and wrapped it in gauze.

Finally feeling a bit relaxed, she turned back toward her brother. He shifted on his feet and then rolled his neck. Satisfied, Anna started looking for the pile of clothing that contained her trousers.

"They said they were looking for a map," Markus said, watching the pirate carefully.

She saw it too, the moment the pirate tensed.

"What map?" she asked anyway, forcing her gaze away from the redhead.

Dread infused itself into her bones at hearing this was about a map. A *map*. All of this over a little map. A single scrap of paper or—her stomach clenched, blood cooling in her veins—a bit of leather she suspected might actually be a weathered scalp.

She stood, needing something to do with her hands, with her body, while her brother recounted the events. The pirate stood as well, likely waiting for her to buckle. The skin around her stitches was tight with swelling and warm with irritation, it wouldn't take much to tear it. Anna knew he was thinking that as much as she was, but he kept his distance, shucking his hands into his pockets and keeping his facial expressions disinterested.

Her fingers found the waistband of her breeches as Markus made a rather big deal about the marshals stampeding into his room and tracking dirt everywhere. Anna snorted. That sounded like her brother. As he continued to tell his tale, he became more animated, settling back into his skin. She stuffed one leg through and then the other, leaning against the cavern wall for support.

"They said they were taking me to a blasted admiral for trial before we left Charleston. But…" He took a deep breath, looking at the ground. "But once we were on the train it was made clear that I wasn't going to be given a trial. Instead, they were handing me off to the Coalition. Said it was an act of good faith if I couldn't come through with the map." Markus gnawed on his lip and stared just over her shoulder. "And they said if I didn't come through, they thought you might."

Anna tipped her head, considering.

It certainly lined up with what she and Mihk had gathered, though the bit about finding her was new. Something about it wasn't sitting right, stirring up all kinds of feelings in her gut.

"'Tis no' how that fucking works," the pirate laughed.

"What was that, wretch?"

"The Coalition. Sorry to inform ye, prick, but those five do no' bargain, nor do they take trades. Us pirates, we're a bit of a *take all leave none* sort. Best case? The bastards are stringing your Senate along. Worst case, your precious Senate is stringing *ye* along."

Bugger.

Anna hadn't thought about that.

"Oh, yes. You would know all about pirate politics, wouldn't you?" Markus hedged. Judging by the sharp glitter of his eyes, he *knew* something.

"Aye."

Anna kept both the men in her sight, unsure if she would have to jump in or not. Whatever bit of settling Markus had done had evaporated the second the pirate disagreed with him. He started pacing, clearly wound up and itching for a fight. Not that he'd be finding one, not if she had anything to say about it. They weren't teenagers anymore, solving problems with their fists no longer applied.

By the time her brother concluded his story, he had an irritated look on his face, glaring daggers into the side of the pirate's head. Anna played with the end of her shirt as she leaned against the wall. She only knew of one map that would have that much bargaining power.

Markus might have been the last one to be physically seen with it, but Anna had stolen it right out from under the Pirate King's nose.

"That's...all you recall?" she asked, closing her eyes tight, hoping, just *hoping*.

"They could not have been clearer with their wishes and intentions, Anna," Markus said dryly. At the look on her face, he sighed and ran his hand through his curls and stared up. "Hand over the map or they'd hand me over. Luckily for all of us, I didn't have it on me, nor in my quarters. Their methods of persuasion were becoming increasingly difficult to ignore."

"Which naval map?" Anna asked, still holding out hope that this fiasco wasn't entirely her fault.

"You're not going to like this," he told her, straight-faced. When Anna showed no signs of backing down, he winced. "It's not a naval map, Anna, darling. You know it well."

"Sometimes I hate being right," she groaned, sliding down the rough cavern wall. She held her head in her hands. From where she was, Anna could just see the pirate. He was entirely too still, his body made of calm, careful lines.

"If it's any consolation," Markus started, "at first, I couldn't wait to tell you it's your fault for once; but now that I have, I feel horrible."

"Thanks, Markus," she muttered, still staring at the redhead. He turned toward her, as if feeling the weight of her gaze. She gnawed at her cheek, considering the handsome scoundrel. "I suppose that explains why you're here."

The pirate cocked his head, hearing the open ending of her sentence. Anna wasn't entirely sure she wanted to hear his story, but it was an important part of the narrative and if she planned on figuring this out, she needed it.

"I…reckon so…" he said slowly.

When he didn't elaborate, Anna focused entirely on him. "Though I still wish to hear your opinion of the events."

"It's a simple tale, ye'd be bored, aye."

"As you can see, pirate, I'm rather free right now and have plenty of time on my hands."

He ran his lip through his teeth. "Well…the Coalition sent others off to find the damn thing, so I'm finding it before them."

"That was three years ago," she told him.

The pirate nodded his head in agreement. "They're still looking for it. I don't have any bloody intention of giving it to them. The Senate can't have it, either—just trust me on that. Coalition typically gets what it wants, but I happened to be privy to where the map was last seen. Put two and two together wi' your brother's arrest. Simple as that."

Who was this pirate and how had he known Markus was the one with the map?

Anna's heart raced in her chest at the implications. He'd been on Tiburon and seen her, that much was obvious. But somehow, he'd seen her give her brother the damn thing and lived. How, though? As far as she knew, every single one of the pirates that had been there that day were dead, their throats slit and dumped overboard after their attempt to waylay Markus's ship.

"That is a very short story." Anna sighed hard through her nose.

Anna waited, there had to be more.

Markus continued pacing off to their right.

"Some stories are, lovely."

"Don't call my sister that," Markus bit out.

"Call her what, mate?"

"You know what."

Of all the times Anna had cursed her brother's hard-wired biological need to protect her, now was the time she rued it most. She tried to catch one of their gazes as they snarled and scowled at each other, but neither of the men dared glance away from the other.

"You're upset I called her lovely?" The pirate laughed. His grin was crooked and sharp and delightfully familiar in a way she didn't understand as he finally turned to look at her. He made eye contact with her, something shy and small in his voice. "Why would I call her anything else than what she is?"

Heat prickled at Anna's traitorous cheeks. She broke eye contact, quickly looking at his feet, but in her periphery she saw the knowing grin light up the pirate's features and the pleased way his dark eyes seemed to shine.

CHAPTER 22

He was going to kill the pirate.

The bastard had to be Tate Lovelace.

He *had* to be.

Markus had seen the quartermaster of the *Pale Queen* enough times to recognize him from a distance. There wasn't any other pirate, aside from Trevor Lovelace, with that wine-red hair and those dark eyes. Couldn't be the Pirate King though, he was too young. And as much as Markus hated admitting it, too handsome.

He sucked on his teeth, wanting to beat the pirate within an inch of his life. He had too much pent up energy and not enough ways to expend it. Not in this broken body. Not in this hellish labyrinth. Not after being on that damnable train spending all that quality time with the Senate's dogs, and certainly not after watching the blasted pirate stand between his sister's legs while making eyes at her and listening to his piss-poor attempts at flirting.

Markus would be damned if he let another Lovelace anywhere near his sister. She'd nearly died after the last run in with the crew of the *Pale Queen* and, being the younger brother of the Pirate King, Tate was probably here to kill her after getting his brother's cursed map back.

The wretch grinned at his sister, drawing a scowl from Markus.

He would have preferred literally any other member of that black-hearted bastard's crew. Tate was known for his accolades with women, for getting what he wanted and tossing it aside when he was done. Tate would make a blasted game of this, of repaying what Anna had done to his brother. Markus couldn't stand the thought.

"...lovely."

He almost laughed, a bit of red creeping into his vision. Of course, of course. The games had already begun. They'd begun the second the pirate found himself sitting across from Anna. It made sense now in a horrid sort of way, why the pirate was there, why he was dressed as a marshal. Why he was willing to tolerate his sister and her blasted tricks. He'd come for Markus and the map and then had the splendid luck of stumbling upon Anna.

Markus's teeth ground against each other as he looked between the two. Watching how his sister kept glancing at the pirate, how the pirate sought her out too when she wasn't looking. He was more than easy enough to look at, Markus could admit that, but he was a pirate. A scoundrel. A man who couldn't be trusted with a sack of shit, let alone with someone as precious as Anna.

She should know better.

"Don't call my sister that," he snapped.

Bollocks, this was three years ago all over again, except Anna had traded in for the younger model.

What was with Anna and pirates?

I should have let you drown.

He twitched, nearly laughing because the fetish must run in the family.

"Call her what, mate?"

"You know what."

The pirate squinted at him, mouth twitching into a scowl as he searched Markus's face for something. Whatever it was, it apparently didn't take long to find. The pirate laughed, looking down on him even though they were practically the same height. The pirate was broader in the shoulders and wider in the torso, but that would hardly make up for the raw feeling burning in Markus's chest.

"You're upset I called her *lovely*?" The pirate broke away from Markus's glare and turned to Anna, a grin pulling at his lips.

But Markus didn't hear what else the pirate had to say or see what other expression he might have made. He could only stare at how it made his sister look, a bit of pink tainting her cheeks.

She *liked* that he called her lovely.

CHAPTER 23

"Blasted *peacocks!*" she growled at about the same time her brother connected with the pirate, arms around his torso, slamming onto the stone flooring, fists swinging before they even landed.

Bugger, Markus was faster than she remembered.

Anna used the wall to stand, every inch of her body protesting the act. Her head swam from the sudden motion, nausea hot in her stomach. Most days Anna recognized and honored the fact that it was safer to watch Markus pick a fight, that a single rogue punch could put her down hard and fast.

Today was not most days.

She ran headfirst toward them, intent on breaking up their pissing contest. It took far longer than she wanted, or would be willing to admit, to reach her brother. Anna looked over his back as she approached, hands already reaching for his arms. She stopped, confusion tugging at her. The pirate seemed content, buffing off each of Markus's blows like they were no more concerning than drops of rain. His lip had split back open and blood poured from his nose and mouth, yet the pirate was laughing—joyless and jagged. It twisted her up inside.

"'Tis all, mate? Surely a big man like yourself can hit harder than this!"

"Shut the hell up!"

Anna struggled to pull Markus back, knee giving out and slamming into the ground as the two men rolled away from her, limbs flying. Her world tilted and whirled, the taste of bile climbing up her throat. Every hit, every grunt, echoed up and bounced off the walls.

Markus was on top once again when she reached them and she had the suspicion it was due to the lack of effort provided by the pirate more than anything else. The pirate's hands were up in fists in front of his face, forearms brushing off or redirecting each of her brother's swings. He still had that worrisome grin, the rest of his features calm and uncaring, and Anna stilled when she realized why.

This was a regular occurrence for the pirate.

If not now, then it had been in the past.

"Markus!" Anna snapped in a voice she didn't recognize, fingers wound tightly around his elbow.

"Get out of the way, Anna!"

She pulled, throwing all her weight backward, muscles straining to gain ground against the hulking mass of practiced muscle that was her brother. She hardly moved him, but at least she had the one arm trapped. The pirate hadn't been returning any of her brother's blows, so Anna wasn't exactly worried about getting hit by accident.

"Enough!" she yelled at her brother, grabbing at his forearm and twisting until he started moving away from the pirate. Markus turned and thrust his arm back, palm catching her sternum where the plate of bone met clavicles, and shoved.

Normally, Anna would have been able to catch herself because of the strength in her legs. She stepped back, gritting her teeth as the stitches in her thigh pulled taught. Her knee wobbled and gave, hitting hard against the stone. It cracked and Anna thrust her hands forward, hoping to catch herself before her face met a similar fate.

She sucked in a tight breath, a yelp of surprise and pain leaving her lips as she pushed herself up into a sitting position. Her hands stung and her knee throbbed but none of that compared to the pain coming from her thigh. Markus hadn't noticed any of it, he'd already turned his attention back to the pirate, to the danger he was so sure of.

But the pirate?

His attention darted between her knee and face before turning toward Markus, lips curling in rage and eyes deadening into something feral. Anna's stomach dropped, both in confusion at his expression and in sensing what was to come. She'd seen the end result of those who scuffled with him both on the train and in the bazar.

Death.

"Wait!" she yelled, but it was already too late.

The pirate was a vicious and brilliant creature, cold and impossibly practiced in a way Anna and Markus could never be. Their upbringing was not the sort to cultivate, nor encourage, such a ferocity. She had enough time to swallow before the pirate had pinned her brother down and was beating him into the ground. His head snapped sideways but his fists never stopped hammering.

"Stay back, Anna!" Markus yelled through a mouthful of blood.

Anna lunged forward anyway, fingers curling around the pirate's bicep.

It was a stupid idea, she knew that.

He very well could turn around and break her neck. He owed her nothing and without the poison running through his veins, she had nothing to hold over his head. But the second she touched him, he stilled, gaze sliding to her, deep breaths rattling in his chest. She watched as blood dripped from his raised fist, his knuckles split and raw.

That's enough, she shook her head, pulling him back by his arm.

The pirate listened to her unspoken words, already leaning away from Markus when her brother bucked his hips and planted both feet on the pirate's chest, sending him skidding backward. His arm slid through her hands until just his fingers were touching hers—something sparked, pulling her attention to his eyes.

Markus turned toward the pirate with a snarl; he was on his feet and lunging again before Anna could blink. She pulled the pirate back by his shoulder and threw herself between the two men. Chest heaving, Anna pinned her brother down with a look that could cook him alive and held her ground. Shock passed over his face, brows high and eyes wide.

Markus stumbled to a stop and then dropped back onto his haunches. "Anna—"

"You have done quite enough!" she hissed, fists clenching at her sides, voice rising with every word. "Whatever this is, it is *done*."

"But—Anna—he's a pirate!"

The laugh scraped at her throat, loud and angry. Anna put her hands on her hips and shook her head. "Yes, we established that. Is this about what happened three years ago? Do you really think I'd be daft enough to attempt another stunt like that?"

"Yes! I mean, no! I—" Markus groaned loudly in frustration and threw his hands in the air. "Just get over here! That's Tate Lovelace, Anna, would you just listen—"

She turned enough to see the pirate from the corner of her eye. He stood as still as a statue, hands in his trousers, but the bunched muscles at his shoulders told Anna he was ready to act if need be. She dragged her gaze from his head to his toes and then centered her attention on his right cheek. The bit of panic that was just blossoming blew away with her next breath.

"No, no, he's not." She sighed. "The quartermaster has three scars on his cheek. I remember that much about him. Right coloring though, I'll give you that."

Anna tried to smile at her brother but he was too busy glaring at the floor to notice her olive branch. Fine, if he wanted to be a grump, she'd let him. She took another breath, heart still hammering away in her chest, and rubbed at her upper thigh. It pulsed and throbbed beneath her touch.

The pirate's knuckles brushed her lower back. When Anna turned, he had stepped closer, looking down at her with concern in his eyes. "Are ye all right, beastie?"

"I'll be fine," she said quietly. And she would be. Of course, her injuries and the pain they brought would hinder her, but she didn't have the time to think about that. Not when a plan to keep her brother from the noose needed to be thought up and enacted.

The pirate shook his head and a grin broke across his face. Anna's heart clenched; despite the blood, the bruises, and the crack down the middle of his lower lip, he was still beautiful.

"I don't know, old girl." Markus squinted at the pirate, frown deeply engraved on his face. "Still might be Tate."

"Shite, mate, Tate Lovelace wishes he was this pretty."

Anna laughed, quick and surprised. The pirate waggled his eyebrows at her and stepped away. She hadn't realized just how much heat radiated off him until she felt the absence of it like death's cold embrace. Slowly the pirate took another step back, toes dragging on the ground. Did he want to remain close to her in case her brother decided to do something impossibly stupid?

She smiled at the redhead, going for reassuring, before turning toward her knucklehead of a brother. He had moved to sit against the wall, his elbows propped on his knees. She cocked a brow at him and folded her arms against her chest. Markus made eye contact with her and shrugged his shoulder. A second later he spat a bit of blood from his mouth and wiped at a bleeding cut on his cheek.

Served him right.

The pirate was still on his feet on the opposite side of the cavern, closer to her than she was to Markus and keeping a vigilant eye on her brother. Anna doubted he would try brawling with the pirate again tonight, but Markus had surprised her before and she wouldn't put it past him to do so again. After a long moment, Anna cleared her throat. It would be best to get this out of the way, no more letting her brother stall his way out of talking.

"Now that you two are quite done, Markus, where is the map?"

He glared at the ground.

"Markus?" she sighed, a bit of the exhaustion she felt creeping into her voice.

"I put it where I put everything precious to me, Anna," Markus said quietly, voice as small as a child's.

It took a minute for his clue to sink in and when it did, it struck Anna like a bolt of lightning. She put her face in her hands and groaned, "*Please* tell me you didn't put it where I think you did?"

Markus met her gaze, an uncharacteristically tired grin on his face. "Oh, but I did."

The pirate looked from one sibling to the next, squinting at them. "Would either of ye care to share where the bloody map is?"

Markus glared.

Anna shot him a dirty look before turning back to the pirate. "It's in the capital—"

"'Tis no' so bad."

"—in our father's estate, beneath Markus's bed."

The pirate blinked, staring hard at Markus before turning back to Anna. She watched his gaze slide skyward, head sagging back. She imagined he was looking to the heavens, praying for mercy or patience. Anna certainly felt like doing so and hoped he asked for a bit of luck as well. They were going to need it.

"Fuck."

"Aye," Anna mocked the pirate in his roguish brogue. "*Fuck.*"

"Things are never easy wi' ye, are they?"

"Afraid not."

His snort descended into a chuckle, eyes bright when he turned to her. They remained quietly staring at each other until Markus cleared his throat rather forcefully and Anna looked away with a small smile, forcing herself to think about the problem at hand.

The Pirate King's map.

It was a rather unfortunate situation that the blasted thing would be at their father's estate. To think the Senate sent their dogs after her brother for a map that was already sitting in the home of one of their members. Normally she would have found that bit of information rather comical but not today; not with Markus's life hanging in the balance and not with the importance of the map to the Coalition and the Senate.

Even with Markus's help, it would be difficult to sneak into their father's estate and steal the map back. But Anna doubted Markus would even be able to help. With the Senate's dogs hunting for him, he wouldn't be able to set foot on the grounds, let alone show his face in Bellcaster—and that was without her father's birthday celebration coming up. The event pulled nearly all the Senate's resources and security every year.

The pirate's boot scuffed against the ground, drawing her attention. She stared at him hard enough to cause him to fidget back and forth. His brows drew together and he straightened his shoulders beneath her gaze. He'd been helpful before on the train and in the markets. Maybe...

She rubbed the outside of her thigh. The pirate missed nothing in her movements, one brow twitching at the action. "It would appear we are after the same map and I believe we have similar goals of obtaining it," she said quickly, looking between the two men.

"When did we decide that?" Markus asked at the same time the pirate spat blood from his mouth and purred, "Aye, *lovely*."

An intentional grin stretched across his mouth like a cat settling into the sun. They were both aware of what he was doing and even knowing that, Anna couldn't help the smile tickling at the corner of her mouth. She squashed the blasted impulse as soon as her brother noticed it.

Anna shifted, brows drawing together. Surely, there was a way to satisfy all their needs—the pirate's for the map, her brother's for his life, and hers for—hers for what? Adventure, notoriety, something more? That's what stealing the damn thing the first time was supposed to do. Anna sighed. It felt a bit like coming full circle.

The map, the terrible scrap of weathered leather. It had been loathsomely difficult for her to find in the first place, let alone get her hands on, and the only reason Anna had even attempted it was because Markus had shown an interest and their father said no one would be able to accomplish such a task.

And she had, despite not being able to tell anyone but her father and brother.

It hadn't been easy and Anna had made some rather questionable choices, but she'd been victorious. She thought of the warm, satin-like feeling of the little rolled up map in her hands. It had been tied with a string of twine and at the time she could have sworn it had been inked in blood, though the thought seemed a bit ridiculous now. Anna had only looked at it briefly before tucking it away, not nearly long enough to decipher it. Not even close.

Anna had never bothered finding out where it led or what was at its end. That had never been the point of her expedition. Successfully thieving it had been an accomplishment in and of itself, and any map belonging to the Pirate King couldn't possibly lead anywhere good. That would explain why the Coalition wanted it, but not why the Senate did.

Anna chewed on her lip, the knowledge that both the Coalition and Senate wanted the map with the desperation of a starving man certainly sparked her interest. Surely, they wanted it because of where it went or what was there.

Bugger, now she really wanted to know.

Her heart thundered, skin heating. It called to her then, the map and where it led, and what was at its end. The conundrum of being accomplished at finding things, often old and forgotten, gave Anna the feeling she had a duty to do so.

Markus took one look at her and frowned. "I know that look. Whatever you're thinking, my answer is no."

"I was only thinking it would be a good idea if we worked together."

"Like hell it is. You want the map for yourself."

"Fine," Anna admitted, seeing no point in arguing. "I want the map and I want to see where it goes. But I also realize we need that map if we are to pacify the Senate and possibly clear your name."

Markus folded his arms and leaned back against the wall. "I knew it. My answer stands. We can find another way. Handing the map over will only further implicate me in all of this."

She eyed Markus carefully. "Who are you and what have you done with my brother? The Markus I know would never turn down the opportunity to go treasure hunting."

"If this was about treasure, Anna, you could count me in. But that map..." He shook his head and closed his eyes. "That map will probably lead to an island full of rocks and certain death. I want jewels if I'm going to go treasure hunting. Gold. Diamonds. Beautiful fabrics. Not rocks. Not death."

The pirate snorted, wiping at his face now that his nose was under control.

Markus shot him a glare before turning back to Anna. "No."

"Oh, come on, it'll be fun, Markus."

Markus scowled. "Absolutely not. That's exactly what you said the last time you went looking for it and you nearly died."

"That is neither here nor there." She waved him off, though the scar along her chest itched in response to his words. "I know where the map is now. I stole it once, I can steal it again."

He shifted, crossing one foot over the other in outrage. "You can't do that! That's cheating."

"You never said no take-backs. Now quit whining, it's unbecoming."

"What about the blasted trouble I'm in, Anna? I'd rather not hang later just so you can go on some daft adventure."

"Fine, fine, fine," she said, leveling him with a knowing look. "I happen to know an extremely gifted cartographer. We'll copy the map and hope that's enough to clear your already-tarnished name. Though I doubt it will be." Anna smiled at her brother and turned to the pirate. "So, will you be helping us or will I be poisoning you again? The fact of the matter is my brother is a wanted man and I don't think I can do this on my own."

"Ye and these threats, luv. If ye want my help, all ye have to is ask."

Markus laughed, disbelief plain on his face. "You can't be seriously considering bringing a scoundrel like him with us! He'll just hand the map right over to the Coalition."

"Fuck that." The pirate snorted. "I told ye, Coalition 'tis no' getting the map. This cartographer of yours is making mistakes when they copy it, aye. Senate can no' have a bloody copy either."

"I think he can do that."

"Anna—" Markus pinched the bridge of his nose.

"Now, we'll need a ship and a crew and last I checked, pirates had those in spades."

"—even if he is telling the truth, how are you planning on crossing the sea? You know you can't."

The pirate's brows drew together, a frown finally tipping at his lips. His voice was low when he spoke, hardly a whisper. "What the hell is he talking about?"

"Superstition. It's nothing," Anna huffed, tucking a stray curl behind her ear. She turned her gaze on Markus and pinned him to the ground with it, *not one word.*

You're marked, Markus's gaze seemed to whine. *Marked by the Coalition and the Pirate King.*

Instead, he said, "It'll be dangerous, Anna."

"All the best adventures are," she shot back stubbornly.

"Reckon 'tis no' more dangerous than running around wi' ye," the pirate commented off-handedly from beside her. He was still staring at her warily, thoughts swirling behind his eyes like smoke under glass. In one slow movement he leaned back against the wall and slid to his haunches, stretching out his legs with a wince. "Right, *lovely?*"

The pirate certainly wasn't wrong.

"Honestly, I wish that were true." Markus laughed angrily in response, causing Anna to take a deep breath.

When she was certain she wouldn't flay Markus alive with the next look, she turned to face him. He looked close to foaming at the mouth at the prospect of spending another second with the pirate. Anna could only wonder why. If she had the choice of working with the pirate or against, she would choose with.

Whatever it was, it had to be more than their conflicting background or the pirate's perusal of her features. Markus was an idjit, but he had to have figured out the pirate was goading him. It wasn't possible he was genuinely infatuated with her.

"Which is why it will be both safer and easier to work together." She held up a finger when Markus opened his mouth. Anna turned toward the pirate, folding her arms across her chest and tilting her head at him.

He closed his eyes and tipped his head back against the wall. The motion exposed the column of his throat and the ink that decorated it. "Do ye know where that cursed, wee map leads?"

Anna shook her head, watching him carefully.

The pirate stilled, his breaths coming in and out slowly. His throat bobbed and then he peeked an eye open. "On that train, ye asked me if I covet death, but I have to wonder the same about ye, luv. Nothing good will come of it. Reckon a noose will be the least of your problems if you're caught."

"From Senate or Coalition?" Markus asked rather pointedly.

"Rope's a rope, bucko, I don't think who's slipping it around your fucking neck matters."

"If you're trying to scare her away, brigand, it won't work," Markus grumbled from the side. "Once her interest has been piqued, it knows no bounds."

"And treasure maps and peril are what pique her interest?"

Anna wasn't facing the pirate, but she could hear his teasing tone easily enough. Even if she hadn't heard him, she would have known his tone for what it was by the flash of anger in her brother's gaze and the curl of his lip. She swung her head around, staring hard at the pirate. He sat against the wall, frame deceptively relaxed with one ankle crossed over the other.

"You're right. A pirate would suit ye fine, luv. We're as treasure-obsessed and drawn to danger as they come."

Anna ignored the way her heart stuttered in her chest.

There was something familiar about the angle of his jaw in the low lighting, in the darkness that pooled in his gaze. She brushed that aside. There was a map to be stolen and treasure to be found and of all the circumstances in her life that had nearly ended her, Anna refused to let a *rope* be the reason for her expiration. There was an answer somewhere in this sea of possibility. An answer that didn't lead to her or her brother's execution. Not even that of the pirate, if she could help it.

Anna tipped her head back and closed her eyes. She had to plan, the quicker the better, but she had no reason to be visiting her father, let alone be in Bellcaster to begin with. She only returned between trips and never to say hello to John Savage in his estate. He would suspect something immediately, maybe nothing to do with the map at first, but with Markus's escape circulating…

She pressed the heels of her hands into her eyes. Her father was a patient man and his estate could lock down into a stronghold if he wished it. They might never see the inside, or outside, if he figured it out. Anna started cataloguing what staff would be present this time of year. The ground would be flooded for her father's birthd—

Anna's head snapped up, grin twitching at her lips.

Of course.

The pirate shifted, stretching his arms above his head. She stared at him, unblinking. He blinked back in response, slowly lowering his arms. His jaw ticked and Anna sucked on her teeth. It would be risky, bringing another into the Savage Estate instead of going alone. Even more so considering he was a pirate and after the map same as they were.

Would he really help them when asked? Or was he just trying to lull them into a false sense of security? Anna slowly let out her breath. There really was no way to know.

A plan slowly strung itself together in her mind. One that would excuse her presence in Bellcaster and allow her access to her childhood home in one fell swoop. She'd need a dress readied for her, which meant she had to write Mihk, and her father would expect Anna to arrive with a companion of some sort and she couldn't possibly bring Markus without being arrested by marshals on sight.

And she might need help getting out, if things went poorly.

"Aye, luv?" the pirate asked at her questioning gaze.

"Your answer, pirate."

He was quiet for a long minute, gaze unwavering and chest stilled with a held breath. "Long as ye give me that map, I'll take ye anywhere ye wish to go. Anywhere on any sea. Even to the end of that cursed map if that's what ye fancy. I can't say I'm excited but, bloody hell, if you're going, so am I." He sighed, that shy shine back in his gaze.

She cleared her throat and turned back toward her brother. "Excellent, we leave at first light."

The pirate shot her a curious look. "That was quick, luv."

"I do everything quickly, pirate. Do try to keep up."

CHAPTER 24

Trevor scrubbed at his jaw, a wee impressed.

Only man that could go toe to toe with him was Tate, but 'tis only because they had been fighting since he was a wee lad. The victorious grin still forced itself to the surface each time Trevor felt the heat of the prick's gaze. The fem had asked if he was a prince or a frog and Trevor had proved he was a king, for better or worse. Usually bloody well worse, but he'd try no' to dwell on that. Thinking of the feeling of her hand in his, Trevor closed his eyes.

The wee female had jumped between them wi'out a thought and something about it twisted him up inside. Trevor still hadn't figured out which version of the story he liked best—that Anna had done it to keep him from being bloodied and bruised, or because she was confident Trevor could kick the ever-loving shite out of her brother.

Matters naught, he decided.

Either way, Trevor still felt two times his size.

He heard the shuffle of her step long before she reached him. His chest tightened at the limp and every bit of pride he had been feeling was sucked right out of him. If they had been on the *Pale Queen*, Trevor would have lobbed both of the prick's bloody hands off for touching her so carelessly. He stilled, watching as Anna brushed her brother off and kept walking.

Maybe he shouldn't have pushed Markus. At the time it had seemed the obvious choice. The prick clearly needed to get some energy out of his system and Trevor didn't mind a bit of rough and tumble, he needed to get his own bloody energy out too.

Are ye okay? He cocked his head toward her leg as she stepped wi'in reach.

She leaned her weight off it and shrugged a shoulder, tucking a strand of blonde hair behind her ear.

Trevor stretched out against the wall, taking the candle from Anna when she offered it. It was lit, wavering wi' each breath she took. The female stood in front of him like some chaotic goddess. Trevor didn't think he'd ever lose the sense of awe that bloomed behind his ribs.

Bloody hell, he had been around the world more times than he could count, but never in his life had he met anyone quite like her. Anna was curious, adventurous, and genuine. The lass was daft the same way Tate was, but she was better for it.

They stared at each other.

Clearly, the lass wanted to say something to him and he wanted to hear it. He was beginning to wonder if Anna was a fucking witch. She'd *seen* him earlier, stared at his tattoos, the damage he could do, and no' shied away. From what Trevor could tell, the lass hadn't wanted to look away either. He'd felt every second of her gaze like the sun on his skin as she inspected him.

But shite, Trevor did no' like the way it made him feel, like he should be preening and that wasn't befitting a man of his bloody status. And he wasn't at all concerned with Anna figuring out who he was and he should be. They were about to walk into the den of a senator and any of those fucks would love nothing more than to put Trevor in one of their pretty nooses and parade him around.

"Thank you for not killing my brother," Anna said, looking away in what could have been embarrassment. The lass had no reason for the feeling. If anyone had reason, it was him. He'd finally had the chance to wring the bloody prick's neck and chosen no' to.

Tate was going to get a good bloody laugh out of that.

"Are you all right?"

Trevor nodded his head. "Aye, naught is wrong."

"I…" Anna cleared her throat, pulling his attention to her mouth. A second later he looked back to her eyes to find something curious and calculating staring back at him. "Why didn't you fight back?"

"Why…didn't I…?" he repeated dumbly. That hadn't been what he was expecting. "No'…no' all fights are worth it. And that one wasn't, no' until he pushed ye."

"No one likes being hit. No one likes being in pain. That's why people struggle, pirate, to get away from it." She laughed but there was nothing funny about the sound. "It's *always* worth it."

"No' every time, luv," Trevor said quietly.

He dared a glance upward; Anna had narrowed her eyes at him, looking for something.

Trevor took a deep breath, sitting up straight. The sun was long past setting, casting the space around them in shadows. The flame of the candle in his hand danced wi' each of his breaths. She nodded curtly, having come to some decision about him.

Bloody hell, Trevor wanted to know what it was but wasn't willing to ask.

The words caught in his throat and then she was turning as quickly as she could, walking away from him.

"I—Anna?" he started, putting pressure against the wall to stand, one hand reaching out toward her. "Where the hell are you going?"

"To write a letter."

Trevor swallowed, feeling tense and loose and hot and cold, like he couldn't find his own damned head even though it was attached to his bloody body. He leaned back against the wall and watched the lass limp away from him, her steps slow and unhurried. Sighing, he slid down the wall and dropped his head into his hands.

Markus bloody Savage chose that moment to chuckle and shift along the ground. "Careful, pirate," the prick whispered, voice naught but smug attitude. "Anna has a bit of a temper when she doesn't get her way."

Trevor tipped his head back and turned his best smirk on the male. "'Tis a good thing I plan on doing everything to please her then, aye?"

Markus growled in response.

Good. This was all his fault anyway.

If he wanted to play games, Trevor would play the fucking games.

CHAPTER 25

"Ticket!"

Anna turned an ear toward the noise but otherwise kept her gaze on the velvet runner. The collar of her jacket was turned up against prying eyes. They passed row after row of occupied seating until they stepped between train cars and into the section that was reserved for the closest thing Briland had to royalty—the Senate and their families.

She ducked her head into the car before fully entering, making sure there wasn't any staff in view. They'd take one look at Anna and her companions and kick them straight off the train. She wouldn't have blamed them either, not with how they looked and smelled. A week of hard travel hadn't done them any favors, especially Markus.

"Come on," she whispered, muddy boots leaving a trail of dirt in their wake.

"I'm far too dashing to die so young," Markus groaned quietly from a step behind her.

The pirate snorted and Anna rolled her eyes.

"For the last time, it's a headache. You're dehydrated, Markus, not dying."

"You're not a physician, you couldn't possibly know these things."

"It doesn't take a physician to notice you've only drunk one bottle of water in the past few days. Ergo, dehydration."

They passed several private compartments, all of which Anna knew would remain empty. Five on their right and five on their left; ten total compartments for the ten members of the Briland Senate. Each sliding door was adorned with one animal or another. A wrought-iron wolf hung on Hayhurst's door; across the way, Anna spied the wildcat of house Frost and the Cunningham's proud lion.

Anna and Markus stopped outside a cabin with a gilded wrought-iron snake on the front. She let out a breath and her lips twitched into a frown. They both stared at the Savage crest with matching expressions of dread. Markus was nearly as excited as Anna about returning to the estate. He might not be going with her physically, but his thoughts would be with her when he could not be.

She still wasn't entirely sure if this was the right course but now that she'd stepped upon it, there was little else to do. Either the pirate would help her or he would hinder her. Either they'd succeed or fail and it would all come down to a single second—things like this always did. Anna only wished it was her life hanging in the balance and not Markus's.

The pirate opened the door to their cabin with a sliding snap, breaking whatever spell seeing the crest had put them under. He crossed the threshold first, eyeing the cabin carefully. Something about his critical gaze made Anna nervous, like she was the one on display.

His dark gaze skipped from the brass adornments to the plum-colored velvet bench seats. Intricately hand-painted screens with dark wooden frames separated the space and the pirate was careful to peek behind them, lest some nasty monster sneak up on him.

"Anna, luv," the pirate started, swallowing thickly. When he turned back toward her, his face held a hint of emotion. "There's goose down comforters back here. And bloody flannel sheets. So many pillows..." he trailed off, breathing deep.

"Aye, pirate," she mocked with a smile, walking toward where Markus had sagged onto his bench seat. The bone-deep exhaustion in Anna's soul called to the feather mattresses hiding behind the screens, but now was not the time for sleep. "We'll have plenty of time to sleep later."

And they would. If nothing else, Anna intended on sleeping the last leg of their journey away. She'd need the extra rest if she was to be expected to interact with their father, let alone the rest of the Senate, in a civil manner.

"Longing for the finer things in life, wretch?" Markus asked, stretched out on one side of the bench, his forearm stretched across his eyes.

"Aye," the pirate answered with a shark-like grin. "When ye grow up wi' nothing, ye tend to grasp at everything."

Anna swatted at her brother's foot as she approached; they didn't have time for his shenanigans. She needed to get her weight off her leg and to do that, her brother had to scoot his monstrous body over. Her leg was healing well enough—a bit fast in her opinion—but the constant travel and use was setting her back. She'd torn stitches twice and each time the pirate had stitched her back together.

"LAST CALL!"

It wouldn't be long now.

The pirate plopped onto the seat opposite them, gaze trained on the brass light fixtures around the cabin, at the intricate scaling they had been shaped with. He scratched at the scruff on his face; it had gotten longer in the last week. The pirate had already decided he was getting rid of it for her father's birthday gala and the thought of his clean-shaven face made her a little sad. Anna would never admit it, but she rather enjoyed his scruff.

"Are ye sure we have to wait?" he asked quietly, gaze darting toward the sliding door.

Anna nodded her head with a sigh.

He frowned, crossed his arms, and turned to look out the window. Anna followed his gaze and watched as men and women walked about the platform, all dressed finely in their Sunday best. Men with their collars turned up and hats pulled low, women in their silks and scarves and heavy coats. The winter chill had come early this year and despite being a few days from Bellcaster, it was evident even here.

Closing her eyes, Anna wondered how much snow would be on the grounds of her father's private estate. Bellcaster sat at the base of the mountains but their father's estate was located farther up, climbing into the thinner air and surrounded by towering coniferous trees. While Anna didn't have any plans to run around in the snow, it was a variable to consider.

At hearing the clink of glass, Anna opened her eyes. The pirate tipped his head back, throat exposed as he drank deeply from a thin-necked bottle of water. He wiped at his mouth with the back of his hand and slouched, propping his elbows on the table that spanned the distance between them.

"Bloody hate waiting," he grumbled, closing his eyes.

Anna smiled. "Me too."

He returned her grin before looking away nervously, knocking his knuckles against the tabletop in what Anna had identified as a nervous habit. She focused on his hands, on the dirt beneath his nails and the swirls of ink on his skin.

That bloody chanty had been on the tip of her tongue for days now. The sound of the tune had nearly been enough to drive her insane. It appeared in her dreams. It followed her during the day. The pirate had even taken to whistling the tune while they traveled.

Can't ye remember? it seemed to sing, night, day, and all the hours in-between.

The pirate caught her staring and grinned something small and sweet enough for heat to flood her chest and cheeks. He really was handsome, especially when he looked at her like that. He rubbed at the side of his jaw with a finger, tilting his chin upwards, and opened his mouth to say something when the blare of the train's horn interrupted. Then the slow pulls tugged at them as the train sank into motion.

They each exchanged a look and a small breath.

And then madness ensued.

In seconds, Anna and the pirate were stripping off their thick outer layers while Markus tried to stay out of their way. It was an explosion of cotton and thin fur, wool-lined coats and insulated leather. Her brother collected their strewn clothing and packed it away out of sight, to be burned later. As the pirate stripped, she caught glimpses of tanned skin, ink, and scars.

Anna grabbed the bottle the pirate had been drinking from and wetted a rag with it before throwing the rag to him. He scrubbed at the kohl she'd put around his eyes, quickly wiping at the rest of his face and then down his neck and lower between his pecs—

Markus coughed pointedly.

Anna glowered as she lifted her arms and pulled her wild blonde curls from their plaits. They fell around her shoulders, ending just past her breasts. Standing in nothing but her underthings, Anna snapped her fingers in the direction of her brother and pointed to another torn piece of cloth. He doused it in water before throwing it her way.

As soon as the cold cloth hit her fingers, Anna started scrubbing at her arms and chest, in-between her breasts and down the line of her stomach. She cleaned the dirt out from beneath her nails and tossed the cloth, dropping to the floor to tear through her bag. Anna quickly found what she was looking for, a pair of thick, dark, fur-lined breeches. They slid up her legs, feeling snug against the remaining swelling of her thigh. Next was wool socks and supple, knee-high, leather boots. With a snap, she unfolded her corset, grinning at the monstrosity.

"A hand, Markus?" she whispered hastily, gesturing wildly to her corset while she laced her boots.

"Exhale!" He rushed, fingers tightening her corset expertly.

Anna held the cough in, swallowing hard around her need to breathe. Her brother always pulled a bit too tight. She breathed deeply, noticing only briefly that the pain from her broken rib was no longer there. The instant Markus backed away, she pulled her arms through the sleeves of her pearl-white button-up. It had taken some digging to find, but the fabric felt like butter against her skin and the brass buttons gleamed in the light. She adjusted the collar, looking over her shoulder to see the state of the pirate.

He had already clothed himself in a clean shirt, his fingers fastening the buttons at his wrists. She frowned at the action, glaring at the leather gloves that now adorned his hands. This pair was finer than the pair she'd met him in and spoke to the allowance that would be at his disposal if he'd caught her interest. It was such a shame to cover up something so lovely.

Anna turned and buckled her waist cincher loosely. It was made of thin leather in the same color as her boots, ending below her breasts and just above the waistline of her breeches. The pirate was pulling the tight leathers up his legs and tucking in his shirt when Anna turned around next.

They froze at the rapping of knuckles on the door, the sound resounding around them like a gavel passing judgement in a crowded room.

A quick look passed between all of them and then they were scrambling about the room without making a sound. Markus scooped their clothes into the bags and kicked them behind the screens before diving behind as well. The pirate threw himself into one of the booths, all the way toward the window where he could hide his unlaced boots, pulling on his leather jacket as he went.

She ran her hands through her hair, sitting down across from the pirate, who glared violently at the sliding door with his arms crossed against his chest. The leather of his jacket only emphasized the swell of his biceps and the curve of his shoulders. She grinned; it would certainly encourage whoever was there to leave promptly.

"Is…is there someone in here?"

Anna licked her lips and then cleared her throat. "Well, of course."

"Miss Savage?" the man asked and the sliding door opened. "I hadn't realized you would be accompanying us this evening."

She turned from her position of gazing out the window and offered the man a small smile. "I do try to travel discreetly, Sebastian."

Sebastian's throat bobbed, focus centered on the pirate.

Anna marked the action, turning back to the window. He had been in this position on this particular train route for as long as she could remember and had been a longtime friend of their father. Sebastian was a stout, broad, grizzled old man. He reminded her quite a lot of a masculine teapot, actually. She and Markus had long suspected he was older than their grandfather, but despite his age, he still managed to work and conduct business without any hitches.

He breathed deep, nose twitching at the smell coming from behind the screen. Anna rolled her shoulders back, frowning. "I apologize for the smell. We may be clean but the clothes we were wearing in the jungle are not."

"Think nothing of it, Miss Savage. I am well accustomed to the unusual smells that hang about you after a dig." Sebastian assessed her before winking. "This might be the cleanest I've seen you yet."

She rolled her eyes. "It's not that bad."

"I beg to differ," he huffed, rolling up his sleeves, revealing powerful forearms covered in hair, and stared down his nose at the pirate. Sebastian stood about the same height as Anna, he could only look down on the pirate because the redhead was sitting down—and slouching at that. "Will you be stopping in Bellcaster?"

"Oh, yes," Anna replied. "It's Father's birthday gala, I couldn't miss that even if I wanted to."

"I'll be sure to send word ahead to prepare your accommodations then, miss."

Anna was sure Sebastian would be mentioning more than simply her need for accommodations once reaching Bellcaster. He was likely to send a letter to her father as well, indicating where she was and who she was with.

"Accommodations?" she asked, turning to look at the old man.

His thick brows pulled together critically. "Yes, Miss Savage. Your father is putting all you nice folk up at the hot springs."

"How lovely," Anna said a bit stiffly, holding in the sigh that wished to escape. "Thank you, Sebastian."

"Of course, Miss Savage. Please ring if there is anything else you need."

The door closed with a soft click and they all breathed a sigh of relief. Markus cleared his throat, leaning out from behind the screen, his hair mussed from the mad dash. The lack of shirt made her think he was in the middle of cleaning up, just as tired of dirty clothes as Anna and the pirate were. A soiled cloth hung over his shoulder and he stared at the pirate.

"I hope you realize it's your sinful stench that good Mr. Sebastian smelled," Markus said, leaning a shoulder against the wall.

"He was looking at your hiding spot, mate, no' at me." The pirate didn't even bother turning to address her brother. Instead, he rested his forehead against the window and stared out at the ever-changing landscape.

When they had begun their journey to this train station, the deserts had quickly transformed into oceans of grass, stretching as far as the eye could see. They passed through marshes and into forests full of ancient redwoods. The landscape became greener and colder as they traveled north toward Bellcaster. The pirate had seemed a bit enchanted at every step of the journey, especially when they traveled at night.

The sky had been clear, a dark tapestry full of bright pin pricks. He'd stared up at the stars and grinned with his arms behind his head, looking from one constellation to the next before settling on the moon. Anna had watched him as she fell asleep every night, never quite able to turn away from the boyish look on his face, wondering who he actually was.

Another knock at the door had Markus scrambling back behind the screen and the pirate looking bored. She gave quick permission to enter and not a second later, the sliding door opened and revealed a middle-aged man. The name above his breast read: *Garret*. He had dark hair and grey eyes and a spindly sort of body that was most likely much taller than at first glance. Even now, Garret hunched over, going so far as to tilt his head down in their direction.

The pirate angled his head upward and his eyes widened. He blinked several times in surprise at the man's height. Anna felt a bit of amusement. It could be argued that Garret was taller than Markus or the pirate, but the man lacked any sort of muscle mass to make him appear anything other than willowy.

He cleared his throat and spoke, the deep baritone surprising her at first, "May I offer any beverages or snacks, Miss Savage?" His attention darted between Anna and her very grumpy-looking male companion. "Our chefs are baking those pastries you favor, they should be ready within the hour."

"Excellent." Anna grinned, narrowing her eyes on the pirate. "I'd love some tea as well, Garret."

"We've a beautiful jade green blend at the moment, it has a hint of citrus and mint."

"That sounds lovely, thank you."

The pirate snorted, rolling his eyes until he was gazing out the window. Garret dipped his head, saying he would return in a few minutes with tea. As soon as the door slid shut, Markus was out in the open again, this time with a cotton sweater and socks, missing his trousers.

"Come on, mate," the pirate groaned. "*Again?*"

"Do I make you uncomfortable, wretch?"

The pirate looked down and scoffed, a bit of a chuckle leaving his lips. "Oh, aye. I'm trembling."

"Both of you behave yourselves."

"Reckon that shouldn't be too difficult," the pirate answered.

"You're absolutely right." Anna glared at the two men. "It *shouldn't* be difficult. But I have a feeling the two of you could muck anything up."

After traveling with the alpha males for the last week, she would put nothing past them.

"Ye wound me, lovely." The pirate gasped in mock pain, clutching at his chest.

Anna rolled her eyes and noticed Markus tensing, shoulders bunching and lips tightening into a thin line. The idjit was still having a difficult time with the pirate's rakish behavior. Anna hadn't figured out if it was because the pirate insisted on flirting with her, much to her brother's behest and in spite of his threats, or because Markus couldn't intimidate him.

This, of course, was unprecedented. To date, there hadn't been a man that her brother couldn't frighten away with a growl or a sour look. Even Bryce had balked. Yet here they were, with a pirate who made a show of winking suggestively in Anna's general direction even now. She was certain he would stop if she asked, but…

Never mind that.

Anna coughed lightly on her next inhale, still acclimating to the stiff, shallow breaths the corset forced her to take. She rubbed at where the ribbing was beneath her shirt and frowned. It had been on the small side to begin with and Markus had done more than a fine job of cinching it up. Had he done that on purpose? A small bit of retaliation?

"What is the point if ye can't breathe?"

"Well," Anna started with a grin, "they're extremely fashionable in Bellcaster."

"Ye bloody jest," the pirate said in surprise.

"I really don't. And"—Anna scowled at her brother—"they make my breasts look damn good, even bigger than Markus's."

"*Anna*," Markus groaned, clearly embarrassed. "For the last time, I do not have breasts."

She shrugged, ignoring her brother's antics with a full smile on her face. Anna turned back toward the pirate, who was staring at her with a light flush and a confused expression on his face. His lip twitched and he cocked his head and sighed.

"What?" she teased, looking down at the shape the corset created.

"The men appreciating that contraption are fools." The pirate shook his head, a disapproving frown forming on his face as his line of sight dropped to her breasts. He flushed further and looked away. Anna's cheeks warmed in response. "Your breasts were lovely before, beastie. Though if ye think I should inspect them further, I shan't say no."

Markus stomped forward, shucking one leg through his pants and then the next as he glared at the pirate fiercely. Anna couldn't help the laugh. It felt good and right and crazy with the situation they had landed themselves in.

The pirate tipped his chin back defiantly. "What, mate? I suppose ye'll be making your beautiful sister the same offer?"

Markus looked like he might vomit all over the pirate's freshly shined boots.

"We have an accord, then." The pirate winked. "I do so for the greater good."

Anna waved him off, adjusting the thin leather cincher over her shirt. She steeled both her nerves and her lungs at the thought of the tasks before them. This would be an arduous twenty-four hours, rife with danger and intrigue—only to be followed directly by more danger and intrigue. Anyone with their sanity intact did not attempt to sneak a pirate into the Savage estate, let alone steal the most infamous of the Pirate King's maps.

It was a good thing Bellcaster aristocracy had always believed her to be a little daft.

Anna grinned, leaning her head back against the booth, and looked out the window.

She couldn't wait.

CHAPTER 26

Markus had never understood pacing.

He had grown up watching Father pace in that damnable office in front of floor-to-ceiling windows with drapes the color of greed pooling on the floor. Dark wood floors and matching bookshelves stretched to the eaves. Markus even had memories of watching Grandfather do the same.

Ten steps to the right, about face, ten steps to the left. Hands folded behind backs, brows furrowed in contemplation of one issue or another. Bright, ashy blond hair slicked back against their skull and pale skin drawn tight over bone.

Markus had never understood pacing, not until now.

He'd had this energy in him ever since Anna rolled through that train car door, guns blazing, with an unknown and undoubtedly handsome man at her side. It had only worsened at figuring out the man was a pirate, turning to rolling nausea whenever the wretch insisted on flirting with his sister. It wouldn't have bothered Markus nearly as much if he was being insincere—he would have preferred that, actually.

But the prick came off as genuine about it.

Like he *liked* Anna.

That wasn't obscene in and of itself; Anna was a lovely woman with a heart of gold and a mind that couldn't be matched. Any man would be lucky beyond compare to be graced with her hand, even if it was only to hold.

But he was a dirty pirate.

And Anna seemed to like the dirty pirate back, even if she didn't realize it.

Bollocks, it was the worst.

Every god and goddess his mother had ever taught him about knew Markus had made mistakes, ones he needed to atone for. It made a man wonder. Was this some sort of cosmic retribution for past wrongs?

Thus, the pacing.

It was the only way Markus could get that energy out, each nervous flicker of his stomach, every flash of electricity in his veins. It was all that was left after Anna made her opinion on gutting the pirate clear; all he had was walking from one side of the train car and then turning to start again.

One more thing, that's all it would take for something in him to bend.

Maybe even break.

"Careful, Markus, you're beginning to look like Father," Anna commented from behind him.

The blasted pirate was asleep in one of the bunks behind the screen, a light snore the only sign he was even there. Markus had nearly clubbed the wretch earlier when he'd suggested Anna climb in with him. She had declined, albeit with a grin. Now, she sat on the bench with her shoes on the floor and her knees pulled to her chest. Her gaze had settled on something outside the window, somewhere far beyond the horizon.

"I don't like it," he said, turning away.

"I know."

"You know what sorts of tricks Father will play."

"I know that too."

"And you expect the pirate to stay quiet when Father sets his sights on him?" Markus pinched the bridge of his nose and closed his eyes, stopping in his infernal pacing. "Father is angry, Anna, and spiteful, and the full extent of his wrath will be pointed at you when you arrive with that man on your arm. You will have the

Senate to contend with. You will be with a brute who knows nothing of high society…and—and you know who else will be there."

She sighed, turning on the bench seat to face him. The blanket dropped from her shoulders and her hair glowed in the sunlight. "I do. Bryce Cunningham will be there, but he's no fool, Markus. He won't make a fuss in front of all his father's friends."

Markus snorted, crossing his arms. "Of course, he isn't a fool. He wanted to marry you. That's a stroke of genius in my opinion. I just worry because I won't be there."

And he will be.

He didn't say it, but he knew he didn't have to.

Anna nodded her head. "I know."

Both their gazes wandered to the screens and who they both knew slept behind them. Markus deflated, shoulders curling with a wince. "How can you trust him? He's a pirate, Anna. Some of the most despicable beings I've met have been pirates."

But not all of them, the thought came sudden and hard.

"I don't know," she said, finger twirling around a curl, brows scrunched together. "I've always believed actions speak more honestly and intentionally than words, and he hasn't given me a reason to doubt him yet. He helped both of us when he didn't have to." She swallowed, the action slow and purposeful. "And there's something familiar about him."

"Even if you asked the scoundrel who or what he is, he'd probably lie," Markus croaked. "Bet that's why he won't tell us his name."

God, Markus was going to have a blasted stroke.

There were very few reasons his sister would think the pirate familiar and each one was worse than the last. He dropped into the bench next to her, his arm wrapping around her shoulder and pulling her close. Markus planted a kiss on the top of her head, settling into a calm as Anna leaned hard into his side and adjusted the blanket so it laid over his legs as well.

"You have nothing to worry about while I'm here." He looked down at her matching blue eyes. They'd always been a pair, like gems chipped from the same stone. "Never while I'm here."

"I know." She yawned.

Markus cleared his throat, dropping his gaze to the tabletop. "I'm sorry for all of this. For all I've put you through. For your leg—I know it still pains you. And I'm thankful too, Anna. I know I haven't said it yet, but thank you. Thank you once, thank you a thousand times. I'd be in a very bad place right now without you." He choked on his laugh. "I'd always be in a bad place without you. And I'm sorry for being an ass. I just…I love you, Anna. Don't ever forget that."

"I love you too, Markus. That has never been a question."

"That's not…even with our mother, we didn't hear it enough. I think I forget to say it sometimes because of that. I should say it more."

"Actions, Markus." Anna bumped him with her shoulder. "Quit worrying or you'll give yourself wrinkles."

Markus laughed, opened his mouth to say something else, and realized she was sleeping. Something caught in his throat as he looked at his twin. Anna had been there from the first moment. His very first breath. He couldn't imagine a life without her in it. The thought had occurred to him before but it had never seemed as loud as it did now. Markus had gotten them into plenty of trouble before and Anna had always gotten them out, but this was something else.

This was their father.

This was a cursed Pirate King's map.

This was insanity.

He leaned his head back and made small, slow adjustments until he sat comfortably, gazing out at the changing landscape as his sister had, and tried to reconcile the fact that the pirate would be going with Anna. It was difficult to swallow, difficult to think past the roaring panic. Their father was not a kind, forgiving man and despite it all, sometimes he worried Anna forgot that.

There would be hell to pay for showing up with some un-known man in front of all their father's friends and the families entrenched in Bellcaster high society, the aristocracy that the Senate lorded over. It was going to be a tall order for something that potentially wouldn't have any pay off.

Anna stirred from next to him, drawing his attention. Her nose twitched and her mouth curled into a frown. She rubbed her forehead into his side as her brow crinkled. "What is that smell? I thought we threw out those soiled clothes," she muttered sleepily.

"No," the pirate replied rather obnoxiously, voice rough from sleep. Disgusting. "Your brother's bloody boots are still back 'ere. I can toss 'em if ye wish, luv."

"Toss my boots and I'll toss you," Markus snapped, think-ing of the note in his heel.

"Aye, aye. I leave it to ye, mate."

The compartment quieted, nothing but Anna's soft snores and the pirate's shuffling as he tried getting comfortable once more. He had every intention of throwing the boots out, there just hadn't been a spare second to grab the note from his heel, let alone time to find a place to hide it. He'd have a hell of a time explaining the note to his sister.

I should have let you drown.

He was such a damn hypocrite.

CHAPTER 27

Unfortunately, Anna seemed to do a lot of waiting.

The rest of the day and night passed slowly. Bellcaster arrived and with it a carriage to take them to the hot springs. Time again rolled by at a leisurely pace, the only real difference being that the scenery passed by slower now that they were out of the train.

It was both a blessing and a curse, as most things were. The time was a god-send but the wait was enough to drive her over the edge. Markus and the pirate were suspiciously civil, choosing to play a game of "Go Fish" to pass the time on the way up the mountain, the creak of the carriage the only other sound.

Anna was honestly surprised they could do anything without glaring or arguing, but perhaps roughing it together for a week with her temper looming over their heads had done the men some good.

"Ye got any fives?"

"Go fish," Markus muttered.

"If you're fucking lying mate, I'll—"

"You'll what?" Markus drawled sarcastically, completely unconcerned.

Anna looked over just in time to see the pirate's lip twitch and curl into a smirk. "I might just take the wee beastie on a fancy date. Get her some more of those little shell things she likes so much. Are there certain foods ye like?" he asked, turning toward her.

"Dessert." Anna grinned, pulling the heavy wool blanket over her shoulder. Even with the foot warmer and her heavy coat and gloves, the carriage maintained its status as an ice box and would only grow colder as they continued to ascend.

Markus glared at her from over his cards and rolled his eyes. "You know any suitor has to go through Father first."

"And here I thought they had to go through you. Good thing we're going to his birthday gala together then, isn't it?" she teased.

Markus groaned. "How is it his birthday again? I swear we just celebrated the blasted thing."

Anna smiled, shaking her head.

"Ye'd really go to dinner wi' me, luv?" the pirate asked, perking up and leaning up off his elbows.

"Anything is possible. Look at us now."

"Careful, pirate," Markus cautioned. "The man that courted her last is an expert swordsman and a *bit* bitter that Anna wouldn't marry him."

The pirate scoffed, looking back to his cards. "I fear no man, mate. And I'm no' too bad wi' a blade myself."

She frowned. "Markus is right. We could rarely best him two-on-one on his worst days. He's always been brilliant with a blade, so if anyone challenges you to a duel, decline."

A moment had not gone by without dancing around the idea that Bryce would be there. She hadn't seen the captain since declining his proposal and did not look forward to the experience. She hadn't done so on purpose but it had been easy to avoid each other. She had always been in various ruins or performing research and he had been tasked with combating the slave trade and the Pirate King.

Truth be told, Anna was more nervous about a possible confrontation with Bryce Cunningham than she was with her father. Senator John Savage would play at words and try to tear her and the pirate down verbally with no real consequence. And while she didn't think Bryce would try to spill blood, he had always been hot-headed and quick to act.

"I've never backed down from a fight in my life," the pirate said stubbornly.

"Might want to put that to the side for tonight. Pick it back up tomorrow," she said quietly.

The pirate looked at her curiously. "Are ye asking me no' to fight for ye, luv?"

"If you lose, you lose your life. Our goal tonight isn't defending my honor from a past suitor, it's nabbing that map and getting out alive. Stay focused."

"But if I win?"

"You win nothing." She laughed, unsure why this mattered to him. "Nothing except for bragging rights."

The pirate shrugged, seemingly pleased with his potential spoils.

A knock sounded on the carriage roof before the stable hand's voice echoed down. "Miss Savage?"

Anna turned toward the ceiling and cleared her throat. "Yes, Griff?"

"Five minutes until arrival. The Ascendant knows we're on our way and your room has been readied, miss."

"Thank you," she called back, a grin on her face.

They might be closing in on her father's estates and potential ruin, but from here out they'd be in a state of motion. No more of this waiting nonsense. Go to the hot springs, take a quick dip, get dressed, and go. They'd be fashionably late, but was there really any other way to arrive at her father's gala?

No, not as far as Anna was concerned.

Markus looked her over with a critical eye. "Anna, I do believe that concussion might have done some lasting damage. You look…excited to see Father."

She stretched her arms above her head. "God, no. I'm excited to find this map and see where it leads."

"I wish ye would reconsider, luv."

"And why's that?"

"It's a dangerous stretch of water. Full of beasts and plagued by heavy storms. The Black Line 'tis no place for a treasure hunter and the island is even worse. Guardians patrol by night and the bloody jungle—"

"Good God, man, would you shut up?" Markus snapped, throwing his hands up angrily. "You're only making her want to go more!"

Anna practically vibrated with excitement though the pirate was less than amused when she turned to him. "I'll have you know I'm paid to find and excavate long-lost treasure troves born under ancient pretenses. Cursed is not a word I fear but a prerequisite for my research. This is right up my alley."

It could be no worse than one of Khan Granbaatar's allegedly cursed tombs. Those were a tricky sort of business that, more often than not, ended in the expiration of the explorer. Anna had spent too many of her days spelunking through booby-trapped corridors or in obscenely small air shafts to fear a little map or where it led. And she'd have a guide for this. The pirate had been there before and if he was willing to take her, Anna was willing to bet he'd show her around too.

They'd make a date of it.

Beyond the excitement of following the map and unearthing what it wished to hide, a small pit of dread burrowed deep in her stomach. What was on that island that the Coalition, the Senate, and the Pirate King wanted? It couldn't possibly be good, but Anna believed very few things in life were inherently malicious. The only way past the dark hesitancy she felt was through it, forging blindly ahead until it dissipated.

The carriage came to a halt, no longer swaying with the pull of the horses on uneven cobbles. Anna heard Griff jump down outside, his boots thumping on the frozen ground and cracking brush. He knocked and then the door swung open. A gust of air breathed into the carriage, bringing soft flakes of snow.

"Me first, luv," the pirate said, standing slowly.

Her breath fanned in front of her face and Anna leaned around the pirate to catch a glimpse of the ground. There was a light dusting of snow visible even in the low light and it was full dark now, no hint of the setting sun that turned the ceramic roof tiles of Bellcaster orange and pink. The sky was black as pitch, the clouds almost purple in color. Snakes of fog threaded between trees and thickened upon the ground. And if Anna thought the night sky above was dark, the shadows between the trees were darker yet.

The pirate stopped in front of Griff, his brows drawn in thought. He turned toward Anna, crossing his arms against his chest, then stepped back so the stable hand could help her down from the carriage, as was fitting for their roles.

Griffin was the stable master's son at their father's estate and as the stable master himself was prone to drinking and deep sleeping, Anna wasn't all that surprised to see him at the train station. She and Markus had five years on the boy, but age had done little to deter him over the years. He had grown into a strapping young man, tall and broad from the time he spent working in the stables with his father. Big, bright green eyes with hair the color of wheat, all things he'd inherited from his mother.

She squinted, gaze drifting between Griff and the pirate. Standing next to him, Griff looked more like a child who had recently grown into a man's body. It occurred to Anna then that she had no idea how old the pirate was. Based on his stature, she had to assume he was closer to her and Markus's age, likely a little older.

At catching her glance at the stable hand, the pirate's own gaze narrowed to little black pinpricks. Griff cast a curious look at the pirate as he dipped into an extravagant bow. "Bath fit for a goddess straight ahead, Miss Savage," he said, holding out his hand to assist her.

"I'm terribly sorry you had to fetch us, Griff." She grinned down at the boy.

"Wouldn't miss your arrival for the world; you know that."

"Surely you were sleeping; it's past dinner time and you rise before the sun."

He grabbed her hand and brought her gloved fingers to his lips before helping her step down and out of the carriage. "I was already up thinking of you, so if anything, 'tis a dream come true."

Anna laughed and the pirate's throat bobbed. He stiffened but only for that second. If she hadn't been watching, she would have missed the look of confusion before the pirate smoothed it over with a rakish grin that didn't meet his eyes. It was so incredibly fake. Did anyone else notice that, or had she been the only one to catch it?

"Shit, mate, how else are you to stay warm on a cold night?" the pirate said, doing his best to smooth over his brogue as he had done on the train before. "Can't say I wouldn't be doing the same."

Griff chuckled, deep and throaty. "Finally, someone who understands!"

Anna stepped away from Griff, her hand sliding through his as she stepped closer to the pirate. Markus's dark mood was a thunderhead of static energy behind her. She didn't have to look to know he'd be scowling at the ground or at the pirate.

The pirate relaxed beside her in his own heavy coat and thick cap; strands of red had escaped and danced in the breeze against his forehead and Markus's hands were stuffed in his pockets with his collars turned up around his ears.

She swallowed tightly and looked around the front entrance of the Ascendant. There were no carriages in sight, which was to be expected. Their father's birthday gala had already begun and the guests would have taken their carriages there. A parallel line of posts with lanterns hanging from them sat on either side of the recently shoveled walkway, casting warm yellowish-orange light on the fresh snow and dark cobbles.

The pirate's jaw fell open as he squinted past Anna, gaze darting from one side of the tree line to the other. She grinned at his speechlessness. At the opposite end of the path towered a retreat built in the fashion of a log house. It wasn't the monstrosity of a building that caught her eye, but what lay behind it.

The trees cut an impressive arc on either side before opening to the night sky just behind the log house. The stars were mostly tucked behind billowing, dark clouds. From the look of them and the smell in the air, Anna figured it would start snowing again. She wasn't too excited about that, for as much as she loved the snow, she hated the idea of having to trek through it to escape her father. Numb fingers and toes had never done anyone any favors.

"Seems a bit cold," her brother commented off handedly.

"It's always cold this time of year." Anna clenched her jaw and tucked her own hands into her coat pockets. "You're just never in Bellcaster for it."

"Probably because I hate the cold," Markus grumbled, pulling his collars tighter about his neck.

The pirate whistled his sea shanty as Griffin unloaded their meager luggage. Anna turned toward him in surprise to see his lips working in such a splendid way with the frigid temperature. He seemed right at home in the frost. Or perhaps his blood ran hot enough that the chill didn't bother him. She found herself leaning toward him, looking for any of the warmth he clearly had, clenching her jaw to keep the damn thing from trembling.

"You don't seem too bothered," she said.

"Aye." He smiled down at her. "Ye lot clearly have never been to the north seas."

Anna nearly snorted; there was nothing but snow and ice past Bellcaster. It was a strange land that spent most of its time in either full night or full day with an ever-changing landscape. The land wasn't solid, but shifting, moving masses of ice floating atop a nearly frozen sea. Anna had never had the inclination to go spelunking around it. She rather liked having all ten fingers and toes.

"God, no." Markus laughed, breath puffing in front of his face. "Not with Marshal MacGrath in those waters. And even if I were daft enough to tangle with him, you couldn't pay me to go near the Ice Queen."

The pirate winced. "Aye, she is no' a fem to be trifled wi', 'tis true. And MacGrath is...well, he's just a wee unconventional."

Markus and Anna both gave the pirate a look. It was her brother who continued speaking, "I consider him the most dangerous of the Coalition chiefs."

The pirate looked surprised. "True? Even with Kidd?"

Markus nodded. "Kidd has a pattern, a consistent way about him that makes him...easy isn't the right word, but it makes him easier to navigate. MacGrath has none. He's just as likely to blow his own ship as he is one of ours."

"What about the Pirate King? Where's he fall on this list of yours?"

"The navy's? Near the top, enemy number one. On mine? Near the bottom."

The pirate laughed. "Ye can't be bloody serious."

"Oh, but I am." Markus sighed. "Though my opinion isn't widely shared. The wretch seems to be blamed for a great deal of grievances. Honestly, I'm not convinced he's responsible for the slave trade." Markus finished quietly.

Anna snorted. "Unlikely."

Markus shot her a look and frowned. "He might have been the meanest bastard on the seas in his prime, but I have yet to catch him doing more than plundering cargo ships with hulls full of finery."

"Ye complaining the prick hasn't been causing enough bloody chaos lately?"

"Good God, no. I've heard stories of the blasted debauchery he got up to in his youth and I have absolutely no interest in combatting it. Fighting sea monsters, destroying entire fleets."

Markus shook his head. "What I'm saying is his appetite for adventure and treasure rivaled my sister's once. Now, I have little evidence to suggest he does more than collect pretty pillows and bedding."

"Suppose that's fair." The pirate shrugged and turned to his feet, kicking a small rock. She smiled at the action, at how boyish it seemed from a monstrously sized man. His cheeks had pinkened from the cold but it also could have been a blush. He raised his gaze to meet hers and held it. Anna refused to be the one to look away; if he wanted to be challenged, she was more than willing to do just that.

Her brother cleared his throat and Anna looked toward him only to find Griff standing behind him with a raised brow. He stepped forward, placing several of the bags in front of Markus and the pirate.

"Miss Savage's belongings go to her room," Griffin said. "Top floor, last room on the left."

"I'm sorry, mate," the pirate spoke up, crossing his arms and tipping back on his heels. "But are you Miss Savage?"

Griff rolled his eyes and caught Anna's gaze.

A grin broke through and she turned to raise an eyebrow at the pirate.

The man clearly did not like being told what to do any more than she or her brother did. She cocked her head at him and dragged her gaze from his toes to the tip of his hat. He wasn't just any pirate, then—a master gunner maybe, or a quartermaster? He clearly wasn't used to being told what to do, though he hadn't shown any signs of minding when Anna asked for something.

At least the bugger had his priorities straight.

Griff rolled his eyes. "I don't suppose you'll make the miss carry her bags?"

"What about you, bucko?" the pirate fired off.

"I'm the stable hand." Griff grinned, pulling himself back up to his carriage. "You honestly believe they'll let my boots anywhere near the Ascendant's flooring? Ring the front desk when you're ready to depart, Miss Savage. We'll be ready."

"C'mere, lass." The pirate nudged her with his elbow as the carriage rolled away. "Let's get ye inside."

She nodded her head, listening as Markus and the pirate hefted their bags and started toward the Ascendant. It was a quick walk through the main lobby. She waved to the staff she recognized and marched across the battered floors and beneath the vaulted ceilings, ignoring the hail of *Miss Savage* and bows that followed in her wake. The smell of pine and cedar flooded the space. The Ascendant was four floors and her room was at the top on the left-hand side, overlooking the hot springs below. It was the same room she always stayed in.

The door opened without a creak or protest. The hinges were well-oiled and the floors had been waxed recently. A king-size four poster bed lounged against one wall with what looked like ten thousand pillows and a thick down comforter. Beneath it, and covering most of the floor, was an exotic, tasseled rug. A floral-patterned chaise lounge sat at the foot, matching the vanity in the corner. Everything was set in warm reds and dark woods with accents of cream and chocolate throughout the room.

Anna leaned back, stretching. Her leg ached something fierce, drawing her gaze to the balcony and what she'd be able to see below. With everyone else already at her father's gala, the hot springs would be empty. She swallowed, thinking of the medicinal waters soaking into her battered body.

The men dropped their bags, the pirate creeping forward until he sank into the chaise as Markus slumped into her vanity chair. Both sat with their arms crossed and legs splayed out in front of them, each a mirror of the other. The vanity chair creaked from Markus's weight, drawing a wince from Anna. God, if her brother broke her chair—

"He have a bloody death wish?" the pirate asked with a tilt of his head, meeting her brother's gaze.

Markus frowned. "Griffin has been smitten since the day he laid eyes on Anna. I recall the day well. Spring. Noontime. We were eleven and she threw dirt at him."

She watched suspiciously as they exchanged a look, an agreement made. Anna squinted at them, rubbing a hand against her sternum, a prickle of fear making itself known. Surely their agreement on anything was an omen of terrible sorts. Anna strode across the room and looked out the blinds to the sky, waiting for the fire and brimstone.

The pirate leaned forward, elbows on his knees. He glanced at her comically before dropping his voice into a mock whisper, "He the sort she fancies, though? Seems a wee young..."

"If only. I wouldn't mind being related to Griffin. He's a respectable, hardworking man—though Father would never approve. Usually it's scholars and the unsavory I'm chasing away."

"Unsavory?" The pirate perked up.

"No," Markus said curtly.

Anna grinned with a shake of her head and walked to the bathroom, sensing their tentative truce was about to come to an end. If they wanted to hash it out, she'd let them. Her body needed to soak in the hot springs and she would not deny it that. Another thirty minutes wouldn't change how late they would be; late was late, whether it was five minutes or fifty.

It was a quick strip. A large clawfoot tub sat against one wall, a mirror and sink across from it. She wrapped a soft cotton robe around her body and tied it tight at the waist. It would be a brisk walk with the robe ending at her thighs but the reward of soaking in the waters would be worth the brief bite. The pirate and Markus were still at it when she exited, pulling her hair up into a messy bun. Markus pinched the bridge of his nose, his elbow resting on his other arm.

"Clearly the lass doesn't like her da'. I got to get a blessing from *someone*."

"Well, you're not getting the blasted thing from me."

"C'mon, mate."

"You're insufferable."

"I'm an unsavory sort, no' a scholar. Keep the words short."

Anna pressed her lips into a thin line at the irritated look on her brother's face. They were acting ridiculous and she wasn't entirely sure which she preferred, this odd state of companionable limbo or the fussing and disagreeing they had been doing prior.

She stepped into a pair of sandals and reached for the door. She smiled as she thought of the scorching, medicinal waters that awaited her. Their magic would do Anna's body a great deal of good before the gala. The poor thing had suffered grievously in springing Markus and escaping the slavers.

"Where do you think you're going dressed like that, Anna?" Markus asked quickly, stopping her in her tracks.

She looked over her shoulder, one hand on the frame of the door. "Where does it look like? I'm going to soak." And then she walked out the door, leaving the men to scramble behind her.

"Wait up, luv!"

"You can't walk around naked, Anna!"

It was just as quick of a walk down to the hot springs as it had been up to their room. Down, down, down a spiraling staircase carved from a single cedar trunk. She caught the eye of an attendant she knew well, though she'd never asked his name. They had gotten along swimmingly in the past and he'd always had a glimmer of professional mischief in his gaze.

He quickly fell in line with her, opening the door to the bitterly cold outside where the hot springs were. The man dipped into a bow as she exited. "Miss?" he asked quickly, stepping out of the way and letting go of the door as Markus and the pirate both tried to walk through it at the same time.

"Yes?" she asked, soaking in the scent of the hot springs, listening to the rush and gurgle of water in the near distance.

"Mr. Tamm left you several gifts. He requested that we delay their delivery to your room. He wished them to be sent up upon your arrival. The bags will be on your bed."

"Thank you, I appreciate that," she told him, turning toward the path that led out to the tree line.

The trees here were centuries in the making. Their needles were an ominous dark green with frost clinging to their tips. Fog hugged their bases and shadows hung between them with their own conscience, making Anna feel like she was being watched. Even with the slippers, the stepping stones were cold beneath her feet and goosebumps formed on her legs, slowly creeping up beneath her robe. A minute later, the heat from the steam wafting off the water hit her like walking through a cloud.

"They're a bit feral," the attendant commented from just behind her.

"Quite." She grinned, listening to her brother and the pirate mock fight.

The path opened and then all Anna could see before her was stars and the moon off in the distance. She paused, taking it all in. The sky, the moon, and the waters in front of her that reflected the heavens. The pool was vast, cutting into the cliff face and bubbling over the edge, feeding smaller pools below. The water itself was the color of ink, as black and fathomless as the pirate's eyes.

She heard the crunch of leaves and twigs and turned to look over her shoulder. The pirate stood as still as a statue, staring at the sky. There was an unrestrained awe in his features, a wondering that was so innocent it reminded her of a child's. Even Markus's features relaxed, a small smile on his face. She caught the pirate's gaze as he stepped forward.

She inclined her head and spoke softly, afraid to break the magic. "You said you missed the night sky."

He nodded his head once, looking from Anna to the sky and then down to the pool that reflected it all perfectly. His lips twitched into a full smile, his head tipped back as he stared up. Anna's breath caught. She had to turn away, heat rising to her cheeks at the embarrassing response. Anna wasn't a blushing maid, but the pirate had a way with smiles and grins and a knowledge of what they did to those he wielded them against. The butterflies that danced in her stomach were evidence enough for her.

The attendant continued to follow her before stopping abruptly. She heard the shuffle of feet and the quiet gasp of surprise. Anna looked at the others; the pirate had a hand on the attendant's bicep and Markus loomed behind them, brooding in a way only a grumpy, over-protective brother could. Just like that, the magic was gone.

Markus cleared his throat and dropped his voice several octaves. "Excuse me, sir," he said in his orchestrated voice. Despite the niceties, there was venom in it, venom that could bite and rot. "But what exactly are you still doing here?"

The attendant looked toward Anna for help and she winked with a grin. She saw his brow raise a hair and the twitch at the corner of his lips. Her brother and the pirate could use the goading. They deserved it with how they were acting and Anna was positive the attendant wouldn't come to any harm for the good, clean fun.

Seemingly forgotten, Anna stepped back and crossed her arms, ready to enjoy the show.

"I...well," the attendant started, voice mockingly bashful. "Sometimes...sometimes Miss Savage requires *other* amenities."

Oh, yes, she did.

Like snacks and a good drink. But she knew her brother and could guess where his mind would wander, and as soon as he realized what the attendant was implying his nostrils flared and he tucked his hands deeper into his pockets. She watched the heave of his chest as he inhaled, heard the hiss of his exhale.

But the pirate?

He flushed and blinked several times, his throat bobbing as his grip slackened.

"If you stick around…" The attendant cleared his throat, slowly removing the pirate's hand from his bicep, finger by finger. He stepped away and smoothed out his sleeve before straightening his lapels. "I'm sure you'll hear…"

Anna had to bite her lip to keep from laughing and drawing the attention back to herself.

Markus barked out an irritated chuckle, face flushed with anger. He started shaking his head. A second later his hands were out of his pockets and he was rolling up his sleeves. His head continued to rock back and forth as he muttered to himself beneath his breath.

Anna watched as the phrase, '*I guess I'm fighting the fool,*' dropped from his lips.

Meanwhile, the pirate paced backward, opened his mouth, closed it. He squinted at the attendant before nodding his head slowly, coming to a decision with glowing cheeks. Anna felt something warm in her stomach at the look. Her robe slipped from one shoulder, the bite of cold on her neck and arm hardly even noticeable while watching the pirate flush.

"I volunteer as tithe." He swallowed hard again.

"Only the Pirate King takes tithes," she said, stepping forward with her hands on her hips, thinking of all the tales she had heard of men at sea offering pretty maidens for no other reason than to escape the Pirate King themselves.

Is that what he was suggesting now? That he would offer himself up in place of others? Anna nearly flushed at the thought.

"Like bloody hell—" the pirate responded immediately, turning to look at her.

Anna watched his entire body stiffen as he took her in. A grin threatened her lips as his jaw slackened and his gaze dropped to her feet and trialed upward until he was staring into her eyes. The contact only lasted a second before he looked away. It didn't make sense to her, he'd seen her in less. Surely, this wasn't impressive.

But she wanted it to be.

He cleared his throat. "Pirate King does no' take tithes, luv. 'Tis a lie."

"Is that so?"

"Aye, though plenty seem to believe throwing maidens at the man will keep their heads on their bloody shoulders." His throat bobbed as he held her gaze. "But it doesn't."

She turned and casually dropped her robe, heat rising in her cheeks and along her neck at her own brashness. First it slid off her shoulders and then down her body, and then she was striding forward and stepping into the first pool. Behind her, she could hear the pirate choke something and then Markus was at it again. The brush on the ground shuffled back and forth but as she continued to sink into the scorching waters, all the extra noise sank to the background.

"Thank you for your assistance, you're dismissed," she said to no one in particular. The attendant would depart and Markus and the pirate may even leave her alone with the command. She was Annaleigh Rae Savage, few were willing to go against her requests.

For a long moment, all Anna could hear was the sound of displaced water lapping at the edges of the hot spring. Not even the insects hummed now. Surely cold snaps had chased them away some time ago. Steam rose from the waters in tendrils, curling around her face and shoulders as if they were the fingers of a loved one. She exhaled, dropping her shoulders beneath the water, and closed her eyes.

"As you wish, miss. The stable master's boy is in the stables. Ring the front desk and he'll bring the carriage around. If I don't hear from you, breakfast is at eight in the reading room."

"Thank you. Have a lovely night," she replied automatically.

"You as well, miss."

Her brother and the pirate continued discussing something, but their voices were nothing more than whispers of wind. She rolled her neck briefly before massaging her thigh. Her thumb carefully brushed over the pirate's stitching as she basked in the scalding waters. Anna wasn't entirely sure how much time had passed but her limbs were beginning to tingle with the effects of the water.

Then, a splash.

Her heart jumped into her throat as she ducked into the water and wheeled around in a panic. But then—she stopped, staring with wide eyes. The pirate was…he was waist-deep in the water and casually strolling closer to her. The heat rose to her cheeks with a fury. She gulped, blinking slowly. Anna had known he exercised daily, she had often exercised with him. This shouldn't have been a surprise and yet—and yet…Anna was gawking.

Her gaze jumped from his musculature to his tattoos, all out on display for her for the first time. They rose over his shoulders and spilled down his pecs and biceps, ending at his fingers and sternum in hard angles. Her gaze dropped as his tattoos did, lower and lower, following every row of muscle. His abdomen twitched as he crossed his arms.

The pirate asked something, a playful tone to his voice, but all she could hear was blood pounding in her ears. The most Anna had seen of him thus far had been his forearms and a small triangle of his chest. This was—this was rather distracting. She looked up quickly, catching a shy smile on his face.

Anna cleared her throat and looked away. "What?"

God, she was an idjit.

He cocked his head at her. "Where are your manners, Miss Savage?" the pirate teased. It was an excellent question. "No' inviting your favorite pirate for a swim?"

"Mm." She nodded her head absently, glancing back only to watch water trickle down his torso.

He settled lower into the water, assessing her carefully, wading several steps closer, head cocked in concern. "Are ye unwell, luv?"

"Favorite?" She cleared her throat, trying to recover. Her brain stumbled toward some semblance of awareness, toward the vocabulary she had somewhere inside her. She knew plenty of words, now where the hell were they? "Who said you were my favorite?"

He grinned, hair damp and sticking to his forehead. He brushed it out of the way and sat up a little straighter. Anna tried to focus on his face, on the eleven or so freckles over his nose and on the few that disappeared in his hairline. "Surely ye don't know many pirates?"

Anna laughed; if only that had been the case. Her laughter slowly died off into a soft chuckle and she tipped her head back to look him in his eyes. "Markus is going to strangle you. I'm certain of it."

"Do I look that bloody easy to kill?" he scoffed, motioning to himself.

It was difficult not to stare, especially when he was inviting her to with that gesture. But, somehow, Anna managed. He was a dangerous man—such a dangerous, dangerous man. And not at all in the way one might believe at first glance. Of course, he was deadly with a weapon or his fists.

But that *grin*.

Anna was so sure it had killed far more than any weapon had.

"All men die," she said quietly, choosing to look up and anchor her gaze on the stars.

"I assure ye, lass, it takes a wee more effort to kill me than most."

"Does it?" She grinned.

He winked, hearing the challenge for what it was, and sank beneath the water, past his shoulders until all of him was submerged. Anna counted to ten, waiting for him to rise. With him below the water, she felt her head clear, felt more centered in herself, but only slightly so.

When the pirate broke the surface of the dark pool, he shook his head like a dog, sprinkling Anna with water. She laughed and splashed him back, appreciative of his attempt at disarming her and breaking this tension between them. She flicked a bit more water at the pirate as he sat back on his haunches, his shoulders barely breaking the surface. The tattoos at his throat seemed to strain upward, intent on strangling him.

He cocked a brow. "Notice something, luv?"

"You're not just a pirate, are you?"

He shook his head. "Hate to disappoint, but I'm exactly that."

Anna pressed her lips into a thin line to keep herself from smiling. "No, you're not. Not just any pirate. That...to think *that* would mean I believe you're just one of the many cogs in a machine. And you're more than that in the same way I'm more than what everyone sees too. More than a cog. More than a lady. What a pair we make," she mused quietly.

He stared at Anna, brows drawn in thought, though his expression was unreadable. She swallowed and waded to the edge of the pool, the very one that ended in a sheer drop until a hundred feet below where the more public pools were. She pressed her chest against the rough rock and rested her head on the edge.

Anna had already made the mistake of thinking him one thing when he was so clearly another. She listened as the pirate joined her, the water lapping eagerly at his skin. In seconds, he had propped himself beside her, his arms crossed and hanging over the edge. The night sky was endless from here and Bellcaster seemed so small.

"Afraid that's no' how I see myself," he murmured at long last.

She looked at him, at the soft tone of his voice.

His eyebrows were drawn and for once his features took on a stern, contemplative edge. Something tightened in her stomach, distraught and appalled. How could he think so lowly of himself that he would see himself as something less than what she did? Sure, the man was a scoundrel and a criminal, but he was a man with plenty of good qualities too. He'd helped her when he needn't. He hadn't left her to die.

Anna leaned her cheek against her forearm. With his chin atop his arms, he stared out at the night sky like it had the answer to a question he so desperately wanted. Like it was sustenance and he was hunger.

"You may not see it," she began, "but it doesn't negate the truth of what others see. Of what I see. You are a scoundrel and a rake, but you're more than that too."

He nodded, thoughtful. They were silent for a long time, listening to the water trickle over the edge, feeding the pools below.

"If I am more," he finally said, "then what am I?"

There it was again, that challenge in his voice, in his eyes, as he turned to her.

He wanted her to ask.

To *know*.

The reason scared her. Why would a pirate want her to know who he was, explicitly and without a doubt? If she didn't know his name, he could at least disappear back into that wicked abyss without a fear that she might tell someone it was he who helped her, who went against the Coalition and the Senate.

Against the Pirate King.

Bugger, it was knowledge she did not need. Not now and not in the future. She looked away, back out at Bellcaster's small, sparkling lights. But she could play along. "If I'm being honest, I'm not sure. I've thought a lot about it. The son of one of the Coalition chiefs. A quartermaster aboard a larger vessel. A well-known gunner. A master-gunner, even."

The pirate snorted. "Seems grand, any of those titles. Has a captain no' crossed your mind?"

"I would have recognized you."

"Aye?"

Anna smiled, tilting her head toward him enough to catch his eye. "You're a bit memorable, pirate."

"A male such as I? Memorable?" He laughed, puffing out his chest.

"Aye," Anna mocked, flicking more water at him. "Before I stole the map, I did a hefty amount of research on the pirate captains and their ships. On the Coalition, too. The only crews that don't have updated pictures are…" Anna trailed off, brows pulling together.

"The *Pale Queen*," he whispered, a knowing in his voice. "And Kidd's crew."

Anna nodded her head. "That's right. But the *Pale Queen's* crew is established, older. And Captain Kidd's quartermaster has green hair and his master-gunner is dark-skinned. So that rules you out." She swallowed, turning back toward the stars. "I have yet to hear of a captain with red hair and dark eyes that's your age. Quin of the *Plight* has blue eyes and Kallum of the *Red Fortune* has brown. But…"

Anna stopped and swallowed, thinking of the *Pale Queen* and her crew. Her night aboard the Pirate King's ship was a blur at best and a black hole at worst. She distinctly remembered meeting the quartermaster and in a way, he looked like the pirate to her right. Dark red hair and bottomless eyes, though he wasn't as broad as the man next to her.

A detail was escaping Anna. Something about the quartermaster or the Pirate King? She wracked her brain for more memories of the night, for them to sharpen. But Anna had made the unfortunate mistake of helping them clear the rum cellar. She had asked herself that night, what would Markus do? And lo and behold, she had done something irrevocably foolish in a fashion that only Markus could contend with.

"Something bothering ye?" he asked gently.

"No. Yes. I don't know," she admitted. "The only two with your coloring that I can think of are the captain of the *Pale Queen* and the quartermaster. But you're much too young to be either of them. Maybe some long-lost cousin or son, I suppose."

"I guarantee the Pirate King looks no' a day older than twenty-eight," the pirate said, sounding offended.

Anna shrugged.

She didn't care how old he looked or how old he was, that wouldn't change the fact that he'd hang her if given the chance. "That matters quite little. He is still the most notorious pirate of this age. He still runs the slave trade, takes women as tithes, shatters families. He could be the most handsome man on the seas and it wouldn't lessen how despicable he is. He's not the only one, but he's the worst."

The pirate went quiet.

"Ye know who else?"

The pirate fought against the slave trade, that's right. She exhaled deeply. Was that where his change in mood came from, discussing the despicable thing? Maybe she had found an ally in the Coalition, someone who saw what was wrong with the world no matter what side of the line they were on. Maybe he was like that. At least Anna could hope so; she was choosing to trust him with her life, with her brother's life. Choosing to trust him to take her where she wanted to go, to not burn her at the end of this.

She swallowed, feeling the pressure of his gaze. "Some...I know some of the pirates sailing about as slavers. I could likely guess at a few more if I saw them."

"How?"

She closed her eyes, smelling the piss and gun powder of the cages below deck of *Devil's Gold*. She remembered the crying, remembered the hunger and the bruises on her wrists.

"To get the map, I needed a way to Tiburon. I...I caught passage on *Devil's Gold*, captained by Cashton Black. But...they weren't all his men. Some had snake bites on their neck or on their arm."

The pirate paused again, a curious look appearing on his face. "If I recall, his ship burnt at sea."

Anna gave a quick grin. "You would do well to remember that no cage can hold me."

Of course, that was only part of the truth, but, bugger, how could she explain the rest without sounding absolutely daft? She couldn't. Anna wasn't entirely sure she even believed what had happened, especially with the distance between now and then.

The pirate turned toward her, flicking her nose and tucking a strand of hair behind her ear. His thumb brushed across her cheek tentatively and Anna forced her muscles to lock, otherwise she would have leaned into his touch. The pirate stood, his torso once again on full display.

She cursed him with a grin, leaning away.

"Don't stay too much longer, luv," he said and then made his way from the pool. Anna turned away, choosing to look out at the night sky instead of watching the amount of his skin on display increase. "We've a party to attend and I've an ex-suitor to embarrass in a duel."

"I would really advise against it."

"Kettle, meet pot." He laughed, his throaty chuckle growing quieter.

It was silent again for several beats.

Anna listened to the water and pretended she was somewhere else, doing something else. While excited about her adventure, something still wasn't sitting right in her stomach. Something beyond why the Pirate King's map was such a wanted commodity— about how it had become such a wanted commodity.

Markus.

Anna's brow furrowed.

She still hadn't figured out how the Senate knew Markus had the map. It was a variable she couldn't work around, couldn't plan for. The not knowing could come back to bite her, bite *them*, the consequences of something like that...

She sighed, her skull beginning to pound.

Who told the Senate?

She hadn't mentioned the map to anyone but her father. Markus of course knew, but only because she had brought the damn thing directly to him, right along with a fleet of pirate ships. Her mouth dried, words and feelings caught in her chest and throat.

Anna shook her head; the idea was preposterous.

Her father would never sell Markus to the Coalition.

He would never trade his only son for a map. He wouldn't…he just wouldn't. Her father was a monster, but even monsters had their limits.

CHAPTER 28

Bloody hell, Trevor felt like hitting something.

He had always wondered how the wee lass had ended up on Tiburon. He'd known how she came to be on the *Pale Queen*—he had Tate to thank for that fucking mess. But Tiburon? No one simply stumbled upon the damned island. It wasn't a destination anyone was interested in, despite its beauty. 'Tis pirate country. An island full of criminals and the forgotten.

And yet she had found her way there because she had—*willingly*—been taken into the slave trade. Wi' how lovely she was, it was no' hard to figure Cashton's thinking. The lass would have sold better in some market on the island than taking her anywhere else.

Bloody fucking hell, it was a gamble. Trevor still couldn't believe it. Couldn't believe *her*. Coalition was going to be in for a fucking surprise when he saw them next. Forgiveness was no' a trait he was known for and they'd be reminded of that soon enough.

"What's wrong with you?" Markus glared from his seat on the vanity as Trevor entered their room, legs kicked out in front of him.

Too many fucking things.

Trevor shrugged instead, pulling his shirt over his head. He needed to bathe and change, get the image of Anna in that starlit pool out of his head while he still could. Needed to drown the bloody image of her below deck in a cage too. Things like that

255

could drive a man mad and he was well on his gods-damned way. He'd always wondered if Jean Black had something to do with the bloody slave trade and Anna gave him an answer.

The fucker did; Cashton was the Coalition chief's nephew. If anyone knew what Cashton was up to, it was Jean. He scrubbed his hands against his head a few times, his movements driven by frustration of all bloody kinds.

Trevor clenched and unclenched his fists, remembering the feeling of her soft hair and skin beneath his fingers. That had been a terrible idea. He'd known it in his head when he'd stripped his clothes off and had known it in his soul when she had stared at him, cheeks pink.

"Does it have something to do with my sister?" Markus hedged.

"No' everything is about her."

Markus snorted. "I think she'd take offense to that."

Ignoring the blond, he paced straight into the restroom and began filling the tub. After shucking his pants, he glared down at his traitorous hand. The fucker. Trevor did his best to let it know any more infractions and he'd lob the whole thing off. Who needed two bloody hands, anyways? A man only really needed one unless he was talented in verse, then he did no' need any. Or at least, that was what Tate always spouted.

Trevor glowered.

He wasn't a man talented in verse.

Bright side, Trevor could just get himself a hook and complete the whole bloody image. Most thought he had a hook for a hand or a peg for a leg as it was. Frowning, he climbed into the tub. It was a wee thing, his knees nearly touching his chest.

Trevor snorted, leaning his head back against the lip of the tub. Apparently, the masses also believed him to be old. Anna thought so, at least; she'd certainly be surprised when she found out the bloody truth.

Part of Trevor desperately wanted to tell her who he was. He could tell she knew, she *knew* he was more than a bloody pirate. More than a grunt. Someone who had status because they might be related to the Pirate King. She just wasn't willing to put the pieces together and see the whole picture. Thank the fucking gods for that, because the other half of Trevor dreaded her finding out. She'd hate him.

Probably try to kill him.

Again.

And Trevor wasn't ready for that, ready to leave behind whatever this was.

So, he'd wait.

He'd attend this fancy party wi' her, probably embarrass himself dancing. Trevor would drink and eat and raise glasses to men and women he had no respect for. If he was lucky, Trevor would be dueling that shite of an ex just to make a damn point. Didn't know who the fucker was, but Trevor couldn't wait to find out. They'd steal the map and as long as he had it in his hand, he'd take the lass wherever she wanted to go. And maybe one day she'd know who he was and no' hate him.

Probably no', but he was allowed to dream.

Markus's fist cracked against the door several times. "Hurry it up, wretch. Anna is on her way back. You try anything with my sister and I'll know."

Trevor scoffed. He fucking doubted that. "Anything that bloody well happens will be 'cause your sister wanted it to fucking happen. Ye best take this conversation up wi' her, mate. I'll deny her no' a thing."

And he wouldn't. Didn't think he could. Where the wee beastie was concerned, Trevor had found it nigh impossible to tell her no. He'd even agreed to take her to that damned island, and that was something he swore he'd never do again.

No' after Taylee.

Gods, no' after Taylee.

CHAPTER 29

"Markus, we'll be fine," Anna said over her shoulder.

Her brother had been doing his due diligence in hindering their departure, going over the plan again and again and *again* until it had seared itself into Anna's very soul. She explained more than once that he needn't fret. That, thanks to him, this was within the normal realms of shenanigans she had become accustomed to over the years.

Normally, it was a decimated tomb or temple ruins she went spelunking in, looking for the remains of long-lost kings with tragic backstories or an item of irrelevant value that had been rumored to be cursed. It was honestly the same situation if you squinted.

Anna reached for her heels as she sat on the floral-print chaise. "This mother hennery is unbefitting of a man of your stature, Markus."

He grumbled something unintelligible beneath his breath and crossed his arms.

Anna squinted at him and then tipped her chin in challenge.

A frown twisted his features as Markus looked away from her. "I'm worried about you," he said before his voice dropped an octave lower. "Especially since you'll be alone with our resident scoundrel. He has nefarious intentions, Anna."

After their quick dip in the pool, Anna wasn't entirely sure she was opposed to the pirate and his hypothetical nefarious intentions. She glanced toward the restroom where the pirate was dressing in the finest silk, cotton, and leather that Mihkel Tamm had been able to dig up. Part of Anna wished the door was open, if for no other reason than to catch another look at the pirate's tattoos and the way they danced on his skin.

She leaned back on her palms and tipped her head to the side, ignoring the bit of heat in her cheeks. "I was alone with him earlier and I escaped that encounter unscathed."

"Yes," Markus sighed ruefully, sliding his hands down his face. "I do recall him traipsing back smelling like the waters you were soaking in."

"We were talking, Markus, for the very last time."

"Is that what they're calling it these days?" Markus mused with a frown. "Children and their colloquialisms...I suppose it *is* a conversation of sorts. A give and a take."

"You're taking this rather well."

He shrugged. "The wretch returned in a mood I would hardly expect if anything *had* happened." Anna raised a brow and her brother rolled his eyes. "...and I could see you from the balcony."

"Ah, there it is." She stood, making her way to the vanity behind him. Her earrings sat out, waiting to adorn her. They were absurdly large things, circular diamonds that dangled and glimmered in the light, a matching necklace laid next to them. "Spying is a rather nasty habit."

"Can you blame me for trying to protect you?" he asked. For the first time in his life, Markus looked exhausted. He clenched his jaw and looked up at her with a raised brow. "It wouldn't be the first pirate you've tumbled and we both remember how *that* turned out."

Anna's fingers fumbled with her earrings, eyes widening in surprise. Both their gazes dropped to the mirror and then to her scar. The jagged, white line ran from the side of her neck and through the notch in her collarbone, all the way to the middle of her sternum. The dress Mihk chose highlighted the damn thing perfectly.

She tried to swallow past the growing knot of anger in her throat. "That was too bold," she told Markus stiffly, hands shaking as she finished with her earrings and started on her necklace.

"Anna, I didn't—"

She shook her head, leaning back and adjusting the skirts of her gown with a flick of her wrist. It was more akin to glittering cobwebs than fabric; every inch of it twinkled in the light, shimmering silver, white, and pale blue. The sleeves ended at her wrists and the front cut across her chest, dipping low between her breasts in a scandalous V. The dress hugged tight at her waist and thighs before tapering out and spilling onto the floor like liquid starlight.

A loud crash sounded from the restroom, quickly followed by creative cursing on the pirate's part, something about his *gods-damned bloody tie*. Anna's cheek twitched and she turned toward her brother with a long, drawn-out breath. She crossed her arms and stared hard at him. Markus flinched beneath her gaze and leaned forward onto his knees, folding his hands. Now wasn't the time to fight but Anna wasn't about to let him get away with acting like an ass because he was a bottomless pit of worry.

"I'm not a child anymore."

"I know." He nodded quickly.

"I can take care of myself."

"I know that too."

"And technically," she said, poking him hard on the chest, "I'm older than you."

He smiled softly. "By five minutes. But only because I was born with manners...unlike some reckless heathen we both know."

"Are you speaking ill of our pirate?"

"Not this time, I'm afraid."

More rustling came from the restroom, drawing her attention back to it. She pressed her lips into a thin line and walked back to the chaise, moving her skirt to the side as she sat down, one elbow slung against the plush armrest. Looking up, she sighed. Her conversation with the pirate hadn't escaped her yet, no matter how hard she pushed it away.

Thoughts of the Pirate King and this curious little map ate at her like a dog gnawing a bone. Her musings of what happened that night aboard the *Pale Queen* had worsened and, for whatever reason, kept bubbling to the surface. Something about that night tugged at a loose thread in her head.

Anna looked down, sucking on her teeth to keep from ruining her lipstick. "What…" She said, raising her gaze to meet her brother's, "what do you know about the *Pale Queen*'s crew?"

He eyed her suspiciously, leaning back against her vanity. "Why?"

She brushed a strand of hair behind her ear. Most of it had been contained in a thickly plaited crown that wound around her head. A few strands had been left to curl here and there about her face. "Something…I don't know, but something…bugger, Markus, I have this silly little puzzle in front of me and I'm trying my best to solve it."

Markus nodded his head slowly. "We're after the Pirate King's map, of course the miserable wretch and his crew are haunting you." He licked his lips and sighed. Anna didn't have to wait long for her brother to continue. "You already know most of what I do. Lovelace prefers a small company he can trust. The quartermaster is his younger brother and their sailing master defected from the Briland Navy. Word is two of the cooks used to work for the Senate in their private offices."

"I thought it was just one?"

He shook his head and looked at his hands, his left leg bouncing. He swallowed hard and cleared his throat. "Lovelace has the best master-gunner ever seen. Anytime we ran into the woman, she'd blow the shit off our ships and leave us marooned. And I'll be damned, Anna, she has the loveliest golden-green eyes you've ever seen. It's hardly fair."

Anna squinted at her brother, a brow slowly rising in intrigue. When had Markus gotten close enough to the Man-Eater to see what color her eyes were? Juliana Gray was not a woman to be trifled with; she would have chewed him up and spit him out without a second thought.

He noticed her curious look and cleared his throat again, looking down at the floor. Whatever she had seen on his face smoothed over immediately into something surer, something less interested in the conversation. She let it drop. When Markus wanted to talk about it, he would. Until then, he'd remain locked up tighter than Chesterhale.

"What can you tell me about Lovelace?" Anna asked instead, pulling his attention back to the matter at hand.

He cocked a brow. "Which one?" Anna narrowed his gaze and Markus snorted. "Surely, you're the expert on that scoundrel, Anna. What could I possibly know that you—"

Anna leaned forward, uncrossing her legs. "That. I. *What*?"

"Noth—" Markus's gaze darted from one side of the floor to the other, a look of absolute horror washing over his face.

He stood, looking to the restroom door just as it opened and their pirate strode out. His mouth snapped shut and his gaze dropped from the pirate's feet and traveled up to his head, clearly searching for something. Anna thought it was a funny time to gain an appreciation for the redhead. He had cleaned up well, though she preferred him a bit more rugged. There was just something about it that fit him better.

The pirate locked gazes with her brother, running his hand through his hair. He had shaved earlier on the train, yet already sported a bit of shadow on his jaw. He looked absolutely dashing in the clothes Mihk had found for him. His trousers and jacket were dark, nearly black. His waistcoat was a soft dove grey, striped and lined with charcoal. The shirt was dark as well, all the better to hide any tattoos that might try to creep up his throat. Anna grinned at the cravat; he'd tied it quite well despite his earlier protests. Dark leather gloves were tucked in his coat pocket. Anna nearly frowned at the thought of the pirate hiding his hands.

She turned toward Markus, but he was eyeing the pirate far more cautiously than he had the past few days. "Markus, are you all right?"

He nodded his head, stepping slowly toward the pirate.

"Did I hear talk about the King? Reckon I know the man best," he said, attention cast toward his fingers, which were checking and double-checking all the weapons on his person. "Ask and I'll tell, luv."

"Isn't that against the rules?" she asked quietly, unsure of the sudden tension in the room.

It was different than it had been in the past. Before, it had been volatile and indulgent, full of vicious remarks and scathing intentions. Anna looked between the two men. This was a ghost sitting among them. This was stiff and scared, like a secret about to be shared.

"*Pirate*, lovely, we don't—" he stopped short after raising his gaze to meet hers.

His jaw slackened and his fingers fumbled along the buckle of one of his revolvers, nearly dropping the gun to the ground. A nervous flutter made itself home deep down in her stomach, a stubborn heat growing on her cheeks. Anna drew her arm up across her chest and over her shoulder, covering a majority of her scar. Stepping forward, her gaze dropped to his lips before returning to his eyes.

The pirate cleared his throat, a smile growing on his face, back straightening. Pink dusted his cheeks, making him look younger. He opened his mouth and then closed it with a shake of his head, looking away from her. Anna's grin widened. She took another tentative step toward him.

He motioned to her head vaguely. "Is that a crown?"

"God, no," Anna said, remembering their conversation in Heylik Toyer. "Mine will be made of real gold and jewels."

The pirate rocked back on his heels, offering his arm. "For no' being a bloody pirate, ye sure are interested in treasure, luv."

"I'm an archaeologist," she said, taking his arm. "All things glittering and gold interest me...especially if they're old."

"Ye don't say?"

"Aye. The older, the better."

Markus beat them to the door, wary in the way he walked around the pirate. It was a curious and intentional thing, circling the pirate on Anna's arm as if he wasn't sure whether to treat the man as predator or prey.

Something had changed, something in their conversation had triggered this new caution from her brother, only she didn't know what. If Anna had to guess, she'd say it clearly had something to do with the Pirate King, or quite possibly Juliana Gray. Anna canted her head to the side in question but Markus ignored the action, choosing to clap the pirate on the arm in some mock display of camaraderie.

"Be careful with my sister, pirate."

There were warnings and unspoken threats hiding behind his teeth. Both curiosity and caution wanted to know where the change in Markus's demeanor came from, but time dictated she would ask later and hope he answered.

"I'll be fine," Anna said.

"Aye...mate, worry no' about my wee beastie. I'll be there to cleave heads from bodies yet." The pirate paused, the grin on his face looking more and more like that of a shark. "That is, if Anna leaves anything left of the men."

Markus looked distressed but the clock on the wall chimed, signaling it was time to go. She patted him on the arm and then strode from the room with the pirate tucked tight against her, wondering why brothers were so incredibly strange.

CHAPTER 30

All Markus heard was the ringing in his ears.

The door closed behind his sister and then the thumping of his blood through his blasted head was the only sound in the room. The only thing left, like the air had left with his sister.

How—*how* had this happened?

Why hadn't he noticed it sooner?

Of course, Tate was the likelier of the two. The quartermaster had been known to step foot on the continent, he was younger, and known for his exploits with lovely women. Before Markus had been horrified at the thought—enraged, and worried. Now, he only wished it had been Tate Lovelace traveling with them.

Tate at least—

He might have—

The walls warbled and Markus clutched at his chest. A wheezing sound he had never heard before came from his throat, from somewhere deep down in his blasted soul. He stumbled backward until he ran into the bed and thumped to the floor, cradling his head in his hands as he rocked.

Markus had only felt such fear once before, when he'd watched a cutlass bite into Anna and peel her skin back like a hot knife carving through butter. He swallowed and closed his eyes, gasping as he tried to force his breathing into some semblance of calm.

But how could he be calm with his sister in the arms of the enemy and about to willingly walk into a den of lions that had spent their time sharpening their claws? How had this happened?

Was it cosmic retribution for something he had done or the things he wanted to do?

Or the things still yet to come?

Markus didn't know and he wanted to find out even less.

He didn't know what he would do if anything happened to his sister. Blame himself, of course. But after that? He'd probably want to curl up and die, to dig a hole and lie in it. Anna had been there since his first breath and she was supposed to be there when he took his last. He'd promised—*promised*—that nothing would ever happen to her, that he would take care of...

"How did this happen?" he asked himself, the question repeating itself over and over, the question mark louder than cannon fire.

Did the answer matter?

Would looking back and searching for it *do* anything to change the fact that Anna walked from the room on the arm of that man? He took a deep breath, held it. No. No, it wouldn't. Markus wouldn't feel better and it wouldn't change who she was with or where they were going.

"God-damnit." He laughed, throwing his forearm over his eyes. "That was Trevor Lovelace."

CHAPTER 31

The carriage ride from the Ascendant to John Savage's private estates had always taken roughly thirty minutes. It was a steep incline, the estate itself nestled in the middle of the forest with nothing but the smell of fresh snow and pine to surround it. Anna held her breath at seeing the monstrosity, a man-made establishment that looked completely out of place here in the mountains. At least the Ascendant with its log cabin feel fit the aesthetics.

The ride had left Anna with little else to do but ponder Markus's odd behavior and the Pirate King. It was infuriating, really. Her memory was one of her best assets, one that she could usually count on in times of need or distress. But right now, it was a withered and pitiful thing, cowering away from questions and answers that pertained to Trevor Lovelace.

Anna shook her head as she stared out the carriage window, watching the shadows slowly roll by. She may have spent four months at sea, but Anna had been in the company of the Pirate King aboard his flagship for only a single night. Despite that, one would think she could remember something of him—*anything* of him—after what they had done.

But nay, extreme alcohol consumption and a wicked concussion had wiped the slate clean where the Pirate King was concerned.

Frustratingly enough, Anna recalled the quartermaster with near-perfect clarity. He had a long, lean build reminiscent of a competition swimmer. His dark red hair had tangled around his shoulders with beads and priceless metals hanging in the strands. Unfathomably dark eyes, like staring into a bottomless pit.

Probably the most notable feature of the quartermaster had been the three thin scars on his cheek. They were deeper near his hairline, the imprint fading as they angled down like he had been scratched. Being brothers, Anna imagined the Pirate King looked similar. Reports had confirmed dark hair, red or brown, and dark eyes.

She looked from the darkness outside the carriage window to the man half asleep across from her. Her pirate fit the bill of a Lovelace; he could most definitely be related to the quartermaster or the Pirate King. The thought terrified her. It would certainly explain what he wanted with the Pirate King's map. But for the life of her, Anna couldn't figure out why he wouldn't be bringing it back to Trevor Lovelace or the Coalition. Why he would be willing to take her wherever it led.

Unless it was a lie and he intended to deliver her to the Pirate King or Coalition.

That would certainly piss her off.

"Trevor Lovelace," Anna mumbled, the name like acid on her tongue.

Bugger, why couldn't she remember him?

"Mm?" the pirate answered, eyes still closed but body moving to sit up. After another minute, the pirate rubbed at his eye with the heel of his palm. "Did ye say something, luv?"

Anna smiled, discreetly rubbing the smudge on her palm. "Just talking to myself, I'm afraid."

"Ye could talk wi' me instead. Might seem less daft, aye?"

Anna pretended to contemplate her answer, tapping a finger to her chin. It wasn't the thought of talking with him she minded, it was the feeling of eagerness that lumped in her chest at the prospect. But if he was willing to talk, Anna figured she should listen.

The pirate dragged his hand through his hair but before she could answer, several knocks on the carriage roof sounded, quickly followed by Griff's voice. "We've arrived, Miss Savage."

The carriage came to a slow halt, effectively bringing their conversation to a standstill. Anna and the pirate stared at each other as they listened to the blond's feet hit the ground. The sound of the door opening followed quickly after, bringing a gust of icy air with it. Anna pulled her fur cover up tightly about her shoulders and held her hand out to the stable hand.

The pirate frowned at her. It didn't take much effort for her to discern what he was thinking. Anna rolled her eyes at him, placing her hand in Griff's anyway and allowing him to help her down. If she thought the breeze in the carriage was cold, the air outside of it must have come straight from the north, a gift to her father from the Ice Queen.

Anna dropped Griff's hand and her skirts as the pirate came to stand directly at her side. She tilted her head toward the blond and smiled. "Thank you, Griff. I really do appreciate your hard work tonight."

Griff shrugged and tucked his hands deep into his pockets. "No need for that, miss." He paused and then looked up at the sky, a bit of a blush on his cheeks. "You suppose you brother will make a surprise appearance too?"

A brief bit of relief found its way into her chest. If Griffin didn't know about Markus's arrest and detainment, perhaps it meant the general public didn't either. Anna doubted her luck would run that far or fast, but she hoped it would. She sighed. At least Griff hadn't realized it was Markus with them earlier; that was something.

The pirate's head cocked ever so slightly, gaze narrowing curiously.

"Afraid not."

Griff sighed. "What a shame. I imagine he's grown quite a bit in three years."

"And here I thought it was *my* ass you looked forward to seeing."

"Yes. But his looks just as good as yours in tight pants." Griff grinned and winked before striding back to the carriage. "I'd keep the new company, miss. They're delightful to look at."

The pirate's gaze narrowed further, lips pressing together in thought. She waited for it, for the moment he would realize what Griff implied. After another second, he blinked and turned toward her in surprise.

Anna tried to contain her amusement at the pirate's reaction by biting her tongue. It broke through anyway, her chuckle deep and joyous, bringing a laugh to the pirate's lips as well. She looked up, watching the amusement dancing in his dark eyes, his grin crooked and unbelievably handsome.

"Yes?" she asked, holding her skirt with one hand as they approached a flight of stairs, her other arm threaded through the pirate's.

His grin widened. "Ye don't seem to be disagreeing wi' him."

"I already know my brother is a feast for the eyes; we are twins, after all." Anna paused and looked up at the pirate playfully. "Though I'm surprised you think so as well. I never would have guessed that you fancy men."

He frowned, looking down on her. "'Tis no' what I bloody well meant and ye, fem, know so."

"Mm," she hummed, barely keeping the smile off her face. "Of course."

Anna was still laughing beneath her breath when the merriment and music trickled into the air, cascading down from the open doors at the top of the stairs. The floor-to-ceiling windows had frosted over with cold. Bright light poured from behind them, casting the dancing figures inside in shadows and rough outlines.

Guardsmen stood stock-still at the door, clothed in black with a glimmering green snake at their breast. Instead of stiffening like most men would at their intimidating frame and the weapons they openly carried, the pirate rolled his shoulders back and grinned. His gait slowed, pulling Anna back with him, and when she looked up to catch his eye, he had relaxed completely.

She tipped her chin up as they approached the guards and were hailed with a chorus of '*Miss Savage*,' as they passed. Every single one of her father's personal guards dipped their heads in deference upon her arrival. Only one stepped forward as she and the pirate crossed the threshold into her father's estate.

"Your father will be pleased you're in attendance, miss," the guard said, eyeing the pirate.

Anna didn't bother with a reply—not a verbal one, at least.

She removed her fur coverup and placed it in the guard's hand. Pulling the pirate closer, she leaned her head against his shoulder for all to see as they left the guards behind. Her heels clicked against the hardwood and the hem of her gown whispered behind her. The pirate let go of a breath, head tilting this way and that to take in the extravagance of the Savage Estate.

Dark floors and glamorous wallpaper. Brass fixtures and pictures worth thousands on every wall. They turned down a hall, a sculpture of a naked man throwing a disk in the corner, and Anna's steps slowed. A vaulted entry huddled at the end of the hall. It led to the larger of two ballrooms on the grounds where the public celebration would be. Bellcaster high society would be dancing beneath the glittering glass dome, glasses would be clinking and speeches made.

"I should probably warn you," she said suddenly.

"Ye did no' poison me again, did ye?"

"No." She laughed, smacking at his chest with the back of her hand and pulling him forward once more. "There will be gossip and everyone is going to stare."

"Wi' a dress like that, I can't imagine why they wouldn't... shan't say I'll bloody well enjoy that."

"Not just at me. They're going to be staring at you quite a lot, too."

She saw his throat bob from the corner of her eye.

When the pirate spoke, he sounded far surer than he looked, tone full of bravado. "Ah. Well, I'm a bloody handsome man, I would expect them to—"

He stopped, stiffening slightly beside her as they crossed beneath the threshold and into the ballroom. Sound had carried down the hall and outside, but it was nothing like walking into the ballroom. Music played and everyone in the room conversed, some laughed loudly and others murmured in quiet, dark corners. As if all as one, conversations died out, glasses lowered, and even the orchestra stumbled. Heads turned, eyebrows rose, and then everyone in the room stopped to stare at who had entered.

Time seemed to slow, dragging by as every man and woman in the room took measure of them. Anna raised her chin. Let them talk, they always did anyway. The pirate's chest rose and held, but he didn't break his pace as they entered the room. In seconds, the whispering picked back up into conversation and Anna could see and hear her name leaving nearly every mouth in the room.

She had expected that.

That wasn't why her blood was boiling.

What she had not expected was the women's jaws to drop nor their gazes to turn so hungry at the sight of the pirate. Even some of the men looked on with something cruel and ravenous in their eyes. She found herself grinning at them and pulling the pirate a hair closer.

The crowd parted around them, allowing her to take in the ballroom. The room was full of freshly bloomed red roses. The floral arrangements interspersed with varying wreaths of garland, peppered with bits of dried holly berries and pearls. Beyond the smell of roses were undertones of incense and a dizzying amount of perfumes and colognes.

The barrel-vaulted ceilings rose high into the air, beams of dark-stained pine stretched across as a glass dome and continued to rise above. Roses and garlands wrapped around the beams even as crystal chandeliers hung from them at uneven heights. They were bright and glittering, causing candlelight to cascade in every direction and making the pale white marble of the ballroom shine.

Beyond the opulence of the ballroom were individuals in every shade and color imaginable, dressed to the teeth in their finest. She paused, staring up at the ceiling where the sky stared down at her. Every star seemed to be out tonight, shining bright against the velvet backdrop of the night.

The pirate jerked Anna to a stop, a stainless-steel tray of something that smelled delicious passing in front of her face. It had been shined until she could see their reflection and what a pair they made, the pirate grinning down at her when she wasn't looking.

Anna stared at the empty space in front of her for several seconds, the image of them imprinted in her mind. As handsome of a pair as they made, something about it was off. Like she was staring at a version of them she didn't quite know. She swallowed. It had to be the finery. The sparkling clothes fit them no better than they had fit her growing up.

"Anna, if these bloody pricks keep staring at ye like this, I might have to fucking fight them," he grumbled beneath his breath, dipping his mouth to her ear.

She shivered, his breath hot against her skin. His bicep tightened beneath her hand, surely anticipating one fight or another. She squeezed the muscle beneath her fingers and looked up at him, trying to catch his gaze. But the pirate was scanning the area, a nonchalant expression on his face despite what he had said and what she could feel.

273

"I'm not interested in any of them," Anna found herself, inexplicably, saying.

"No?"

She shook her head against his shoulder as they strode forward. "None of them have ever been right for me. They see the value I present, the climb in the social ladder, the connection to my father and brother. They all want *something* but who I am isn't it."

He cocked a brow. "So what you're saying, luv, is that you're waiting?"

"I suppose you could say that." Anna turned her head with a small smile, spying the western wall.

It was completely composed of floor-to-ceiling windows, the very same one she had looked at when first climbing the stairs. From here, just through the frost on the panes of glass and the clinging fog outside, Anna saw the forest and its league of shadows. The stream that bubbled through the forest and across their estate looked more like a black ribbon in the dark.

"Afraid I've never been to one of these."

"Considering you're a *pirate*, that seems rather understandable," Anna said quietly, steering them toward a cluster of tall, circular tables with silk tablecloths. Just behind the smaller tables were long stretches of rectangular ones with every delight imaginable and sculptures made of ice.

"Aye, most pirates tend to stay at sea. For good reason too. Coming to something like this is a good way to lose your bloody head."

"*Most?*" She waved to one of the senators across the way when they made eye contact. Senator Wallace Ackerman stood in the center of a small group of men, a drink in hand and his heavily pregnant wife, Nora, next to him. She scanned the floor around their legs. They must have left their toddler, Cora, at home.

"Aye, *most*," the pirate said, interrupting her thoughts. "Lesser known pirates or those who've kept their faces a secret might attempt it. Well, them and the fucking idiots. The Old Crow was daft like that. Coming to land just to see what he could get away wi'."

The Old Crow.

He was the Pirate King before Trevor Lovelace caved his face in with his fists.

A chill crept down her spine. "Would…the Pirate King— *Trevor Lovelace*—" she clarified, "ever come on land?"

"No' unless he had to, no," he answered, ducking a shoulder beneath a server's tray. "'Tis no' a good idea. He hates the Senate and likes land even less."

"What a shame," she said, breath catching in her throat. "I bet he cleans up well."

"Oh, aye. I've heard the man is delightful to look at."

"I have a feeling Trevor Lovelace would object to being called delightful," she said absently.

Anna tried to look up and over the crowd, certain she had seen a blond man, short of stature and in the sharpest dinner clothes she had ever seen. Mihk was back there somewhere and Anna owed him thanks. But the blond would only make himself known when he felt like it.

"And you're an expert on him?"

"No." She shook her head. "I've had enough practice with alpha males to confidently make an educated guess."

"I reckon he would no' care what ye call him, luv."

She chuckled, threading between conversing groups and continuing to wave and tip her head at the aristocracy she was required to greet. She'd seen Senator Cameron Fry with his wife, Hazel, ten paces back and just to their left was Jude Bourke, son of Senator Thatcher Bourke.

"Doubtful," she finally told him after glaring at a passing woman for staring too long.

"Why's that, beastie?"

Anna swallowed hard, feeling her cheeks heat. This bit of information wasn't common knowledge. Mihk might have suspected but only Markus knew and she'd rather keep it that way. But the pirate had been open with her and she wanted to be honest with him. And, while she didn't believe in this bit of pirate lore, Anna figured he should know before going out to sea with her.

"I'm…on the Coalition's naughty list," she mumbled, pulling him toward a table with bubbly, pale drinks in long crystal flutes. She raised her left palm for him to see, revealing a dark smudge about the size of a fingerprint on the center of her palm. "The relationship between the King and Coalition, as you know, is strained as it is. Out of respect for the chiefs, I'm sure he would hand me over without a word—if he didn't kill me himself first."

The pirate coughed a laugh, turning his head down to catch her gaze. It took him a second to realize that Anna had not misspoken, nor was she jesting. His features sobered as his attention centered on the mark on her palm. It was a shame, really. Anna much preferred his laughter over the cool appraisal and questions hidden in his eyes.

"How…" His jaw tightened and his face paled, gaze still trained on the smudge. "How did ye manage that?"

She shrugged, picking a flute off the table and swirling it. "The Coalition and the Pirate King do not take kindly to those who steal from them."

"Reckon 'tis why that prick brother of yours said ye couldn't sail?"

She nodded her head.

The pirate's gaze swept over the table, taking in the pyramid of bubbling drinks in shallow, wide glasses and bright popping pink ones in long flutes like Anna drank from. He took a mushroom stuffed with sausage gravy from the table and popped it into his mouth. He turned as the orchestra changed its tune and the dancing started up again.

"Do you dance?" she asked quietly, swirling her flute.

He shook his head. "No. No' unless ye wanted to. I'd be willing then, lass."

It was Anna's turn to shake her head. "No, I don't much feel like dancing tonight. There is too much to do and…" She breathed deep. Raised her glass to her lips. Hesitated. "You said…you said he—the Pirate King, he doesn't typically come on land?"

"Ayyye."

"Is there…?"

She didn't want to ask but she knew she had to. Hoping the pirate had been speaking the truth wasn't enough, Anna needed some sort of confirmation. She had tricked the Pirate King and stolen from him, making him appear a fool in the eyes of the Coalition. Death by his hands seemed a weary and, quite possibly, prolonged fate. One she had diligently avoided the last three years.

"Lovely?"

"Might there be a reason he decides to step foot on land?"

"Ah, aye." The pirate chuckled. "There's this matter of a rather bloody dangerous map and the wee bonnie lass who stole the damn thing. She's caused a wee bit of trouble, ye understand."

Anna froze.

Bugger.

Bugger it all to hell.

She looked up to him slowly, fingers trembling on his arm. Anna wasn't entirely sure what she was expecting, but the playfulness in his features and in his frame? That wasn't it. She squinted at him, a sort of knowing sinking into her bones and waiting for her to remember.

"So. You've known?"

"Aye."

Bugger. "And you've known it was me?"

"Since ye hummed that adorable lullaby on the train."

"Isn't that just splendid?" she grumbled, feeling like a fool.

Anna led him to a more secluded section along the wall, one where the light from the sconces didn't quite reach. Standing still had not been an option. There were too many women oohing and aahing at Anna's gown. And at the handsome man at her side, the one they had never seen before but wanted to see more of. Anna couldn't help but agree with them, even as she glared at those ogling like he was a piece of meat. The pirate was so much more than that. He was clever and wicked in a fight and he was kind.

Anna flinched when an elbow bumped into her and she tried to ignore the venomous look the pirate shot the man in the tweed jacket. She looked away and feigned interest in the dancing once more upon realizing it was Senator Chelsea Cunningham, Bryce's father. He glowered at her, his silver eyebrows thick accents above light green eyes.

With her left hand, she rubbed at her scar, finger digging into the divot in her clavicle. She had to get to the wall, away from prying eyes and ears. Had to ask some questions. The pirate glanced down and frowned.

"Know about that too," he said a few beats later.

Anna dropped her gaze to where her finger touched her clavicle and then looked back to the pirate, breath catching in her throat. There were very few reasons he should know about the scar and how she received it.

Bugger.

CHAPTER 32

Trevor couldn't tear his gaze away from the wee fem.

He'd thought he was leading but a minute later Anna pulled him behind a marble pillar and no' for the reason he wished. Bloody hell, she was a vision and he wanted nothing more than a single touch of her lips. His gaze dropped to the red paint before raising back to her eyes; they were rimmed in kohl and dramatically done.

Witch, she was definitely a witch.

"How much do you know?" she whispered hastily, pressing him up against the pillar wi' one wee hand on his chest. His back bumped against the marble, bringing them to a halt. Her tone may have been cool but the flush on her cheeks and the frantic way her gaze darted from one part of him to the next said differently.

How much did he know?

Shite, he knew everything.

He knew what she looked like beneath those cobwebs, knew what she sounded like in the still night wi' nothing but the tide to muffle her—to muffle *them*. He knew the way her skin felt beneath his shaking fingers. Trevor didn't remember much of that night but he remembered that.

He reckoned that was no' what she wanted to hear, though. She'd probably try to tear his throat from his neck right then and there and all he'd be able to do is apologize for bleeding on her dress like a fucking prick.

"Enough," he finally said, voice rough.

"...*enough*," she repeated, hand still pressed against his chest, right over his heart. The other twirled her pink bubbly drink in its elegant flute. She shook her head, squinting at him. "You knew who I was. What I was doing on that train." It was not a question. "You didn't say anything, not once."

"Luv, ye never asked."

Something flashed in her eyes, something hurt and trying to hide. And she would, even if it meant rebuilding the wall between them brick by brick after he had spent these weeks tearing it down wi' his bare hands. Shite, he could never tell if he should step in or away. But her hand was warm against his chest and Trevor wanted to circle her wrist and pull her close, to crush any doubts she might have about him.

He tucked his hands into his pockets lest the fuckers get any ideas of their own.

Anna stepped away, the absence of her hand on his chest immediate. Fuck, there was a cold spot over his heart that sank into his damned soul. The look in her clear blue eyes turned icy and expectant. She swirled the flute again before knocking the contents straight back and narrowing her eyes at him. Trevor understood fucking perfectly.

Talk.

"I was there because of the prick's arrest...it presented an opportunity and all that to get the bloody map back. 'Tis been a wee pain in my ass the past three years, luv."

"Oh, has it?"

"Aye. Many ships were told they couldn't return unless it was wi' that fucking map."

"Return where?"

"Tiburon."

One of Anna's brow arched. She was curious. "By whose authority?"

"Coalition."

"Not the Pirate King?"

Trevor shook his head, swallowing past a knot in his throat. He felt a bead of sweat drip down his spine. The interrogation was apparently making him more nervous than he'd fucking thought. Every question she asked brought them closer and closer to the bloody truth and he didn't want to share it, to ruin what they had right now. But he would if she asked.

"How unfortunate."

"Unfortunate? That doesn't—" He rubbed the back of his neck, eyes nearly closing wi' the memory that overtook him. He'd had to scrub nearly every inch of himself afterward, had picked her blood from beneath his nails for days. "Oh, aye, I knew ye, luv. I don't think I could ever forget ye. Especially no' after that." He motioned wi' his head to the scar on her chest. "Bled all over me while I stitched ye back together."

"You were on my brother's ship?"

"Aye. Snuck aboard and borrowed a bloody uniform. Wi' all the pirates swarming about, it was easy to blend in."

"You seem to do that a lot. Take other's clothes," she said quietly, touching where the scar cut into her collarbone.

He followed the trail of her finger and had to hold the wince in. Her scar was thin, jagged in some parts, going from her neck, through her collarbone and down between her breasts. He'd killed the fucking man that put it there and a haze tinted his thoughts whenever he saw the thing. It made her no less beautiful but, shite, did it make him angry and nauseous to see.

She shook her head and then laughed, bright and clear and so unexpected it fucking stunned him.

"Anna, luv, are ye—are ye all right?"

The lovely female turned to him and then started laughing again, one arm across her torso. She looked to the right and left and then tossed her empty flute of pink bubbly in a ceramic pot before turning back to him and shaking her head, lips pressed tight.

Shite, he might have broken her.

"I," she started, looking up to the ceiling, "I suppose it makes sense now."

"What does?"

"Why you didn't look at my breasts on the train. You've already seen them," she teased.

Trevor quickly realized they were moving past the conversation and this was Anna's attempt at smoothing everything over. It was something he'd come to like about the fem—she valued peace, didn't want any parts of a fight if she could avoid it. But she would fight if she had to. Especially for the people she loved. She'd fight tooth and nail and break herself again and again for them, like a tide crashing upon the shore.

Fucking scared Trevor, if he was being honest.

But he saw her nerves in the way she covered her chest, her scar, and rounded her shoulders. The heat in her cheeks and the way she couldn't meet his damn eyes.

Was she embarrassed by the scar?

Trevor swallowed thickly; he hadn't thought about that. About how the bit of torn flesh would make her feel. Did she think herself less lovely because of it? Bloody hell, if that was the case, he'd have to change it. He stepped away from the wall and offered her his arm. She pulled it tight against her body, drumming her fingers.

Anna looked to the glass dome above where the North Star shone brightest. It truly was a masterful bit of construction. Shite, Trevor never thought he'd compliment anything of John Savage's but this bloody ballroom was a breath of fresh air and so was his daughter. But he doubted either of those things had anything to do with the senator.

No, some gentler hand has crafted them.

"My mother," she said quietly, gaze still anchored above. "She commissioned the dome. We used to lay blankets in the middle of the floor and stare up at the stars. She told us all kinds of stories then; I don't remember them very well but I remember her being very good at it."

The more the lass spoke of her mother, the more Trevor loved the woman.

"I—" The hair on the back of his neck stood up as a creeping feeling made itself home in his spine.

Trevor looked left and then right. Wasn't sure what the fuck it was, but he wasn't about to let it go wi'out investigating. His gut had saved him more times than he'd like to admit and wi' Anna on his arm, he wasn't about to take any chances.

It took several passes to realize the pit developing in his gut stemmed from all the gods-damned staring and whispering behind hands. He wasn't shy, but this was bloody ridiculous. Everywhere he looked some bastard smirked at Anna or a gaggle of females pointed at the two of them, judgement in their eyes and spite in their mouths.

"'Tis like this all the bloody time?"

"Aye." She grinned up at him. "High society enjoys gossiping when they have nothing better to do. I'd just ignore it, I think they're jealous."

"Of?"

Anna's wee shoulder brushed against his in a glimmer of fabric. "I'm here with a very mysterious and handsome man of unknown origins. Minus the paperwork, I live a bit of a reckless life filled with intrigue and wonder where I travel to potentially exotic destinations. I want for nothing, my father and mother ensured that."

His heart thundered in his chest.

Anna thought he was handsome.

They should get the hell out of there before anything could fuck up his night, because right now, it was going a wee bit too well. He cleared his throat and leaned down. "I hear a *but* in there, beastie."

She nodded, chewing on her cheek. "But I am expected to be who they are and to want what they have. And I don't. I want none of it. Not unless it is authentic and fought for and lived in. I want a life and a love loud enough to rattle the stars."

Trevor had thought something similar once—that he wouldn't live unless it was wi' fucking fame and fortune, a life he didn't have to scrap for, a place where everyone knew his godsdamn name. He remembered his pulse keeping time to it, to that blasted want for *more*.

The price he'd paid for it had ripped his fucking heart out. It was a price he'd never pay again and he'd live the rest of his despicable bloody years regretting ever wanting anything above his bloody station.

"Come on, pirate." Anna grinned, staring at a corridor in the distance. "We've a map to steal."

More, more, more.

"Aye, lass."

Always more.

CHAPTER 33

Anticipation hummed through Anna.

It was finally time to go and claim that horrible little scrap of leather. They'd arrived and been noticed. Bugger, they had been noticed all right, especially the pirate. Word was sure to reach her father that his less-than-dutiful daughter had shown her face at his birthday gala and that she had decided to spit on it by coming with this man on her arm.

Speaking of the mysterious man...

Anna glanced up at him. His gaze roved from grandfather clocks and statues, looking from paintings to the other odd trinkets her father kept on the walls. Always diligent, this one. On the lookout for poor unsuspecting monsters. Little did the beasts know the man at her left was far more fearsome in a fight.

The pirate gnawed on his lip, looking up at a golden chandelier with chains of crystal hanging from it. They sparkled in the low light cast from brass fixtures on the walls. Anna studiously ignored the various bundles of mistletoe interspersed with her father's trinkets and other party decorations. If the pirate noticed them, he made no mention of them. They rounded another corner, a suit of armor on their right. He slowed, head canting to the side as he frowned at the axe in the suit's gauntlets.

As a child, the Savage Estate had always seemed more akin to a labyrinth than a place to live, and Anna's feeling on the matter hadn't changed. If anything, they had grown stronger, throwing down roots and burrowing deeper. Winding wood floors passed gilded trinkets and priceless works of art. Stairs spiraled upward and, in a single case, downward into a cellar stocked well enough to feed royalty. There were more rooms than Anna knew what to do with, many with furniture hiding under sheets—ghosts of rooms, really.

Every step through the monstrous building brought them closer to Markus's room and closer to the map. Closer to another adventure, wrought with intrigue and treasure. She didn't know where the map led or what was at its end, but Anna wanted to find out. The matter of clearing Markus's name still loomed before her, but they'd find a way after handing in the poorly copied map. She doubted her father would let his sole son and heir rot in jail. It honestly wouldn't have surprised her if Senator John Savage was already hard at work greasing palms and sweet talking.

Finally, they came to the top of a staircase. Rooms lined the hall to their left and right like soldiers standing at attention. It was nearly dark as pitch, none of the sconces had been lit. The only bit of light came from the moon shining through skylights. She stepped forward, a board creaking beneath the thick rug that ran the length of the corridor.

They were halfway down the hall when she finally deigned to speak. "This—"

Anna stopped, squinting ahead. A faint glow lit the end of the hall where it curved and wrapped around. The pirate stilled, leaning in front of her. Did he intend on using himself as a shield again? Anna nearly shook her head at him; that may have been an option at the beginning of this adventure but it wasn't one now.

With her heels on, Anna could easily see over his shoulder. They watched the dull glow brighten and soon the sounds of murmurs and steps echoed their way.

"Bugger," Anna swore, grabbing at the pirate's hand and pulling him with her.

The door creaked fiercely.

Anna pinched her eyes shut and shoved the pirate in, stumbling against each other as they tried to catch their footing. Her hip glanced off his thigh and he slid against the wall. Good God, the sound of his coat catching the wall seemed impossibly loud in her ears. They settled, Anna pressed tight against the pirate. She grasped the knob, attempting to close it, but the traitorous thing whined the whole way.

"Ann—" he started but Anna pressed a finger to his lips, the other still wrapped around the knob. She swallowed hard, unable to see anything. Heavy drapes covered the windows and with the door closed, there was absolutely no light.

"I told you," one of the guards finally sighed, "'tis haunted."

"Nahh," the other scoffed. "P'rolly just rats."

Their steps picked up again.

"Shit, I hope not. Rats are worse than ghosts. Now what's this you were saying about the Pirate King?"

Anna held her breath as their steps drew closer. She closed her eyes tight, slowly freeing her fingers from the knob and placing her hand on the pirate's shoulder. She lowered the finger pressed against his lips as well, placing this one against his chest.

The pirate was strung tight, pinned between Anna and the wall, her body pressed against his. In the scramble to enter the room, he had frozen with one arm wrapped around her waist. She wasn't entirely sure what he was doing with the other, but she couldn't feel it on her.

"You fucking jest!" one guard spoke in a harsh whisper.

"I do no such thing, Gareth."

"Pirate King goes missin' and the bloody Man Eater is at the helm? Omen if you ask me. Doubly so with that bitch in lead," Gareth continued. "How long?"

The pirate twitched but said nothing. Anna opened her eyes to see him, to gage his reaction, but it was too dark in the room to see. Even with their close proximity he was nothing but sharp planes of shadow. It occurred to Anna then just how close they were. Close enough to kiss. Anna flushed and turned her attention back to the door, embarrassed. The pirate surely couldn't see her, but she could feel the weight of his gaze regardless.

"No one knows. Some say two weeks; other blokes say the old bastard has been gone longer."

"If he's not on the fucking *Queen*, where the hell is he?" Silence followed. Anna assumed the other guard must have shrugged. "Where was the *Queen* spotted last?"

"Off the coast of the Emerald Isles, heading west."

The pirate twitched again, his arm jumping and tightening around her waist. Something was bothering him, though Anna couldn't guess what. She sucked on her teeth and whispered, "What's wrong?"

The pirate didn't reply.

Gareth cleared his throat. "What about that brother of his? Where's the wee Lovelace run off to?"

"Heard he went looking for the prick. It's not lookin' pretty for the Coalition at current."

"Let 'em all burn in hell."

Again, his arm tightened, forcing Anna up against him. His breaths were short and choppy. She turned to look where she assumed his head was, feeling her way back up his chest and neck, fingers shaking as she felt his jawline and found his lips once more. Wind rattled the windows behind them, loud and furious.

"You hear that? I told you, this place is fucking haunted."

The guard's footsteps trailed away, their laughter lingering in the air. Anna cocked her head, listening as the cadence of their feet on the hardwood changed from walking to descending stairs. She reached, feeling for his nose, and then flicked him.

"What's wrong?" she asked again, cracking the door open to chase some of the dark away.

"What the fuck isn't?" he sighed.

Anna drew back.

Something furious burned deep in his gaze, a depthless void that appeared to whorl and crackle. She hadn't realized the dark could be so incredibly nuanced and layered until then. Until the shadows darkened the planes of his face and tricked her eyes into thinking his irises were twirling like a whirlpool made of ink. She swallowed, looking deep into his eyes and then with a deep breath, poked him hard between the pecs.

He glanced at her and then returned his gaze to the door.

Anna frowned; something about the intensity of his anger reminded her of someone. It was an uncomfortable feeling, one that had her reaching out and jabbing him hard again. Oh, the stupid man thought he could ignore her? Not today. It wasn't until the fourth poke that he closed his eyes, took a deep breath, and anchored his gaze to her face.

The pirate's expression lost some of its animosity, though Anna wasn't fool enough to believe it was far from reach.

"Ignore the guards," she told him, flicking his nose again.

"'Tis blood easy for ye to say," he grumbled.

"*Aye*," Anna teased, pulling away, savoring the feeling of his hand sliding over her lower back and her hip.

The pirate didn't reply, simply leaned over and poked his head into the corridor.

"Shall we, luv?" he asked, holding the door open for her.

Anna nodded her head, all her thoughts jumbling around with the movement. If the Pirate King wasn't on the *Pale Queen*, there really wasn't a way for her to track him. The ship was beautiful, white-washed with an ethereal figurehead and black sails. There wasn't a soul alive that couldn't recognize it. Just as there wasn't a ship alive that could outrun it.

Anna and the pirate passed overly large portraits of Markus and her as children. He paused to look at one but Anna dragged him along, not at all interested in her twenty-two-year-old self or the scar her father refused to have painted in the portrait.

"Ye were adorable, luv," he murmured, staring at a picture of Anna and Markus and two of their hounds before a fire. She had been six then. They rounded another hall and three steps later they were standing in front of her brother's door.

She sighed, looking at the thick, decorative molding and then down to the brass knob fashioned in the shape of a snake eating its body. Anna pursed her lips and tentatively turned the knob only to meet resistance. Sighing, she bunched up her skirts and settled onto her knees. A few short seconds later had Anna picking through her curls, procuring pins and a hammer to pick the lock.

"Problem?" the pirate asked, tilting his head and lounging against the wall with his hands in his pockets.

"Not for me," she replied. True to her word, the lock clicked and the door swung open less than a minute later. Anna stood, using the pirate's hand to help. She hastily turned a brass fixture near the door. Light flared into the room as lamps roared to life with newly born fire.

She stopped in her tracks and frowned.

Markus's room was a god-awful mess.

She tried to rationalize it. It had been years since her brother had been in this room. But it wasn't like Markus. He had always liked his things orderly despite the chaos that reigned over every other inch of his life. Anna had always been the opposite, her professional life organized and orderly where her personal quarters were the disaster.

"Is...that fucking cannon powder I smell?" the pirate asked from behind her. She looked back just in time to watch him close the door with his foot. "Definitely fucking cannon powder."

She sighed, slumping a little at the mess and dreading what they might stumble upon beneath the layers of dust. It was absolutely splendid that they knew where to find the despicable little scrap of leather. Anna had never gone snooping through her brother's things before and she wasn't about to start today.

Markus's bed sat across the room, a thick, dark rug in front of it and long narrow windows behind it. It had been carved from pale wood with nautical imagery in the headboard. Ships and sailors and the constellations they find their way by. Anna recognized a few. Mother might have always told them stories about myth, but Markus had told her stories about the stars.

She largely ignored any of the other trinkets in the room. The books, the sailing devices. A child's telescope to chart the stars and old parchment paper where Markus had clearly been penning his own maps. No, Anna made a beeline for the bed and hopefully the little box beneath it. The pirate's steps ate the space between the bed and the door, keeping time with her own.

"The prick's room always look like shite?"

Anna ignored the feeling of unease that built deep within her.

"No...normally you'd be able to eat off the floor."

Careful once more of her dress, Anna kneeled and looked under the bed with a cough. A thick layer of dust coated the floorboards. An old pair of undershorts was the only thing to be seen. She flicked them over her shoulder with a scowl. Markus had said the box slept beneath his bed, but the state of his room...

"Something wrong, luv?"

"There isn't anything...but maybe..." She trailed off, tapping one floorboard with a finger and then the one next to it. Squinting at the neglected boards, she tapped and slid her nail between them until she found one that wiggled. Anna grinned, prying the board up slowly. "Hello, beautiful."

"Appreciate the compliment, luv, but I think now is hardly the bloody time."

Anna rolled her eyes and set the board to the side, revealing a narrow, dark cavity beneath. She reached and rooted around until she grasped something cool and smooth. Sitting up, she stared down at the little metal rectangle in her hands. It has been made beautifully. There wasn't a seam that she could see, all flat grey edges except for an intricately crafted lock on the front.

Anna stayed on her knees, fiddling with the lock. What an interesting little box. It was rare that Anna encountered anything that gave her trouble. She tipped it upside down carefully and examined the bottom.

Pesky little bugger.

Markus had done his research when he purchased this devilish thing. If his intention had been to keep Anna out, he had certainly achieved it. She hoped it had cost him a fortune. Turning, she slid it to its side and applied pressure to one of her picks, a stray curl of blonde falling in her face.

She shook her head, glaring down at the damn thing. If her dress had been less form-fitting, she would have suggested they just take the box with them. But it was too bulky to fit even in the pirate's dinner jacket. He'd probably be patted down for weapons and then they'd be in real trouble. Not only would her father's personal guard find the box, but also the weapons the pirate had carefully tucked away.

Minutes passed and with each one her hands grew sweatier. Anna wiped them off on Markus's bedding several times, turning the damned box this way and that as she chewed on the inside of her cheek. With another few twists, the lock popped and the resistance she felt in her fingertips dropped away. Anna looked up to the pirate with a grin. The victory written in every inch of her features matched the dread in the pirate's.

"Shall we have a look?"

"Might as well," he said, bending at the hip to see inside the box.

She popped the lid open and reached inside, pushing a few things from her finger's path to grasp the only bit of leather. She unrolled the small parcel, scanning its contents. None of it meant anything at first glance, but continued exposure would only reveal more. She rolled it up upon realizing she didn't immediately recognize this language, nor the rather interesting symbol in its corner.

Anna smiled down at the map in her hands. This would be a true adventure, one fit for an archaeologist who had never wanted a stale life—a life questioning whether or not she had truly lived. The pirate cleared his throat, one of his hands turned in question. She looked at the leather of his glove and then up to his eyes.

"Is this where you whisk me away to the Pirate King?" she asked quietly.

He shook his head, speaking with a finality she hadn't heard from him yet, "Bloody hell, fem, no. Ye and I made a deal, aye? I'll no' be taking ye anywhere ye do no' wish."

The choice was easy enough. She trusted the pirate despite her better judgement. Well, that, and Anna wouldn't be able to conceal the map on her person in this particular gown. It lacked pockets, among other things. And he would be easy enough to keep an eye on.

She held out the map. His fingers brushed hers. "You swear?"

"On my fucking life."

The pirate sat down on Markus's bed directly in front of her. Anna remained on the floor, watching his expression shift. He rubbed the back of his neck, dropping his head down. He looked at her from beneath his long lashes, hair mussed from all the times he'd run his fingers through it. The pirate sighed, smacking the map against his thigh once.

"Tell me, beastie, how did ye come across this?" he asked, tentative and soft.

Anna sat up straight.

Now, that was a tale fit for a rainy day and much, much more rum. Anna had only disclosed all those details to one man and he was probably pacing his way through the floor at the Ascendant. She shook her head at the prospect of telling *this* pirate what she had done with *that* pirate. It had been years and yet Anna still felt jittery when she thought back to those few hours despite not being able to remember them.

What a curious thing the body was, always remembering what the mind might forget.

"It is an old, tedious tale, I assure you." She swallowed, waving her hand flippantly. She cleared her throat and stood, stepping back toward the door. "We should be leaving, anyway. We have what we came for and if we stay much longer we'll only press our luck."

The pirate remained seated on Markus's bed.

Anna crossed her arms and stared up at the ceiling, at the chandelier, at the stars her brother had painted. "I stole it."

"Why?"

"Because I wanted to," she said, meeting his gaze head on. "Because my father said no one could and I thought if anyone would be able to, it would be me. Turns out I was right."

The pirate dragged his hand down his face, exasperated in a way that was bone deep. "Shite, female, do ye *ever* think to ask?"

"Does the Pirate King think to ask before he whisks all those sons and daughters away?" Anna snapped, hands trembling. "Does he go door to door before they're loaded onto ships in chains and forced below deck?"

"It's—shite, he's no' the one doing that, luv," the pirate raised his voice, flustered.

"He is despicable and dangerous and the worst of what humanity has to offer. If not him, then who?"

"I've an inkling, and they'll pay their fucking due."

She waved her hand. "Well, good luck with that. The Coalition and its king are rather hard to pin down."

"Aye, they are." He nodded his head. "And yet ye, beastie, no' only got aboard but found your way into his cabin. So how did ye manage it? He doesn't take females there often."

"I was invited aboard. At the time I thought he was the Pirate King, later I learned he was the quartermaster." Anna laughed, turning away from him. Heat rushed to her cheeks. When she thought of Trevor Lovelace, she couldn't remember anything clearly. It was like seeing something from the corner of her eye, only for it to disappear when she turned. "One thing, well…one thing led to *another*."

"Do ye…regret it?"

Her gaze wandered from his eyes to the windows behind him. She could see out and across the grounds of her father's estate. The trees had blurred together into a single dark wall. Anna hadn't thought about it before, hadn't given any energy to contemplating how she felt about sleeping with the Pirate King only to steal something from him.

Let alone poisoning him.

She supposed that made her a bit of a rogue.

Anna pressed her lips into a thin line, brows pinching together. She'd been victorious, giddy, and accomplished in a way no one else had. She'd even dare say she had been satisfied completely. Sore. Disappointed with herself for bedding a ruthless skin peddler.

Then scared for her life once that pesky little smudge appeared on her hand. She wasn't one for superstition, but there was something about a mysterious black spot materializing on her palm that made even Anna apprehensive.

Regret, though?

She exhaled. "No. And if I did, I don't remember feeling it."

"Ye don't remember? I'm sorry, luv, but I reckon tumbling the Pirate King would be rather memorable."

She quirked an eyebrow, stepping back toward him. "I wasn't opposed to it," she said, feeling that was important information. He relaxed a hair, leaning forward onto his knees. "But we cleared out his rum and snuck off—" Anna paused, glancing away from him, the heat returning. "Afterward, I nabbed the map and walked back off the ship with almost none the wiser. I hit my head, it was a really nasty concussion."

The pirate stared hard, head canted just so. It gave him a predatory look, one that made her stomach flutter and her hair raise on end. He watched her, every breath she took, every contraction of her muscles. It was a heady feeling, knowing someone observed her so thoroughly they could count each of her heartbeats.

Anna wondered if she could do the same with him.

Finally, his throat bobbed. "Ye remember nothing else?"

"No."

It was the pirate's turn to stare at the ceiling. "Reckon it was at least enjoyable, aye?"

"I…" She trailed off, tilting her head and crossing her arms. "Honestly, pirate, I don't remember. It couldn't have been utterly terrible." She shook her head. "I guess we'll never know; the likelihood of repeating the events are slim to none on account he wants me dead."

"Coalition wants ye dead, no' the Pirate King."

"Semantics."

The pirate shrugged. "He might surprise ye. Reckon ye surprised him wi' that wee stunt." And then he laughed, shaking his head. "Knowing the Pirate King, it was fantastic, most like."

"Or perhaps he was average—uninspiring, even?" He opened his mouth to protest but Anna plowed ahead. For whatever reason, this topic concerned him greatly and she was enjoying making him squirm. "Or, maybe, since he did help me drink all that rum, he couldn't—"

"Shite, no." A brief note of panic flared in the pirate's voice. "'Tis no' enough rum in the world for that, lovely."

Anna chuckled, waving him off and spinning on a heel. She listened as he stood from the bed, his steps slow yet soft. "Come on, you. I've answered your questions."

"No' all of them."

"No?" She looked over her shoulder, reaching for the door knob.

"Why did ye do it?" the pirate asked quietly. When Anna only raised a brow, he rolled his neck and looked in the full-length mirror in the corner. "Tumble him?"

Anna took a deep breath, turning to lean back against the door. "I don't…I don't do that with just anyone, but I was there on the *Pale Queen* and wasn't sure what else to do, so I asked myself '*What would Markus do?*' I find most of my worst decisions come from that little wondering."

The pirate's jaw slackened and he turned toward her in surprise. "And Markus would do *that* wi' the Pirate King?"

"You mean the ol' in-out, in-out?" she teased.

Anna laughed outright at the contemplative look on his face and then covered her mouth to stifle the sound. He looked away from the mirror, brows drawn and jaw set. He shoved his hands deep down into his pockets, the map no longer out in the open. Anna scanned his body. Where had he hidden the blasted thing?

"He fancies men?"

She nodded her head. "Yes. And women. What of it?"

"Think naught of it. Anna, I have no' a problem wi' one male fancying another. Two of my gunners are married—"

"That is very progressive of you," she whispered, her heart thundering in her chest.

"No' progressive, *right*. Love is love." He paused, running his hand through his hair yet again. "I just…didn't fucking expect he'd fancy the Pirate King. 'Tis it the star-crossed lovers shite?"

"Oh, no. Markus would have no interest in that beast beyond an appreciative glance. But it is exactly the kind of reckless stunt he would dare attempt. I mean, he would have slept with *someone* while he was aboard the *Pale Queen*, but it wouldn't have been the Pirate King."

He turned a rakish, breathtaking smile toward Anna, raising his gaze to meet hers with a shyness she hadn't been prepared for. "Can't really blame the prick. I've heard Lovelace is as fine a specimen as they fucking come."

Anna pushed off the door. "I think I could drink to that, from what little I remember. But Markus prefers dainty individuals."

"The Pirate King is no' dainty," he announced with finality, maneuvering around Anna so he could open the door and peek out into the hallway.

"Aye," she played, bumping her shoulder against his. She turned away as he pulled his lips through his teeth, looking down on her with a brilliant smile.

The hall was as empty as it had been before and dimmer than Markus's room. Anna wasn't looking forward to the shadows that tucked themselves into every corner, to the monsters that would appear if only she would let her imagination loose. The pirate bumped her with his shoulder and then held out his elbow.

They were halfway down the hall when a faint tapping had Anna tipping her head. It sounded like it was coming from behind them. She turned, seeing a faint light coming from one of the rooms beyond Markus's. A denser set of footsteps followed the lighter pair. Her father had certainty outdone himself in staffing the halls tonight.

Anna glanced down the hall at the growing light, a small bit of panic flooding her veins. She turned in a circle, looking for an escape. Anna reached for the nearest door, turning the knob only to find it locked. Bloody hell. Could she pick it in time to shove the pirate in? Anna wasn't sure. She closed her eyes. There had to be a way out. There was *always* a way out. If she couldn't think of one, she would make one.

What would Markus do?

Something surely idiotic with dramatic flair.

She opened her eyes and stared at the pirate.

Her brother would create a distraction, one that would explain his being in a dark hall this late at night with none the wiser. Why he might be hiding away. One that would make it impossibly awkward, one that would deter questions from being asked. She dragged her lip through her teeth, watched as the pirate's mouth moved without sound coming out.

The steps grew louder.

"Trust me," was all she had time to mutter before his back thumped hard enough against the wall that it would certainly draw attention. His eyebrows skyrocketed, mouth opening in question. Anna's throat bobbed, taking all her insecurity with it. They needed a distraction to provide a reason for their being in this wing.

Anna would give them on—and she might even make a show of it.

His gaze dropped to her lips and she pretended not to notice. Surely, she could have come up with a better excuse, a better plan, but seeing him stare at her lips evaporated the urgency to find one. Only one thought occupied space in her head.

Anna wanted to kiss the pirate so very badly.

The feeling was fierce, leaving her raw and breathless. She looked to his lips and then back up to his eyes. Her hands shook but she forced them to move and to do so quickly. Like ripping off a bandage so fast the body didn't realize what had happened to begin with. So fast that the prospect of doubt would remain in her head. Anna's fingers curled around his neck and her thumbs brushed either side of his jaw. And then she yanked his head straight down and pressed her lips to his, listening as the steps drew closer.

Something warm zinged through her as the pirate stilled completely. Anna wasn't entirely sure he was breathing but then she opened her mouth and drew his lip through her teeth, coaxing a small bit of movement from him. His tongue brushed Anna's, unsure and shy. He was careful and gentle, keeping his hands at his sides. Restrained, so completely and pointlessly restrained.

Anna leaned back, eyes closed, sharing the pirate's breath.

He cleared his throat as her hands slid from his jaw and down his neck only to come to rest against his chest. He was breathing hard, chest rising and falling noticeably beneath her fingers.

She opened her eyes, tipping her chin up to catch his gaze. His irises had been dark before but they were impossibly so now. She was close enough to tell they were solid black, like the night sky. No hints of blue or brown or green.

And they were hungry.

Anna pressed her thighs together, arching her back and leaning away to gain some distance between their faces. His throat bobbed and the weight of his hand landed on her hip, his thumb tracing bone. The other splayed against the wall, fingers outstretched. Anna figured he must have kept himself from falling by throwing his arm out like that.

The pressure of his fingers increased, a slight tug. A question, she realized, leaning toward him. He was asking her a question, waiting for her to make the next move. Anna's breath grew tight; she knew what she wanted, but she also knew what a splendidly horrible idea it was.

His eyes twinkled. *Ask me to move.*

But she couldn't.

Ask me to stop.

And she wouldn't.

Instead, she pulled him closer, fingers clenched around the lapels of his coat.

It was like a switch flipped in the pirate.

Where his mouth had been tentative and unsure, now it was heavy and hungry. She opened her mouth, grinning against his lips on a small laugh. One second Anna stood in front of him, his back to the wall, and then she felt the cool plaster through her gown, the pressure steady against her back, silk buttons pressing into her spine.

The pirate's hands were gentle and warm as they traveled up and down. His lips dropped from her mouth to her jaw and lower still as Anna's fingers threaded through his hair. His hands slid down until they were beneath her ass. He lifted, pressing his hips into Anna's, effectively pinning her. Wrapping her legs around his waist, she tipped her head back, heat flooding her cheeks and growing lower. Her gown bunched around her thighs, exposing her skin to the cool air.

Anna moaned softly, lips pressed into a tight line between her teeth. The pirate answered, the rumble starting in his chest before tickling against her throat. She had the strangest feeling of déjà vu, like she had done this before. It was absurd. Anna would have most definitely remembered being pinned against the wall with the pirate's hips grinding into hers. With his lips and teeth and tongue at her throat.

She had experienced want before, but never like this. The world tilted and Anna could feel the pirate growing between her legs. She cocked her head to the side, exposing more of her neck. She was hardly an expert in this field but it had never been like this. Not with Bryce nor any other.

The reminder doused a bit of the flame but not enough to put out the embers. The reminder of what they still had to accomplish and who they were crashed over her like a wave, but Anna couldn't find it in herself to really care. She had read enough stories about star-crossed lovers growing up to know they only ever ended in tragedy, but that didn't stop the characters then and it wouldn't stop Anna now.

"More," she breathed.

The pirate chuckled against the bit of skin where her neck met her shoulder, drawing it between his teeth and tongue with a suck. His left hand slid up, a lovely pressure around her ribs and then higher. A thumb brushed over her breast.

Anna sucked in a tight breath as that thumb pressed against the scar on her sternum and slowly traced it upward, the rest of his palm trailing over her sensitive skin. She was nearly nauseous, she hated that the horrible little line was out, disliked it even more that the pirate gave it attention instead of the parts of her that so desperately wanted it.

But then his hand curled around her neck, tracing the topmost bit of her scar with his thumb, his lips on the other side of her jaw near her ear. She could feel it, that there were words he was searching for and unable to find. The hand still around her ass tightened and his mouth opened to speak, his breath hot against her ear.

A man cleared his throat.

The pirate froze, muscles coiling tight beneath her fingers. Anna winced, looking over the pirate's shoulder, his lips just grazing her skin. She had been expecting a guard; she had planned for a guard. One that would be flustered by the sight of them. One that wouldn't ask questions, that would just chastise her and turn around after smelling the champagne on her breath.

That is not at all who was there. Her cheeks grew warmer, eyes widening as she recognized the small masculine frame, the bottle green eyes and golden blond hair.

God, she might die of embarrassment.

Mihkel Tamm leaned against the opposite wall, arms crossed against his chest with a thinly manicured brow raised. "If I had known your quarter-life crisis would look like *this*, I would have requested one as well."

She swallowed, opened her mouth, snapped it closed. The pirate's fingers loosened as the pressure from his hips lightened. Anna slid back to the ground, heels clicking as they connected with the wood flooring.

Anna straightened her gown, pulling it down. "Hello, Mihk."

"Should I inquire as to what this is about?" He motioned vaguely.

"Helping Markus, remember?"

"And helping Markus involves snogging outside his room?"

Anna shrugged. "Seems a fitting punishment."

"All jesting aside, he is going to be absolutely appalled."

The pirate kept his gaze on the floorboards, one hand coming up to rub at the back of his neck. She forced the grin from her face at the soft pink that colored his cheeks. Anna was entirely sure her cheeks were a similar color but seeing it on his face made the butterflies in her stomach flutter all the faster.

"Good," she told Mihk. "We've caught him doing worse."

Mihk's cringe quickly turned into a smile. "That we have. Now"—he clapped his hands together—"I do believe it is time for you to abscond with your handsome stranger. Our dear friend Bryce has just arrived and I thought you should know. I have been diligently searching every room for you to deliver the very news."

"Including the closets?" She grinned, bringing a light blush to Mihk's face.

"Especially the closets," a taller man chuckled, leaning out a door ten or so feet back with a devilish grin.

Anna dragged her gaze from his shined boots to his dusky brown eyes. His hair was shorn close against his scalp, a rich brown in color, the same as his eyebrows. If not for those rather bold bits above his eyes, she would not have been able to remember his hair color. It had been years since she'd seen Senator Hayhurst's son. Anna supposed that's what happened when one joined the Briland Navy.

"Bastian, it is simply splendid to see you."

Bastian scoffed. "Quit acting the part of the lady, we both know you're not one." His brown eyes centered on the pirate and Anna stiffened. Bugger, she hadn't planned for this. Bastian squinted. "Do I know you?"

The pirate stood up a little straighter and then a mischievous smile curled at his lips and he relaxed into his frame, keeping his hands in his pockets. He rocked back on his heels and tilted his head to the side. "No, mate. But most wish they did."

She cleared her throat, lacing her fingers through the pirate's. "This is Bastian Hayhurst. He's a captain in the Briland

Navy. Senator Spencer Hayhurst's son…" She trailed off, unsure of what else to say.

"I know of him." The pirate continued to grin, though it was turning into a darker thing. One made for a shark, for all things that might swim around in the dark.

"And this is?" Bastian tipped his head, brows pulling together as he once again looked the pirate over.

"My companion."

"Does he have a name?"

She laughed, really laughed. "I suppose so, but if we knew it he wouldn't be nearly as handsome."

The pirate stepped forward, wrapping a hand around her waist and tugging her to him. She knew the meaning of the act; he thought they should go and she couldn't agree more. "If you'll excuse us, it is time to leave. Thank you for the warning, Mihk."

"Of course, Anna." He grinned, but his smile slowly fell from his face. "Did…did you sort the business with Markus?"

Anna glanced at the captain nervously.

"He can keep a secret," Mihk said quietly.

She swallowed. "It's a work in progress; we'll have to speak later about clearing his name. I'm hoping it'll be over soon. Is it unlocked?"

Mihk nodded, glancing at Bastian. "Is he okay?"

"I hope so."

Anna thought of the dark circles that had made themselves home beneath his eyes and of the haunted look Markus occasionally wore when he didn't think she was watching. He tossed and turned at night and he was still healing physically. Anna knew it would be a while yet before he began healing in his head or in his heart. His soul had been bruised with the experience. Time might not even be enough to heal him.

But she hoped it would be.

CHAPTER 34

"This way," she whispered, pulling him toward a spiraling staircase. "We won't have to go near the ballroom if we use these stairs."

Trevor nodded, no' entirely hearing the lass. He couldn't handle this kind of multitasking. He was hot and cold and his skin was too tight against his bones. He'd never been one to let nerves bother him but, hell, they were bothering him now. There were too many things needing doing and yet he couldn't focus on a single bloody thing.

No' the fact that the shite left *Jules* in charge of the *Queen*. No' Tate deciding *now* was the time to run off on a bloody adventure. No' even the cursed spot on Anna's wee hand concerned him at current and that fucker presented the biggest problem.

All Trevor could think about was Anna shoving him against the wall, of her hands on his neck and fingers in his hair. Of what she tasted like and the sounds he could coax from her. It had been a taste, a small bite, and, fuck him, he wanted more. His cheeks heated and he looked out into the shadows on the other side of the banister.

Shite, he was all twisted up inside.

He chewed at his lip, watching the steps and decorative rug they jogged down, Anna's delicate fingers laced through his, pulling him forward through her da's estate. He breathed out; he had to focus. There wasn't much Trevor could do about his babe of a brother's poorly timed adventure or the shite leaving Jules in charge. The distance was too grand and he hadn't a bloody clue where to start aside from the nearest bakery.

"Just down that hall and out the door." Anna stopped at the bottom of the stairs and stared at the end of the hall, one hand in his and the other lifting her skirt.

The gown was one of the loveliest things Trevor had ever seen, glimmering like starlight even with the brass sconces turned low. Long, elegant sleeves and delicate silk buttons along her spine. Bloody hell, and then there was the neckline, cutting its way to her sternum and showing off that scar of hers.

She looked up at him right as he glanced down; her eyes were the clearest blue Trevor had ever seen in his life, like the shallows of Tiburon. The very same where many a ship dug their grave, wrecking against the sudden change in depth.

Oh, aye.

He'd take the lass wherever she wanted to go, all she need do is ask. But her worry gnawed at him. Worry about the Pirate King and who she thought he was. Of what she thought he would do to her. He wanted to tell her but that ship had sailed, it was too late now. His heart tightened behind his rib cage.

She was a bloody witch.

How else could she squeeze his heart wi'out reaching into his chest?

Trevor realized she was staring at him again when her fingers tightened and relaxed several times. When he turned to her she was looking up, brow raised. He tried smiling to let her know she had naught to worry about. Gods-damned idiot, as if a bloody smile could protect her.

"Miss Savage?" a man called from down the hall.

Anna froze, head snapping in the man's direction. Trevor followed her line of sight, jaw tightening enough to crack his teeth. At the end of the hall stood three men in matching dark uniforms. He squinted, keeping track of every step the bastards took. As they grew closer, Trevor realized he'd seen the guards at the door wearing the same fucking thing.

These were her da's guards and Trevor wasn't sure if that was better or worse than marshals.

She cleared her throat, stepping toward him until her arm pressed into his. "Hello, gentlemen. Is there something I can help you with?"

"Yes, miss. Your father has requested your presence at his private dinner with the other senators."

She frowned. "I don't suppose this is one of those optional offers, is it?"

"Afraid not, miss."

"Ah, bugger."

Worse.

This was definitely fucking worse.

CHAPTER 35

Awkward was not a strong enough word to describe this dinner.

A long table carved from a single tree with rings exposed on its lacquered top dominated the middle of the space. A red velvet runner ran its length, plates of every dish imaginable between Anna and the Briland Senate around her. Bowls of grapes and blueberries, sliced apples dipped in caramel. Fatty slices of prime rib and lemon-scented salmon. She even spied lamb chops off in the distance. They were Markus's favorite—what a shame he wasn't here enjoying this horrendous family dinner.

Anna glanced left and then right, taking in every member of the Senate. There were ten in all, including her father. Every member was a varying shade of white or cream with eyes that were blue or brown. Chelsea Cunningham's were green, a sickeningly light shade like his daughter's. Their hair ranged in shades of blond, brown, black, or...well, bald. Anna tipped her head at Thatcher Bourke, one in the latter category, who was dabbing his napkin against his brow.

Cameron Fry cleared his throat from across the table, a nervous pink shade that only accentuated his beak-like nose. Another one of the senators twitched, clinking his glass against his plate. They were nervous, quite nervous, and rightfully so. John Savage's icy stare hadn't lifted from Anna since she had walked in the room, thoroughly interrupting his birthday dinner with the good old boys club despite being summoned.

He had expected Anna, but not at all who she was with.

"They—they're requesting a hearing," Pell Trafford murmured, his voice a gravelly scratch from a sickness he'd had years ago. Though Anna suspected that attempting to reign in his four boisterous daughters might be the real culprit.

"Of course, they are," Spencer Hayhurst said. "And I think we should. One of them might have a good idea on how to solve this blasted mess."

She lifted a small square of roasted salmon to her lips, gaze still on her plate. The fish was buttery and delicious, smothered in a lovely lemon butter dill sauce. Next to her salmon laid stalks of asparagus seared in oil and seasoned with salt and pepper.

Chelsea Cunningham grunted, his greying brows pulling together in thought as he cut into his lamb chop. His voice wasn't quite as deep as his son's; it had always struck Anna as strange. "Tremble's Bay is hardly in our waters. A mile to the south and it wouldn't be."

"I do believe we all remember where Tremble's Bay is." Raleigh Vance rolled his light brown eyes, chin resting on his fist.

"I was just—"

"I know what you were implying," Vance interrupted. "But Tremble's Bay *is* in our waters and *is* our responsibility. I agree with Pell, we should host a hearing."

She glanced at the pirate through her eyelashes, wondering if he thought this entire farce as comical as she did. They would decide nothing now and likely would decide nothing later as well. Tremble's Bay would continue to be a topic they danced around.

The pirate shifted, tilting his head in the direction of a conversation happening down the table between Cameron Fry and Thatcher Bourke. What were they saying to catch his interest? He sat relaxed enough, back straight and powerful shoulders curled. The dinnerware was positively tiny in his hands. He had a fatty slice of prime rib on one side of his plate and a biscuit and mashed potatoes smothered in gravy on the other.

"We'll discuss it later," her father finally said.

She looked up, briefly meeting his gaze before returning to her dinner.

If her father's icy stare lifted from her, it was only to seek out the pirate.

The only sound in the private dining hall was dinnerware on porcelain plates, their edges gilded in gold. Anna reached forward, swirling her wine before taking a sip, gaze lazily roving the table.

They had been crammed in around the table with her father at their head. Anna sat directly to his right and the pirate on the other side of her. Raleigh Vance and Ramsey Frost sat across from them, Vance raising his clear flute in salute and Frost winking.

Chelsea Cunningham sat to the right of the pirate, Anna knew her father had done that intentionally with her past relationship with his son looming about them like a storm cloud. The pirate's presence certainly wasn't helping Senator Cunningham's mood, but if the pirate noticed the older man's animosity he didn't show it.

Anna's gaze continued to wander around the table. She swallowed another mouthful of wine and wondered if the pirate knew any of the men at her father's table by name. Perhaps they only looked like faceless, old men with hardly any distinctions between them.

"Bloody delicious, this," the pirate murmured.

Anna nodded her head in agreement, lifting another bite to her mouth. "My father enjoys borrowing the Senate's private chefs for all of his gatherings. Lovely men. They make the best biscuits."

He grunted, shoving another bite into his mouth with his weensy fork.

"Anna, darling," John Savage finally deigned to address her. "How thoughtful of you to join us."

She gritted her teeth at his sweet tone and at the shards of glass contained within it. Swallowing, Anna put her silverware down and turned to her father. He sat back in his chair, one elbow resting on the arm. "I wasn't aware that was an option."

"You could have chosen to ignore me—like you do about most matters."

Anna reached for her flute of wine, swirling it before downing it in a single gulp. "And miss this fine dinner with all your friends? I think not. You know how much I enjoy these parties. Especially the desserts."

A server appeared from one of the many darkened arches behind the tables to fill her glass before slipping back into the shadows.

"It does appear you've been partaking in one too many. Your mother had the same unhealthy relationship with sweets."

The room silenced, silverware settling down against plates and glasses hovering before mouths. Even the pirate at her side stiffened, his dark eyes turning on her father. His mouth had set in a thin line, a frown bracketing his lips as his brows pinched in displeasure.

"You are the only man I have ever met who has a problem with my thighs." Anna laughed, the grin on her face a vicious thing. "I assume you requested us for a reason?"

"Us?" John Savage's frown deepened almost into a snarl. Anna steeled her spine and held his gaze, refusing to look away even as he motioned to the pirate with his stout crystal glass. "I did not request him."

"Did you expect me to leave him with my coat?"

"I did not request a lowborn criminal from the Emerald Isles. Not unless he can pay your weight in gold." John Savage tipped his head back, the well-trimmed beard around his mouth threaded with grey.

"He's not a criminal."

No, worse—he was a pirate.

But she wasn't about to tell her father that. Good God, that would have been a death sentence for the redhead and institutionalization for Anna. She swallowed. This couldn't be a drawn-out affair. She couldn't go to battle with her father with the Senate watching, not if she wanted answers to her questions. Luckily, she knew just how to offend John Savage. She'd had years of practice, after all.

"Every man and woman from the Emerald Isles is a criminal, darling," her father said slowly.

"Well, that's too bad," she breathed, a bit of red creeping into the edges of her gaze. "We were planning on, what, fifteen children? I already emptied my savings"—she paused to take another bite. Based on her father's expression, he already knew that.—"to buy a lovely little cottage on the coast of Aidanburgh. I think the sea air will do wonders for the babe," she said, lips curling into a small smile as she dropped one hand to her lap.

Her father's gaze narrowed as it tracked the movement. He stared at her stomach, pausing in raising his glass to his lips. Senator Cunningham's knife squeaked across his plate as he dared to lean past the pirate and glare at her. She felt the heat of his stare on the side of her head as the pirate choked on his bite of food, a blush high on his cheeks.

John Savage's glass thunked against the tabletop. "Excuse us."

Anna froze, glancing from left to right as every member of the Briland Senate stood and filed from the room. Senator Fry glanced at her once before exiting and Frost's lips had pinched tight, face flushed. There was nothing but the sound of their footsteps against the flooring. Senator Chelsea Cunningham turned, a smug expression on his face as he closed the doors behind them.

The pirate stiffened, his hand finding her thigh and giving it a squeeze.

"I wondered when you would send your friends away."

"If you wanted to have a private conversation, Anna, you need only ask."

She cocked a brow. "Fine, what is this about? It's not like you to make a spectacle of me in front of the Senate. You usually reserve that for Markus."

"You're here because I want to know where that brother of yours has run off to. I was expecting him and I figured, being his twin, *you* might know where he is. You haven't heard from him, have you, daughter?"

"I don't expect you to keep up with my escapades, *Father*, but I've been spelunking about in the jungles for over a month now. It was rather fortuitous that I returned when I did, otherwise I would have missed your birthday."

"Escapades. How apt a description." He sighed, looking at the pirate, clearly unimpressed. "I assume that's where you stumbled upon this one."

Anna glanced at the pirate and then back to her father. "Actually, I stumbled upon him on the train. One might say it was love at first sight."

"I tire of your games. Where is my son?"

"I don't know," she said, turning back to her salmon, knife in one hand and fork in the other with the pirate tapping his shanty against her thigh. "It's not my job to keep track of him. Is he not wasting away at the Charleston Naval Base or blistering beneath the sun on the *King's Ransom*? The poor man's talents are wasted in the navy."

John Savage laughed. "What talents, darling? Fighting and fucking and gambling away every last penny he has to his name? I've had to invest a great deal of time figuring out ways to save his good name."

"He *is* quite good at it, isn't he?" Anna asked around a small mouthful of salmon. "But there are worse talents Markus could cultivate than cartography."

"Like traipsing through the jungle with strange men beneath his standing?"

"Traipsing? That's not even the best part." Anna grinned. "Could you imagine if we both walked arm in arm with strange, mysterious men beneath the sweltering sun, unaccompanied? If Markus could remove his clothes half as fast as I can, you would certainly be in trouble."

"Your brother has been arrested," he said severely. "This is not a jesting matter, Annaleigh."

Anna stilled in lifting her flute of wine to her lips. It was a fraction too long, her body much too stiff to be natural. Bugger. She blinked slowly, swallowing a sip of wine before putting it down. "I thought you said you didn't know where he was."

"I don't. Just the circumstances around his arrest. Marshals apprehended him and—" He stopped, a scowl deeply engraving itself into his face before he snarled. "—*lost* him."

"That's excellent news!" Anna pretended to brighten. "If it's your dogs after him, you can simply call them off and sweep the whole thing under the rug. Like everything else."

He ignored her slight, swirling his glass again, the movement slow and purposeful, his gaze narrowed on the redhead at her side. To the pirate's credit, he didn't flinch under John Savage's stare, he simply let it glance off him like rain.

Anna remained quiet, watching the way the wheels turned behind her father's eyes as he glared at the man at her side. She didn't like the way her father squinted at him and found herself leaning forward to intercept his stare.

The pirate had done an excellent job of remaining outside her father's interest so far. Anna was actually quite pleased that he had listened to her warning for as long as he had, but, now that father's gaze was anchored to the pirate she felt him stiffen from next to her and glanced at him in response.

Keep your mouth closed, she glared at the pirate.

The pirate shrugged his shoulder imperceptivity and Anna's heart began beating harder in her chest.

"Can I help ye, mate?" the pirate asked, staring at her father from the corner of his eye.

"Surprisingly enough, I do believe you can." Her father's lip twitched, swirling the crystal glass with his fingertips. "Would you care to introduce us?"

"Not entirely," she replied lightly. "I'd much rather talk about Markus and your opinion of his perceived unfortunate shortcomings."

He set his glass down, ignoring her. "I suppose the little details really aren't all that important. I named your brother and I named you. I can name this man as well."

Anna put her flute down, gaze lifting to her father's. "What are you talking about?"

"Someone has to attend Chesterhale, but it will not be one of my children."

"Attend? Is that what we're calling *hanging* these days?" She laughed, slow and deliberate, a nervous sweat gilding her spine. "What fine form, Father. Cleaning up your children's messes by pinning blame and consequence on an innocent man. Tell me, what is it you think Markus has done that is so terrible that it warrants sacrificing a man you do not know—one you do not even *wish* to know?"

"Conspiring with pirates. Possession of a pirate map. Resisting arrest. Worsening the friction between Briland and the Coalition. Threatening our precarious peace. The list goes on," he rattled off, each accusation sounding more akin to gunfire than her father speaking. There was a force behind his words, a purpose she did not understand. "The Senate knows about the Pirate King's map but not about who has it. Secrets do not remain secrets forever. If I'm to keep him from hanging, we must act with haste, Anna."

"I don't know anything about this and I won't be caught up in your murderous schemes," she growled, throwing her napkin onto her plate as she stood.

"Sit back down."

"No."

A knot developed in her throat. Her father knew. Her father knew why Markus had been detained and that he had escaped the marshals. She closed her eyes. It must have been John Savage who had sent the marshals. It explained why her brother's room had been tossed as well. Her father wanted the Pirate King's map but wasn't sure where Markus had put it. Anna hadn't thought him capable and he had gone and plucked that last bit of faith she had in him.

Her father snapped his fingers, a smug gleam in his eyes.

A marshal stepped from every archway, a total of ten in all— five in front and five in back.

"Shite," the pirate sighed, hand tightening around his steak knife.

Anna sat.

Shite, indeed.

CHAPTER 36

Fucking hell, Markus was a gods-damned copy of John Savage.

Was no' important at the moment, but Trevor could hardly focus on anything else. At least Anna's prick of a brother had a good idea of what he'd look like in thirty years. Trevor chuckled, drawing the man's icy gaze. Anna peeked over her shoulder, brows drawn in confusion and concern.

Apparently now was no' a laughing time.

"Shite, sorry. 'Tis a serious moment," he muttered, looking from Anna to her bastard of a da.

Two decades and no' a thing had changed.

He was still one of the biggest asses Trevor'd ever met. As a captain in the Briland Navy, John Savage'd been a pain in the ass, knee-deep in all sorts of shite. Blowing holes in ships and stealing from the Coalition. He'd seemed honorable at the time, even Trevor could admit that, but then Savage'd created a fucking armada out of merchant ships and they did no' follow any rule unless it passed through John Savage's lips first.

But the men on his ships? They were no' honorable. Nay, he'd filled his ships to the fucking brim wi' mercenaries and worse. Anything and anyone to keep his cargo safe. Trevor'd never dealt wi' him directly but he remembered the Old Crow cursing about it to anyone that'd listen.

The marshal across the way leaned against the arch, one of his meaty hands coming to rest on his rapier. Trevor exhaled, moving his gaze from one to the next. They all looked prim and proper in their matching uniforms, revolvers hanging from their hips wi' rapiers in stiff leather sheaths. Five in front and five in back. Trevor breathed deeply; it was a fair number of men to cut through but he could do it. It wasn't himself he was worried about.

"Fine, we'll do this your way, darling. Arrest them both. Take my daughter to her room and the man to Chesterhale. Do not leave her, though, someone must keep an eye on her."

The marshals stepped forward, focused on Trevor. Oh, aye, he was the one to worry about. Anna could hold her own in a tussle but even Trevor'd have a difficult time in that bonnie dress. There had to be a way out of this, he just hadn't found the wee fucker yet.

Did the lass have a plan?

He glanced at her, to the wee arch of her brow.

Oh, aye, lass had a plan.

"*Arrest* us? Are you out of your damn mind?"

John Savage held a hand up and the marshals stopped in their advance. Trevor shifted, grip tightening around his steak knife. Another one laid a foot away. John Savage did no' think this through, leaving so many knives at their disposal. Should have waited until the desserts. Reckon he could still do some damage wi' a spoon though.

Then again, the bastard had thought he was summoning his daughter and had no' realized just who he was inviting to his dinner table.

"Would you care to explain?"

"That is a very sad story about wanting to keep Markus from hanging but I don't believe it for one second." She slid forward, rump on the edge of her seat, leaning those lovely elbows on the table. "You arrest us and you'll never find the Pirate King's map."

"And *you* know where it is?"

She snorted. "Don't play dumb, its unbecoming, Father. Of course, I know where the Pirate King's map is. That's why I'm here at dinner with you, isn't it? To get it out of that splendid little box for you?"

Trevor saw it then, he did. John Savage's jaw ticked, a vein in his neck bubbling to the surface.

"Ah." Anna leaned forward, placing her chin on her fingers. "That is why. It's a nasty little box, isn't it? All the king's horses and all the king's men couldn't get into the box again." Anna paused, squinting at her father. "You want the map. But the Coalition wants it too and you have to contend with them."

They sure fucking did.

The Viper'd been hounding Trevor for the damn thing for a decade. The cunt'd never be getting the wee map, no' wi' where it led. That island was a hollow place, a husk of what it should be. He'd had nightmares for fucking years about what slept in its waters and swam through its jungles. Of what had happened the last time he set foot there. Just thinking of the damned place sent a hot shiver up and down Trevor's spine.

John Savage sighed, focusing the intensity of his gaze on Anna. "The problem, darling, is that you think you are so very clever and you are not."

"What?" Anna twitched at Trevor's side.

"Let me tell you how this will play out. The criminal will be going where he belongs, charged as a pirate trying to abduct my daughter and taking the place of my son at the gallows because that little map you think I am so interested in will be found on him and returned to me. You, my darling daughter, will be taking a rather extended vacation with your brother somewhere warm and remote to promote better health. Hysteria, they'll say. It's in the blood, they'll say. No one will question it."

Trevor glanced at Anna; some old fearful, feral thing stared back from her irises. Blood drained from her face, leaving behind rosy cheeks and pale skin. Something in her da's words terrified her, Trevor couldn't place exactly which one of the bloody things had done it.

"But it doesn't have to be that way, darling. What is it you want? That seat on the Board of Antiquity? Consider it done, you need only give me that map and let the marshals walk this man from the room. You can go back to your dirt and ruins, Markus can run a debt of the likes I've yet to see and sleep his way through half of Bellcaster. I do not care."

The lass leaned forward and Trevor started sweating. He didn't think she would let him go to the gallows for her brother, but crazier shite had happened in his life. Crazier shite had happened in the last gods-damned month. Her gaze dropped to her hands, which were folded atop the table now.

He closed his eyes briefly.

If the lass gave him up, he'd think naught about it. Just react. React. React. Trevor was fucking king of reacting to shite that could no' be planned. And even if the marshals caught him and sent him on his way to Chesterhale, he'd bloody live with it. He couldn't escape the devil every time the bastard came knocking. But he didn't have to make it easy.

Anna and her da continued arguing in the background. He didn't care much for the outcome, he was fighting his way out of here regardless. Either the lass would be wi' him or she wouldn't. A sweat broke out against his back and chest and he tried pretending like neither of the options fucking mattered to him. He'd known the bloody lass a few weeks, what was fourteen days?

Trevor shook his head, fucking bitter.

Everything. Fourteen days could be everything to the right people.

Their bickering quieted and Trevor opened his eyes.

"A seat on the Board? You could truly guarantee that?" Anna asked, brows drawing together. "And Markus wouldn't be a wanted man anymore?"

Bloody hell.

"The map for a seat and the man for your brother. It really is that simple. All of this will go away."

Trevor had no' always been everyone's first choice and this reminded him of that. Shite, knowing Anna might no' choose him stung and brought him back to Aidanburgh. Back to nights his stomach growled while Tate and Taylee feasted on fucking rubbish. Back to the Old Crow taking a lash to his fucking back.

Back to setting foot on that fucking island.

More, more, more.

Always fucking more.

It brought him right back to that.

Anna nodded slowly—considering. Closing his eyes, he breathed deep. Counted to ten and then did it again. When he opened his eyes, the lass's gaze hadn't moved from her da but there was something cold in it. Bloody hell, he did no' want to fight the lass too. He had the map, he and his crew could go home to Tiburon but—

"I'll earn that seat myself," she said, gown shimmering like a gods-damned dying star and then threw a butter knife at her da.

It landed next to his head, a clear warning as the wee lass spun, a steak knife tumbling through the air behind Trevor. He didn't react right away, instead staring at the wee lass in disbelief. She picked him. She fucking picked *him* and he could no' bloody believe it.

Anna turned to him, just a peek over her shoulder. The concern on her face shocked him, forcing his body to move of its own fucking accord. That's right, he had a bloody job to do. He threw three knives across the room. Each found a home in a marshal, like pins in a cushion. Twisting, he picked up his chair and lobbed it too.

There was work to be done and he was happy to do it if it meant he and Anna were on the same side of the bloody line.

He took one marshal down.

And then another.

John Savage yelled orders in the background, some shite about being careful wi' his daughter, and Anna's heels clicked against the flooring. As the haze settled in, Anna grabbed his hand and pulled. He heard the revolver go off, felt the rain of splinters as the chair he'd been in front of fractured. She sprinted toward the door, her skirts bunched in one hand, his hand in the other. She rammed the door open, deep, gasping breaths raised her chest as she forced it closed behind them.

"Luv—"

"We'll bolt the door. I didn't want them to—never mind," she heaved out, already running to an old suit of armor. Trevor leaned against the doors to keep them closed. She grunted as she lifted the overly large axe, bringing it back and sliding it through the handles.

She leaned back as the thumping started, eyes closed and breathing deep. Bloody hell, she was beautiful, some hairs falling from her braided crown. She had a small scratch along her cheek and a bruise already purpled on her collarbone.

Fucker was lucky Trevor did no' see it happen.

Trevor's brows drew together as she tipped her chin up and gazed into his eyes. His hand acted of its own damn accord, raising and brushing his thumb against the scratch. Anna leaned into the touch, eyes fluttering shut a moment as she pressed her cheek into his palm. He felt her breath on the inside of his wrist and stilled.

Her throat bobbed. "I'm fine, pirate."

"Ye sure?"

She nodded her head, lacing her fingers through his. "This way. The marshals will use the staff corridors to exit since we barricaded them in. I don't want to waste our head start."

Bloody hell, if it meant keeping her hand in his, he'd run to the edges of the damned earth.

CHAPTER 37

Bugger, they'd almost shot him.

She couldn't get the image out of her head, it pounded in her skull with each footfall. Anna had turned around and there a marshal stood behind the pirate with his revolver raised. She hated to think about what could have happened had she been a second later. Instead of the chair fracturing, it might have been him and she couldn't—she just couldn't.

Anna heaved a breath in and then another out, her hand tightly laced with the pirate's. His breathing echoed hers, his gaze jumping from one part of the corridor to the next, looking for trouble in every nook and shadow. Anna hoped they didn't find any.

This was enough trouble.

Senator John Savage would not forget his daughter spitting his deal in his face and refusing to let the pirate take the blame for something that wasn't his fault.

"What a lovely da' ye have," the pirate huffed, looking around a corner before letting her round it.

"I admit he's a bit rough around the edges," she replied, scanning the windows to their right.

"But?"

"No, that's it."

"Ye worried me there for a wee second," the pirate said stiffly.

She glanced up, noting the serious look on his face. "Oh, please, as if I'd give you up for a chair. Chair can't carry my shopping bags."

He laughed a brief, anxious sound as they rounded another corner, matching how Anna felt nearly exactly. He looked down at her, the smile still on his lips, boyish, brilliant, and fierce. He had cleaned up well, his eleven or so freckles standing out against the light tan of his skin. Anna grinned back and then slammed into something solid, stumbling in her heels.

She blinked, focused on the three pairs of black boots standing just in front of her and the black leather pants tucked into them. She glanced to the side, noticing the black coat and the hand that wrapped around her bicep; it had probably been the only thing stopping her from crashing to the floor.

"Excuse us." She chuckled, embarrassed to have been so absorbed that she had stopped paying attention to where they were going.

The pirate stiffened, Anna could only wonder at what. Her gaze continued upward until it snagged on the matte button at the man's throat. Bugger, that's why the pirate stiffened. He was a marshal. Which meant the other boots belonged to marshals as well. And it was a marshal's hand wrapped around her bicep.

"Excuse us," she repeated with a swallow, pulling her arm back only for the marshal to tighten his grip. She winced. "Your grip is quite tight."

Turning her head, Anna glanced at the pirate to see what he was thinking. But his attention remained anchored to the hand wrapped around her arm, something dangerous burning to the surface of his dark eyes. In a blink, her pirate was gone, replaced by whatever beast he kept tucked away beneath his skin. The same one who had come to life on the train and in the bazar. The very one she'd seen staring back at her when she'd grabbed his arm earlier to run.

"My lass says your grip is too tight, bucko," he said plainly, gaze rising to meet the marshal's. "I suggest ye let go."

"Afraid Senator Savage has requested his daughter's presence." The marshal grinned, tugging her forward.

Anna threw her other arm out to catch her balance. Of course, they couldn't catch a break. The pirate's growl rumbled from deep in his chest, his step forward a promise, not a threat. She cleared her throat, fingers just brushing the pirate's sternum, trying to rein him in. They might be able to talk their way out of this yet. He stepped forward, her hand flattening against his chest, elbow bending at his proximity.

"Do you have a decree from the Senate?" she asked, turning back to the marshals. "Or just a request from my father?"

Their silence was more telling than any venomous words could have been.

All three had thick stubble along their faces, two with blue eyes, one with brown. They weren't as tall as the pirate but they were nearly as broad, revolvers sitting at their sides and rapiers threaded through their belts. She scoured their surroundings; there had to be a way out.

One where Anna didn't play the part of bait.

One where the pirate wasn't scrambling to protect her while fighting the marshals off.

They were outnumbered, three to two. Anna in a dress and heels and the pirate dressed immaculately with weapons stashed away. He'd decimated the marshals on the train and in her father's private dinner room and she knew he could wipe the floor with these three easily enough. Some instinct from an era now gone must have informed the marshal of the same, as he was leveraging her. Using her to deter the pirate from acting.

Anna knew what game the marshals were playing because it's the same one she would have played if the situation were reversed.

"Shall we?" the marshal said, looking down at her.

The pirate's fist slammed into the marshal's head, dropping him to the floor. Anna blinked several times at the man now splayed on the ground, unconscious and bleeding from the ear and nose. One hit. One hit and the pirate had fractured the man's skull. She almost laughed. Good God, he had been playing with Markus! She had realized it then but the reminder roared at the forefront of her mind.

Anna shook her head, she could contemplate the pirate's strength later. Right now, they had two marshals in the corridor to best. She inhaled, blinked.

Correction.

Only one marshal left to best, the other laid on the ground. Before Anna could do anything about the remaining marshal, the pirate put his head and shoulders through the wall with a sickening crunch. His hand laced with hers and then he pulled her into a run next to him.

"Which way, luv?" he breathed.

"Left!"

It was only a short minute before Anna and the pirate heard the echoing calls of the marshals and her father's private guard. She'd known they didn't have much of a head start. Their footsteps thundered behind, the accumulation and overlap of sounds almost like the angry hum of a hornet's nest. Anna peeked over her shoulder just before sliding around another corner, four or so men behind them.

Splendid, just splendid.

Anna slammed into the pirate's back, just able to see around his arm and to the four marshals in front of him. They were outnumbered. God forbid this be easy. Anna spent no time deciding what she should do, mind racing faster than the adrenaline flooding her system.

It was these marshals or her.

These marshals or her pirate.

These marshals or Markus, and she knew who she'd choose every time.

She reached under the pirate's jacket for the revolver hiding at his lower back, ducked around him, and fired. One marshal took a bullet through the gut, another in the side of his neck.

She'd been aiming for his head. Anna coughed at the thump of a baton against her back as she slammed into a wall, teeth gritted.

Well, at least they wanted her alive; batons were not a weapon of choice when a marshal had been ordered to kill. The marshal leaned hard against her, one hand coming up to thread through her hair one moment, and then it was gone the next.

The pirate grunted.

A muffled scream echoed behind her.

It all happened in the span of a breath. Anna looked over her shoulder and to the floor, quickly stepping back as a pool of blood reached for the hem of her gown. The remaining three guards laid face up on the ground. Dead. One with a snapped neck and the other opened at the throat, a knife carelessly tossed near his head.

Anna looked from the marshals to the pirate, flecks of blood sprayed across his face in a crude imitation of freckles. Her gaze dropped to the dark spot at his side and then to the river of red dripping from his gloved fingertips. She lifted the hem of her gown, focused on the growing patch of darker fabric at his ribs. If he bled out…

"Are you hurt?" she whispered, fingers trembling as she reached for the probable wound.

Could she cauterize it?

Anna glanced around the corridor, pinpointing where they stood in her father's estate. The library wasn't far. Anna had always thought it rather arrogant to keep a roaring fire so close to the thousands of books in her mother's collection. She thought it a rather splendid thing right now, grateful for the potential flames.

There had been no gunfire, which meant she didn't have a bullet to dig out. It must have been the knife. The marshal had pulled a knife on the pirate—he was apparently dispensable. Her father had the truth of it and it made her furious, a haze blurring the edges of her vision.

He stepped back and away from her, batting her hand to the side. "I'm fine, lovely. Now which way out of your da's gods-damned house?"

"That doesn't look—"

"No' my blood. I said I'm fucking fine." He frowned, gaze more intense and charged than the darkness between lightning strikes. "Just gonna need a nap, luv."

This man and his naps.

She opened her mouth to argue but the sound of boots thumping interrupted her. They both whipped around, seeing the first marshal round the counter. The pirate swore something vicious, grabbed her hand, and pulled her along as the first gun-shot rang out.

"How many?" she asked, heels sliding through blood.

"Does that matter?"

"It might." She paused to breathe, thinking of the four or five she had seen before. "I imagine we could take...four or five."

"Ye mean *I* could take four or five."

She heard the amusement in his voice, the flicker of a grin on her lips. "Well, yes. I'm afraid pirates aren't good for much else. Killing and shopping, that's it."

"No' kissing?" He huffed a laugh, glancing over his shoulder.

The pirate's cheeks darkened and judging from the flutter-ing of her heart and the heat in her own, Anna likely blushed worse. Bugger. The pirate cleared his throat, his grin making him every bit the predator with the speckles of blood masquerading as freckles upon his face.

Another shot ran out, causing him to duck, snarling some-thing foul beneath his breath. A pit of worry grew in her gut, her gaze landing on that growing dark spot at his side and the pale color of his face. They had to get out. Bugger, there had to be a quicker way. But on this wing of the estate the only clear exit was behind them. She cocked a brow, lips pressed thin.

Unless they took the window.

The pirate wasn't going to like this one bit.

Didn't have to like it though, he just had to survive it.

Anna shoved him to the side, catching the reflection of a marshal far behind them as he raised his revolver. The pirate barked another curse, turned, and fired several times. She didn't have to look back to know every bullet hit its mark. He was an excellent shot, reliable in a scuffle, honest, and not at all difficult to look at. Anna enjoyed his company and even Markus had warmed up to the man.

He clearly wasn't an idjit and yet he had somehow decided on piracy as a career. She didn't understand how a man like him became a pirate. Anna sucked on her teeth. There was that darkness he kept locked away, the one he harbored deep within, tucking it behind his teeth. A story nestled deep within this puzzle of a man and if Anna loved anything more than puzzles, it was a good story.

She chanced another glance at him. He held one of her hands with his, looking over his shoulder with his revolver, aiming precariously. He pulled them to a stop, eyes squinted before his trigger finger tightened.

That's when Anna saw it. The crack in the frame of the window. Out beyond the panes of glass, ancient trees stood sentinel. Somewhere in the shadows game trails meandered, some leading to the main road, some leading farther out into the mountains. With all the gunfire, Bellcaster high society was surely evacuating the estate with haste. She cocked her head. They could certainly steal a carriage.

Another revolver went off, this one ricocheting and grazing her arm. She bit back a cry, looking at the blood staining her sleeve at her shoulder, the tear in the fabric. They had no choice. If captured, the pirate would be shipped off to Chesterhale in chains and left to rot away under the withering stare of Bryce's delightful older sister. Her father would likely send her to a convent, spouting some nonsense that she'd lost her sensibilities like her mother before her.

God only knew what would happen to Markus.

They slid to a stop, her father's guards appearing at the other end of the hall. The one in front yelled something but Anna didn't hear any of it. The pirate tugged her hand, walking backward only to see more marshals round the corner. Bugger. There really was no choice.

"In for a penny, in for a pound," she muttered, gaze darting toward the window frame with the crack.

Somewhere between one frantic beat of her heart and the next a sense of calm enveloped her, like a cool breeze on a hot summer day. A trellis leaned against the far side of the window, one they could climb down. They just had to make it there first and it really wasn't the window Anna worried about.

It was the drop.

"We—we're at least forty fucking feet up!"

"Forty-four if memory serves!" she said, shooting out the window.

"L—luv, *no*."

"Luv, *yes*," she mocked on a cackle, heels crunching through broken glass.

"'Tis no' a good idea. And I'd fucking know. I'm the king of terrible fucking ideas." He groaned when Anna didn't reply, her focus on the howling wind coming through the window. "Bloody hell."

The wind ripped at her hair, pulling curly strands loose. Anna laughed, loud and free, the icy breeze leaving goosebumps in its wake. The pirate screamed, nostrils flared and glaring at the shadows below them. A smaller roof rose to meet them, breaking one of her heels clean off. Bugger, had the incline always been this steep? She didn't think so but that didn't stop it from pitching both her and the pirate forward. She lost her footing, staring at the shingles as they came impossibly closer.

Oh, no.

Oh, no, no, *no*.

She grimaced, the shingles of the roof like splintered ice. Dropping the pirate's hand, she pulled her arms around her head to protect her face. The night swirled around her, the glimmer of her dress the only real light left. Based on the grunts, Anna assumed the pirate tumbled just as she did, ever closer to the edge.

Her dress ripped as she scrambled to find a hold, the sound nearly deafening.

Bugger it—

Anna spilled over the edge of the roof, fingers digging into the gutter.

—all to—

Metal groaned. Her body swung, knees cracking into old bricks and mortar. Something dark barreled over her.

—hell.

Anna screamed, reaching out against her better judgement. She clutched a bit of fabric at the pirate's shoulder as the gutter squealed from his added weight. Both leather-clad fingers dug into the thin sheet of metal, his eyes wild as he gulped mouthfuls of air. She glanced at his gloves; they would be absolutely splendid right about now. Her fingers were freezing.

"There are easier ways to die, beastie," he said, voice hoarse.

She nodded rapidly, shivering and teeth chattering. "That actually went better than I—"

The gutter groaned.

Anna scanned the metal but couldn't see much in the dark and twisting fog. She heard the next crack, though. Her heart and stomach dropped, panic chewed away at her focus with broken teeth. Anna heard another pop and hoped it was the last complaint from the gutter, but it was quickly followed by a *popopopop* as the gutter came loose, screaming as it came down.

The thin bit of metal swung, ripping an entire section from the roof and slicing into her palms at the drop. Anna screamed as the chill air cut through the thin fabric of her dress. The pirate screamed louder. Between one breath and the next, Anna and the pirate crashed into lattice. Wood and ancient plant life crunched, cushioning their impact, and then the gutter completely broke away.

Anna was weightless.

Then she was falling.

And then she hit the blasted ground.

Luckily, it wasn't a horribly long distance after all that. Upon impact, Anna folded her legs, rolled and skidded. She grunted through it, coughing as she laid there. Blasted ground was more akin to granite than dirt. Slowly, Anna patted sections of her body and let her gaze rove the ground, searching for her pirate in the dark. He had to be here somewhere. As she scoured the shadows, Anna set about righting her breasts as well. They may have been small but the plunging neckline of this gown certainly allowed for potential disaster with all that tumbling.

It wasn't until the marshals above directed light in their direction that she saw him. Crawling forward, her hands trembled at how completely still he laid. If not for the barest rise and fall of his chest, she might have believed he'd broken his neck in the fall.

"Pirate..." she whispered, swallowing past a knot in her throat.

He groaned and stiffly rolled onto his stomach. It was another long moment before he pulled his arms and legs beneath himself and tried to sit upright. Anna placed a hand on his shoulder, tipping her head down to try and catch his expression. His eyes pinched shut and his grimace deepened upon his next breath. She didn't miss the way his arm moved to favor that suspiciously dark patch on his side.

Someone else's blood?

The bloody idjit.

She had hardly believed so before and believed it even less now. If he bled out before she cauterized it or stitched it or whatever he might need—Anna shook her head. She'd lose her mind. Possibly research necromancy and find a way to raise the bugger. Plenty of the old civilizations believed in such superstitions, perhaps one of them had gotten it right.

"Are ye all right, Anna?"

Something fluttered at hearing the pirate whisper her name in such a gentle, wholesome tone. He lifted his head, turning until his gaze met hers. His focus didn't remain on her eyes for long, instead jumping to what he could see of her body—which wasn't much in this unfathomable dark. Her heart skipped a beat again as his brows drew tighter, his attention entirely on her. Anna pushed the feeling away to examine later, when she wasn't running for her life or nearly costing the pirate his.

"I'm all right."

"You're sure, aye?"

"It certainly could have been worse," she whispered, forcing her stiff and aching muscles to stand. Riddled with bruises and scrapes, the cold wasn't doing Anna any favors, but she lived and so did the pirate.

With a wince, she kicked off her heels. Those woods were going to do a number on her feet between the brush and the snow but Anna couldn't run in a pair of broken heels. She raised onto the balls of her feet, hoping to spare some of her skin.

Just in the background, the voices of marshals drifted down like snow. Anna doubted her father's personal guard and the marshals would attempt a similar stunt. Anna and the pirate had the head start, they only needed to keep it and meet up with Markus in the harbor.

"How ye figure?" he asked as he stood, joints popping.

Anna snagged his hand, pulling him in the direction of the woods, listening for the gurgle of a nearly frozen stream. "Well...we're still breathing."

"Aye." He coughed. "Seems a wee thing."

"And like all small things, often taken for granted."

They ran as well as they could toward the forest, the trees reaching higher and higher. From the ground, the forest looked like it held up the heavens. The night around them thickened and Anna couldn't see which direction led to safety, but she could hear it. The stream on this side of the estate ran straight into the main road where an adorable little bridge spanned its narrow width. As long as they followed the stream, they ran in the right direction.

Torn fabric and wisps from her gown caught on nearly every bit of flora. They tangled between her legs, leaving her ripping at them as she ran with one hand while holding the pirate's hand with the other. She winced and squeaked, trying to keep everything in, but the rocks were sharp and the broken sticks precarious. Even the pine cones marched against Anna. At some point she closed her eyes; this was hardly the first time she'd run through the forest barefoot, though some part of her hoped it really would be the last.

It wasn't long before the stumbling sound of many booted feet followed them, sounding as close as their own shadow in the dark. Branches whipped across their faces as they crashed through the forest. Anna found herself holding her breath, certain the marshals and her father's men could hear them. How couldn't they, with all the noise she and the pirate made?

She wanted to laugh. To curse. Almost everything was drowned out by the adrenaline and the need to survive, the feeling of excitement. Never let it be said that Annaleigh Rae Savage lived a boring life. But then there was also dread, the fear of failure. Her father would surely disown her, have her committed. Anna tried to remind herself that her father would have to catch her first.

She shook her head—bugger.

Could they still exchange the map for her brother's freedom? Maybe turn it into another senate member instead of her father. Or give it straight to the Coalition and cut the middleman out? The Coalition would have no need of her brother if they had what they wanted. But that did not resolve the trouble they were in with their father. Or the fact that someone had to hang for possession of a pirate map.

Anna chanced a glance at the pirate. Maybe he'd let Anna and Markus join his crew, let them battle the slave trade with him. She found a life at sea to be far preferable to a life in a cage—and her father would try to put her in one after the stunt she had pulled tonight.

"Just a little farther," Anna whispered.

Several times they had to stop and hide, several times the pirate shielded her against a tree, his breath hot on her neck until the steps faded away. Each time all Anna could think of was the heat of his body on hers, of how his lips had tasted before Mihk had so rudely interrupted them. Even now, it was hiding behind every thought Anna had, below the thrum of adventure but above the despair.

How far would things have gone if Mihk hadn't found them?

Anna didn't know and it terrified her.

She inhaled deep, the sound sharp. The water here at the stream flowed freely, coming to her thighs. Anna waded slowly, feeling her legs numb. Her teeth chattered worse than before, her body trembling. She clenched her jaw. Good God, had she been the one to think of this ridiculous plan? Why had she decided this would be a good idea? As she emerged on the other side, her legs locked up.

"Ye should have let me carry ye, luv," the pirate said, picking her up.

Anna wrapped her arms around his neck and pressed her forehead to his warm skin. "You're absolutely right, pirate. I really should have."

"Which way?"

"Forward." She sighed, closing her eyes.

The forest's silence was a tangible thing, coiling around Anna like a blanket of ice. If not for the occasional hoot of an owl or the sound of the pirate's boots against the brush, it might have swallowed her whole. She inhaled—God, he smelt wonderful. Something dark and spiced and absolutely fitting for the feral edge he walked between man and monster. And the pirate radiated a heat Anna hadn't realized she needed. A heat more like air than anything.

The pirate shivered, clearing his throat. "Tell me something about yourself. 'Tis much too quiet."

She swallowed thickly, curling and spreading her toes. The act itself pained her so she did it again and again. "Like what?"

"Something no one else knows."

"Only if you tell me something of my choosing as well."

He remained quiet a minute, sticks snapping beneath his dress shoes and ferns whispering in his wake. "Deal."

"You already know I bedded the Pirate King. It's the heaviest secret I carry," she muttered, letting her head lull against him. "But once, when I was fifteen, I kissed a girl just to see if I liked it. I wondered if Markus and I were similar in that way too. Sometimes it's a hard thing, being a twin, wondering where one of you ends and the other begins."

He was quiet, and then, "Did ye like it?"

"It was fine. But I find I prefer men, especially ones who know what to do with a lady. How did you become a pirate?"

He chuckled, the sound more of a rasp than anything. "Out of everything, why would ye want to know that?"

"You are kind and honest and everything I have never known a pirate to be. How does a man like you fall in with criminals and their ilk? Become a captain of it?"

"Ye figured I'm a captain?"

She grinned against his neck. "It's rather obvious. You don't like being given orders, and how else would you take me everywhere I wanted to go? You'd need a ship and a crew for that." The pirate huffed a laugh, shaking his head. "So, how did that happen?"

"We don't always have a choice," he said quietly, his words heavy.

"We always have a choice."

"No' when the damn thing is become a bloody pirate or let my family die." He sighed. "My mum, a very popular whore on Aidanburgh, died when I was a lad. It was for the better, she had been a husk for a while yet. My auntie took care of us after that but...she did the best she could, but it wasn't enough. Disease was everywhere, lads and lasses rotting on the streets. But the hunger was worse, always there, always clawing from inside my stomach.

"After a year or so of scrapping on the streets, a pirate ship docked. I snuck aboard, hoping to be a cabin boy and earn a wee living. At least some coins to send back home. I remember it so clearly, looking down and counting Tate's ribs and seeing nothing but hollows in Taylee's cheeks...I thought, '*I have to do something, anything.*' I wasn't much more than skin and bone myself, getting into fights just for scraps out of the rubbish. All fucking day, fists swinging and blood dripping. But Tate and Taylee had to eat."

"Did they let you stay on the ship?"

"No." He chuckled. "Was the Pirate King's ship, the *Devil's Advocate.* He gave me a lash and sent me on my way. Did that four more times, every time he docked over the next year, until finally he let me join his crew. I worked my way up, made a wee name for myself and eventually enough to buy my own ship. Once I had that, I took my brother and sister from Aidanburgh and never looked back."

Anna was quiet, brows pulling together in thought. The *Pale Queen* had been the Pirate King's flag ship for as long as she could remember. She chewed on the inside of her lip and leaned against the redhead. Before Trevor Lovelace became the Pirate King he had a different ship, perhaps it was called *Devil's Advocate.* Something about it didn't sit quite right with her, but Anna had other questions.

"How old were you?"

"Hm? Maybe seven when my mum passed."

"Why…why did you stay a pirate? You could have quit, you were so young. Just a boy."

"Once you're a pirate, luv, there's no taking it back. That kind of freedom sinks into your soul, especially for a captain. Ye see, I loved the stars and the sea even then. I could read and navigate a nautical map wi'out aid by ten. At fourteen, all I needed was the stars. At sixteen, I didn't need even those anymore," he said wistfully, his hands tightening around her briefly.

How could one man go through so much and retain who he was in his heart? The confidence and swagger of a pirate, but clearly the love and sense of honor of someone more. He had lived a hard life, which was not something Anna could say.

Despite her differences with her father, she had never gone a day without food unless it was her own doing, stumbling through jungle ruins or forgetting to eat when engrossed in her work. Even everything that had happened after allowing herself to be abducted into the slave trade to get that blasted map had been her fault. Her idea, when she got to the base of it all.

"I am so sorry," she whispered, aching for the boy he had been, the one who had been forced to grow up fast and hard. "You were only a little boy. You shouldn't have gone through any of that."

"Don't be. Sometimes we have to make do wi' what we have. Life…it's like the seas, luv. No' all of 'em are calm or loving or kind. Some are fucking savage and rough, vicious things that test ye." He inhaled, chest expanding beneath her. "But we make our way anyway. We make our way any way we bloody well can. I know I can survive damn near anything. Can ye say the same?"

Anna opened her eyes and blinked. The pirate stared down at her, gaze focused and intent. She shivered and not at all from the cold. "Maybe not anything," she whispered. "But my seas didn't teach me to survive by going through them. They taught me to go around—they taught me to pivot, you stubborn man."

He chuckled, bringing a light smile to her lips.

"How did you survive it, though?" she blurted against his neck.

"The same way ye survive anything, luv. By looking to the light, to the next horizon, and every one that comes after."

They broke out of the tree line, mist wetting their skin.

Anna cocked her head, tapping the pirate's shoulder rapidly.

He stopped at the edge of the road, just beyond the bridge. Lanterns hung on either side of it, ensuring drivers knew where the small stone contraption stood. No sense driving a team of horses straight into a stream. Slowly, the rhythmic thumps grew louder, the beating of hooves on frozen ground as the team dragged a carriage behind them. She wiggled until the pirate put her down, legs nearly buckling and feet screaming at her for the affront. It was a curious thing, they didn't hurt nearly as bad as before.

She lifted the withering remains of her gown and breathed deep, focusing on the task at hand.

Trust me, she thought, meeting his gaze.

He stepped back, farther into the shadows where the lantern light wouldn't reach.

And then she screamed, blood-chilling, high-pitched, at the top of her lungs. Anna gathered her iron will and ran forward on feet that were cut and surely bleeding. She scraped her way up the small incline and into the direct line of the carriage, whipping around in a frantic, confused circle.

Anna faced the carriage and four big black horses slid to an impressive stop, their hooves raking deep grooves into the ground. She screamed again and became a sobbing mess for good measure, stumbling around to the side of the carriage.

"Good God, woman. What happened?" the driver inquired, loosening his hold on the reins.

"There's—there's—" Anna stammered, not entirely sure where she was going with this. "I—"

The pirate snuck around the other side of the carriage, his dark eyes just catching the firelight. The driver disappeared, sucked back into the shadows shrouding her pirate. She heard the thump and nothing else before the carriage rocked and the pirate climbed over the driver's seat and hopped to the ground.

The carriage moved as if whoever inside stood.

Anna almost groaned and the pirate threw her a revolver before drawing his own. She turned to the door, squinting at the emblem on its side. A lion stared at her, proud and unflinching. Then she hissed a breath of annoyance. Of course, it was Senator Cunningham.

"Fredrick!" The carriage door banged open. "What in the hell is—An—Miss Savage?"

She paused, arm slackening. "Mr. Cunningham?"

It wasn't the senator.

It was his son.

Anna couldn't quite fathom what Bryce was doing here. He had never been one to run away from gunfire in the past, but here he was staring at her like she was a ghost. His warm brown eyes ate her up, starting at her bleeding feet and raising to the bits of flora nestled in her hair. Every scratch, the state of her gown, the smudged makeup beneath her eyes from fake crying. His throat bobbed and he leaned from the carriage door, the heat wafting out prickling her skin.

"God, Anna, what happened?" He paused, and shook his head. "You don't need to tell me, darling. You escaped him, didn't you?"

"Escaped…?" She blinked, unsure of what Bryce was saying.

"All that matters is that you're all right," he said, stepping from the carriage.

She turned her attention to the revolver in her hand, the one now pointed at the ground at seeing the familiar face of her past suitor. Of the man Anna might have married if she had been okay with settling or doing what she was told.

You're—what?

This—us—it isn't working.

I don't understand.

It's not you, I swear it's not. You're lovely and—

She blinked.

He hadn't aged a day since the market.

Bright, light brown eyes with a slight tilt, a narrowing that showed his Xiang heritage, and straight dark brown hair. Normally he kept it shorn closer to his scalp but it'd grown out. It was a few inches in length and he'd combed it to the side. He was taller than Anna—not like the pirate was, but only by an inch or so. She had never been able to wear heels. Solidly built with shoulders that tapered to a narrow waist.

A waist where two rapiers currently slumbered. Stiffening at the sight of those blades, she watched very carefully where his hands drifted. "I am commandeering your carriage, Mr. Cunningham. You may leave your weapons and vacate. If you do so willingly, I won't shoot you in the face."

"Shoot me in the…?" He smiled with a laugh that quickly ended when Anna raised her revolver. He sobered, realizing she was serious. "What's going on? Your father said you've been kidnapped by a blasted pirate and Markus is in the Pirate King's custody. Some business about a trade." His throat bobbed once more, his focus on her revolver as he brought his arms up in a clear sign of surrender.

"Markus is…?"

"Despicable business, if you ask me," he said quietly, taking another step forward. "Taking a man's children and trying to use them to barter. Come, get in the carriage and I'll take you home." He cleared his throat, something stiffening in his features. "Somewhere safe. I won't let anything happ—"

Anna stilled, gaze narrowing on Bryce. "He's already fabricating lies, isn't he?"

His façade fractured then, a slip in his smile that she never would have caught if Bryce hadn't courted her for those two years. His throat bobbed and his focus slowly moved from her revolver to meet her gaze. "Shh, darling. You never know who is listening." He cleared his throat. "Let's just get in the carr—"

"Ye ready, luv?" the pirate called, stepping around the horses and into the light.

Bryce Cunningham whirled around, his eyes widening in recognition. "*You're* the blasted pirate?" he breathed out, anger collecting on his features.

The pirate, not at all concerned, comically rubbed the back of the neck and looked up at the night sky. "Bloody fucking hell. No' ye again."

Anna's gaze darted between the two.

What to do, what to do?

She chewed on her lip, heart sinking as Bryce's fingers splayed and started for his rapiers. She flipped her revolver, lunged forward, and swung hard. She caught him off guard, the butt of the revolver cracking hard against his temple.

He crumbled into a heap of unconscious muscle.

She stared down at him and then looked about the rest of the road. Anna couldn't very well leave him here in the middle of it to be trampled by horses. Bryce wasn't a bad man, likely just following her father's orders and listening to his narrative.

So, she dragged him by his ankles to the side of the road and hurried back to where the pirate stood, still making sense of what had just happened. He crossed his arms and cocked his head, weight leaning to one foot. "So…ye two know each other?" he asked, motioning between Anna and Bryce Cunningham with his finger.

She winced. "One could assume such." The pirate's brow rose. Anna rolled her head. "Remember that ex-suitor I told you about…?"

He blinked.

And then blinked again.

"Ye…" The pirate made a face, stepping back. "Ye and—ugh. Fucking hell, I wish I hadn't asked. There's an image," he said, gesturing to his head. "And I can't get it the fuck out. Bloody hell, I'm going to be sick, lass."

"Just don't think about it," Anna snapped with a frown. "What I find more interesting than Captain Cunningham and I tumbling in this very carriage"—the pirate gagged, glaring at her and then the carriage—"is how you two know each other."

He pulled himself up into the driver's seat with one swift tug, a frown etched onto his face. Anna's lips twitched at his dramatic reaction. He shook his shoulders before leaning forward onto his knees. "I…well, I'm a rather famous pirate, he's a captain in the Briland Navy, of course we bloody well know each other." He nodded slowly. "I run into that shite quite frequently."

Something tugged at Anna from inside.

Bryce had spent most of his time chasing after the Pirate King and working to eradicate the slave trade. Is that how they knew each other? Both working on opposite sides of the law to accomplish the same goal? It couldn't be because the pirate had anything to do with Trevor Lovelace. Anna didn't remember much about that night or the Pirate King but she would know that, wouldn't she? It couldn't be buried so deep she wouldn't recall this man.

Bugger.

It couldn't be, right?

She leaned into the carriage and pulled several fur blankets from inside. They were still warm from the heated bricks within. As much as she wanted to sit within the carriage and regain the feeling in her fingers and toes—hell, her arms and legs—she wanted to keep an eye on the pirate even more.

"Famous?" She grinned, holding the fur blankets in her arms. Gunfire sounded in the distance, for what, Anna couldn't be sure. But she knew what the baying was. She turned and looked out into the creeping mist. The hounds were fast; hopefully crossing the stream would buy them time.

"Aye, probably the most famous," he muttered, staring at the reins in his hands, brows pulled in concentration.

Anna pulled herself into the driver's seat next to her pirate and wrapped the fur blankets around their legs before leaning against his shoulder. He remained still as a statue, lips pressed into a thin line as he stared down at the horses.

"Any time now, pirate," she whispered.

He tensed. "I don't know how to work this blasted contraption," he muttered. "Give me a ship—nay, anything that fucking floats—and I can make it go. But this bloody thing—"

Anna leaned away from him, brow cocked. "Do you require assistance?"

"From the bloody wood nymph?" He chuckled, finally turning to look at her. "I reckon no'."

"Wood nymph?"

"Aye, look at ye," he whispered, picking something from her hair and tucking a loose strand behind her ear. Anna didn't have to look to know. Dirt and blood everywhere. All manner of flora tucked within her dress or hair. Her braided crown had started coming out as well, some strands falling to her breast while the rest remained up.

"Let me remind you that I did everything you did tonight," she said flatly. "Except for in a dress and heels."

"Would ye like a cookie, lovely?" the pirate cracked back with a grin, eyes warm and smile mischievous.

"Actually…" she said, wrapping her fingers around his and leaning her head against his shoulder. She snapped the reins and the carriage lurched as the horses pulled into a steady canter. "That sounds absolutely splendid."

CHAPTER 38

Trevor wasn't an idiot.

But shite, he should have put two and two together. Bryce. Bryce fucking Cunningham. Bloody hell, he must have been wearing some blinders no' to realize who the lass had been speaking of this entire time. Then she'd nearly smashed the shite's face in wi' the revolver. Fucking poetic. He deserved it, as far as Trevor was concerned Tate'd be laughing for years at this rate.

Beyond Cunningham and John Savage, beyond the business wi' his brother and his lovely ship, there were images he couldn't get out of his head. They were frozen there, a different flash every time he blinked, and damn it all to hell.

One blink and Trevor had Anna pressed against the wall, his mouth at her throat.

The next, he sat next to her at dinner, watching that life in her eyes dull at her da's cruel words.

Another and a fucking marshal smashed her into a wall, one hand ripping at her hair.

And the next?

She jumped out a gods-damned window, nearly rolling off a roof to her death.

There had been a sick second where he almost couldn't look; he wouldn't have been able to bear seeing her splattered upon the cobbles below. Shite, then he'd felt her little fingers curled in his jacket and turned to see her staring at him. His night vision was better than most and so her big blue eyes were the first thing he saw.

Trevor hadn't been worried about himself. Oh, nay. He would have been just fine after hitting the ground. Might have had to sleep for a while, but he would have been fine. The lass? Fuck, he wasn't sure. Part of him hoped, of course, but he'd hoped for plenty of things only for them to turn to ash in his hands.

He stared at the winding road, damn near in shock.

Anna was certifiably mad, had the self-preservation of a fem who'd been to the bloody gates above, met their maker, and had been anything but impressed.

Trevor glanced down to where the wee female slept against his arm. If anything, he checked to make sure she was still there, that she had survived. That it wasn't like last time. Her head rolled and lulled against him. The blanket refused to stay over her shoulders and sank into her lap where her hands hid below it.

"Yes, pirate?" she asked, eyes slowly opening to show off those beautiful blues.

His heart fluttered. "What, luv?"

"You're staring." She smiled softly, yawning. "And you really should be paying more attention to where we're going."

"Was no'," he replied, looking to the road wi' a small grin.

"Were too," she chimed, the amusement in her voice music to his ears. When she next spoke, her voice had softened, laced with concern. Concern over him and, fuck, if it didn't gut him. "Are you sure you're all right, pirate?"

"Aye, fem. I'll be fine."

And it was the truth.

The gods-damned truth.

Trevor would always be fine, whether he liked it or no'.

That was the deal he'd made.

"Say what you will. But when we reach Markus, you're stripping and I'm looking at that."

"Ye just want to see me naked." He chuckled, grinning down at her.

Anna shrugged, eyes fluttering shut once more. "Could you blame me," she yawned, "if I did?"

Several minutes passed in silence he liked a wee too much. It was comfortable and warm, this silence between them. Anna coughed, curling closer to him.

"Are ye okay, lass?" he asked, glancing back down at her.

She nodded against his shoulder, dark smudges beneath her eyes and several deep scratches on those lovely round cheeks. Her face was warm against his dinner jacket despite the shivering.

Trevor gulped, his chest constricting painfully. He scratched at the wound at his ribs, poking and prodding where he'd been stabbed. The blood had completely soaked through his first few layers but at least his jacket was mostly dry. At the very least, it would keep her from freezing. The stubborn female refused to sit in the passenger's seat where it was toasty and warm.

Carefully, he pulled his jacket from his body and handed it to her. "No' much, luv, but it'll keep those rosy shoulders of yours warm."

"Thank you," she whispered, threading her arms through his sleeves and buttoning it clear to her throat. Once done, she leaned against his shoulder again and pulled the cuffs over her hands, adjusting how the fur blankets sat over their legs.

The heat rose high on his cheeks and against his neck.

Something bloody intimate about sharing a jacket wi' Anna, wasn't something he did for any fem. The seas he sailed were warm, the sun beating at the crew's back. And if they ended up in cooler waters, the crew packed accordingly. He'd never had a need to share his clothes wi' a female.

He liked it though.

Fucking hell, he liked seeing Anna in his jacket, how small she looked settled in something he'd been wearing. It wasn't long before her head lulled back and forth wi' the motion of the carriage. He'd never been gentle with anything in his life, but he was wi' Anna when he carefully moved his arm and wrapped it around her shoulders. Figured it'd keep her warmer while she slept and at the very least it'd keep her from falling off the bloody carriage.

"Idiot," he told himself with a shake of his head. "Such a fucking idiot."

But he had the map.

And he had the lass.

So, he considered it a job well done.

CHAPTER 39

In Anna's opinion, they had made it in record time.

The horses panted and sweated profusely by the time they arrived in Bellcaster proper. Entering the boundaries of the city, they ditched the horses and carriage, instead choosing to walk to where Markus would be waiting. They took the dark back alleys and tomb-like side streets, the pirate's hand pressed to the small of her back.

"No need to worry," she told him, thinking the pirate must be reminiscing about the last time he'd strolled with her down shady-looking streets. "The only pirate in Bellcaster that would whisk me away has already declared he would never take me anywhere I do not wish to go."

"Aye," he grunted. "'Tis no' pirates I'm fucking worried about. Ye've more jewels on ye than a senator's wife."

He said no more and neither did Anna, but the pirate kept his hand exactly where it was. If anything, it slid farther around her waist, his gaze turning sinister. She'd hate to be the individual who ran into him in the middle of the night.

Anna rolled the sleeves of his oversized jacket up her forearms and attempted to remove as much of the ruined fabric of her gown as she could. The tear started at her left knee, ripping upward in a ridiculous angle until the middle of her thigh. It wasn't much warmer in Bellcaster proper, but the ground was solid and flat, free of sharp rocks and sticks, and so part of Anna believed her feet to be feeling better. Either that, or numb enough to cause worry.

They arrived at the shipyard much later than anticipated.

Anna supposed the events of the night were to blame, not necessarily her planning. It was a grand place, miles upon miles of docks in every scale imaginable. Out in the port slept every vessel a well-seasoned sailor could name, both large and small, and off in the distance, masses of ice ambled by. Fog curled here too, a foreboding cloud off the water sending fingers forward to lead the way.

In Anna's head it took half an eternity to reach the harbor and even longer yet to find the tin building. Anna swallowed hard, unsure if Markus would be behind the door. The shed belonged to Senator Hayhurst for his family's personal use.

She stared at the less-than-elegant metal shack, the door closed but shivering in the light breeze nearly as hard as Anna was. The pirate bumped her with his elbow, stepping forward, always first.

He ducked beneath the entry, one hand hovering at a revolver, the other holding a blade. Where it had come from on his person, Anna wasn't entirely sure. She placed a palm at his back, following him into the near darkness. One lamp had been lit, the fire exposed instead of hiding safely behind glass. She sighed, that was a safety hazard Markus wasn't prone to. Plenty of supplies in this shed could catch if the lamp fell over.

She turned in a small circle, taking note of the spider webs and layers of dust. Clearly, Senator Hayhurst had not kept up on his dusting. Judging from the lump of sail, Markus had made camp between various supplies and nets needing repairing. Farther in, a figure shrouded in shadow sat on a crate, their back to Anna and the pirate.

She stepped forward and cleared her throat.

Their head whipped around, revealing Markus.

He looked so worried, face pale and shadows beneath his eyes. He blinked once and then again, recognition and relief flooding across his face. Then he was up off the crate, lunging across the room. The pirate twitched, defenses rising at the sudden motion. His fists followed as Markus rushed forward and—

He ran straight past the pirate.

She laughed, eyes stinging.

Markus knocked into Anna, arms wrapping completely around her, crushing her to him. She reached up and around his back, squeezing Markus to her. He was here and he was alive and they had the map. They had the map and a pirate that could take them anywhere they wanted. She'd have to break the news to Markus, but he'd find a way to live with it.

"Hello to you too, Markus." She laughed, clutching at the fabric at his back.

"I was so worried," he whispered, voice thick.

"I know."

"Anna, I've never been so scared in my life."

"I know that too."

Bugger.

Anna hadn't realized just how distraught Markus must have been. It was easy enough to see with the track he had paced into the packed dirt floor. She'd known he would worry, of course, but this unfathomable fear? She hadn't expected that.

It didn't make a lick of sense.

Not with the trouble the two had gotten into together. This night had been no more dangerous. Perhaps that is where the rub lied, that Markus had to wait in anticipation instead of being in the thick of it with her. That she had gone out with some mysterious man whose words were only as good as his intentions. She sighed; Markus's imagination possessed the potential to create far worse fates than what had transpired.

Anna stepped back, biting her lip, unable to look her brother in the eyes. Markus did not pull away from her, instead he turned. Squinting at him briefly, she noticed he took up residence between her and the pirate. Bugger, they were back at this? Just when they had finally made nice?

"Did you find it?" he asked, his focus clearly anchored on the pirate.

Anna cleared her throat, forcing herself away from him, and glanced between the two. A charge lingered in the space, one that had not previously been there. This wouldn't do, not if they were to be at sea together, following wherever this map might lead.

"Of course, *we* did."

Markus turned a sharp look on her. "What happened?"

She blinked, looking up at him with her arms crossed. "I don't know what you're talking about."

He squinted, turning from Anna, to the pirate, and back again. "Something happened."

"Nothing beyond becoming wanted fugitives of Briland. All in a day's work, really."

"That's not it. I can tell that's not it, Anna," Markus muttered, turning toward the pirate with an expectant glare. "Talk."

Anna glanced at the pirate, his cheeks flushed.

The redhead rubbed at the back of his neck furiously, staring Markus down. He was uncomfortable, and reasonably so. She tried catching his eye and mouthing threats and when that didn't work, Anna proceeded to glare at the side of his head. Feeling the weight of her stare, his cheek twitched. The pirate turned toward her, lips turning into a grin as he settled his gaze on Markus.

"Got into a few scuffles, we did."

"That is typically the natural progression of things when Anna is involved. I could have as much based on the state of her dress. What else?"

"She kissed me as a bloody distraction."

Markus gagged, turning away to pinch the bridge of his nose and groan. "Anna. *Anna*. Why would you do that?"

"It seemed like a good idea at the time." She winced. "I thought some guards were sneaking up on us and asked myself what you'd do in the situation."

He turned slowly to face her, expression stuck somewhere between stunned and disgusted. He cleared his throat and closed his eyes. "Why is it whenever you ask yourself what I would do, you end up snogging the nearest pirate? Why is that your first instinct?"

"Not one word." She shook her head at him. "Not *one*."

Markus slumped onto an old crate and Anna was quite surprised the dusty box didn't cave right in from her brother's considerable weight. He dropped his head into his hands. "I knew you two couldn't be left unsupervised. Now, what is this business of being fugitives? I thought you said you have the map."

"I do. It all went perfectly splendid. Got the map, had dinner with Father. Turns out, the Senate wants the map for their own nefarious purpose. Didn't hand it over and now we're criminals."

He raised his head, blond curls sticking out to the right like he'd tried to sleep at some point. "I—why didn't you just hand the blasted thing over to him?"

"He wanted the pirate too."

"I'm well aware you hate sharing, old girl, but if there ever was a time to do so, that was it."

"To hang, Markus! He wanted to hang him instead of you. I couldn't do that. He's innocent."

"Hardly," her brother scoffed, turning to look at the pirate.

Anna followed his gaze, noticing how pale the redhead's face looked. His freckles stood out against the flecks of dried blood. He ran his hand through his hair, the thick strands sticking up on end, and leaned back against the wall with a cough. She squinted at his side. Bugger. The spot had grown, looking shiny now in the dim light.

She stepped forward only for Markus to block her. "Easy, Anna," he whispered, motioning to the small lamp in the corner. If that fell over, the whole shed would go up. It wasn't like her brother to be so careless. "Do you have a plan?"

Anna stared into her brother's matching blue eyes. "I do. We still make a copy of the map and turn it directly into the Senate. Still need to think up a way to clear your name and the whole needing to hang someone, but I can do that easily enough while we sail wherever the map leads."

"I should have expected you'd want to do that."

"You really should have." She shrugged. "I should also warn you that we might have to become pirates, anyway. I imagine Father is going to disown us after tonight."

Markus stared at her and then closed his eyes. "So...you suggest we give the map to the Senate and then become blasted pirates ourselves to avoid being grounded?"

"Yes. And I want to go wherever that map leads. There is something at its end and I want to know what."

"I suppose it's not the worst outcome. Do we live in it?"

"It's probable," Anna answered and Markus nodded his head.

"In over your head, beastie," the pirate said quietly, a sluggish quality to his voice.

"Are you all right?" she asked again for what felt like the hundredth time.

"Aye, aye. Just need to sleep. I'll be fine in the morning, lass," he said, sliding down the wall and landing with a thud. The pirate winced, stretching his legs out in front of him.

"It's settled, then. We sail in the morning. Don't get too comfortable, pirate, you'll be taking that shirt off here in just a moment."

Markus groaned and the pirate chuckled, eyes sliding shut.

There was something larger at work here, something pulling her forward, ebbing and flowing through her veins. Some might have called it a knowing, others might have called it coincidence. But the Aepith seafarers would have called it Fate. They would have said Anna had waded into one of Fate's tides and now had to wait and see where it took her.

Anna turned to the grimy window against the far wall and grinned.

The pirate would say it was time to look to the next horizon. And she rather liked the idea of that.

LATER

Anna rummaged through various crates and boxes, looking for medical supplies. Damn what the pirate said, she knew an injured man when she saw one. His head lulled to the side, chest rising and falling sluggishly. Markus took up residence across from the pirate, staring at the ceiling with his legs crossed at the ankles.

"Fugitives," he groaned.

"Yes."

"Criminals."

"That too, I suppose." She grunted, lifting one crate and digging into the one below it. She sat up straighter and mused, "Does this make me a cat burglar?"

"Cat burglars scale *up* to a high vantage. You fell out a window, I don't think it qualifies." He sighed. "We are no better than rogues."

"I hear the rogues have all the fun."

"That's what they want you to think." He paused long enough for Anan to look over her shoulder. He closed his eyes and tucked his arms behind his head. "I can't believe Father. I mean, I can. But—blast it all to hell, he's the one that started this. I was—I was detained because of him. And he knew what they'd do and he did it anyway."

Anna nodded her head and opened her mouth to answer. But the tin door swung open, cracking against the inside of the shed with a brutal force. Anna and Markus turned toward the sound as one, both tensing. Bugger, what now? She prayed it was only the wind even as the cause of the sound strode into the small shack.

First it was nothing but shadow and then it was dark leather boots and an impeccable ensemble of clothing, black trimmed in gold. Ah, this one oversaw the marshals. Anna continued to follow the man's form to his face and froze, any air in her lungs whooshing out in surprise.

"Hello, little bird," Bryce Cunningham said as a contingent of sailors and marshals filled the space behind him.

Bugger.

ACKNOWLEDGEMENTS

Just publish it, they said.

How hard could it be, they said.

Well, here I am a year later with my sanity intact and a book in your hands. So, I consider that a bit of a win. When I set out (read as: when my husband's pestering finally won out) to publish This Savage Sea, I knew it wouldn't be a walk in the park. Turns out, I was right. Self-publishing is no joke and I couldn't imagine setting out on that adventure by myself.

So, thank you to Brittany for fielding all my ideas—no matter how weird. For reading my messages in the middle of the night and asking questions I hadn't even thought of yet.

Thank you, Dane & the rest of the Ebook Launch Crew for the gorgeous cover and formatting my book baby. My point of no return for publishing This Savage Sea started there, staring at the cover.

Gratitude is not a strong enough word to describe what I owe RaeAnne (follow her on Instagram, she's amazing @lavender-prose.editing) She found a home for every comma I missed and made the entire editing process as painless as possible.

It wouldn't be a proper acknowledgement without the list of names, so thank you: Dane, Phil, and Geoff for offering to co-splay as my characters and sell my book at Comic Con.

Thank you Tiff, for nodding your head and smiling whenever a rant struck me.

Thank you: Ashley, Michael, Rainbow, Dawn, and Scot for being so incredibly excited to read This Savage Sea, and for always offering input when I needed it.

Thank you, Scarlett St. Clair, I would have eventually done the self-publishing anyway, but I'm not sure it would have happened as quickly without you. You may not know it, but you're changing lives by being there and being you, and showing it can be done.

I wouldn't be where I am now without any of you, but I most definitely wouldn't have been able to start this journey, let alone finish it, without my family. Thank you, Martha and Eric for spending as much time with my crazy toddler as you do, it sure gives me the time I need to write. A huge thanks to my mom and dad, two of my biggest supporters. I love you both.

Thank you: Glenn and Bella, without you two I'm not sure Markus and Anna would exist. And if they did, they wouldn't be the same. I know I wouldn't be.

And last, but not least, I would not have accomplished this without my husband. Thank you, Travis. I thank you now, and I thank you later—you know, when I'm crying over book two. I've always wanted a life and a love to rattle the stars, and with you I have that. Quick question, though: Did you read the book, or just skip to the end to see if I said anything about you?

I love you, babe.